# FALLING IN LOVE

Tobias cleared his throat. "I had better be on my way. I have lessons to prepare for next week."

If she was surprised by his sudden decision to leave, she was too polite to show it. "I'll walk with you a little ways," Miranda offered simply.

She walked with him to the open space beyond the willows where he had picketed Romeo. After Tobias coiled up his picket rope and tied it to his saddle, he turned to face her.

The formal words of thanks he meant to say died in his throat as he looked down at her. She'd taken off the shapeless jacket she'd worn this morning, and the old, gray dress she wore emphasized her womanly curves. Tobias swallowed hard. Miranda Kilpatrick and the love she gave so generously to her nephews represented everything he'd had torn from him violently years ago. He longed to pull her into his arms and feel her softness against him. Before he could stop himself, he reached up and touched a lock of her hair, which had tumbled free from the bun she wore. Her hair felt softer than corn silk between his fingers.

She stared back at him, her eyes dark and wondering. Dizzy with sun and a hunger far more complex than desire, Tobias was stunned by how much he wanted to taste her mouth with his own. Some remnant of sanity prevented him from dipping his head toward her and doing exactly that. Instead, he raised the lock of her hair to his lips. It smelled of lavender and willows. Over the rush of the stream, he could hear a hermit thrush trilling its sweet song. This moment washed by the warm fall sun spun into infinity. The world disappeared around them, and their sensual awareness rose in a dangerous tide. . . .

# BOOK YOUR PLACE ON OUR WEBSITE AND MAKE THE READING CONNECTION!

We've created a customized website just for our very special readers, where you can get the inside scoop on everything that's going on with Zebra, Pinnacle and Kensington books.

When you come online, you'll have the exciting opportunity to:

- View covers of upcoming books
- Read sample chapters
- Learn about our future publishing schedule (listed by publication month *and author*)
- Find out when your favorite authors will be visiting a city near you
- Search for and order backlist books from our online catalog
- Check out author bios and background information
- Send e-mail to your favorite authors
- Meet the Kensington staff online
- Join us in weekly chats with authors, readers and other guests
- Get writing guidelines
- AND MUCH MORE!

**Visit our website at**
**http://www.zebrabooks.com**

# THE COURTSHIP

## Anna DeForest

Zebra Books
Kensington Publishing Corp.

http://www.zebrabooks.com

For Joseph,
my loving husband and best companion

Acknowledgments

I would like to thank my wonderful proofreaders—Maureen,
Laurie, Theresa, Julie, Nana Jane, Dawn, Beth, Jill, Sherry,
Jane and Evelyn. Your comments and input improved this
book so much! And once again, my gratitude to my loyal and
capable agent, Pam Hopkins.

ZEBRA BOOKS are published by

Kensington Publishing Corp.
850 Third Avenue
New York, NY 10022

First Printing: October, 1999
10  9  8  7  6  5  4  3  2  1

Printed in the United States of America

# Prologue

*Montana Territory*
*August, 1880*

The man they called Jonah knew he was dying. His shirt was wet and heavy with blood. His legs had gone numb, and he was cold to the marrow of his bones despite the blazing sun which bleached the color from the green-gray sagebrush all about him. Habit and a stubborn refusal to give up kept him in the saddle as the weary buckskin plodded onward.

He felt a flash of anger at the young fool who had brought him to this. Calling himself Arizona Jack, the wild kid had come to the sorry little town where Jonah had hidden himself and challenged him to a gunfight. He had laughed at the kid at first, trying to save his life. He had seen only the boy's youth and ignored the coldness of a born killer in his eyes. For that mistake, Jonah was about to pay with his life—not that it really mattered. Nothing seemed to matter anymore.

Still, he was glad he had sent that murderous, drygulching

Arizona Jack to meet his maker. The punk had waited for him in a canyon and drilled him in the back. Playing possum, he'd shot the young killer when the boy had come to gloat. Although Jonah already had too much blood on his hands, he reckoned the world didn't need any more killers. Which was why it was probably just as well the two bullets the kid had put into his body were going to kill him now.

Jonah closed his eyes against the bright sun. For the past ten years he had struggled and schemed and fought to stay alive. Now he was just too tired to care anymore. Why fight to survive when another bloodthirsty youngster hunting a reputation would just come along and plug him when he wasn't watching?

There was one thing he had to do, though, before he packed it in. After he reined up the buckskin, he slipped from the saddle. Just before his knees buckled, he managed to catch hold of the pommel and swore under his breath. He had to stay conscious for just a few minutes more. The buckskin was a damn fine horse, and he deserved his chance to survive in this rough country.

Forcing back the waves of darkness threatening to engulf him, Jonah loosened the cinch strap and tugged the saddle from the horse's back. The heavy weight knocked Jonah to his knees. Fighting his way back to his feet, he reached out and used the horse's neck to steady himself. Frightened by the scent of blood, the buckskin blew and shifted uneasily.

"Whoa, now, fella, steady there. Let me get this bridle off you, and then you're free to do as you please." With shaking hands, Jonah stripped off the bridle and let it fall to the ground. He stood there panting from the effort it cost him simply to raise his arms.

The buckskin snorted and rubbed his sweaty, itchy head against him. Jonah raised his hand to give the horse a final pat; but his legs gave way, and he slumped to the ground. He crawled over to his saddle and laid his head back on the seat. He stared up at the empty blue sky. If there was a God, he would be meeting Him shortly. But Jonah had his doubts about God. How could any self-respecting deity create a creature as mean, quarrelsome, and just plain ornery as man?

With his poor luck, chances were he wouldn't even get an opportunity to ask God that question. Considering all the killing he'd done, they would probably just send him straight to the fires of hell. Damned if he cared. His mouth couldn't be any drier than it was now.

So, he was going to die alone, in the wildest country left in the West. That seemed fitting, all and all. He'd lived most of his life that way. It was a sad thing, though, for a man to die leaving no family, no friends, no woman, no children to mourn his passing. Those human ties were all that truly mattered. If only he could have a second chance, what different choices he would make.

But there were no second chances for a man like him. The gunfighter known only as Jonah closed his eyes and let the darkness take him.

# Chapter One

*Northwestern Colorado*
*September, 1887*

Morning sunlight burnished the grove of aspen trees beside the road bright gold as Miranda Kilpatrick and her young nephews, Sean and Rory Broden, drove into town. They all laughed when a breeze swirled aspen leaves in a shimmering coil around the buckboard. To the north and east, snow already crowned the jagged crests of the highest peaks. Old-timers were predicting it was going to be a long, hard winter here on the western side of the Rockies.

Miranda frowned as she considered that prediction and its implications for her new saloon. Winter could be a good season in the saloon business, as long as she could still obtain supplies of whisky and her patrons could reach town to drink. And she needed a good season, needed it desperately with so many people counting on her to provide for them.

She roused herself from her worrying as they approached the outskirts of Pine Creek.

"The new schoolmaster is here!" Rory's freckled face flushed with excitement as he pointed to the buckboard tied up before the schoolhouse. Miranda smiled at her nine-year-old nephew's exuberance while she moved one hand closer to his shoulder to keep him from falling off the seat. Rory had inherited his blue eyes and bright red hair from the Kilpatrick side of his family. Ever since he was little, his sweet nature and unbridled enthusiasm for life had won Rory a special place in her heart.

"Aw, I don't see what you're getting so het up about. A new schoolteacher just means school's gonna start next week after all." This glum comment came from Sean, sitting on the other side of her. Sean was a strong, sturdy boy with his father's brown eyes and blond hair. Miranda loved Sean fiercely, too. She respected his strength of will, his loyalty, and the soft heart he hid beneath his tough boy exterior. The sullen, guarded look she saw in his eyes too often these days saddened her. Because he had just turned twelve, Miranda was trusting Sean with the reins, but she was also keeping a weather eye out for possible collisions.

"We're lucky the school board was able to find such a capable schoolteacher willing to come to our little town. Surely he'll have brought with him a new book or two you'll not have read," she said lightly.

Sean perked up at that idea, just as she had guessed he would. Even though Sean pretended to hate school, he did love stories and books, an enthusiasm she encouraged all she could. The dirt road twisted then, and they turned onto the one and only street of Pine Creek.

It was still early enough that a few of the shopkeepers were out sweeping the boardwalks before their false-fronted stores. No one tipped their hats to Miranda or smiled at her. Instead, all she and her young nephews received were disapproving stares. Miranda straightened her shoulders and held her head high as Sean carefully reined the team to a halt before Mr. Peabody's General Store and Dry Good. She thanked Sean gravely when he handed her down from the buckboard. Afterward, with a self-important air which made her smile, he turned to tie up the horses.

"Can I run back to the schoolhouse?" Rory asked, his eyes alight with curiosity. For once, there was something more fascinating in town than Mr. Peabody's striped candy to hold Rory's interest.

"That you may, but don't you go pestering the man," Miranda said, making an effort to keep her tone severe. "I heard he's come all the way from St. Louis, and he's probably weary from traveling."

"Can I go, too?" Sean asked. "That's some horse he has tied up behind his wagon."

Miranda sighed. She would have liked the distraction of their company while she went through the ordeal of placing her weekly order at the store. But she didn't have the heart to say no when both boys were so eager, and she had so few ways she could indulge them.

"All right, Sean, you can go, too." Both boys went racing off like the ruffians most of the townsfolk undoubtedly thought them. "Mind neither of you get into trouble, now," she called after them, but she doubted her warning would do much good. Trouble seemed to follow her two lively young nephews wherever they went. Since she had been much the same when she was their age, it was hard to hold their spirited ways or their knack for making mischief against them.

She turned about to face the store and drew in a deep breath. Randy Murchinson and Red Smith, two of the town's worst idlers and bullies, lounged in chairs on either side of the door.

"Howdy thar, sweet Miranda." Randy leered at her.

"You're lookin' mighty fetching today." Red winked. The men's greetings were cordial enough on the surface, but the tone in which they were uttered and the way the men looked at her made Miranda's skin crawl.

"It's Miss Kilpatrick to you both, for I've not given you leave to use my given name." She met their lewd gazes with a level look of her own.

"She shore is uppity for an Irish whore," Randy leaned over and told Red in a mock whisper.

Miranda gritted her teeth and strode past the two grinning men. There was no use trying to change their minds. She wasn't a whore and never had been, but she realized most of the citizens of Pine Creek regarded her as such.

A bell tinkled as she pushed open the door to the dry good and stepped inside. At once, the rich scents of spices, peppermint and tobacco enveloped her. Her heart fell when she saw Mrs. Reed and Mrs. Goodwin at the counter already conducting their business with Mr. Peabody. The women stopped talking with each other the moment they turned about and saw her standing in the doorway. Deliberately they turned their backs on her and resumed their conversation, in lowered voices now.

Cheeks burning, Miranda went to browse the shelves while she waited for Mr. Peabody to fill Mrs. Reed's and Mrs. Goodwin's orders. Of course, two of Pine Creek's most estimable matrons wouldn't lower themselves to speak to an Irish girl, particularly one who ran a saloon. As soon as they finished making their purchases, they hurried from the store.

"Good day to you, Mr. Peabody," she said politely to the storekeeper. "Here's the list of what we'll be wanting this week."

The storekeeper didn't even bother to return her pleasantry. Instead, he grabbed her list and began filling it in surly silence. Reining in her rising temper, Miranda marched away from the counter and pretended a fascination with a bolt of blue gingham she hardly felt.

She had known it would be like this, known the moment folks found out she was going to run the saloon they would

brand her a fallen woman. But she hadn't known how hard it
was going to be to cope with their contempt on a daily basis.
Some days, she longed to throw their hypocrisy back in their
faces. What would Mrs. Goodwin say if she realized her precious Thomas came to the Shamrock at least once a week and
stared at Miranda's ankles and bodice while she sang? Even
rude Mr. Peabody patronized her establishment on a regular
basis.

Miranda let out a long breath. If she faced the same dilemma
she had six months ago, she would make the same choices all
over again. She finally had a sure way of providing for her
small family. During the past few months since she had taken
over the Shamrock, the saloon's profits had risen steadily. Word
had gotten out she kept a clean, well-run place with fair gambling and good music. She doubted the saloon would ever make
her rich, but it was going to keep a roof over her head and
food on the table. From bitter experience she had learned never
to take those two commodities for granted. She simply had to
ignore the scorn of her fellow townsfolk.

Mr. Peabody was just finishing up her order when the boys
came rushing into the store to find her.

"We just met the new schoolteacher. He doesn't say much,
but he seems real nice, and he's coming here to talk with you,"
Rory announced.

Miranda closed her eyes. Sweet St. Agnes grant her patience.
The boys had been away from her for a half-hour, and already
they had gotten into trouble.

"What did you two heathens do?" she asked them, suddenly
feeling weary despite the fact it was only nine o'clock in the
morning. How on earth had her own dear grandmother managed
to raise ten children and keep her sanity? The last thing she
had wanted was for the boys to alienate the new schoolmaster.
Education was the only way her nephews were going to better
themselves.

"We didn't do anything wrong, Aunt Miranda, honest. Sean

helped Mr. Johnston carry a crate of books inside and unpack them. They started talking about the books, and the schoolmaster got excited when he realized you'd been reading Shakespeare and that Sir Walter Scott fellow to us.''

"Is this true, Sean Shamus Broden?''

"Yes, ma'am. You should see the books Mr. Johnston brought with him. The schoolhouse is starting to look like one of those libraries you told us about back east. He has three whole crates of books, and he said I could stay after school and read them all if I liked.''

Miranda realized she was fast running out of time to interrogate her nephews. Through the open door of the store, she spotted a tall man wearing a pair of gold spectacles and a somber suit walking across the street to the store. He surely looked like a schoolteacher, and she had never seen him about Pine Creek before.

"Well, looky what we have here,'' Randy Murchinson sang out from his chair by the door. "If it ain't a real city gent come to live in our poor little town.''

"Feller looks like an honest-to-gawd professor to me,'' Red chimed in.

The schoolmaster slowed his pace and eyed the two men warily. Miranda bit her lip. Clearly Randy and Red had decided he would be easy prey.

"Say, professor, you got time to recite us a poem or two?''

"As a matter-of-fact, I'm afraid I don't, gentlemen. I just arrived in town, and I am eager to get settled. I'm looking for two boys I just spoke with over at the school, and their aunt.'' While he talked, Miranda closed her eyes and simply enjoyed the sound. What an elegant voice that man possessed. He spoke with a clear, precise diction she knew she could never master, no matter how hard she tried to shed the last of her Irish accent. His deep, rich voice made little shivers chase down her spine. If he could carry a tune, he would be a wonderful singer.

The two men exchanged looks and snickered. "Why, I don't

believe we've seen any boys today, have we, Red, much less any aunties?''

"Nary a one. That seem a bit strange to you, Randy? You'd think a nice town like this would be full of boys and aunties.''

Miranda hustled through the doorway, meaning to stop their cruel teasing before it became any worse.

"A good day to you, sir. My name is Miranda Kilpatrick, and I believe you just spoke with my two nephews. We were just finishing up our business here. Rory and Sean—'' she glanced back over her shoulder ''—please go fetch the supplies Mr. Peabody has set out on his counter for us and put them in the buckboard.''

She turned back toward the schoolmaster and stepped off the boardwalk into the dusty street. "If you wished to speak with me, I'm afraid you'll have to accompany me to Doc Wheeler's office. I'm in a bit of a hurry this morning." A part of her cringed at her forwardness, but she couldn't think of any other way to get him away from Randy and Red before the two became truly offensive.

She paused when she stood three steps away from the schoolmaster. She glanced up and found herself looking into a beautiful pair of gray eyes rimmed round by long, dark brown lashes. His hair, what she could see of it under his hat, was cropped short. It was a handsome brown-gold color with a tendency to curl at the ends. His nose was regally straight, his jaw firm and strong. A forceful brow and stark cheekbones gave him a forbidding look. Yet the expression in his gray eyes seemed quizzical, almost as if he guessed that she was trying to rescue him. His tone when he spoke to her was serious and polite.

"Hello, Miss Kilpatrick. It's my pleasure to meet you. My name is Tobias Johnston, and as you may have surmised, I am Pine Creek's new schoolmaster. I would be delighted to escort you to Doc Wheeler's office."

"Well, then, that would be grand." She let go a breath, wondering why she suddenly felt so flustered. Since she started running the saloon, she had spent a great deal of time around men. She couldn't remember the last time one of them made her heart beat faster. But this one definitely had the blood pounding in her veins. He seemed more appealing the longer she looked at him. He was tall and lean, and he surely had a fine set of shoulders beneath that somber suit he wore. She'd always been partial to broad-shouldered men.

When he found out she owned and ran a saloon, he wouldn't be so quick to escort her anywhere, she reminded herself sadly. In fact, he probably would never speak to her again. Proper schoolmasters didn't consort with improper saloon keepers.

She stepped back up onto the boardwalk and started off toward the doctor's office. The schoolmaster fell into step beside her, automatically shortening his long stride to keep pace with hers.

"What is it you wanted to speak with me about?" she asked when she could contain her curiosity no longer.

She risked a quick peek at him. The correct and formal schoolteacher appeared to be fascinated by her hair. Folks often stared at it when they thought she wasn't looking. It was a particularly eye-catching shade of red. Her father had called it the glorious color of living flame, but he was a poetic soul and hardly a man to be objective about his daughter's looks. Since she was a small girl, the fiery color of her hair had been one of the greatest trials of her existence.

Then again, the schoolmaster might just be looking at the battered and bleached flowers on her old bonnet. That notion was hardly more comforting. Miranda's chin went up a notch higher. What money she had these days went to her nephews' clothes, not her own.

When Tobias Johnston obviously realized she had caught him staring, he looked away and cleared his throat. "I was quite impressed to discover your nephews seemed so familiar with the works of Shakespeare, not to mention Scott and Tennyson."

"Ah, well, the boys love stories, and I found out reading to them was one sure way to keep them out of mischief. Not that they are bad boys, mind you," she added hurriedly. "It's just that they are so active. The tales keep their minds occupied, and they give them something to play act when Sean and Rory are running about together."

"But what made you choose Shakespeare? I doubt that's the usual choice adults read to young ones here in Pine Creek."

Miranda glanced up at him, wondering if she heard irony and humor in that perfectly correct tone of his.

"I suppose it isn't. But my da was an actor, you see, and so I was raised from the cradle on Shakespeare and the poets." She waited to see derision in his expression. Usually Americans seemed to think acting was as great a sin as being Irish. Instead, when the schoolmaster glanced her way again, she could read only the same mild, polite interest he had shown toward her all along.

"That explains Sean's fascination with my books. That also probably explains how a young Irishwoman living in a frontier town came to be named Miranda. 'Oh brave new world, that has such people in't.' "

There was no mistaking it now. That dry note in his voice was humor. "I see you've more than a passing acquaintance with the bard yourself," she exclaimed delightedly.

"My own father had a passion for Shakespeare," he admitted. "He was a preacher. Although many men of the cloth in this country disapprove of Shakespeare's writings, my father always claimed William Shakespeare understood the heart of Christianity better than some of the apostles."

"My father believed most of the human experience is reflected in Shakespeare's writings," Miranda offered. "The day I was born, he decided there were already plenty of Cathleen and Colleen Kilpatricks in the world. When I reached out and grabbed his finger, yelling like a banshee all the while, he decided right there and then I deserved a different sort of name.''

"Any young woman brave enough to take on raising two nephews in a rough western town like this one surely must possess a sense of adventure. Your father obviously named you well.'' He smiled at her, and Miranda felt her heart do a somersault in her chest. When the schoolmaster smiled, his lovely gray eyes lit up, and years seem to fall away from him.

Again, she smiled back, wishing with all her heart that Pine Creek was ten times bigger and it would take them an hour to reach Doc Wheeler's office. Suddenly, the schoolmaster seemed to remember himself, and his smile disappeared.

"Well, Miss Miranda Kilpatrick," he said, returning to his formal, correct tone, "I was wondering if you would allow Sean to stay after school a few days a week to do some extra reading. Rory would be welcome, too, if he's interested.''

They were passing the Shamrock now. Miranda resolutely refrained from glancing through the window to see if Otis had swept up the saloon properly after she left last night. Mr. Tobias Johnston would find out quickly enough what she did to make a living.

"Sean already told me you suggested something of the sort,'' she replied. "He has chores he's to do after school, but I'll figure out a way to get by without his help. I'd love to see you encourage him any way you can with his studies. Sean loves to read, but he doesn't care much for the rest of his schoolwork.''

"We'll just see what we can do about that,'' the schoolmaster said with another smile, a more guarded one this time.

Tobias Johnston had the most wonderful, sensitive mouth, she decided dreamily, but that sensitivity seemed at odds with his firm chin and strong jaw. In fact, the sternness of his jawline seemed to contradict his gentle demeanor and the almost hesitant way he carried himself.

With a little start of disappointment, she noticed they had reached Doc Wheeler's office. It had been a long time since any gentleman, much less such a fine-looking one, had treated her like a lady. Soon the townsfolk would tell him what business she ran. Chances were, the next time she saw him, he wouldn't treat her with such respect. *Well, Miranda Kilpatrick,* she told herself bracingly, *Mr. Johnston is welcome to think what he likes of you, but you're going to hold him to his offer to let Sean read his books after school, come hell or high water.*

As they stood on the boardwalk before the door to Doc Wheeler's office, she wished she could think of some topic to keep Tobias Johnston standing there talking with her a few minutes longer. But then she spotted Mrs. Reed watching them from across the street, her disapproval and outrage obvious. At once, Miranda realized the painful truth. Because they taught the young, schoolmasters were supposed to be beyond reproach. It could only hurt Tobias Johnston's reputation to be seen with her.

Miranda glanced up at the schoolmaster and sent him a bright smile of dismissal. "Here we are. I'll be thanking you most kindly for your escort, Mr. Johnston, and I thank you for your interest in my nephews. I wish you the best of luck getting settled."

She thought she saw a gleam of curiosity flash in those intelligent gray eyes of his. He glanced the way she had just looked, across the street toward Mrs. Reed, who was still glaring at them both. When he looked back at Miranda, his gaze was unreadable. "Once again, Miss Kilpatrick, it was my pleasure." He tipped his hat to her and turned about to walk back the way they had come.

Despite Mrs. Reed's dour presence, Miranda allowed herself to look after him for a few moments. Tobias Johnston was surely one fine figure of a man, she decided wistfully. Ah, well, she could look forward to the times she'd see him about town, for he was easy on the eye. She had no real interest in courting and marrying any sort of man, respectable or otherwise. Her dream was to put down roots, have a house of her own and a reliable way of providing for herself as an independent woman. Now, thanks to the Shamrock and her dear departed Uncle Shamus, a good part of her dream was coming true. Of course, she'd always longed for good friends and the respect of her community. That part of her dream would never come true in Pine Creek, but the desperate times she had survived these past few years made her grateful for what she did have now.

Trying to put the new schoolmaster from her mind, Miranda knocked on the door to the office. Doc Wheeler made a special liniment for his patients with rheumatism, and Lucas Ransom, the oldest member of her household, had recently run out. When the damp weather came, the old gambler's joints ached and his knuckles grew so swollen it was hard for him to deal cards for her at the Shamrock.

Doc Wheeler opened the door and greeted her with a smile. She returned his greeting warmly. Doc Wheeler and her uncle had been great friends, and the doctor was one of the few in town who refused to treat her like a leper for taking over her uncle's saloon business.

Ten minutes later she emerged from the doctor's office with a good-sized bottle of his liniment. She hurried back toward the dry good, wondering if Rory and Sean had managed to stay out of trouble during the brief time she had left them alone. She heaved a sigh of relief when she spotted them both perched on the front seat of the buckboard. As she drew closer, she noticed they were staring at something happening on the other side of the buckboard with great interest.

When she reached her team, she saw with a sinking heart that Tobias Johnston stood in the street before the store, Randy and Red on either side of him. Clearly he had returned to the dry good to make a few purchases of his own, for he now held two brown-wrapped parcels in his hands. The sun glinted off his wire-rimmed spectacles. He no longer wore his hat, however, for Randy Murchinson was twirling it about on his hand.

"You want your hat back, Mr. Schoolmaster, you're gonna have to ask for it, nice and polite-like," she heard Randy say.

"Please, gentlemen, I would like to have my hat back," Tobias Johnston said slowly, his deep voice completely devoid of emotion.

Randy made a great show of starting to hand it over. When the schoolmaster reached for his hat, Randy caught it back suddenly. "Shucks, I think I changed my mind."

Miranda bit her lip. As much as she longed to plunge in and help the schoolmaster, she knew she couldn't interfere again. He would lose face before everyone if he was rescued by a woman. He would have to learn to deal with the less savory characters in Pine Creek even as she had.

Her heart still ached for him. He stood, his head bent, his hands clasped into fists as the two bullies began to toss his hat back and forth between them like naughty boys. At last Randy and Red grew tired of their game. It was clear they weren't going to provoke him into a show of temper or into the fight they wanted.

"Schoolmaster, wherever you hail from, the men must not be worth spit," Red declared with disgust. He deliberately dropped the hat and kicked it across the dusty street. Tobias Johnston never moved. Laughing between themselves, the two men swaggered away.

The schoolmaster stood quietly for a long minute, looking at his hat. At last he leaned over and picked it up. He turned and slapped it against a nearby porch post, his motions strained and taut.

Miranda eased toward the buckboard, for she didn't want him to see her standing on the boardwalk and think she had witnessed the entire scene. He must have noticed the motion out of the corner of his eye, however, for he spun about warily. Their eyes met. His gray gaze burned with a wild rage which made Miranda reach a hand to her throat. In that instant, he didn't look like a mild-mannered schoolmaster in the least.

And then he glanced away from her. He clapped his hat on his head, turned about, and strode off toward the schoolhouse. Miranda stared after him, wondering if she had imagined the violent anger she had just seen in his eyes.

# **Chapter Two**

Miranda stood on the back porch, enjoying a stolen moment of quiet in the midst of the hurly-burly which always took place before meals in her household. The evening sun slanted across the hardy yellow and lavender asters and purple fireweed which had survived the first frosts of autumn. She loved this little garden, just as she loved with all her heart the simple white clapboard house Uncle Shamus had left her.

He'd originally built it for his beloved Kathleen, a sweet young Irishwoman he'd met and married in New York. He'd refused to let her face the discomfort and dangers of living in the mountains of Colorado until he'd built a home fit for her. Sadly, though, the very summer Uncle Shamus finished this house, his Kathleen caught typhoid in New York and died. Da claimed Uncle Shamus had never been the same after that blow. He kept on with his gold hunting and his saloon keeping, but much of the joy went out of him with Kathleen's death.

Miranda cherished the home her uncle had built with such loving care for the bride who had never seen it. After years of traveling about the country like tumbleweeds with her parents, Miranda had come to treasure permanence. After nearly starving in Nebraska a year ago, she had come to treasure security.

"Miranda, supper's ready to serve up," Christina called from the doorway.

Miranda smiled at her young Swedish housekeeper. "I'll be right in," she replied.

She took a final look at her garden. Next season she planned to try transplanting some of the delicate wildflowers that grew in profusion in the meadows about Pine Creek. Many women sneered at those wild plants as weeds, but she loved their glorious colors. Nodding to her garden in promise, she went inside.

Soon she was bustling about the table, making sure Rory and Sean had enough stew and biscuits for their supper. She dished out a generous second helping to Lucas, the lean old gambler who had become a second father to her. No matter how she tried, she never seemed to be able to fatten him up.

"Don't you be leaving those carrots," she admonished Sean when she came to his place and saw most of his first helping was gone already. Sean ate like a young wolf these days; but he was none too partial to vegetables, and carrots were among his least favorite. His mouth tightened at her nagging, but he never said a word.

She was surprised, therefore, when she glanced over a few minutes later and saw Sean had indeed eaten every one of his carrots with no more cajoling from her.

"I got something you're supposed to read," he announced with the air of someone determined to get an unpleasant chore over with. "It's a note from the schoolmaster." He reached into his pant's pocket and fished out a mangled note which he handed to her.

"Oh, Sean, surely you didn't get into trouble already? School's only been in for two days now."

He made no answer, but the way he dropped his gaze to the table told her all she needed to know.

"I was so hoping you'd make a good impression on Mr. Johnston. You two seemed to start off well."

"Who cares what a lily-livered piece of milk toast like him thinks, anyway?"

"Sean Shamus Broden, you'll not be speaking of your elders in such a disrespectful tone, most especially the man who is going to be teaching you your letters this next year."

"But we all saw him. We all saw the way he let Randy and Red push him around."

"So you'd think better of the man if he'd started a brawl in the street just to get his hat back?"

"At least I'd know he had the guts to stand up for himself." Sean dropped his spoon and pushed back his chair. "Can I be excused?"

"But Christina made apple pie for dessert. It's one of your favorites."

"I don't feel like dessert tonight," he replied sullenly.

"All right, you may go, but don't forget to finish your chores." Miranda watched, perplexed, as Sean stalked away from the table.

"May I be excused, too?" Rory piped up.

Miranda smiled fondly at her younger nephew. It was a sign of the hero worship he felt for Sean that he was willing to forego his dessert to keep his brother company. The two boys were unusually close because the gradual decline and death of their mother last year had forged a strong bond between them.

She nodded her permission and sank down into her chair. Suddenly, her own portion of stew no longer seemed appealing. Although she had been hungry moments ago, Sean's news had stolen away her appetite.

"It's only natural, you know. Boys respect strength at his age," Lucas said quietly.

"There's different kinds of strength, and well you know it.

I'm thinking Mr. Johnston possesses the strength of restraint, but Sean is too young to understand that idea yet.'' She shuddered inwardly, remembering the look she had seen in the schoolmaster's eyes. She still wondered about that look, and whether she had just imagined the violence in it.

She thought about Tobias Johnston at the most peculiar moments. The handsome planes of his strong face came to her when she was washing glasses at the saloon. Suddenly, while she was helping Christina in the kitchen, she'd picture the way his nice, broad shoulders filled out the simple suit he wore. And at night, before drifting off to sleep, she'd remember the deep timbre of his voice, and her body would shiver beneath the covers.

She couldn't remember the last time a man had caught her fancy this way. And now her eldest nephew had probably alienated the schoolmaster for good. Indeed, Tobias Johnston was probably wondering just what sort of an aunt she was.

She shook her head, opened the wrinkled note, and spread it out upon the dinner table.

*September 14*

*Dear Miss Kilpatrick,*

   *I discovered your nephew fighting in the school yard today and yesterday. I would appreciate your coming to the schoolhouse at your earliest convenience so that we may discuss this matter.*

                                   *Yours Respectfully,*
                                   *Tobias Johnston*

Such a polite note it was, written in a clear, masculine hand. She would go to see the schoolmaster after school let out on the morrow. She'd been looking forward to the next time she saw Tobias Johnston about town. Now she could only feel chagrin and embarrassment about their upcoming meeting.

Miranda forced down several mouthfuls of stew because she had a long night of work and singing ahead of her at the saloon. When she had finished, she rose to her feet and took her dishes to the dry sink.

"I'll see to the washing up," Christina spoke up softly. "You go get ready."

Miranda sent Christina a grateful smile. Christina was the newest and quietest member of her household, but already Miranda didn't know what she would do without her. Miranda had met her back in Keene, Nebraska, after she had started singing at Nolan's Saloon to earn money to feed her family.

Miranda had liked the lovely young Swedish girl with the sad blue eyes from the start. Shy Christina had worked as a hurdy-gurdy girl, but she also had been Johnny Nolan's mistress. Miranda discovered this fact the night she had found Christina sobbing in her room. Nolan had beaten her savagely for dancing one too many times with a handsome young cowboy who was smitten with her.

Two weeks before she left Keene to move to Pine Creek, Miranda had gone to see Christina. "I'm leaving town to take over a saloon of my own in northwestern Colorado," Miranda had told her. "My Uncle Shamus left it to me in his will. I wouldn't want you to work upstairs or dance with my customers. But I do need someone to look after my nephews while I'm running the saloon. I can't pay much, but I can promise you a roof over your head and a chance to get away from Johnny Nolan once and for all."

Christina had accepted her offer immediately. Despite her youth and her quiet ways, she was surprisingly firm with Rory and Sean. During the trip to Colorado, Christina had confided that she once had seven younger brothers and sisters, but they and her parents had all died in a cholera outbreak which had wiped out much of their settlement in South Dakota. For a time, she had been passed from family to family, never really fitting in anywhere. When she was only fifteen, Nolan had traveled through the settlement and spotted her at the general store. He had talked her into coming to work at his saloon to dance with his customers, promising her good money and lots of pretty dresses.

Christina clearly regretted that decision, and the three years she had spent with Johnny Nolan had left their mark. She avoided men like the plague now, with the exception of Lucas. Miranda hoped that time would help heal her, but she feared Christina might never be truly happy again.

Miranda sighed as she hurried upstairs to change into the flashier clothes she wore at the saloon. From her days on the road with her father, she had learned the importance of dressing properly for a role. At night, she played the part of a worldly saloon keeper and sophisticated barroom singer, and she played it well. The hems on her saloon dresses were a little shorter, the bodices tighter and lower than the dresses she wore during the day. She couldn't bring herself to dress like a harlot, and she told herself it wasn't appropriate that she should, for she was the owner and proprietor of the Shamrock.

She was well aware some men rode miles simply to look at her or listen to her sing. That was fine, as long as all they did was look and listen. She didn't tolerate anyone pawing her.

Lucas Ransom wouldn't tolerate it, either. Even now, the old gunslinger was changing into his fancy gambling clothes. He insisted on accompanying her every night to the saloon. He ran the games for her, and ran them fairly and cleanly. No matter how busy the gambling grew in his corner of the saloon, she knew he kept a careful eye on her, and she was grateful for his protection.

Miranda grimaced at herself in the mirror as she pulled a few curls loose to dangle seductively beside her ears. Would the schoolmaster have found out by tomorrow what she did to make a living? Even though Tobias had only been here for three days, Pine Creek was such a small town, she rather guessed he would. She would have to endure his contempt along with the contempt of everyone else in this town.

But a small voice in the back of her mind kept warning her 'twould be the hardest slight she had endured yet if tomorrow Tobias Johnston looked at her with scorn and loathing in those clear gray eyes of his.

Tobias smiled to himself while he watched Teddy Clausen write laboriously for the thirty-second time, "I will not tease girls," across the blackboard. Tobias had a strong hunch the writing part of the exercise did not constitute a particularly effective punishment for young Teddy. What did pain the boy was the fact he had to stay inside for an extra hour after school while his friends were all having a fine time outside. Teddy sighed, looked longingly out the window, scratched his nose, and started to write, "I will not tease girls," for the thirty-third time.

Tobias swung about when his instincts warned him that he and Teddy were no longer alone in the schoolhouse. Miranda Kilpatrick stood in the doorway, looking apprehensive and uncertain. He guessed she'd made a special effort to appear respectable for her meeting with her nephew's schoolmaster. She wore an indigo dress and a black shawl. If she meant to look demure, she had failed miserably. The simple lines of the dress emphasized her womanly figure, and the deep blue color of the fabric brought out the remarkable shade of her eyes. Beneath the simple hat she wore, she had tamed that magnificent red hair of hers into a severe bun.

The bun was a mistake, too, he decided after studying her for a long moment. By taming the wayward wisps of copper and cinnamon hair, which had curled about her face the last time he saw her, she showed off the delicate line of her jaw. Seeing that mass of hair confined so strictly made a man fantasize about pulling it down in luscious waves about her shoulders.

Tobias cleared his throat. "Ah, there you are, Miss Kilpatrick. I will be with you in a moment." He nodded to her and turned away, ostensibly to scan the blackboard.

"That will do, Theodore," he said gruffly. "I trust you will practice more restraint in the future. As tempting as Miss Henderson's braids may appear to you, you will not go pinning them to the back of her chair, or dipping them in your inkwell, or do anything else to torment the young lady in question."

Grateful for the distraction his wayward pupil offered, Tobias found himself warming to the lecture. "If you do, the next time I will take a paddle to your backside, and I promise you will find it a most unpleasant experience. Do I make myself clear?"

"Yes, Mr. Johnston."

"Very well, Theodore. You are excused."

Young Teddy Clausen caught up his cap and books. The relief on his face as he hurried past Tobias's desk was palpable. Tobias followed Teddy down the aisle between the desks. The moment he reached the door, Teddy bolted down the steps to join two of his friends lingering along the edges of the school yard.

"Poor Teddy." Tobias looked after him with a shake of his head. "I'm afraid he's lost his heart to Miss Henderson, but he hasn't the slightest notion of how to go about winning her regard."

"It sounds like your students have given you a lively start to your school year," Miranda offered with a tentative smile.

When Tobias looked down into her blue eyes, he was surprised by the fact his heart was beating faster. The sweetness in her smile gave him pause as well. He had been startled last Thursday when Mrs. Reed had stalked into the schoolhouse to inform him that the young Irishwoman he had escorted to the doctor's office ran a saloon. Mrs. Reed had proceeded to stay almost a half hour, telling him every scandalous rumor she'd ever heard about Miranda Kilpatrick. Mrs. Reed had also gossiped shamelessly about many of the parents of his students before he could get rid of the garrulous woman. Her stories about Miranda had surprised him. He'd known plenty of women who worked the row in his time, and Miranda Kilpatrick just didn't seem the type.

If she was a prostitute, she had to be relatively new to the business. She didn't have the world-weary, cynical look in her eyes they all had after years of selling themselves to rough western men. There was pride and spirit in her, and compassion. His lips twitched as he remembered the way she had tried to save him from those blustering bullies before Peabody's Dry Good.

"My pupils have given me an interesting time, indeed," he said, his mind hardly aware of the words he spoke. "I had no idea what a wide variety of wildlife the boys would smuggle into this room in their pockets and lunch pails during the past three days. To date, I have confiscated and liberated two frogs, one mouse, a snake, and several grasshoppers. If I had just thought back to my own school days, I should have known what to expect."

She smiled with less caution in her expression this time. "Is this your first year teaching?"

"I taught students in the eighth grade back in St. Louis for three months, long enough to know I enjoyed the work, but not long enough to realize what a challenge it was going to be to manage eight grades at once in the same room."

Annoyed to find himself prattling on like a smitten schoolboy, he took refuge in his most stern, schoolmasterish tone. "I realize you didn't come today to hear about the trials of an inexperienced schoolmaster. We need to discuss your nephew's behavior. Please, Miss Kilpatrick, would you like to sit down?" He gestured to a nearby bench.

Her expression cooled instantly. "Thank you, no," she replied. "I would prefer to stand."

"As you wish. Unfortunately, I had to break up a fight again today between Sean and Jimmy Smith, and your nephew was involved in a scuffle the first day of school with Robby McGregor as well. Three altercations in three days is quite a record, even for a twelve-year-old boy."

"It certainly is," she allowed in a stifled voice. The glint in her eye made Tobias think young Sean was going to receive quite a talking-to this evening.

"Neither Sean, Robby, nor Jimmy Smith would tell me what the fights were about, but there were several witnesses, and I was able to get them to spill the beans, so to speak. On each occasion, the other boys teased Sean until he lost his temper."

Her eyes darkened, and her face grew pale. Tobias guessed right then she knew exactly what he was going to say.

"At first Jimmy and Robby teased Sean about being Irish. Your nephew managed to take that well enough in stride, but when they began to call you names, it was too much for him."

She looked so stricken, he cleared his throat again. "I wanted you to know I've taken steps to discipline Jimmy Smith and Robby McGregor as well as Sean. I'll be talking with their parents this afternoon, and hopefully we'll soon have this matter cleared up. Although in many ways I respect your nephew's loyalty to you, I cannot tolerate his brawling in my school yard."

"Of course you mustn't tolerate such behavior," she said in her musical voice, her chin held high. "You may be sure I'll speak with Sean this very night." Her cheeks burned with color now, and her eyes swam with tears she clearly refused to shed in his presence.

Tobias breathed a silent and most unschoolmasterly curse. Not for the first time, he wished he could have let Jimmy and Robby receive the thorough thrashing they deserved from young Sean. The matter would probably have been laid to rest by now, for Sean Kilpatrick was a fierce and capable fighter. But the children had expected their schoolmaster to interfere, and he'd had little choice but to break up the fights before Sean could give either boy a real licking.

As Tobias gazed at her, he couldn't help wondering if she was one of the finest actresses he had ever come across. Could a hardened harlot possibly be so upset to discover that her nephew had been fighting to protect her reputation? What Miranda Kilpatrick did or didn't do upstairs in that saloon of hers, he reminded himself sternly, was none of his business. Miss Kilpatrick could only mean trouble for Pine Creek's new schoolmaster. He wanted this new life for himself, wanted it with a fervor that surprised him. Keeping her hotheaded nephew in line was the matter, and the only matter, he should be concentrating on now.

"If he gets into another fight, I'll have to take the paddle to Sean and keep him after school." Tobias's tone was harsher than he'd meant it to be, for much of the harshness was directed at himself.

"I understand," she replied and turned to go.

Something about the vulnerable set to her mouth made him add against his better judgment, "I do not envy you your responsibility, Miss Kilpatrick. It must be quite a challenge raising your two nephews on your own. But Sean is a fine boy. I'd like to help him if I could. I understand his mother died last year."

He left the subtle query hanging between them. She turned back to face him, her blue eyes guarded once again.

"The doctor told us she died of pneumonia, but I think it was a broken heart which killed her in the end. My sister Mary married a handsome gunfighter when she was only sixteen, a man who could never stay in one place for more than a few months at a time. She asked him to give up his guns and settle down for her, but he never would. He drifted from town to town, working as a lawman or taking fighting wages during range wars.

"Two years ago he ran off and left her for good. Something inside Mary died when he left her that last time and told her he was never coming back. She came to live with my parents on their farm in Nebraska, and bit by bit she just gave up living. It was so hard for both Sean and Rory, for they adored her, and they couldn't understand why she wouldn't fight harder to stay with them."

Something in her tone told him she couldn't understand that choice herself. Right then he decided Miranda Kilpatrick probably had never been in love.

"What brought you to Pine Creek?" He told himself it was simply professional interest in one of his students that made him ask the question.

"Unfortunately, my father was much better at acting than he was at farming."

Tobias wondered if she realized how her whole expression softened when she spoke of her father.

"He turned to farming to please my mother, but he just wasn't cut out to work the land. Year after year he fought to make that benighted piece of dirt produce a living for us all, but the land won in the end. One day when he was out plowing, he just dropped dead right there in the field. A year later, Mama up and died of typhus. She caught it helping some poor Irish settlers traveling through our town."

"You didn't try to run the farm by yourself, did you?" He was appalled by the notion of this beautiful young woman out plowing fields herself. Once, several lifetimes ago, he too had lived on a farm, and he knew what brutal work it could be.

"I tried, all right," she admitted grimly. "It was the only home we had. But the farm was too much for the boys and me to manage on our own. I was just about at my wit's end when I received a letter from Doc Wheeler here in Pine Creek. He said my Uncle Shamus had passed away and left me his saloon and his house. I think Uncle Shamus and Doc Wheeler thought I'd choose to sell the Shamrock, but I saw it as an answer to all my prayers. Now I've a way to feed Rory and Sean and keep a roof over all our heads." Her blue gaze met his levelly, daring him to condemn the choice she had made.

He rubbed his chin as he thought about the story she had just shared with him. He supposed most schoolmasters would be shocked, but the Good Lord knew, he wasn't cut from the same cloth as most schoolteachers. For the first time, he considered how few the options really were for a woman in the West, trying to support two boys. If she'd been on her own, with her striking looks and her curvaceous figure, she could have found a husband in no time, but those wild nephews of hers had likely scared off most of her suitors.

Instead, she had made a practical, courageous decision and ruined herself in the process. Whether or not she actually whored for her clientele, she was a scarlet woman in the eyes of the town simply for going to a saloon each night. He remembered the scorn and hatred in Mrs. Reed's voice, and the way the woman had looked at Miranda when she stood on the boardwalk before the doctor's office.

"There's a question I've been meaning to ask you." Miranda's voice, with its lilting Irish accent, broke in on his thoughts.

He stiffened. What could she possibly want to ask him? Could she have sensed the truth about him already? She clearly was an intelligent woman, and he was afraid he had let her see too much that day in front of Peabody's store.

"Will you still be sharing your books with Sean, even though he's been so much trouble for you already?"

He forced himself to relax. "Of course, I'd be happy to let him stay after school any day he wishes. In fact, if he started staying in the schoolroom an extra hour, he'd be less apt to run into Jimmy Smith and his friends."

"That would be just grand. I'll suggest that very plan to him when I talk with him tonight. He hasn't mentioned wanting to stay after school, but I think that might be because he wasn't sure of his welcome after the mischief he's caused.'' One moment, her face was alight with enthusiasm. The next, it was as if a wooden mask had slipped over her animated features.

Tobias looked toward the door and saw Mrs. Josiah Smith standing in the doorway. She was dressed quite fashionably for a matron in a western town. Her light blond hair was done up in a severe style which made her angular face look even more sharp and thin. Her pale blue eyes radiated dislike and disapproval as she stared at Miranda.

''I assure you I will give Sean a long talking-to this evening, and you'll see no more fighting in your school yard from my nephew.'' With that, Miranda Kilpatrick turned and walked toward the door, her head held high. Tobias watched in growing anger as Mrs. Smith remained hovering in the doorway. Clearly the woman wasn't going to enter the schoolhouse until Miranda Kilpatrick left. Miranda nodded to her politely, but Mrs. Smith deliberately looked away from her, derision and distaste still writ clear upon her features. It was that look that made Tobias throw all caution to the wind.

''Miss Kilpatrick,'' he called after her.

She paused and looked back over her shoulder, her eyes wide and questioning.

''I understand it's a tradition for the schoolmaster to take supper with the families of all his students. I was hoping I might be able to begin the rounds at Mrs. Smith's home, and then come to yours the following evening. Would this Thursday night be convenient for you, Mrs. Smith?''

Mrs. Smith blinked and began to preen. ''Why, you wish to come to our home before any other in town? Mr. Johnston, we would be honored. I'm sure Thursday is just fine by both Josiah and myself.''

''That is most kind of you. I look forward to that evening. And Miss Kilpatrick, would Friday night be a good time for you and your household?''

Miranda Kilpatrick was watching him, obviously taken aback. Her fair cheeks were stained with color once more, and she shot Mrs. Smith a quick look.

"We'd be most pleased to have you to supper," she said after a few moments.

"That's settled, then. Now, Mrs. Smith, if you would care to come and take a seat, I'd like to talk with you about your son." Mrs. Smith bustled past Miranda into the schoolhouse. As he turned to speak with the older woman, he felt Miranda watching him curiously for several moments before she turned and left.

As he launched into a polite diatribe on the evils of name-calling and fistfights, Tobias told himself he was ten thousand times a fool. In his old life he'd been crazy enough to stand up for others on plenty of occasions, and every time he'd stuck his neck out, his actions had only brought him grief and pain. One of the new rules he'd sworn to live by was to take care of Tobias Johnston first and foremost. He had no cause to go trying to help an Irish girl with hair like fire just because a stiff-necked matron like Mrs. Smith with too much starch in her drawers had snubbed her.

There was nothing he could do to change Miranda's standing in the eyes of the townspeople. She must have realized what she was getting into when she decided to run a saloon. But still, he owed her, for trying to save him from the bullies by the dry good. By inviting himself to dinner, and showing the rest of the town that he, at least, considered her to be acceptable company, he had evened the score between them. He'd always been a man to pay his debts, and that was all there was to it.

Tobias was just finishing his talk with Mrs. Smith when a rangy man in his thirties dressed like a cowpuncher appeared in the doorway.

"I'm Rob McGregor, Robby's father," he said simply and went back outside while Tobias finished his talk with Mrs. Smith. After he escorted Mrs. Smith to the door, he found Rob

McGregor admiring his bay gelding in the corral behind the school.

"That's a fine-looking animal you have there, Mr. Johnston."

Tobias leaned his elbows on the corral rails just as McGregor was doing. "There's more to him than looks. He carried me most of the way from St. Louis."

Rob McGregor shot him a quizzical look which clearly took in his size. "That animal must have more sand and bottom than the South Platte. But I didn't take time off from my ranch work to admire your horse. I'm sorry that boy of mine caused trouble. I had a long talk with him after I got your note. There's no excuse for Robby to be calling anyone names, or for him to be fighting at school. I don't think you'll have any more problems with him, but if you do, just send another note on out our way."

Tobias turned so that he could study McGregor. Talking to him was a refreshing change from listening to Mrs. Smith's endless excuses for her precious Jimmy. McGregor had the brown, weathered face of a man who had lived most of his life outdoors. Tobias knew from Mrs. Reed's remarkably thorough gossip session about his students and their parents that McGregor owned a good-sized ranch five miles out of town, and that his wife had died in childbirth four years ago. Tobias decided he liked this rancher with his level gaze and his straightforward manner.

"Robby's a good boy. I think he just wanted to impress his friends," Tobias said.

"Well, he picked a mighty poor way to go about it. I think Miss Kilpatrick is a fine woman, no matter what the folk in this town say about her."

So that was the way the wind was blowing, Tobias thought cynically. He must have let his thoughts show, for McGregor pushed his hat back on his head and grinned. "Now, you're probably thinking I'm sweet on her, and you'd be dead wrong.

I've got my eye on that pretty little Swedish housekeeper of hers. If Miranda Kilpatrick's a whore, she must be the most particular one this side of the Mississippi. I don't think there's a man in town who has actually gone upstairs with her at the Shamrock. And that's not for a lack of trying on their parts. I've heard of fellows who rode fifty miles just to come and listen to her sing. Most would dearly like to share more with that woman, but she's not having any of them.''

Their talk turned then to town happenings and McGregor's ranch, the Ladder M. Rob McGregor did most of the talking, but Tobias didn't mind. McGregor had the dry, laconic humor of many western men, and Tobias found his view of life in Pine Creek both entertaining and informative. At last McGregor straightened up and said he had to be going. Before he left, he invited Tobias to stop by the Ladder M for a meal anytime.

As he rode back to his own cabin, Tobias found himself thinking about Miranda Kilpatrick once again. A beautiful saloon keeper with lips to drive a man mad and blue eyes he could lose his soul in had no place in the new life he was determined to build for himself. Despite his many failings, he had always been brutally honest with himself, and now there was a truth he didn't want to face at all. He was looking forward to having dinner at her home, looking forward to it far too much.

# Chapter Three

Friday night had come. Miranda bustled about the house, making sure all was in order before the schoolmaster arrived for dinner. She paused in the dining room. For the fourth time, she inspected her mother's best tablecloth for wrinkles or lint.

"You've caught up all the animals, haven't you?" she called after Rory when she spotted her younger nephew trying to slip out the front door. "We wouldn't want Mr. Johnston to think this place is a menagerie."

But in actual fact, she'd let the boys turn her home into one. In the small yard beside the house, her nephews kept a remarkable range of animals, all injured or abandoned creatures they had found during their rambles about the Pine Creek valley. She told herself she allowed them to keep the poor creatures to teach Sean and Rory responsibility. Yet well she knew she had a weak spot herself for injured birds and rabbits. She was less fond of the reptiles her nephews constantly collected, and she forbade their presence in the house.

Rory hung his head. "I caught everyone but Oliver and Henry. I can't find them anywhere."

"Sweet St. Agnes, grant me patience. That's the last thing we need is for Mr. Johnston to see Oliver while he's here. Keep looking for him. Perhaps he's in one of the jars in the pantry again."

Rory perked up at that suggestion and went off to find his missing pets. Miranda hurried back to check the parlor for the fifth time. "What time is it now, Lucas?"

"Exactly four minutes later than the last time you asked me," he replied after consulting his gold pocket watch. "I'm lookin' forward to meeting this schoolmaster of yourn. I don't think I've ever seen you in such a tither over a gent," he teased her with a sly smile.

"And why shouldn't I be worrying about making a good impression on the man who'll be teaching my nephews this year? Where is that Sean? I want to make certain he is clean for a change." She plunged into the kitchen where Christina was frowning at the oven in the cast-iron stove.

"I'm still not sure we should have tried a new recipe for tonight," Christina said doubtfully.

"I refuse to serve a schoolmaster something ordinary. Have you seen Sean?"

"I saw him go upstairs just a few minutes ago," Christina replied, still staring at the oven as if she could will the soufflé to turn out properly.

Miranda rolled her eyes. "I asked him to be home an hour ago. I'll never get him cleaned up in time." She raced up the stairs and dashed into the room Sean shared with Rory. She found her nephew lying on his bed.

"For heaven's sake, Sean. Your teacher will be here any minute, and you look as if you've been playing in a peat bog."

"I don't see what all the fuss is about," Sean said with a mutinous thrust to his chin.

"It's an honor to have the schoolmaster come dine with us,

and we're only the second household in town to entertain him. Now, skeddaddle out of those filthy clothes and change into the clean ones I left on the chair for you there.'' Miranda glanced out the boys' window which overlooked the walk leading to the house. She spotted the schoolmaster tying his horse to the hitching rail beyond their front fence.

"There he is. Wouldn't you know the man would be right on time? Mind you wash your hands and face and comb your hair before you dare set foot in the parlor.''

She was flushed and panting by the time she arrived downstairs again. So much for hoping she'd look poised and collected when she greeted Tobias Johnston at the door. She spared a half second to glance in the hat tree mirror to make sure her hair was still pinned properly. At the sound of a strong, firm knock, Rory came running from the back of the house to stand beside her. She smiled down at her eager nephew. Rory was almost as excited as she was about having his teacher to supper.

When she opened the door, she found Tobias Johnston staring in some fascination at the large pot of geraniums she kept on the front porch.

"Good evening, Miss Kilpatrick.'' He seemed to recollect himself with effort.

"Good evening, Mr. Johnston.'' So much for fussing over her appearance. The man seemed far more taken with her flowers than he was with her.

Rory, who had edged up right beside her, suddenly brightened. "There's Oliver. I knew I'd find him.'' Rory darted forward and caught up the huge bull snake coiled about the base of her geranium pot. Oliver had clearly been enjoying the last rays of warm afternoon sun.

Miranda felt her cheeks heat as her beaming nephew held up the six foot snake for Mr. Johnston's inspection.

"That's a mighty fine specimen you have there,'' he told Rory soberly.

"Isn't he a beaut? We caught him two months ago, and he

seems to like our yard real well. He doesn't like cages, though. Sean and I keep trying, but we can't seem to build anything Oliver can't slip out of.''

"That's clear enough, me boyo,'' Miranda said under her breath. "Mr. Johnston, wouldn't you like to come inside?'' She pasted a bright smile on her face, determined to act as if keeping snakes on one's porch was the way most polite, civilized folks did things.

"Why, thank you.'' The schoolmaster took off his hat and followed her in through the door. Suddenly, her front hallway seemed a great deal smaller. Standing this close to Tobias Johnston, she realized once again what a big man he was. She considered herself to be of medium height, and yet the top of her head only came even with his shoulders.

"Something sure smells good. A man living by himself gets tired of eating his own cooking after a while,'' he said with a smile which warmed her right down to her toes.

She ushered him into the front parlor where the simple furniture she had inherited from her parents gleamed from the polishing she had given it earlier today. Lucas rose from the rocker and watched the schoolmaster with undisguised curiosity. The two men sized each other up while Miranda made the introductions.

They made quite a contrast, the lean, old man and the diffident young teacher towering beside him. Yet Miranda was surprised to realize they possessed a similar look in their eyes, a kind of wariness in the way they watched the world. Before she could contemplate that similarity any further, Sean slipped into the room, looking blessedly neat and clean for a change. He'd even combed his hair just as she had asked. She flashed him a grateful smile before going to check on their supper.

She was taken aback to discover Christina was standing before the stove, wringing her hands. "It was supposed to puff up, and it never did,'' she wailed, her Swedish accent much stronger in her dismay.

Miranda stared in horror at the soufflé they both had labored to create this afternoon. Christina was absolutely right. There was no puff in the elegant French dish she had insisted they make to impress Tobias Johnston. Instead, it looked remarkably like a huge, sagging, yellow flapjack. Miranda groaned aloud. She'd never seen such an unappealing mess. The stars must have dictated this evening was going to be a disaster. She refused to feed their guest cold ham, biscuits and cheese, the only other food she had in the house she could serve for so many on such short notice.

"Perhaps it will taste better than it looks," she suggested hopefully. "Besides, no one but the two of us know what a soufflé is supposed to look like." She crossed her fingers and hoped fervently Mr. Tobias Johnston hadn't run across a French soufflé back in St. Louis.

The evening swiftly slid downhill from there.

After they were all seated at the table, Christina gamely brought forth the soufflé from the kitchen. Because she was watching for his reaction, Miranda saw the schoolmaster's eyes widen when he took in the main course. He smiled and claimed he was quite partial to soufflé, which made Miranda's heart sink. That meant Tobias Johnston did know what soufflés were supposed to look like.

As the dinner progressed, Sean would only reply in abrupt, one-syllable answers to the polite queries the schoolmaster directed his way. Christina, who rarely said a word around a man she didn't know anyway, was so mortified over the disaster of the soufflé she never spoke at all. That left Miranda, Rory and Lucas to carry on the conversation, and the old gambler seemed gleefully bent on grilling the poor man for all he was worth. Miranda shot Lucas daggerlike looks when his questions grew too personal. She supposed her da would have been tempted to do the same thing; but Lucas wasn't her father, and the schoolmaster was hardly courting her.

"So, where do you hail from, Mr. Johnston?" Lucas asked

when they were all starting in on the cherry pie Christina had made, the one part of the meal that had turned out well.

"Kansas, but my folks were from Massachusetts originally."

"Miranda mentioned your pa had been a preacher."

"That he was. Folks came from miles around to hear his sermons. My father could preach to raise the rafters, people always told us."

"Coming from New England, I bet he was all for abolition and such."

"He felt all men should be free," Tobias replied more guardedly.

"That could be a dangerous position for a man to hold in Kansas before the war," Lucas probed shrewdly.

The schoolmaster looked down at his plate, a muscle ticking in his jaw. "Bleeding Kansas was a dangerous place for lots of folks before the war."

Miranda decided it was definitely time for a change of subject. "Are you all settled in?" she asked him.

"I am, indeed. I didn't have much to settle except my books when all was said and done," he replied with a rueful shrug of his shoulders.

"Will Ray Ferguson's old cabin truly suit you?" Miranda asked. "I understand most of our previous schoolmasters boarded with Mrs. Fisher. Surely that arrangement would have been more comfortable for you."

"I'm a man who prefers his privacy. The old cabin suits me just fine," he said so shortly, Miranda couldn't help but feel rebuffed.

"How's Romeo like his new corral and shed?" Rory plunged in, oblivious to the currents of tension swirling about him.

The schoolmaster smiled at Rory, and Miranda's breath caught. When he smiled like that, with no caution or reserve in his expression, she thought he must be the most handsome man she had ever seen, spectacles and all. He'd break the heart of every unmarried lady in town if only he'd abandon that serious way he had.

"I think Romeo likes his new corral just fine."

"Romeo, is it?" Miranda couldn't help chuckling at the unlikely name.

Tobias Johnston met her gaze across the table, humor in his gray eyes again. "Well, I am a schoolmaster, after all, and Romeo was a stud for several years before they cut him. As far as I can tell, that fool horse has more romantic inclinations than most stallions I've come across. He's a fine animal, though, and he holds up well carrying my weight across long distances."

"I heard you rode all the way from St. Louis. That's quite a trip to make by horseback," Lucas commented, still intent on prying all the information he could out of their guest.

"I've never cared that much for rail or stage travel," Tobias replied steadily.

"That must have been an interesting trip for a city feller like yourself."

"I only lived in a city during the time I was studying for my degree. I spent much of my life before that living in the country."

"Now, what parts of the country would that be, exactly?" Lucas blithely ignored another dangerous look Miranda sent his way.

Suddenly, there was a crash in the front parlor. The schoolmaster was on his feet in a second, facing the door to the hall. Miranda watched him in some surprise. He'd hardly seemed the jumpy sort, but the man certainly could move quickly when he'd a mind to.

A few moments later, Henry came wandering through the doorway. Miranda wished the earth would open up and swallow her. His face was a picture as Tobias Johnston watched the bright-eyed raccoon amble through the dining room.

"I take it this is another member of your household?" he

asked her, one brow lifted in a purely masculine expression of amusement as he settled back into his seat again.

"Rory, you take that animal outside at once. If I find him indoors again, I swear he'll end up in Christina's stewpot," she said tightly.

Rory stood up and quickly apprehended his raccoon. Miranda stared at her dessert plate and listened to Henry chittering indignantly as Rory carried him through the house. Now she just wished everyone would eat their pie quickly. The supper had been a disaster from start to finish. So much for hoping she could impress the schoolmaster or show him her household was just as genteel as any other in town.

As soon as she saw everyone had finished, she glanced at the clock hanging over the doorway to the kitchen.

"I thank you for joining us this evening, Mr. Johnston, but I do need to be getting ready to go on to the Shamrock soon." She said the words defiantly. There was no use in hiding or pretending what she did to make a living. She'd been foolish to think tonight could possibly make a difference in anyone's eyes, much less the schoolmaster's.

His face imperturbable, Tobias Johnston rose to his feet at once. He thanked Christina for the meal and said good night to everyone. Miranda walked him to the front hallway, where they both paused while she handed him his hat.

"Miss Kilpatrick, I can truly say it's been a remarkable experience having supper with you and your family," he said in that slow, measured way he had.

"I'm sure the food and the company were far more refined at Mrs. Smith's house last night," Miranda countered glumly.

"Actually, Mrs. Smith seasons her roast beef with too much salt for my taste, and her husband talked almost the entire time about his hobby of taxidermy. I discovered that particular topic, explored for an entire evening, can grow to be quite tiresome.

"On the whole," he finished, sending her one of his sudden

smiles, "I prefer to dine with live snakes and raccoons and your charming self. Good evening, Miss Kilpatrick."

With that, he placed his hat on his head and stepped out the door. Miranda stared after him in astonishment. The man was actually whistling as he strode down her walk.


Tobias grinned to himself as he untied Romeo's reins. He'd meant what he'd just said to Miranda. Despite Sean's less than friendly behavior and the old man's efforts to interrogate him, he'd enjoyed himself, wildlife and all. Miranda Kilpatrick had created a warm, caring home for her nephews, the kind of home he'd seen too little of during his past fifteen years of drifting.

Somehow she'd looked just right to him, sitting at the end of the table watching over the little flock of people she'd collected. All he'd managed to collect in the course of his life was three crates of books and a head full of memories he'd just as soon forget.

Swinging up into the saddle, he quit whistling. He'd never thought he was partial to redheads, but that conviction was beginning to change. Miranda's coloring fascinated him. Her fair skin was the color of fine old lace. She had a full pair of red lips to haunt a man's dreams at night. Her body looked soft and round in just the right places. And that hair. In the hallway just now, he had longed to reach out and loosen her pins and bring that wonderful wild hair tumbling down and bury his face and hands in it. Chances were, she would have slapped him for his presumption. He'd caught a couple of glimpses tonight of the temper that undoubtedly went with that particular shade of red.

Yes, sir. Miranda Kilpatrick was one heady package, but she also spelled trouble, of the sort he'd no interest in tangling with just now. He was too busy building a new life for himself. A proper schoolmaster had no business dangling after an Irish saloon keeper, none at all.

With a sigh, he headed Romeo back toward town. It was a clear night, and the moon, even in its quarter phase, shed plenty of light for him to see the road. A few moments later, Romeo snorted and pricked his ears, looking toward a grove of aspens just off the road with a good view of Miranda's house. At the same moment, Tobias felt the hairs on the back of his neck prickle.

A gut instinct he had learned to trust over the years told him someone was watching him and watching the house at this very moment. Instinctively he reached for the rifle in the scabbard by his leg, but his hand touched nothing but air. He no longer carried rifles or pistols or any sort of gun. He wondered if the new principles he was trying to live by were about to get him killed. And all the while Romeo bore him inexorably closer to that aspen grove.

Damnation, he'd no reason to expect trouble here.

"All right, old fellow, let's get on home," he said aloud, for the benefit of whoever waited in those trees, and urged Romeo into a lope. The very least he could do was present a moving target if the watcher in the aspens proved to have an itchy trigger finger. But when he rode past the grove, he drew no fire at all. He told himself the whole incident could have been a figment of his overactive imagination. But he didn't believe that for a moment.

He reined Romeo to a halt a half mile down the road. He dismounted and led the gelding into a dense thicket of brush and tied him there. He pulled a pair of moccasins from his saddlebags and swiftly tugged his boots off. Within moments, he was walking silently back the way he had just come, missing his old Winchester with an intensity that surprised him.

He was almost back to the grove when Miranda and Lucas came driving along in their buckboard. He waited until they passed before he eased his way into the aspen trees. Whoever had been there was gone now. But that person had waited, waited there long enough to roll and smoke three cigarettes.

The butt of the last of the smokes was still warm. Had Miranda attracted herself a shy suitor at that saloon of hers? Or was she in some sort of more serious trouble?

He told himself Lucas Ransom was perfectly capable of handling any danger that came Miranda's way. In another lifetime, he'd heard the name, and the reputation that went with it. Even though he was old now, Lucas clearly wasn't someone to be trifled with.

Tobias strode back to the place where he'd tethered his horse. The watcher was probably just some amorous cowhand too intimidated to approach Miranda directly. Tobias continued to wonder, though, all the way back to his cabin. Surely a shy cowhand could get his fill of looking at Miranda by simply going to the saloon. The more he thought about that mysterious person who had watched and waited in the aspen grove, the more worried Tobias became.

The setup had a feel he didn't like. He didn't like it at all.

# Chapter Four

Miranda drew out the last rollicking notes of "Little Brown Jug." Otis grinned at her from his piano stool and brought the song to a close with a rousing crescendo of chords. After she curtsied with a flourish of her petticoats, most of the men in her large audience jumped to their feet, clapping their hands, whistling, and stamping their boots against the rough-hewn floorboards. She threw them a saucy smile and shook her head with mock regret as they called for a third encore. She blew several kisses over their heads and slipped back behind the red velvet curtains of the small stage she had built at the back of the saloon.

As she hurried out of her stage costume, she blessed the theatrical savvy she had gained from her da. 'Twas always better to leave an audience asking for more. Besides, she had one more set of songs to sing two hours from now, and she needed to save her voice. Those men who truly wanted to see her perform again would remain at the Shamrock, spending their good money on the drinks she and Otis poured for them in the meantime.

After she emerged from her tiny dressing room, she eyed the busy saloon with satisfaction. If business kept up this way, she'd have to hire more help soon. Her patrons tonight were the usual crowd. Most were cowboys in from the closest ranches, a few old sourdoughs lonely for company, a drifter or two, and several men from Pine Creek itself. Before circulating through the crowd, she made straight for the bar and poured three ciders, one for herself, one for Otis and one for Lucas. When Otis came to stand beside her and began tending bar, she passed him one of the ciders.

"You're singing real well tonight, Miz Miranda," Otis told her in his soft voice.

"And you're playing even better. Johnny Nolan will never know what a gem I stole away from him." Miranda grinned at Otis and toasted him with her glass.

Otis was an ex-slave who had drifted to Nebraska after the war. Johnny Nolan had paid him a pittance to empty spittoons and wash glasses at the Silver Dollar, Nolan's Saloon. One night after the saloon closed and Nolan left, Miranda had found Otis playing bar songs on the piano. She had realized with delight that he could play ten times better than she could. She had tried to get Nolan to hire Otis to be his piano player, but Nolan wouldn't listen to her. When she decided to keep the Shamrock and run it herself, she had asked Otis if he wanted to be the piano player at her new saloon. Otis had accepted her offer instantly.

Now he lived in the two rooms over the Shamrock. She paid him as much as she could, for she knew much of the Shamrock's success was due to his terrific talent on the piano. Otis was saving his money carefully. He had a sweetheart back down in Mississippi he wanted to marry and bring west when he'd saved up enough money to pay her rail fare.

Miranda set off across the saloon to check on Lucas. "How

are things going?'' she asked the old gambler after she reached the corner where he ran the gaming tables for her. She handed him a glass and drained her own.

"Been quiet so far," he replied, never taking his eyes from the table as he deftly dealt the faro cards. "You just about lit the place on fire tonight," he teased her with a quick, sidelong look. "Thought we'd have to call for a bucket brigade for sure."

Miranda laughed at his compliment. "No point singing unless I'm going to put my heart into it."

"Reckon that's the way you handle most everything," Lucas said in a more serious tone. "By the way, Andy Harnett came in just in time to catch your act."

Miranda sighed. "I know. I saw him."

"Did he ask you again to marry him?"

"Not yet tonight. I just don't know what to do about him. He won't take no for an answer. Every time I tell him I won't ever marry him, he just smiles that mournful smile of his and says he'll wait."

"You be careful about Andy. That boy's not quite right in the head."

"Andy is a little odd, but I know he'd never do anything to hurt me."

"Anyone tetched like him can be unpredictable."

"You worry about me too much." She leaned over and kissed the old gambler on the cheek.

Lucas made a big show of looking exasperated, but she could tell he was pleased. "Someone's got to look after you, especially since you spend all your time looking after everyone else on God's green earth. Now go flirt with your customers instead of an old coot like me."

Miranda headed off to do exactly that. As she made a tour around the room, she smiled and laughed and bandied jokes with her patrons. To the world it appeared as if she loved being a saloon keeper. She was careful to look like she was reveling in the smoke, the noise, and dodging the groping hands of her bolder customers. But it was all an act. The real Miranda Kilpatrick much preferred staying quietly at home, doing household chores, cooking, reading or tending her garden. But none of those chores helped her buy food, and so she played her role, and played it so well that only Lucas and Otis had any inkling how much she hated what she did.

She was pouring drinks when Andy Harnett appeared before her at the bar. Tall and skinny, Andy wore his mouse brown hair slicked back with bear grease. He had problems meeting anyone's gaze, and a nervous tick often twisted his right cheek.

"Howdy, Miranda. You sure look pretty tonight." Andy was so painfully shy that a sentence or two at a time was about as much as he could manage.

"Why, thank you, Andy." Miranda smiled at him kindly. "How's your mother feeling?"

"Well, she's some better, I reckon." He paused, and his Adam's apple bobbed as he swallowed convulsively. Miranda was aware that his toffee brown eyes watched every movement she made. "You know, if you married me, you wouldn't have to work behind a bar no more."

"Andy, we've been through all of this before. I like tending bar, and I'm not going to marry you."

She picked up the tray of drinks, but before she could walk away, Andy blurted, "Well, I don't think you do like it all that much."

Miranda paused, surprised by his perceptiveness. "Nevertheless, it's my job, and I don't want to marry you, or anyone else," she told him in a gentler voice.

"I guess that's the way you feel now, right enough. I'll just wait and ask you agin next week."

"All right"—Miranda couldn't help smiling at his good-natured tone of resignation—"but I warn you, my answer will be just the same."

Andy wandered off and sat at a table where he could watch

her moving about the room. Miranda shook her head over her one and only suitor in Pine Creek and went back to serving drinks.

An hour later, a stir by the door caught Miranda's attention. She was listening to old Pete Ferguson tell her a tall tale about the time he'd slept in a cave with a mountain lion. She looked up to see five rough-looking men walk into the Shamrock. A shiver frosted down her back. Her years on stage had made her an expert at reading a crowd. These men with their hard faces and swaggering walks meant trouble.

She understood instinctively that the big, unkempt man with the black eye patch was the leader. He stood in front of the others, his thumbs hooked in the gun belt slung about his belly while he surveyed the saloon out of his one good eye. She glanced across the room and met Lucas's gaze. He nodded to her slightly, indicating he knew they could have a problem on their hands.

Three of the men lingered by the door while their leader with the patch and a younger man with restless eyes and two tied-down guns strode to where she stood behind the bar.

"You must be Shamus Kilpatrick's niece. They said you was a looker," the one-eyed man said in a gruff voice.

The way he stared with his bloodshot eye made her skin crawl. She longed to slap that leer off his face. She managed to refrain, though, for fear of starting real trouble. She'd just sunk most of her savings into fixing up the Shamrock, and these men looked quite capable of tearing her place apart.

"Yes, I'm Miranda Kilpatrick. Can I get you something to drink?" she asked with cool politeness. She had found if she treated men with courtesy, they often surprised themselves by acting like gentlemen in return.

"The name's Ben Slaughter. Your uncle and I were partners, and we had some unfinished business to settle when he up and died on me. I figure that business is between the two of us now, since you inherited his place and all. But before we talk,

I want a whisky, and then we'll go upstairs. I ain't had me a redheaded whore in a coon's age.''

"I don't go upstairs with anyone in my place," she informed him curtly. "If you want whores for you and your outfit, Jake Hobbs has several girls working for him at the Silver Jack on the edge of town."

"I don't want one of his whores. I want you. I'm even willing to pay, although you should give it to me for free, seeing as your uncle and me were such good friends."

Slaughter smiled, revealing a mouthful of broken, yellow teeth stained from tobacco. He reeked of stale sweat and horse. Lucas crossed the room and stepped behind the bar. She breathed a silent prayer of thanks for his comforting presence.

"If you knew my uncle well, you never would have made that suggestion. Shamus Kilpatrick would have skinned you alive for insulting his niece that way." Miranda was vaguely aware the entire saloon had fallen silent now. Every man in the place was watching her and Slaughter.

"I don't think you rightly know who I am, girlee. Folks in these parts can tell you it ain't a good idea to cross Ben Slaughter. We're going upstairs right now, and I'm gonna find out if you're a redhead all over."

He reached for her arm across the bar. He froze at the distinctive sound of double shotgun hammers being cocked.

"She's not going upstairs with you, not tonight and not ever," Lucas said in a cold, hard voice.

"And just who might you be, old-timer?" Slaughter snarled, color rising in his cheeks.

"The name's Lucas Ransom. But my name and my age ain't what counts right about now. What does count is the fact this shotgun's aimed at your belly. I'll spread your innards all over this place if you so much as touch this little gal.''

Slaughter didn't look much impressed by the threat. "Lucas Ransom, eh? I thought you done pickled yourself with drink back Nebraska way."

"Reckon I dried out since then," Lucas replied with quiet dignity.

An eager look came into the light blue eyes of the young man standing beside Slaughter. He stood up straighter and stared hard at Lucas. "I heard of you. You shot four men on the riverboats, including Black Jack Mattheson. But you don't look so tough now. I can take you, old man."

"You're welcome to try, boy." Lucas smiled at him thinly. "If you two don't hightail it out of here, I'll let loose with both barrels. I figure I should be able to cut you in half from this distance."

The young man tensed, and his hands hovered above the holsters to his pistols.

"Tyrel, you simmer down," Slaughter said harshly to the young man at his side. "Right now, we're bucking a stacked deck. We'll go, but we'll be back. I ain't through with you, girlee, and I ain't gonna forget you had me thrown out of your place," he finished with such menace, Miranda felt another shiver go down her back.

Aware of all the men watching her, she was careful to keep her face expressionless as Slaughter stalked from the saloon. Even though her heart still raced and her knees felt weak, she couldn't afford to let anyone think she was easily cowed. The moment the last of Slaughter's men stepped outside, she nodded to Otis, who went over to the piano and started to play a lively tune. Gradually, conversation started up again, but the mood was more subdued. Miranda bit her lip when she saw several cowboys grab their coats and slip out.

Damn that Slaughter for hurting her night's business. Drawing on all her skill as a actress, she threw her head back and laughed. "Well, boys, I didn't like the way Mr. Slaughter looked, and he smelled worse. We're much better off without his business tonight. Who wants to dance with me?" She grabbed the nearest volunteer and swung out onto the dance floor with him. After that, she had to dance with every man in the place who wanted to, and most did, so she was worn out when she, Lucas and Otis finally shut the doors to the Shamrock at two in the morning.

It wasn't until they started home that she had a chance to talk with Lucas about the incident with Slaughter. The way Lucas kept the shotgun across his knees and watched the dark road ahead of them while she drove the team gave her pause.

"Lucas, just who is Ben Slaughter?" she asked him the moment they turned onto Main Street.

Lucas sighed. "I won't lie to you, Miranda. He's trouble spelled with a capital *T.* Slaughter's wanted for several murders down Texas way, and the Mexicans would like to skin him for the killing and raping he's done south of the border. Rumor has it he was a Confederate guerrilla fighting in Kansas before and during the war. After it was over, he just kept on killin' until the law in Kansas got tired of him and tossed him behind bars. One of his gang managed to smuggle a gun to him, and he shot his way out. After that, he was smart enough to move out west where lawmen are scarcer."

"I wonder how Uncle Shamus ever got tied up with a man like that."

"I'll ask around and see if I can find out. I'd heard Slaughter's been robbing banks and rustling cattle in these parts on up to Wyoming. He and his gang stay in rough, wild country because there's so many wanted posters out on him now."

"Do you know who the young man was with the tied-down guns?"

"I'm guessin' that was Tyrel Reynolds. I'd heard Slaughter joined up with a punk who was fast with a gun."

"He looked like he was dying to start a fight with you." She shivered when she remembered the eager look in Tyrel Reynolds's pale eyes and the way his hands had hovered longingly above his pistols.

"He's just another young fool hopin' to make a name for himself. The penny dreadfuls back east and the damn newspapers are making gunfightin' sound real glamorous these days. The only problem with this boy is he's fast enough to kill a few men before he lands himself in a grave on Boot Hill."

She chose her next words with care. "I expect Lucas Ransom could handle a boy like that with one hand tied behind his back. In fact, you handled both of them just fine tonight, and I'm grateful. Still, I hope you'll be careful. I would hate to see you hurt on my account."

"Ten years ago, I could have handled a punk like Reynolds. But I'm slowing down some, and I'm not sure I could take both Slaughter and Reynolds if it came down to a fight. I'm not going to lose sleep over it for myself. I figure I'm livin' on borrowed time anyways. If it weren't for you helping me to dry out, I'd be dead for sure. The only reason I'm worrying now about Slaughter and Reynolds is you."

Miranda switched the reins into her right hand so that she could give his arm a squeeze. "Well, I want you to be around for another twenty years to deal faro for me, so I'm going to worry plenty for both of us. I wonder what that unfinished business is he was talking about." Miranda huddled into her coat and wished she'd thought to bring a woolen scarf. The nights in Pine Creek were definitely growing longer and colder with winter fast approaching. That had to be the reason she felt chilled through.

"I expect we'll find out soon enough," Lucas said soberly. "Ben Slaughter meant it when he said he'd be back."


Tobias opened his eyes and came wide awake in an instant. He always woke that way in the morning, immediately aware of his surroundings. He drew in a deep breath and forced himself to relax the wary tension coiled inside him. He smiled when he realized today was Saturday. As much as he enjoyed teaching, he relished the two days a week he didn't have to ride herd on his lively pupils.

He rolled out of bed and winced when his bare feet hit cold dirt floor. *Tobias E. Johnston, there's no question about it. You got just plain spoiled living back east in rented rooms furnished with nice braided rugs, like the ones Miranda Kilpatrick has covering the floors in her home.*

Tobias glanced about his one-room cabin. It did look plain compared to Miranda's cozy house. His log walls were completely bare except for the one corner where he'd built a crate bookcase for his books. The cabin wasn't particularly homey, but it suited him. It was plenty private, and he was a man who liked his privacy. Having to make conversation with other boarders at Mrs. Fisher's house day after day in town would have driven him crazy.

Being private also meant being cold. Right now, he could see his breath in the morning sunlight slanting in through the cabin's single window. Tobias cursed under his breath as he tossed kindling onto the coals inside the old iron stove and hurried into his clothes. While he fixed himself a breakfast of coffee, ham and biscuits, he decided he'd take Romeo for a ride and scout the terrain around Pine Creek. He never felt comfortable in a place until he knew several good routes out of it.

He actually caught himself whistling as he sent his big bay jogging down the road toward town. It was a glorious fall morning. The sky overhead was the deep blue only seen in high country on the clearest of days. The quaking aspen on the hillsides above him shimmered brilliant gold in the morning light, and the fresh fall air filled his lungs. Times like this he realized a part of him had been dead during the seven years he had lived in the east getting his college degree.

He liked what he'd seen of Pine Creek so far, and he wanted to put down roots here. Idly he considered the notion of buying the cabin and the forty acres surrounding it from the widow Ferguson. Whether or not he bought the place, he needed to repair the lean-to behind it to give Romeo better shelter this winter.

Caught up in his plans, Tobias was surprised to discover sometime later that he had turned onto the lane that led to Miranda's place. As long as he was headed out her way, he decided he might as well check around her land for tracks. That incident last night still bothered him.

An hour later, he was even more worried. He'd found two more places where someone had waited and watched her house since the last rain. That someone was a man with medium-sized feet, he rode a shod horse with big hooves, and he liked to smoke.

Tobias frowned as he studied the tracks and butts on the ground before him. He wished there was some way he could tip Lucas Ransom off to be on the lookout for trouble. It was always possible Miranda had an admirer too bashful to approach her directly. But the alternatives were troubling, particularly when he'd seen so much of the darker side of human nature.

At just that moment, Romeo pricked his ears and looked toward the house. Moments later, Miranda and her nephews appeared. Even from this distance Tobias could see the sunlight glinting off that fiery hair of hers. One look at the long poles they carried told him they were headed off for a morning of fishing. Lucas Ransom followed them, a shotgun slung under his arm. Perhaps Ransom didn't need a warning after all.

He meant to ease Romeo back into the willows before anyone spotted him, but at that instant, Rory looked his way and started waving with all his might. Tobias smiled and waved back, wondering quizzically why he was so glad the boy had seen him.

He would have ridden to meet them, but he wanted to find some way to point out the tracks and the butts of the smokes to Ransom; and so he stayed put while Miranda and her family came to him. It occurred to him in the meantime that schoolmasters probably weren't supposed to be interested in reading sign, and Miranda and Lucas were going to wonder what on earth he was doing here. Tobias leaned back and pulled out the specimen net he'd tied on the back of his saddle. A little bug collecting would provide a good excuse for his presence. It also would probably convince Sean once and for all that his teacher was a complete sissy.

"Good morning, Miss Kilpatrick," he greeted Miranda as she and the boys came hurrying up. She was wearing an old cotton dress with a man's gray woolen jacket over it. She should have looked drab, but her ivory cheeks were flushed from the cool air, her hair blazed in the morning sun, her blue eyes shone, and her lips were as red as ever. Miranda Kilpatrick was a woman who could never be drab.

"A fine day it is, too." She smiled at him brightly, but he could tell she was curious about his presence and too polite to ask what he was doing on her land. Young Rory, however, had no such scruples.

"What are you doing out here, Mr. Johnston?" he asked promptly in his piping voice.

"Last evening when I came to supper here, I told myself this is just the sort of place I might be able to catch an excellent specimen of *Speyeria Nokomis*. That's a kind of fritillary butterfly which flourishes in open meadows like this one."

Lucas watched him out of narrowed eyes. The old gambler scented a lie and was so busy sizing him up, Tobias was afraid Ransom would miss the tracks on the ground beside Romeo completely. Suddenly, inspiration seized him. Tobias knew he was going to sound like a preachy schoolmaster, but there was nothing for it.

"Say, I hope you boys haven't been smoking. I saw that pile of butts over there, and I prayed you two hadn't discovered the evils of tobacco at your tender age."

Miranda glanced at the butts. Her eyes widened in dismay. She whirled about and stared at her nephews. "Sean, Rory, do you know anything about those?"

In the meantime, Tobias saw with some satisfaction, Lucas Ransom had circled about Romeo and was studying the butts and the tracks near them carefully.

"Aunt Miranda, we didn't smoke those, honest. We only tried a smoke once behind the barn at Freddie Atkins's place, and it made us both cough like crazy. We ain't, I mean we haven't tried any since," Rory pledged.

"Is he telling the truth, Sean?" Miranda asked her older nephew in a stern voice.

Sean's face tightened, and he shot Tobias a resentful look. "Rory's telling the truth. Neither of us smoked those," he replied and stared at his boots.

"You two are absolutely certain about this?" She looked from one nephew to the other, obviously wanting to believe them but puzzled by the evidence right in front of her eyes.

"Miranda, the boys are telling the truth. Someone else was here." Lucas spoke up from where he'd been studying the tracks.

She looked over at the old gambler. Tobias watched with great interest as the two exchanged a silent message with their eyes.

"Ah, well, I'm glad to hear this is one bit of mischief you two managed to avoid for a change," Miranda declared brightly and smiled at both her nephews. "Now, I think it's time we went to catch ourselves dinner."

The boys seemed unaware of the false gaiety in her tone. Miranda Kilpatrick was a remarkable actress. *That is a fact worth remembering about this woman*, Tobias told himself.

"Would you care to join us, Mr. Johnston?" She looked up at him, a friendly light in her blue eyes.

"You might be able to show us some of those worms you talked about in school the other day, the ones which make their little houses on the bottom of river rocks." Tobias looked down into Rory's eager face, and the polite refusal he was about to make died on his lips. Something about Rory Broden disarmed him completely. Despite his mother's recent death, the boy had yet to let the hard side of life dampen his enthusiasm.

"Why, yes, I think I will tag along, for a little while at least," Tobias agreed.

"We're off, then," Miranda declared and turned toward the clear stream running along the edge of her property. "Sean, you can pick the first place we should try."

Looking puffed up and pleased with his responsibility, Sean went running ahead of them to choose just the right stretch of stream. Tobias dismounted and fell into step beside Miranda. Lucas stayed behind them, no doubt comparing the schoolmaster's tracks against those of Miranda's mysterious visitor.

Feeling at a loss over what to say, Tobias fell back on common courtesy. "Thank you again for the fine supper last night."

" 'Twas a pleasure for us all," Miranda said, looking straight ahead, color rising in her cheeks. "We rarely have company, and I was glad the boys had a chance to practice their manners."

Those pleasantries exchanged, a long, awkward pause stretched between them. Tobias realized he'd rarely talked with a decent woman, and he wasn't sure what to say to her. For all the townsfolk of Pine Creek seemed certain she was a fallen woman, the more time he spent with Miranda, the more sure he became they were wrong about her. Although there was a frankness in the way she looked him in the eye, there was also an essential innocence in her gaze which made him willing to wager all he owned that she'd never shared or sold her body to a man.

He considered asking her about the Shamrock, for he was genuinely curious how she managed to run it and her own household at the same time. Last night, though, she had only brought up the Shamrock once in his presence, and that time he gained the strong impression her saloon was a sensitive topic.

Miranda suddenly came to a stop, her expression earnest as

she swung about to face him. "Mr. Johnston, I'm glad we saw you today, for there's something I've been wanting to thank you for." She paused and drew in a deep breath.

"I know what you were about the other day when you invited yourself to our house in front of Mrs. Smith. 'Twas a kind thing you did for both me and the boys, and I'll not be forgettin' it."

He decided not to pretend that he had no idea what she was talking about. "It was my pleasure. I wish I could do more to help, but people in small towns can be mighty set in their ways and intolerant in their opinions."

"That's true enough," she agreed with a sigh, "but you mustn't think about doing anything else to help us. You've your own position to maintain. You'll do nothing but tarnish your own reputation if you try to help us again."

That thought had already occurred to him, but for some reason it irritated him to hear her state it so plainly.

"I believe I'll do and say exactly as I please. That's the way I've lived my life for the past thirty-two years, and I'd find it hard to change my ways now," he said more shortly than he'd intended.

She looked a little taken aback by his tone, but she held her ground. "That's your choice, certainly, but I'd hate for any harm or trouble to come to you because of your kindness to us." With that, she turned away and started off toward the stream again.

He stared after her for a long moment, wondering when the last time was that someone had worried about him. It was a novel sensation, to say the least. Slowly, he followed her.

When they reached the stream, Tobias expected he'd have to help untangle hooks and lines from willow bushes. He was impressed to discover Miranda and the boys knew what they were about when it came to fishing—Miranda in particular. With only a small grimace, she helped the boys bait their hooks with worms Sean had brought along in a can. Sean and Rory proceeded to drop their lines in the water in a surprisingly quiet and businesslike fashion.

They only had three fishing poles between four fishermen, for Lucas declined to participate from the start. He told Rory with a twinkle in his eye, "I reckon I've already done my fair share of fishing in my day. Besides, once you catch 'em, then you've got to clean 'em. I plan to keep my hands clean and stay nice and dry while I watch the rest of you get wet." With that, the old gambler sat down on the grassy bank with his shotgun within easy reach and kept a watchful eye out.

Tobias meant to wander off someplace quiet and enjoy a book from his saddlebags, but Miranda thrust a pole into his hands before he could slip away.

"There's a fine hole just below this willow bush," she told him eagerly and led the way downstream. "I hooked a trout there two Saturdays ago the size of my arm, but he got away."

"Are you sure he hasn't gotten bigger since then? The ones which get away have a tendency to grow, you know."

She glanced up at him, her eyes dancing with laughter. "Well, actually, he was almost the size of a whale, but I thought you wouldn't be believing me if I told you the truth of it. Now, toss your line right in there, and we'll see if my old friend might just oblige you this morning."

It was hard not to catch her enthusiasm. Tobias tossed the line out where she indicated, and the current drifted his line into a deep hole beside a boulder. Within seconds, the pole jerked in his hands. Startled, Tobias nearly let loose a most unschoolmasterish profanity and tightened his grip on the pole.

"There, you've hooked him. Look at the way he's bending your pole. It's my big fellow for sure. Keep the tip of the pole up, for heaven's sake." Miranda was almost dancing with excitement at his elbow. Tobias looked down at her, amazed by the vividness of her beauty in that moment. Miranda Kilpatrick was an attractive woman, but when she was alight with joy and excitement like this, she took his breath away. He felt

a strong urge to lean over and kiss her, but the pole jerked in
his hands again, so strongly he almost lost hold of it.

She reached over and pulled the pole upright for him.

"Sweet St. Agnes, grant me patience, man, pay attention to
what you're doing, or you'll lose him."

Tobias grinned to himself. Miranda was finally forgetting
the polite veneer she was always careful to show Pine Creek's
new schoolmaster, and her Irish accent definitely became
stronger when she was excited.

"All right," he told her, trying to look suitably chagrined.
"I've got a good grip on the pole now."

After that, he did his level best to keep the tip of the pole
up, but the lively trout he'd hooked gave him a run for his
money. When the trout headed upstream, Tobias felt the whole
pole shiver in his hands, and the line stretched taut. Afraid the
rig was going to break, he breathed a silent curse and stepped
into the stream. It had been a long time since he'd been fishing,
and he didn't want to let this one go. Up and down the stream
he waded, trying to tire the fish out enough to pull it to the
bank while Miranda called a constant stream of suggestions to
him.

At one point Tobias glanced over his shoulder and saw quite
a crowd gathered on the bank of the creek. Sean, Rory, Miranda
and even Lucas were all there cheering him on. Amused by
their enthusiasm and his own determination, Tobias kept splash-
ing up and down until his trousers were soaked and his legs
half-frozen by the glacial water.

Finally the fish tired, and Tobias managed to flip it out onto
the stream bank. It lay on the grass, gills heaving while the
sunlight shone off the iridescent spots on its side. The rainbow
wasn't exactly a whale, but it was a good twenty inches long,
he saw with some satisfaction as the boys and Miranda all
clustered around. Out of respect for a formidable adversary,
Tobias was inclined to toss it back, but the boys wouldn't hear
of it.

Miranda reluctantly sided with her nephews. "He's a handsome fellow, and a part of me would rather see him go back to where he came from, but we meant to catch our dinner this morning, and he's half a meal in himself."

"Then, we'll keep him." Tobias smiled at her and dispatched the fish with a quick rap against a rock. He allowed Sean the honor of placing the trout on a stringer back in the stream. When Tobias met Lucas's gaze, the old gambler quirked a smile.

"That's a mighty handsome fish you managed to catch there, schoolmaster," Lucas allowed in his dry way.

Tobias glanced down at his soaked trousers and boots and grimaced. "You might have had the right idea staying out of this fishing business, when all is said and done."

"You've got us off to a fine start, Mr. Johnston. Would you be caring to try your luck again?" Miranda asked Tobias gaily. "I'm warning you if you say yes, this time you'll be putting your own worm on the hook."

"That's enough fishing for me for one day, thank you, Miss Kilpatrick. I'm going to work on drying myself out in the sun."

"Well, I'm going to do my best to match your effort, but I have a feeling your fine fellow is the prize for today. If we catch a few more, we'll be all set for our cookout."

Miranda, Tobias saw with some amusement, went about fishing with a fierce sort of concentration he found endearing. At Rory's request, he waded back out into the stream and showed the curious young boy caddis larvae and the odd houses they made for themselves from gravel on the bottom of river rocks. After that, they had a fine time catching dragonflies in Tobias's specimen net and picking some examples of the more interesting plants along the stream. Rory was fascinated by anything that had to do with the out-of-doors, and he peppered Tobias with questions. Sean, however, stayed well away from the impromptu natural science lesson.

When Rory finally decided he wanted to fish, Tobias spent

the next hour pretending to read poetry by Robert Burns while he sat in the sun drying out his wet trouser legs. Actually he spent much of that time watching Miranda. No matter how involved she became with trying to catch a fish of her own, she took time to help her nephews and admire the smaller fish they managed to land in their turn.

She would be a fine mother to children of her own some day, if she ever had the opportunity. He wondered if there was some upstanding citizen in Pine Creek who would unbend enough to offer her marriage. With her unique looks and the scarcity of women in these parts, she should eventually be able to find herself a husband. He frowned when he thought of the sort of men who probably frequented her saloon. One of them could easily promise marriage in hopes of taking advantage of her or her business. He hoped Miranda would have the sense to send that sort packing.

In the meantime, Rory and Sean were very lucky she had decided to look after them. He had run across too many orphaned, homeless youths in his time. Many came to a violent end out west, without a stern, loving guardian like Miranda to set them on the right course in life.

When he wasn't thinking about her relationship with her nephews, Tobias studied Miranda Kilpatrick's hair. She had taken her straw hat off early on during the fishing expedition. The fall sun brought out a remarkable variety of colors in it. Her hair wasn't truly one shade of red, but a rich palate of shades, including cinnamon, copper, dark cedar, and gold. A man could spin dangerous fantasies about a woman with hair like that.

Before he could spin one of his own, Tobias looked away from Miranda to find Lucas Ransom watching him out of icy blue eyes. That look was like a dash of cold water. Tobias had no wish to prod the old gambler. Besides, the look in Ransom's eyes served as a good reminder that schoolmasters had no business spinning fantasies about anyone, much less lovely Irish saloon keepers.

After that, Tobias was more careful to keep his eyes on his book. When Christina appeared just before noon bearing a picnic basket giving off luscious aromas, Tobias decided he was very glad he'd joined the fishing expedition. Christina seemed taken aback to see him. She never once looked his way or spoke to him as she laid out the food she'd brought on an old quilt. Yet when Sean and Rory came to her and insisted that she see all the fish caught that morning, she smiled brightly and went with them at once.

With her pretty blond hair and cornflower blue eyes, Tobias could see why Christina had aroused Rob McGregor's interest. He wished the rancher plenty of luck if he meant to try courting the girl. Perhaps she was only shy, but he sensed a deeper hostility in her which puzzled him. Did she dislike all men, or was she wary of him for Miranda's sake just as Lucas was?

Tobias pushed those questions to the back of his mind as he helped the rest set to work building a fire, cleaning fish, and cooking them in a frying pan. Soon they all sat down to a delicious meal of pan-fried trout, fresh-baked bread, pickles and chocolate cake. The trout was light, sweet, and fluffy, tasting the way only fish can when they've been newly caught and promptly cooked. Tobias couldn't remember when he'd last had such a delectable meal.

The moment they were finished, the boys jumped to their feet and went off adventuring. Soon they were battling with each other, pretending switches they had made from willows were swords. Tobias's lips twitched when he realized they were playing *Ivanhoe*.

"I don't know where they get the energy," Miranda commented as she watched them shouting and hacking at each other with bloodthirsty zest.

"I ask myself that question every day I teach," Tobias agreed and lay back on the quilt. He clasped his hands behind his head and wondered when he had last felt this relaxed and lazy. Christina brought out her knitting while Lucas leaned against a tree smoking a pipe. Miranda sat crossed-legged, her chin propped on her hands while she talked and watched her nephews. Overhead the fall sun shone down through the bright yellow leaves on the cottonwood trees.

"I've no idea how you handle a whole schoolhouse full of young heathens."

"I'm bigger than you are," he told her mildly.

"I expect size helps," Miranda allowed, "but then again, my grandmother put the fear of God into eighteen of the most mischievous grandchildren ever to plague a family, myself headin' the list, and she wasn't bigger than a leprechaun."

"You sound like you miss her. Did she emigrate with your parents?"

Miranda looked down at her lap. "She did. She was all for us leaving Ireland to find a better life for ourselves, but she took sick on the ship and died before we reached New York. That's always made me sad, for I think she would have loved America and traipsing about with Da while his theater troupe lasted."

"So you inherited your adventurous spirit from her."

Miranda raised her head and wrinkled her nose at that. "I'm the least adventurous soul in my family, except my blessed ma, of course. Both of us could have stayed in one place all our lives. But my da and my brothers loved to travel and see new sights."

"Where are your brothers now?" Tobias asked curiously. This was the first he'd heard that Sean and Rory had uncles. Why weren't they helping Miranda look after the boys?

"Their adventuring got them killed in the end," she replied, her voice bitter. "They both thought it would be the grandest adventure of all to fight for the Union. They went off to war and never came back to us. Fergus was killed at Shiloh, and Timothy died of dysentery with Grant's troops during the siege of Richmond.''

"I'm sorry," Tobias said gruffly and sat up. He wasn't a man used to offering comfort, and he wasn't sure how to go about offering it. "The war stole so many young men from their families.'' He looked over and saw Lucas Ransom sending him another dour look.

"Speaking of traveling"—Tobias cleared his throat—"I had better be on my way. I have lessons to prepare for next week."

If she was surprised by his sudden decision to leave, she was too polite to show it. "I'll walk with you a little ways," Miranda offered simply.

She walked with him to the open space beyond the willows where he had picketed Romeo. After Tobias coiled up his picket rope and tied it to his saddle, he turned to face her.

The formal words of thanks he meant to say died in his throat as he looked down at her. She'd taken off the shapeless jacket she'd worn this morning, and the old, gray dress she wore emphasized her womanly curves. Tobias swallowed hard. Miranda Kilpatrick and the love she gave so generously to her nephews represented everything he'd had torn from him violently years ago. He longed to pull her into his arms and feel her softness against him. Before he could stop himself, he reached up and touched a lock of her hair which had tumbled free from the bun she wore. Her hair felt softer than corn silk between his fingers.

She stared back at him, her eyes dark and wondering. Dizzy with sun and a hunger far more complex than desire, Tobias was stunned by how much he wanted to taste her mouth with his own. Some remnant of sanity prevented him from dipping his head toward her and doing exactly that. Instead, he raised the lock of her hair to his lips. It smelled of lavender and willows. Over the rush of the stream, he could hear a hermit thrush trilling its sweet song. This moment washed by the warm fall sun spun into infinity. The world disappeared around them, and their sensual awareness rose in a dangerous tide.

Suddenly, a wild war cry from one of the boys broke the spell. As Rory charged past them, intent on his battle with his brother, Tobias came back to his senses with a rush. He let go of Miranda's hair and forced himself not to look at where it had fallen against her right breast.

"Thank you for a wonderful morning," he told her in a husky voice. "This is the best Saturday I've had in a long time."

She wrenched her gaze from his lips, and her ivory skin flooded with color. It gave him little satisfaction to realize she looked dazed, too. If she felt the pull as strongly as he did, they both were in a world of trouble.

"Anytime you've a mind to try your hand at fishing, you're welcome to try our stretch of stream again." She managed a smile with some of her former spirit in it.

"I'll remember that. A good day to you, Miss Kilpatrick." He touched the brim of his hat to her and swung up onto Romeo's back.

*Tobias E. Johnston, you are ten thousand times a fool,* he warned himself as he rode away. A minute longer and he would have kissed her and made the simple life he was trying to build for himself impossibly complicated. Tobias urged Romeo into a lope the moment he turned onto the lane that led away from Miranda's place.

At least Ransom knew now that someone had been watching Miranda. Tobias guessed from the shotgun the old gambler kept with him constantly that Ransom was already on the lookout for trouble. Tobias forced himself not to wonder what sort of trouble it might be. *Miranda Kilpatrick and her problems are none of your business. Old son, you best not go riding out by her house again.*

After making that firm resolution, Tobias pulled Romeo back to a walk and wondered why the shine had gone out of his day.

# Chapter Five

"I'm sorry, you two, but Pine Creek will just have to celebrate Founder's Day without us," Miranda told her nephews. "I need your help around here that Saturday, and that's final."

Rory and Sean had cornered her in the kitchen after supper, apparently determined to change her mind about attending the town's festivities next Saturday. The house had just been pummeled by a thunderstorm. From past experience, Miranda knew the receding clouds would create a spectacular sunset she was eager to see. For the moment, though, she was far more concerned about the domestic storm brewing in her own kitchen.

"But there's going to be ice cream. Charlie Rider told us so," Rory pleaded.

Miranda felt her heart twist as she looked into his beseeching eyes. Sean didn't bother to argue, but she knew he was just as desperate to go. She had made up the excuse that she needed the boys to help her that day, for she was afraid the upstanding citizenry of Pine Creek were just petty and vindictive enough to keep the saloon keeper's nephews from participating in the holiday games. It would be a crushing blow for the boys, and she was determined to keep Sean and Rory from that kind of hurt if she could.

"Pleeease, Aunt Miranda," Rory wheedled. "We'll both work extra hard after school all this week and next, we promise."

Miranda simply shook her head, afraid her voice might break if she had to say no to them again.

"Come on, she's not going to change her mind." With that, Sean stomped from the room. Rory followed his older brother, feet dragging.

The moment the boys left the kitchen, Miranda felt tears well in her eyes, so she swore in a low voice instead. "Damn this town and all the benighted bigots who live here."

Christina, who was washing dishes, raised her eyebrows at Miranda's profanity. For all Miranda heard plenty of rough language daily, she rarely used it herself.

"You could try telling Sean and Rory the truth," Christina suggested gently.

"I'd rather they be angry with me than have their feelings hurt."

Christina paused in the midst of washing a pot. "They are growing up fast. Sean's voice is starting to change. You can't protect them forever."

"I know, but they've already had to lose too much of their boyhood too soon." Miranda picked up a dish towel and dried the dishes and pots Christina had already washed. There was little point in trying to make Christina understand. Losing her entire family and enduring Johnny Nolan's abuse had given Christina a darker view of life.

As soon as their chores in the kitchen were done, Miranda escaped to her garden. She wanted to steal a few minutes of quiet for herself before heading in to work at the Shamrock.

She wandered over and sat down on a little wooden bench Lucas had helped her build. The garden smelled fresh and sweet after the recent rain. As she watched the setting sun burn the trailing clouds over the ridges to the west glowing orange and vivid scarlet, she couldn't help wondering if she had made the right decision tonight for Sean and Rory. So often with her nephews she felt like a blind woman feeling her way. It tore her to pieces the times she had to say no to them.

She wished she had someone she could talk to about her current dilemma. Lucas and Christina already thought she protected and spoiled the boys too much. Unbidden, the image of Tobias Johnston came to her mind. She had thought about him often since their fishing expedition last Saturday. She smiled to herself when she remembered the pleasure he had taken in catching that fish, and the picnic after. For a few hours there, the polite and formal Mr. Johnston had become almost human.

She wondered what his advice would be about the boys' going to Founder's Day. He seemed to understand and sympathize with their difficult situation in Pine Creek. She wished she could stop by the schoolhouse and ask him, but she didn't want to take the risk of anyone seeing them together. Briefly she considered going to the cabin where he lived, but that course seemed unwise as well.

She shivered, remembering the moment when he had reached out and touched her hair. She would never forget the reverent way he had held it between his fingers and raised it to his lips. There had been a controlled stillness to him in that instant, as if he were trying to keep some dangerous part of himself in check. She couldn't help but recall the wildness she'd glimpsed in his eyes that day Red and Randy had been taunting him.

She had never been with a man, but she wasn't entirely innocent about matters between men and women. Da, bless his practical heart, had given her a straightforward talk on the subject when her menses came the first time. Over the years, he had answered every question frankly that she had asked him on the same topic. Her days traveling with Da's troupe, singing at Johnny Nolan's saloon, and six months of running the Shamrock had taught her more than she wanted to know about the male gender and their passion.

She was almost certain that polite, gentlemanly Tobias Johnston wanted her, and she was even more certain she wanted him in return. Miranda rose to her feet and began to pace the little path down the center of the garden. She was twenty-three years old, well on her way to becoming an old maid by most people's standards. And now, for the first time, she had discovered she was capable of desire, the kind that absorbed a woman day and night and made her insides quiver with longing. When Tobias had kissed her hair, she had wanted with every fiber of her being for him to kiss her lips instead.

That kind of wanting was new to her. That kind of wanting frightened her to death. Passion had only brought pain and suffering to her sister, and to her parents as well. One night when he was drunk, Da had admitted to her that the fiery passion he had felt for her mother had led to their hasty marriage. Only later on did they realize how incompatible their personalities were, and their goals in life. Miranda had always felt loved by each of her parents, but she had been painfully aware of the strain between them. Her mother had never been happy on the road, and her father had felt desperately trapped on the farm.

As much as she wanted to talk about her current quandary over Founder's Day with the schoolmaster, she concluded it would be much wiser for them both if she stayed well away from him. With a sigh, she decided she would have to stick to her guns and keep the boys home with her next Saturday, for their own sake. *They might even forgive you for that decision, in another twenty years or so.*

Two days later Miranda stood on the boardwalk outside the Shamrock, washing the plate glass windows she'd had shipped in from Denver. She scrubbed at them with more force than was truly necessary, for she was still furious from her trip an hour ago to Peabody's Dry Good. Most of the women in Pine Creek simply ignored her, but today while she was in the store, Mrs. Reed had looked her way and in her high, nasal voice declared, "It is truly a shame the way the degenerate Irish are taking over every town and city in America. Why, I read in the *Rocky Mountain News* that a group of drunken Irish rail workers in Denver tore apart a saloon there, and they were all jailed for disturbing the peace."

The other women in the store had shaken their heads in dismay while sliding sidelong looks Miranda's way.

Miranda had longed to face Mrs. Reed down and tell her the Irish she so loathed had helped to build the railroads which made Pine Creek and the whole country boom these days. She wanted to shout at her that thousands of brave Irishmen including her own dear brothers had died in the Great War Between the States helping to preserve the Union. But if she antagonized the leaders of Pine Creek society, Rory and Sean would pay in the long run, and so Miranda had kept her mouth closed and left the store fuming.

Suddenly she became aware of the fact that someone was watching her. She gripped the rag in her hand tighter while the skin on the back of her neck prickled. Since the incident with Ben Slaughter and finding the tracks on her place, she'd been on edge all week. Miranda swung about, her heart beating faster. The schoolmaster stood in the middle of the boardwalk, his arms crossed, the glint she was coming to recognize as humor evident in his eyes as he studied her. A pulse of pure pleasure shot through her as she took in his broad shoulders, his gold-brown hair, his square jaw and his intelligent gray eyes. Every time she saw him, she liked the look of Mr. Tobias Johnston better and better.

"You're going to scrub away those fancy letters someone painted on your window at the rate you're going."

"Good day to you, Mr. Johnston," Miranda managed, wishing with all her heart that she was wearing something prettier.

She had planned to spend the day cleaning the Shamrock, and so she had worn one of her oldest dresses. The bodice had a stain on it, and the skirts were mended in several places. She crossed her arms, hoping to hide the stain at least.

Quick on the heels of that realization came remembrance of where she stood, in front of the disreputable establishment she owned and ran. Her cheeks started to burn, and she lifted her chin higher. "Is there something I can do for you?" she asked him coolly.

"Not really, not for me at any rate." He stood there pulling at one of his sideburns and looking surprisingly ill at ease. Her curiosity piqued, Miranda dropped her wash rag in the bucket by her feet and waited for the schoolmaster to speak his mind.

"I understand that you aren't planning to attend the Founder's Day celebrations. I overheard Rory and Sean discussing the matter out in the school yard yesterday. They seemed so disappointed, I wanted to ask you if it's really necessary for the boys to stay home and do their chores that day."

"No, as a matter-of-fact, it isn't really necessary for them to stay home." The hurt from Mrs. Reed's remarks was still so fresh, Miranda's temper rose in a burning wave. "Do you truly want to know why I said no to my nephews? Do you honestly want to know why I'm keeping them from the kind of fun every boy longs for?"

He blinked at the anger in her voice, but he replied slowly, "Yes, I do." His deliberate, dispassionate way of speaking somehow made her even more furious.

"For your information, Mr. Johnston, I don't intend to let my darlin' boys go anywhere on Saturday because if they did come into town, not a soul in this Christian, God-fearing community would even speak to them much less let them play in the games with the other boys. Then I'd probably commit murder right there in the sight of God and everyone. Seeing as I don't want me boys hurt or myself landing in jail, I think we'd all be better off staying home that day."

"I see," he said quietly. "I'm sorry. I hadn't thought."

Miranda drew in a deep breath. *It's not Tobias Johnston's fault that Sean and Rory can't enjoy Founder's Day. If fault lies with anyone, it lies with your own foolish self, for not being able to figure out a respectable way to provide for your own.*

"You don't have anything to apologize for," she said wearily. " 'Tis me who should be doing the apologizing here. I shouldn't have snapped at you. I know you care about the boys, and I'm grateful to you."

He was silent for a long moment. "If I could promise you that Rory and Sean would be allowed to participate in the games, would you let them come?"

"In a heartbeat," she admitted. "But I don't know how you could possibly make such a promise to me. Schoolmasters may be able to influence the young, but you cannot change the attitudes of every adult in Pine Creek."

"Perhaps not, but I might be able to change the minds of one or two adults who matter most, and I've always been a man to relish a challenge," he said with one of those sudden smiles that did such strange things to her pulse. He tipped his hat to her and strode on down the boardwalk.

She stared after him, half believing he might actually be able to do it. She was beginning to think this mild-mannered schoolmaster was a man to be reckoned with. She wondered what it would be like to be the challenge he relished. With a little shiver, she went back to washing her windows.


Tobias strode from Mrs. Josiah Smith's overly decorated-in-the-most-refined-way house, gulping in fresh draughts of air. How on earth did he ever get himself into such a mess? He told himself it couldn't possibly have been because he was developing a weakness for a certain Irish saloon keeper. Surely he'd done it for red-haired Rory, who still had dreams, and his older brother Sean, who cared about life more than he should.

For both of those boys, Tobias E. Johnston was about to organize and run the games at Pine Creek's Founder's Day celebrations.

Christ, he couldn't even remember what sorts of games decent folk played on holidays. Of course, he couldn't tell Mrs. Smith that when she'd nailed him with the suggestion. Beneath that polite, properly beruffled exterior lay the mind of a shrewd manipulator. He'd invited himself over to her house for tea to plead Rory and Sean's cause. He'd chosen Mrs. Josiah Smith carefully. From his days as a preacher's son, he knew her type well. She gloried in her power as a social arbiter in this town, and took her moral obligations as a Christian almost as seriously.

He had carefully pitched his appeal to both sides of her nature.

"It's a shame two promising boys are being ostracized because of their aunt," he had pointed out to his hostess between sampling her sugary cookies. "Surely, it's the proper, godly thing to encourage these boys to come to community events and learn civilized behavior from their peers. If anyone in town can make the citizens of Pine Creek see the good they could and should do for these boys, it's you. I know everyone will listen if you say Rory and Sean Broden should be given a chance."

After listening to his pitch, Mrs. Smith had nodded and declared in her perfectly modulated voice, "Mr. Johnston, I quite agree. We've been unfair to allow the sins of the fathers, or in this case, the aunt, to be visited upon the young." She smiled at her own jest with a smugness that made him long to shatter his teacup on her hearth.

"And while we're on this topic, I've been searching high and low for a volunteer to run the games for us this year. Mr. Tyler usually does it for our Founder's Day Committee, but he's been laid up with a broken leg. You would be perfect, Mr. Johnston. You already know most of the children, and it would be a fine opportunity for you to meet more people in our community.''

He met her cool blue gaze, knowing he'd been cornered. She'd help the boys, but he was going to have to run the damn games for her precious committee.

Tobias shook his head and untied Romeo's reins from the elegant hitching post before the Smiths' home. After he swung into the saddle, he urged the gelding into a run. He headed toward Miranda's place. Since he was going to go through purgatory for her boys, he might as well tell her the good news.

After he rode up the lane to Miranda's house, Tobias reined in Romeo and looked around appreciatively. Shamus Kilpatrick had been a good builder. The white clapboard home he had made was sturdily constructed, with a charming porch extending across the front of it. Kilpatrick had situated his house in a pretty little aspen grove, protected from the worst of winter winds by a forested ridge.

Tobias smiled when he took in the purple and yellow flowers growing in old whisky barrels in the yard. He decided those flowers were likely Miranda's touch. Out here in some of the wildest country left in the West, Miranda had managed to make a real home for her family. As he dismounted and tied Romeo to the plain wooden hitching rail, Tobias wondered wistfully if he'd ever have the right to claim a place like it.

When he stepped up onto the simple plank porch, he grinned at his memory of his first visit here. He looked about carefully for Oliver, but the bull snake was nowhere to be seen. He knocked on the door, and Miranda opened it almost at once, looking flushed and surprised. Her apron was covered with smudges of soot, and she had a fetching streak of black across one cheek.

"Oh, lordy, you caught me in the midst of cleaning the lamps. I must look dirtier than a chimney sweep.'' Miranda pushed ineffectually at the bright red tendrils of hair waving about her face. "Have you come about Sean? He hasn't been in more trouble, has he?"

"Good afternoon to you, too, Miss Kilpatrick, and no, for a refreshing change your Sean hasn't been in trouble recently. I've come to talk with you about another matter," he said, enjoying seeing her so flustered. It occurred to him she made quite a contrast to the precise and proper Mrs. Josiah Smith, whose female form was constricted and barricaded by stays and layers of petticoats. He couldn't imagine Mr. Josiah Smith found much warmth or satisfaction in his marriage bed, which might account for the fact that the Smiths' sainted Jimmy was an only child.

Tobias eyed Miranda's simple work dress with appreciation. He doubted she had a corset on right now. She'd be soft and full beneath his hands, with no forbidding stays to keep a man from exploring the most tempting parts of her. Tobias stood up straighter and forced himself to stop thinking about the kind of exploring he'd like to do with Miranda. Schoolmasters weren't supposed to indulge in such lascivious thoughts.

"Thank heavens it's not about Sean that you've come." Miranda straightened her shoulders and seemed to regain her composure by sheer force of will. "Good afternoon to you, too, Mr. Johnston. Would you like to come in?"

"It would be my pleasure," he said and followed her inside. She left him in the front room while she bustled off saying something about fetching coffee and getting cleaned up. Shortly, Christina appeared bearing a tray full of fresh sliced bread, cheese, oatmeal cookies, and coffee. Her expression was stern and disapproving as she slapped the tray down on the table beside Tobias. After she left, he sighed happily and started in on the food. Besides the pleasure of looking at Miranda, a trip to her place was always worthwhile for the grub served up here.

Soon Miranda appeared again, looking a great deal neater. She'd tamed her hair, washed her face, and put on a clean apron. After a few moments, Tobias decided he liked her disheveled state better. When she was seated on the other end of the settee, he related the outcome of his visit to Mrs. Smith's house.

"Oh, Mr. Johnston, you're a miracle worker. This will mean the world to the boys." Miranda gazed at him out of shining eyes. Tobias shifted uncomfortably on the settee. He wasn't at all sure how he felt about being on the receiving end of such admiration and gratitude.

"I'll ask Christina to take Sean and Rory." Miranda was already planning ahead. "It would be good for her to mix more with the townsfolk, and since she never sets foot inside the Shamrock, they shouldn't be too hard on her."

Miranda was going to send her boys but not come herself. Somehow he hadn't envisioned this possibility. He was surprised by how much the idea of not seeing Miranda at the Founder's Day festivities bothered him. With a flash of honest insight, he realized he'd been looking forward to dancing with her. *Hell, it's the only proper way you can get your hands on her.*

"Surely you could come, too?" he asked, even though he already guessed what her answer would be.

"You may have managed to charm Mrs. Smith into giving Rory and Sean a chance," she replied with a self-deprecating smile, "but I doubt any decent citizen in Pine Creek wants to see the shameless hussy who runs the Shamrock Saloon at Founder's Day."

In that moment he wanted to reach out and shake some sense into that lovely head of hers. He hated hearing her talk about herself that way. His anger made him blunt.

"Miss Kilpatrick, are you a harlot?"

She drew herself upright in her chair, and her blue eyes flashed fire. "You may be the smartest, best-educated schoolmaster west of the Mississippi, but you've no right to be insultin' me in my own home. Although I'm grateful for your kindness to my nephews, I'd appreciate if you left at once."

"I take it that's a no," Tobias said dryly.

"I'm saying who and what I am is absolutely none of your business." She rose to her feet, her cheeks bright with color. "Now, do I need to call Lucas to see you to the door?"

"If you aren't a harlot," he countered evenly, "you shouldn't speak about yourself as if you were, and you have every right to go to the Founder's Day celebrations with the rest of the fine, upstanding citizens of Pine Creek."

It obviously took a moment for his words to register. She sat down slowly, her gaze never leaving his face. She let go a long, quivering breath and stared down at her hands.

"No, I am not a harlot. I never have sold myself to a man and I never shall," she said in a low, strained voice.

He couldn't keep from touching her any longer. He reached out and lifted her chin gently. Her skin was as soft as cottonwood down beneath his fingers. He damned every intolerant idiot in Pine Creek when he realized her indigo eyes swam with unshed tears.

"You're the first to ask. The rest just assumed the worst about me. What sort of man are you, Tobias Johnston?" she asked him wonderingly.

He cleared his throat and lowered his hand. He looked away, afraid those perceptive eyes of hers might see the darkness deep inside him. "I hope I'm a man fair enough to look beyond the surface of things, but in your case, I can't believe an entire town can be so totally blind. I knew you weren't a prostitute from the first day you walked into my school."

She was silent for a long time, digesting his words. "Thank you for that, Mr. Johnston. Do you really think there's any point in my trying to change their minds? My da once told me there's no more stubborn creature on the face of this earth than a God-fearing man sure of his own righteousness."

Eager to persuade her, he met Miranda's steady gaze once more. "If you don't try to change their minds, if you act the part they've scripted for you, they'll have won. Can't you see that?''

She stared at him, a cautious hope beginning to bloom in her eyes. "Do you honestly think I have a chance of getting them to accept me and the boys?''

"People can change," he said with a vehemence that surprised them both. "They have to be able to change, to make themselves better, to learn from their mistakes, or what's the point of life itself?''

"I agree with you on the grand scale of life itself," she said with a hint of humor in her tone, "but I'm dealing with the more practical problem of the here and now. I'm none too keen on going to a town's holiday celebrations and being snubbed and slighted by every respectable man and woman there.''

"You'll never know unless you go, holding your head high and facing them all down with that Irish pride you clearly possess in abundance.''

"Foolish Irish stubbornness more like," she muttered.

"Will you come? I doubt your father would have wanted you to walk away from this fight.''

Miranda sat up straighter on the settee. "Mr. Johnston, I can well believe your father was a preacher. You make me believe anything is possible. Aye, I'll come, and if not a soul at that celebration speaks to me, at least I'll know I tried.''

"Miranda Kilpatrick, you are one of the bravest women I've ever met.''

"Or the most stupid. However the day goes for me, I'm more happy than I can say for my boys. I can hardly wait until Sean and Rory are back from their rambling and I can tell them they may go. Rory will be so excited about eating ice cream, and Sean will be thrilled to spend some more time with his new friend Robby McGregor.''

Tobias's lips twitched. "How the worm turns. You know it was Robby he tangled with that afternoon I sent a note home to you.''

"Truly? Isn't that a strange business? Sean never used to talk about anyone at school. Now it's 'Robby this' and 'Robby that.' Sean's face fair lights up when he talks about that boy."

"I think the two of them had it out down by Grady's Creek after school last week. I overheard some of the younger boys discussing it. I gather it was a pretty good row. It ended in a draw when neither boy could get the best of the other."

"That's why Sean's knuckles were skinned and his clothes were such a sight last Wednesday. The young devil told me he'd fallen down a gully during one of his rambles. I guessed he'd been in a fight, but when I didn't hear from you, I thought I'd leave well enough alone. And now Robby and Sean are good friends?"

"I suppose they felt the matter was settled honorably between them."

"You're a mysterious lot, you menfolk." Miranda shook her head, that laughing light back in her remarkable eyes once more. "I'm not sure I'll ever understand how you think, that is, the times you fellows bother to think at all."

He stared at her, and something inside him twisted. The gaiety and spirit radiating from her drew him like a moth to a flame. Miranda was coming to represent all that was good and loving and bright to him. He had been so long in a world where such qualities hardly existed. Being with her made him dizzy with her vitality. He felt an overpowering urge to bury his hands in her rich hair and kiss those delectable, smiling lips of hers.

He decided he'd best get out of there before he took the kind of liberty in her parlor that would make her think he did consider her a loose woman after all.

"I'm glad you mentioned Robby McGregor," he said gruffly. "I think I'll head out to the Ladder M right now and see if I can rope his father into helping me run the games next Saturday." He rose to his feet and started toward the front door. He paused in her hallway while she opened the door for him.

"My thanks for the food," he said as he lingered on the front porch. "Eating in this household is always a treat."

" 'Tis I who have a great deal to thank you for," she replied earnestly. "I appreciate what you're trying to do for Sean and Rory more than you'll ever guess.

"And when I think of the price you had to pay," she added in a more mischievous tone, "I'm even more grateful. Yes, indeed, Tobias Johnston must be one of the most courageous men in Pine Creek. I'm thinking you'll have your hands full next Saturday riding herd on every active child in town."

"Not by myself, I won't. I'm getting Rob McGregor to help me if I have to hog-tie the man to do it," he pledged with a smile.

His smile only lasted until Tobias turned Romeo away from Miranda's place and started out toward the Ladder M. *What on earth possessed you to talk her into coming to the Founder's Day celebrations?* He'd promised himself he wouldn't get involved in her life, and here he'd gone and done exactly that.

One thing was for sure. He was going to feel meaner than a rabid skunk if the townsfolk of Pine Creek spurned Miranda Kilpatrick next Saturday.

# Chapter Six

Miranda smiled at her reflection in her bedroom mirror. Christina had insisted on helping her dress her hair before they all drove into town to attend the Founder's Day festivities. Miranda would have preferred pinning her hair up in a simple bun, but Christina had wanted to copy a hairstyle she had seen in a six-month-old issue of *Harper's Bazaar*.

Miranda had to admit, Christina's efforts were becoming. She had piled Miranda's hair high on her head and allowed several saucy curls to frame her face. The style emphasized her cheekbones. Excitement had brought a flush to her cheeks and an unusual sparkle to her eyes.

*Miranda Kilpatrick, you've not looked this well in a fair long time. If only Tobias Johnston could see you done up like this.*

She wondered where that thought had come from, and then she made a face at herself in the mirror. If she was going to be completely honest, she had to admit she had spent an inordinate amount of time during the last few days just trying to decide which dress she should wear today. In the end, she had settled on her green summer wool which, after her blue satin, was her nicest dress. The bustle was sadly out of date; but the deep green color of the fabric complemented her hair and her coloring, and the old lace she had sewn on the cuffs and collar was pretty.

She frowned when she realized she was worrying over her dress choice again. A schoolmaster with beautiful gray eyes and a stern face had her turned upside down and inside out. One moment she was sure his kindness was all directed toward the boys. Then she remembered with burning clarity the moments he had touched her, and shivers went down her back.

Aware of the time slipping away, Miranda forced herself to look in the mirror again. *You may hurt Christina's feelings if you ask her to change your hair, but today you need to look like a respectable aunty for your boys,* she decided sadly.

"Christina, it's lovely, but I think I look too frivolous."

"Today is a holiday. This is a holiday way I dress your hair. You work hard all the time. You deserve to be frivolous once in a while." Christina planted her hands on her hips and looked so determined, Miranda decided to give in. She was delighted to see Christina assert herself. She had always been firm with the boys, but until recently she had been terribly unsure around everyone else.

"Very well, we'll keep my hair exactly as it is, and I thank you very much. Now, it occurs to me that what is good for the goose is good for the gander," Miranda announced with a smile. She stood up and guided Christina into the chair she had just vacated. For months she had been dying to change the severe, unbecoming braids Christina always wore pinned on top of her head. She longed to buy Christina pretty fabric to make herself a nice dress or two. Since her time with Johnny Nolan, Christina had clearly gone out of her way to avoid attracting attention from men.

Today, Miranda hoped she could get Christina to dance and possibly even talk to a young man. With her silvery blond hair, bright blue eyes, and creamy skin, Christina was very pretty. If she only looked a little more approachable, she would be thronged by partners wanting to dance with her tonight.

"But this is the way I always do my hair," Christina protested, "and I still do not think I should go to this Founder's Day at all."

"But today is a holiday," Miranda mimicked her Swedish accent with wicked precision and a broad smile. "I'm your employer, and we are not going to argue about your attending Founder's Day again. This is a holiday way I dress your hair. You, too, work hard and deserve to have fun today."

Christina gave up with a sigh. "All right, you may do what you wish with my hair. But do not take too long, or the boys will be after us both."

Miranda had just finished combing out Christina's braids when Rory appeared in the doorway to Miranda's bedroom, his face twisted with impatience. "Aunt Miranda, aren't you ready yet?"

"Rory Patrick Broden, that's the third time you've asked me, and the answer is still no. It's only eight o'clock, and the celebrations don't start until nine. We've plenty of time to drive into town, I promise you. Now, off with you, laddie. Every moment I spend talking to you is a minute longer you have to wait."

Miranda shook her head as Rory hastily withdrew and pounded down the stairs. She hadn't seen the boys this excited since Christmas. She just hoped nothing ugly would happen to mar their joy this day. Saying a silent prayer to all the saints above, she turned back to the happy task of helping Christina look her best.

A half hour later Miranda was quite pleased. She had pulled Christina's hair back from her face in soft coils which made her look much younger and less severe. Now if she could only get Christina to smile once in a while in public, she'd look more approachable as well.

Soon they were all loaded on the buckboard. As they drove off into the beautiful, clear fall morning, Miranda launched into a spirited rendition of "She'll Be Coming Around the Mountain" to get them all in the holiday spirit. By the time they reached the main road to town, even Lucas was singing along.

The rider watching on the forested ridge above the house grimaced when the sounds of singing drifted up to him. Hell, he'd always hated that song. He'd never much cared for any sort of music. With a grim sort of satisfaction, Buck Logan tossed his smoke to the ground. He turned his horse to the northwest and kicked the big black into a run. The boss would want to know right away that the Kilpatrick woman and the rest had all left the house. The boss had been waiting for a chance like this. That Irish whore and her family wouldn't have much to sing about when they came home tonight.

When they reached the meadow to the south of Pine Creek, Miranda saw a dozen wagons and buckboards had already arrived. Several makeshift booths and tents had been set up, along with a wooden platform at the center of the meadow for the town's speakers and the band which would play later during the dancing. Rob McGregor and his son Robby walked over to greet them as soon as Lucas pulled the team to a halt.

"Good morning, folks," Rob McGregor said with such warmth that Miranda had to wonder if Tobias had said something to him about her worries over this day. She didn't know the rancher well, but he had always been courteous to her the times he stopped into the Shamrock for a drink. From the way he often lingered at the bar talking with her or his friends and acquaintances from around Pine Creek, she thought he might be lonely.

She smiled when she noticed the official Founder's Day volunteer ribbon pinned to his vest. "I gather Mr. Johnston was successful in persuading you to help him run the games today."

Rob McGregor shrugged his shoulders. "I'm still not sure how he did it. That schoolmaster is one smooth-talking feller. One moment I'm showing him my breeding bulls, the next I've promised to spend my Saturday riding herd on a bunch of wild young mavericks. That mild-mannered Tobias Johnston is not a man to be taken lightly."

Miranda could only shake her head in sympathy. The same thought had occurred to her just days ago. The fact that she was here today was a testament to that same man's persuasive abilities.

"Well, Sean, do you want to help Robby grease up Ray Thatcher's piglet with us?" Rob McGregor asked her nephew.

Sean's face lit up with a grin. "You bet I do. Can I go with them, Aunt Miranda?"

Rob McGregor made a droll face. "Just why anyone in his right mind would want to grease up a young porker is beyond me, but I'd sure appreciate Sean's help."

"Of course you may go," Miranda told her beaming nephew. Sean was off the buckboard like a shot. "Now, mind your manners and try not to get into mischief," she called after him as he went racing away with Robby.

"By the way, Miss Kilpatrick, Robby was hoping we might have dinner with you and Sean later today. I told him I'd be plenty happy to dine with two of the prettiest ladies in Pine Creek, that is, if you don't mind."

Miranda didn't miss the way Rob McGregor was watching Christina while he talked with them. The wistful look in his brown eyes touched her. "Mr. McGregor, we'd love to have you join us." She made up her mind on the spot. Rob McGregor could be just the man to teach Christina that all males weren't cruel and brutal manipulators like Johnny Nolan.

"That's just dandy," he declared with a wide smile. "I'm off to make sure those boys get most of the lard on the pig rather than themselves." He tipped his hat to them and hurried after Sean and Robby.

Miranda and Lucas had just gotten the team unharnessed and picketed when Rory went off with one of his friends from school. Soon Lucas wandered away saying something about trying to scare up a card game. And so Miranda and Christina were left to brave Founder's Day all by themselves. Miranda hesitated, not really sure where to go first, when a familiar, broad-shouldered schoolmaster came walking across the meadow toward her.

Her heart started pounding in her chest. Miranda realized this was a moment she'd been anticipating for days. *Sweet St. Agnes, the case I have on this man is only getting worse,* she told herself, but on this sunny fall morning so crisp and bright with promise, she couldn't bring herself to care. It was enough that he was here, warming her with one of his rare smiles. He gazed at her with an appreciation in his gray eyes that made her very glad she'd kept the hairstyle Christina had fashioned for her.

"Good morning, ladies." He tipped his hat to them. "I'm sure I'm not the first to point out how fetching you both look this morning. I came over to see if you would like me to escort you to a shady place to watch the games."

*Why, the sober, serious schoolmaster almost sounds gallant this morning.* "We'd be pleased to accept your escort, sir," Miranda responded in kind. For the sake of his reputation, they could spend little time together today, and so she vowed to relish every moment she had with him. As the three of them walked across the meadow, he seemed determined to draw Christina out. He asked her about the boys and talked about Founder's Day. He didn't appear to be put off in the least by her brief replies to his queries. Miranda contented herself with listening to their talk while she drank in every detail of his appearance.

Tobias had taken off his jacket, for the day had already grown warm. He wore a simple white shirt and the dark gray vest from his suit. He'd rolled up his sleeves, revealing a strong pair of forearms dusted with dark brown hair. Idly she wondered how he'd developed such strength teaching children. Her gaze followed his hands while he made a gesture encompassing the whole meadow. His hands were big, but they had been remarkably gentle the times he'd touched her.

Not for the first time she wondered if he had caressed other women with those hands. Miranda felt her cheeks crimson at the thought. There was a kind of diffidence to Tobias at times which made him seem less worldly. And yet when he made up his mind, she knew from firsthand experience how forceful and persuasive he could be. Try as she might, she couldn't decide whether or not he seemed the type of man who was experienced with women in a physical sense. She was willing to wager the Shamrock he had rarely allowed a woman to touch him emotionally. He was too distant, too formal, too uncomfortable with people to have spent much time with a woman he loved.

He moved well, with a grace one rarely saw in a man his size. At just that moment, he laughed at something Christina said about Sean. Miranda shivered in delight over the rich timbre to the schoolmaster's voice. She'd loved his voice from the first day she'd spoken with him in town. She still needed to find out if the man could carry a tune. If he wasn't tone deaf, he'd have a singing voice to please St. Peter himself.

All too soon they reached the shady spot Tobias had chosen for them. While Christina busied herself spreading out a small rug to save their skirts, Tobias turned to speak with Miranda.

"I'm glad you decided to come today," he told her quietly.

Miranda drew in a long breath and looked about the busy meadow. Only time would tell if her presence here was a mistake. So far she hadn't caught any scowling looks directed her way, but the day was early. "I'm already glad I came," she declared, lifting her chin. "I have to see my nephews cover themselves with glory."

"Between the pig catching and the pie eating, I'm not exactly sure it's glory they'll be covered with when today is done," Tobias countered ruefully. He shot a resigned look at the growing crowd of children milling about by Rob McGregor's wagon. "I have to go get this show started. I hope you'll save me a dance tonight."

She knew she should tell him that dancing with her wasn't a wise idea. She had already planned to slip away before the band started to play late in the afternoon. By then she guessed she would have had enough of Founder's Day, and it would be too difficult to stand on the sidelines and watch others dance when she loved to dance so much herself. But now she could cling to the knowledge the schoolmaster wanted to dance with her. That fact warmed her through and through.

"Good luck. I think you'll be needing it," she told him with sweet irony.

"Thank you, Miss Kilpatrick. I'll probably need that luck and more patience than all the saints you've ever prayed to." He flashed her a smile and headed toward the wagon.

Just before Tobias and Rob got the games started, Doc Wheeler came and sat with Miranda and Christina. Miranda didn't feel nearly so self-conscious now that she had the kindly doctor to talk to. Once the first event began, she started to relax and enjoy herself. Rory and Sean participated in every game for their age group. She laughed herself silly when Rory, Sean and two dozen other boys chased Ray Thatcher's squealing piglet about a pen made from hay bales. She shouted herself hoarse while her boys manfully ate whole apple pies without their hands in less than two minutes and covered themselves with pie filling and crust in the process.

The high point of the morning came when Sean and Rory

won the three-legged race, in large part because they had been practicing in the meadow behind the cabin after school all week. Miranda felt as proud as any mother when Tobias awarded them two shiny new quarters for their victory.

And throughout it all, Tobias was there where she could watch the tall schoolmaster as much as she wished. He truly was a splendid man. Surrounded by a dozen helpful fathers for much of the morning, he stood out in the crowd of men, partly because of his height and size, and partly because he possessed a kind of quiet presence. Occasionally their eyes met, and Miranda thought longingly of the dance he'd promised her. How could she slip away and deny herself such a treat?

*'Tis just one dance, with a man you've no business to be yearning after in the first place,* she told herself, but somehow the idea of dancing with Tobias Johnston made her blood sing in her veins and her body tingle in anticipation.

When the games finished, Pine Creek's parents collected their offspring and went off to their blankets to eat dinner from their picnic baskets. Miranda and Christina took Rory and Sean back to the buckboard and set out the picnic they had spent much of the past two days preparing. Rob McGregor and his son soon appeared. Miranda was startled to see they had Tobias in tow.

"Do you mind if I join you all?" The schoolmaster stood at the edge of their blanket, holding a small pail which probably held his own dinner. He looked so unsure of his welcome, she threw caution to the wind. Of course, it wasn't wise for him to join them. His eating with the saloon keeper would surely set tongues to wagging. Yet as she looked up into his handsome face and wistful gray eyes, Miranda couldn't send him away.

She offered him her most welcoming smile and said simply, "Please join us."

It was a gay group. Sean and Rory were still cock-a-whoop over their victory in the three-legged race, and Robby was thrilled for his friend's sake. Lucas was in fine form, telling stories of other holiday celebrations he'd seen throughout his lifetime of rambling about the West. Rob McGregor soon proved he could hold his own when it came to yarning, and he had a sense of humor that kept Miranda laughing till her sides were sore.

Christina even smiled a few times at his stories, although she rarely spoke. She sat on the far edge of the blanket, as if she thought her very presence might taint the rest of them. She never looked at Tobias, but Miranda thought she caught Christina sneaking a few sideways looks at Rob McGregor when he wasn't doing the same in her direction.

Miranda and Tobias said little. For her, it was enough to have him sitting near her, unabashedly enjoying the fried chicken, biscuits, cheese, pickles, apple pie and ginger cookies she and Christina had made while his own dinner pail remained unopened. Occasionally she looked away from the others and caught Tobias's gaze upon her. At times he seemed to be admiring her hair, and the features of her face seemed to fascinate him to no end. She knew she should feel embarrassed by his open perusal, but she delighted in the fact he wanted to watch her. She had, after all, spent much of the morning while he managed the games making the most of her chance to watch him.

When the meal was over, Tobias rose to his feet with evident reluctance. "I have to make the rounds now." He spoke to everyone, but it was her gaze he met. "This is an excellent chance for me to visit with the parents of my students."

She smiled at him, careful to disguise the sharp disappointment she felt. This indeed was an excellent time for him to get to know the people of Pine Creek better, and he'd spent far too much time with her already.

"Ladies, thank you for such a delicious dinner," he said in his serious way and strode off to talk with the parents of his students.

Rob McGregor, Miranda saw with some amusement, made

no move to leave. After she and Christina packed up the leftover food and plates, he remained sitting on the blanket next to his son as the various town dignitaries, starting with Mayor Frederick A. Wright, mounted the small stage at the center of the meadow and gave their speeches celebrating the founding of their town six years ago. After the speeches were finished, the children ran off to play in groups while their parents wandered from blanket to blanket, visiting and exchanging gossip, enjoying the holiday from their normal chores. Miranda was acutely aware of the fact that no one came over to be friendly or chat with her, but no one asked her to leave, either. With an inward sigh, she decided she had to be content with that.

In her mind's eye, she imagined a town where she wanted to live someday. There no one would know that she'd been an actress or a saloon keeper, and few would care about her Irishness. In that town she'd have friends, the kind you could turn to during lonely times or hard ones. Lord knew, she had no need to be a social leader in a place, but she longed for simple acceptance, a sense of belonging in a community. She'd only known that feeling once, when she was a little girl back in Ireland, and she had been too young to appreciate it. To be a part of a place, to put down roots, must be grand.

But for now, it was enough to know her nephews were well on their way to enjoying that sort of acceptance. She watched with a wistful sort of joy as Sean and Rory raced about with the sons of the most respectable folk in the community, and she blessed Tobias Johnston with all her heart for making that small miracle come about.

At four o'clock, Mr. Peabody and Mr. Boyd brought out enough ice cream to feed every child in Pine Creek. The beatific expression on Rory's face as he plowed through his heaping bowl made both Christina and Miranda laugh aloud. Several men who played musical instruments gathered on the makeshift stage at the center of the meadow. The sun was just about to slip behind the mountains to the west. As the first chill of evening stole across the Pine Creek valley, two men lit the bonfire which would burn until the dancing and celebrating were done.

"All right, I think that's enough for us today," she told her nephews when they had finished devouring their ice cream.

"You can't mean to leave before the dancing starts," Rob McGregor protested with friendly dismay. "Pete Jenkins plays a mean mouth organ, and the rest of the boys can really scrape their fiddles. The dancin' is the best part of this whole shebang." The way his gaze strayed to Christina once again made Miranda smile. She couldn't deny Rob his chance to dance with Christina, not after he had spent much of the afternoon with them and his interest in her was so obvious.

"Very well, we'll stay for one hour, but no longer." The moment the words were out of her mouth, Rory and Sean took off like bullets to rejoin their friends. Looking after them with a sigh, she decided that it would probably take her most of the next hour just to round them up again.

She was surprised and amused when Doc Wheeler appeared at her buckboard just as Pete Jenkins and his fellow musicians launched into a spirited rendition of "Turkey in the Straw."

"Miss Kilpatrick, may I have the honor of this dance?" he asked with a twinkle in his eye.

"Sir, I'd be most pleased," she accepted his invitation with alacrity. She did love to dance, and she hoped if she left Christina alone with Rob McGregor for a little while, the rancher might have luck persuading her to dance with him. It took great self-control, but Miranda resisted the urge to look back over her shoulder and see if the two were really talking with each other at last.

Christina tightened her hands in her lap and wished fervently that Miranda hadn't left her alone with the handsome rancher. A lifetime ago, she would have been fooled into thinking that look in his eyes was longing mixed with admiration. Now she could only see lust in his expression, and it repelled her.

Johnny Nolan had taught her that most men only wanted one thing from women. She would never be such a fool again. She would never let a man take advantage of her body or destroy her dignity the way Nolan had.

"Would you like to dance with me, Miss Erickson?"

She felt too vulnerable to this man with his lean face and his coffee brown eyes. She looked him straight in the eye and told him coldly, "No."

"You know, I've always admired women who don't waste words," he said with a hint of humor in his tone. "Well then," he added, "do you mind if I just sit here and keep you company?"

"You'd be wasting your time."

"That's for me to decide, I reckon. Just looking at your pretty face makes me happy," he said so simply she almost believed him.

"It shouldn't," she countered, determined to drive him away now. Something about him drew her, and she didn't want to ever be attracted to a man again. "Because of this pretty face, I became a saloon keeper's mistress when I was fifteen. I will never let a man use me for his pleasure again. And if you are looking for a sweetheart, you don't want to court a girl who has been used and soiled the way I have been."

She'd hoped to shock and repel him. Instead, he looked thoughtful. "I figured something of the sort probably happened to make you so skittish around menfolk. Who was he?"

"His name was Johnny Nolan," she replied bitterly. "He was a man who cared more about himself, his own pleasure, and making money than he cared about anything else."

"Not all men are like that. I'm not like that."

"Can you look me in the eyes and honestly say you don't want to lie with me?"

In the fading light, she could see his brown face flush, but he held her gaze gamely. "The thought probably crossed my mind, but there's a whole lot more I want from you besides that. I want to get to know you and what you want from life. I want to know everything about you."

"Well, I don't want to know you. I don't want to know any man ever again."

With that she crossed her arms and stared stonily at the dancers in the meadow.

He was silent for a long moment. "Guess you made your feelings pretty clear on that score," he said at last. "I know you'd rather I moved on right about now, but if I leave you alone on this blanket, you're going to have all sorts of men come a-pestering you. As much as you don't seem to care for my company, I figure you'd enjoy theirs even less."

Christina's stomach clenched. He was right about that. She couldn't bring herself to thank him, but still she was profoundly grateful for his presence. All she wanted to do was go home to Miranda's house, away from all these strangers and this disturbing man who threatened her hard-won peace of mind. She knew this day wouldn't turn out well for any of them, but she hadn't wanted to dampen Miranda's or the boys' enthusiasm.

Since she'd left Nebraska, she'd come to love the members of her adopted family. Sean and Rory had brought joy back into her life, a kind of sweet, clean, uncomplicated joy she'd thought she'd never feel again. And dear, kind Miranda had given her a reason to keep living when life with Nolan had become too grim to endure any longer.

Miranda didn't know. Miranda didn't really understand the darkness inside men's hearts. Christina feared for her headstrong, naïve friend, especially now that this schoolmaster had barged into their lives. She saw how he looked at Miranda. She was afraid Miranda was already starting to care for him. Miranda, with her optimistic nature, would blind herself to the fact a schoolmaster couldn't possibly have honorable intentions toward a saloon keeper. Christina would do what she could to protect her friend from the harsh realities of life, but she was afraid that in the end, Miranda would have to learn the hard way what cruel, uncaring brutes men could be.

Miranda quickly discovered that Doc Wheeler was a fine dancer. Laughing and whirling about with him helped take away some of the pain she felt when she saw Tobias dancing with Miss Emily Danforth, one of Pine Creek's prettiest young ladies. As she watched the two of them circling the dancing area together, Miranda decided Tobias looked positively distinguished, but Miss Emily Danforth's chin was too weak for true beauty.

Miranda reminded herself sternly that she had absolutely no claim on the schoolmaster and never could. Yet seeing another female in his arms made her despair inside. Determined to hide her feelings, Miranda sent him her most brilliant smile. He looked back at her, his gray gaze somber behind his spectacles.

Doc Wheeler insisted on partnering her through three more numbers. On the second, Tobias danced with Miss Katherine Thompson and on the third with Mrs. Josiah Smith. Miranda told herself she was daft to keep track of his partners this way, but she couldn't help herself.

During their third dance together, Doc Wheeler's face grew red, and his breath started coming in gasps. Afterwards he admitted he needed a rest. When Miranda returned to her buckboard, Christina and Rob were sitting as far apart on the blanket as they possibly could. Christina appeared ready to burst into tears, and Rob looked like someone had just shot his best friend. After Doc Wheeler sank down on the blanket, Rob jumped to his feet, his relief palpable. Immediately he asked Miranda to dance.

Wondering what had gone wrong, Miranda accepted his invitation. Rob guided her through a reel, but she could tell from

the look on his face that his mind was elsewhere. In the meantime, she was trying not to mind the fact that Tobias was now
dancing with Miss Anna White, a lovely girl in a rather pale
way who had hands and feet far too large for the rest of her.

Miranda was only too aware of the fact he still hadn't made
any effort to ask her to dance. So much for being silly enough
to think he might look forward to their dancing together as
much as she had. She was careful not to look his way again
and threw herself into the music.

When that dance ended with a flourish, Miranda suggested
to Rob that they go fetch some punch from the table set up
beside the dancing area.

"It looked like a storm was brewing between you and Christina when I came back from dancing with Doc Wheeler," she
commented as she sipped her punch and watched Tobias lead
plump Mrs. Kurtz out for a dance. That schoolmaster seemed
determined to cut the rug with every female here except her.
"Do you mind if I ask what happened while I was gone?"
she asked the young rancher. "I thought you made some real
progress today. I caught her actually smiling a time or two
during your stories."

"I don't mind you askin' one bit." Rob McGregor smiled
at her. "You'd be doing me a mighty big favor if I could talk
to you about Christina. I thought I was makin' a little headway,
too, but the moment I asked her to dance, she told me about
being with that Nolan fellow, and then she said she didn't ever
want to get to know any other man again."

"How do you feel about the fact Christina was with Nolan
for almost three years?" Miranda decided to be blunt. If Rob
couldn't accept Christina's past, then it was better for them
both if Rob never spoke to her again.

"I'd like to ride back to Nebraska and shoot that bastard,"
the young rancher admitted grimly. "But finding out she'd
been with a man like that didn't surprise me much. She's so

skittish around me, I already figured she had to have had a bad time with some sort of skunk.''

He sighed and pushed his hat farther back on his head. ''What I can't figure out is this. If her past doesn't matter to me, why should it to her? Maybe this is just a way to tell me she doesn't want me to come courting her.''

''She just needs time,'' Miranda reassured him. ''You're going to have to be patient with her. Right now she doesn't feel like she deserves to have a decent man pay attention to her. I don't believe I've seen her say more than two words to any man except Lucas and Mr. Johnston in the past two years I've known her.''

''That's consolation of a sort, I reckon.'' He smiled ruefully. ''Well, if I have to take it slow with that little gal, I'll take it slow. My ma always said the best things in life are worth working and waiting for.''

Miranda grinned at him, just plain delighted he'd taken such a shine to Christina. If Rob McGregor would be patient, he could be just the man to teach Christina how to trust men again.

Miranda was making her way back to her buckboard when Andy Harnett approached her. She'd been aware of him watching her much of the afternoon; but he'd been with his mother then, and Miranda was quite sure Mrs. Harnett didn't approve of her son's infatuation with an Irish saloon keeper. A semi-invalid, Mrs. Harnett must have asked her son to take her home early, which meant Andy was finally free to do as he pleased. Miranda disguised a sigh and tried to think of some reason for not dancing with Andy which wouldn't hurt his feelings.

''You sure look pretty tonight, Miss Miranda. W-would you like to dance?''

At just that moment she spotted Tobias heading toward the dance area with yet another young, unmarried woman in tow. ''Andy,'' she said instantly, ''I'd be delighted to dance with you.''

Andy was so stunned by her acceptance, she had to take his

hand and lead him toward the rest of the dancers. From the moment the music began, he was clumsy and stiff. He stepped on her toes repeatedly. Worst of all, she found herself counting the times his Adam's apple bobbed as he swallowed and awkwardly steered them about. At least she didn't have to make conversation. Talking was clearly beyond Andy's abilities while he concentrated on the challenge of dancing with her.

When the dance was over, Miranda thanked him politely. Before he could ask for another, she told him she would be going home shortly and made a beeline for her blanket. She was so busy looking around for Sean and Rory, she ran right into a broad male body. Warm hands reached out to steady her, and she looked up to find the schoolmaster gazing down at her quizzically.

"Where are you headed in such a hurry?"

"It's getting late, and it's time the boys and I were heading home."

He quirked an eyebrow at her. All at once she realized the irony of a saloon keeper who often stayed up most the night claiming seven o'clock in the evening was late.

"I thought you were going to save a dance for me," was all he said in a mild voice.

Her frustration and disappointment over the long day rose up and choked her throat. None of Pine Creek's fine citizens had actively snubbed her, but no one except Doc Wheeler and Rob McGregor had made any effort to talk to her, either. As long as she lived in Pine Creek, she was doomed to live as a pariah. She'd known it from the start, but for a brief, foolish two weeks, this man had made her hope that it might be otherwise.

"I don't think you want to be doing that," she countered. "The good folk of this town wouldn't want to see their schoolmaster dancing with the likes of me."

He sighed and ran a hand through his hair. "It didn't go well for you today."

"I suppose they were polite enough." She shrugged her

shoulders and tried to keep her tone airy. "No one came and chased me off, but no one but Doc Wheeler and your friend Rob McGregor made me feel welcome either. And why would they? I sell spirits, which to many is the devil's own brew, and for all they know, I probably sell myself as well."

"You know you don't sell yourself, and I know you don't, and that's all that really matters," he said in a hard voice, and his hands tightened on her arms until his grip almost hurt her. "If the idiotic people in this town are too blind to see what a generous, loving spirit you possess, that's their loss in the long run."

Miranda blinked. The times he spoke like that, he didn't seem like a mild-mannered schoolmaster in the least. "Well, I know I tried. And now I'm tired, and I just want to gather up my boys and go home."

"Please, Miranda, dance one dance with me before you go. I've made a point of partnering every female here under of the age of forty, just so they couldn't talk when I had my dance with you."

When he looked at her like that, the longing and the loneliness she saw in his gray eyes made her melt inside. "Very well, Mr. Johnston, let's go enjoy one dance together, and then I'll start home."

He took her hand, but he made no move to lead her toward the dancing. "I believe we've progressed to the point we can call each other by our Christian names now, don't you?"

She knew it was reckless to throw away one of the most effective barriers between them—formality and convention. But she wanted to call him by his name and hear him say her name again in his wonderful, deep voice.

"Very well, Tobias," she replied with a demure smile, "are we going to stand here all evening, or are we going to dance? The two of us holding hands like this is a fair good way to get us noticed and start the gossip wheels turning."

"The gossips can go to hell," he said in a most unschoolmasterish tone. "Miranda, it would be my pleasure to dance with you." With that he tucked her arm beneath his own and led her out. As fate would have it, the musicians struck up the strains of "Beautiful Dreamer," one of her favorite love songs.

She slipped into his arms like a ship coming home to a safe port at last. From the first they moved together easily, as if they had been dancing together for years. She was glad he didn't seem inclined to talk. Instead she could simply concentrate on the pleasure it gave her to circle about the grassy meadow with this man, the black mountain sky above their heads glistening with silver stars, the clean scent of pine trees and wood smoke from the bonfire scenting the air about them.

For a time, Miranda closed her eyes and just relished the feel of Tobias. His shoulder was hard and muscular beneath her palm. His right hand clasping her own was firm and warm. She was intensely aware of his fingers splayed across her rib cage. It was a wonderful sort of torture, being this close to him and wanting so much more.

She longed to slip her fingers through his beautiful, tawny hair. She wanted to caress those lean cheeks of his and smooth the frown lines between his brows. She wished she could snatch his spectacles away and see his gray eyes just once without the barrier of glass between them. Most of all, because they were so close, she was tempted to shock all of Pine Creek and tug his head down to hers and kiss him with all the fire his nearness had kindled in her veins. But because she cared about him, and because she knew how much he loved the job he did, she did none of those things and simply dreamed about them instead.

All too soon the music came to an end. He tightened his hold on her. She could read it in his eyes that he was about to ask her to dance a second time. She hastily stepped back, forcing him to let go.

"Thank you for that dance," she said breathlessly. "It was just heavenly. I hope you enjoy the rest of your evening." She turned away and started back toward her buckboard, but he caught up with her within three steps.

"I believe I'll escort you to your buckboard first," he said in an implacable voice.

She was afraid that if she stopped to point out his foolishness, they would only attract the sort of notice he needed to avoid at all cost, and so Miranda bit her tongue.

They were halfway back to her buckboard when a big, drunken cowboy lurched out of the darkness. After a few moments, she recognized him from the Shamrock. Lucas had had to throw Rye Murdoch out of the saloon twice before for pestering her.

"Hey, Irish, I just saw you dancing with Mr. Schoolmaster here. If you can dance with him, you can damn well dance with me," he announced in a belligerent voice.

Miranda bit her lip in mortification. This was just the kind of incident she had hoped to avoid today.

"Miranda, go on to the buckboard. I'll see if I can't talk some sense into this gentleman." Tobias gave her shoulder a none-too-gentle push. She went on, several steps anyway, because of the snap of command in his voice. But then her common sense and concern for Tobias got the better of her. How could scholarly Tobias possibly handle Rye Murdoch? The big cowboy was one of the roughest fighters in Pine Creek. She turned around just in time to see Rye bend over, clutching his stomach. It was hard to see in the uncertain light, but Tobias seemed to be holding on to his arm most solicitously as he led the big cowboy away.

Could Tobias have hit Rye? Somehow she couldn't picture him hitting anyone. Within moments Tobias returned to her side, looking as calm and unruffled as ever.

"Some people just can't handle their drink," he commented. "It's embarrassing when a man loses his dinner in public like that."

Miranda eyed him dubiously, but she had to accept his explanation. She doubted Tobias had learned how to slug a man during the years he'd spent studying and reading his beloved books. When they reached her wagon, they found Christina had packed up the blanket and harnessed the team. Lucas had already gone on to open the Shamrock with Otis tonight. Business would be good with many men from Pine Creek wanting to continue the day's celebrating at the saloon.

Miranda looked around for Sean and Rory. Of course, she could see neither hide nor hair of her nephews. She felt like stamping her feet with impatience. She needed to get the boys back home and settled so that she could return to town and help at the saloon.

"Christina, could you go look for the boys? I'll come help you in a moment."

Christina nodded and slipped away into the darkness. And then Miranda was alone with Tobias in the shadows beside the buckboard, and she realized what a strategic error she had just made. She turned about, determined to send him on his way with a cheerful dismissal, but it already was too late. Before she could say a word to him, Tobias stepped closer, pulled her into his arms, and kissed her soundly.

# Chapter Seven

Despite the fact he was a man who was used to being careful and cautious, Tobias dove headlong into that first kiss. Miranda Kilpatrick felt like heaven in his arms. She was warm and soft and smelled like lavender and roses. She stayed completely still for a long moment, and then she gave a little moan and wrapped her arms around his neck and kissed him back with such enthusiasm Tobias wanted to grin. Of course she'd go about kissing with the same sort of generosity and headlong verve that she tackled everything else in life.

He pushed her back against the side of the buckboard, glorying in the way she yielded against him. He kissed her cheeks, her eyelids, the smooth skin above the collar of her dress, relishing the chance to finally caress the places he had wanted to touch for weeks now. Dancing with her just minutes ago had stoked a fire in him which still raged in his veins. He had longed to kiss her then, but by drawing on a lifetime of self-control, he'd managed to keep from embarrassing them both while they danced in front of Pine Creek's finest citizens.

At last he had her in his arms, in a shadowy place, and he meant to make the most of this opportunity. He wasn't surprised to discover she was inexperienced. The moment he tried to taste her with his tongue, she stiffened, but when he tugged at her chin gently, she allowed him entry. Soon she was following his example, exploring his mouth with an innocent abandon which made his body grow even harder.

He wanted this moment to go on and on, but the watchful side of him which could never quite let go was very aware that time was ticking on remorselessly. Christina would be returning shortly to the buckboard with the boys.

He pressed one more long kiss on her lips and then raised his head. Miranda's indigo eyes were as dark as the night sky overhead. The band was playing a gay polka now, but this secluded spot beside the buckboard was hushed and quiet. Aware of his own harsh breathing, he reached out with his hand. She could have stopped him with a whisper, but she made no sound as he cupped her breast. She filled his hand perfectly. Someone groaned. He was amazed to realize it must be him. He bent his head and kissed her other breast, cursing the layers of cloth that separated him from her flesh. She let go a little sob and ran her hands through his hair, urging him closer.

Need, stronger than anything he had ever known, rose up inside him. He was moments away from pulling her to the ground and taking full advantage of the desire he now knew with glorious certainty she felt for him. Suddenly, he heard boyish voices approaching the buckboard, and reality returned to him in a cold and painful rush.

Tobias stepped back from her, his chest heaving. In the dim light Miranda looked dazed. It gave him little consolation to realize she was breathing just as hard as he was.

"The boys are almost here," he warned her in a thick voice.

She nodded and quickly straightened her dress. Her hair was disheveled, but it already had escaped from its pins during the dancing. Moments later, Christina appeared with two weary boys in tow. Christina watched Tobias suspiciously while she told Miranda she'd found the boys playing with Robby McGregor.

"Where's Lucas?" Tobias asked Miranda as Rory and Sean settled themselves in the bed of the buckboard and Christina climbed up on the seat.

"He's already at the Shamrock," Miranda replied briefly while she took her place beside Christina.

"I'll escort you home, then."

"You mustn't be doing that. You've spent far too much time with me today as it is," Miranda protested.

"The faster we ride out to your place, the faster I can get back here." Her worried expression made him add in a gentler tone, "I need to go fetch Romeo first. I have him picketed on the far side of the meadow well back in the trees. You can start now, and I'll leave in a few minutes and catch up with you. I doubt anyone will even realize I left, and no one will know I went with you."

"Well then, have it your own way. Has anyone ever told you that you can be the most stubborn male since God made Adam?"

"I believe my mother once told me something of the sort." He smiled as he said the words, surprised that for the first time in years he could actually speak of his mother without the old pain and fury clawing at his innards.

Miranda smiled at that, but her eyes remained worried. She slapped the reins and started her team toward home. Tobias walked straight across the meadow, heading to the place he had picketed Romeo. When a few folk hailed him, he stopped and chatted just long enough to be polite. He moved on quickly each time, thinking of the mysterious watcher in the aspen grove near Miranda's house and the fact that Lucas Ransom and his shotgun were at the Shamrock right now.

The more he thought about it, the less he liked the idea that

Miranda was driving anywhere in the dark without some sort of protection. Surprised by the strength of the fear he felt for her, Tobias made quick work of releasing Romeo from his picket and bridling him. Once he was mounted, Tobias sent the bay loping through town toward Miranda's place.

He relaxed only when he caught sight of the buckboard trundling down the road in the starlight.

"The boys are already sound asleep," she told him quietly when he reined Romeo back to a walk and kept pace beside her. "You gave them quite a day, and memories they'll remember all their lives."

"I'm glad you brought them," he replied. "Every boy should have a chance to win a three-legged race." Today had brought back many happy memories of his own childhood, memories he thought had been drowned or scoured away by years of bloodshed and killing. Now he remembered that he, too, had won a three-legged race when he was ten, with his best friend Tommy Fielding, and they both had been full of themselves for weeks afterwards.

" 'Twas a kind thing you did, making sure they could come today, and I'm grateful to you."

Her gratitude made him so uneasy, he could think of nothing to say, and so he fell back on his old companion, silence. He was pleasantly surprised when she seemed content to share that silence as their horses clip-clopped down the starlit road. He'd rarely encountered a woman who was comfortable with quiet.

Once she raised her face to the heavens and said simply, "I love the mountains at night. I've never seen a blacker sky, or so many stars."

"It's a beautiful sight," he agreed, but his gaze was on her delicate profile, and the way her ivory skin gleamed pale in the starlight. Looking at her skin made him remember the exquisite sensation of touching her barely an hour ago. Clearing his throat, he forced himself to look away.

All too soon they came to the little lane that led to her

house. She tried to shoo him back to town, but he insisted on accompanying her right up to the barn where she pulled the team to a halt. He didn't know whether to be relieved or amused when he saw Miranda heft a shotgun quite competently from the floor of the buckboard before he helped her down from the seat. He should have known that Ransom wouldn't have allowed her to drive home in the dark without a gun.

He helped Miranda unharness the team while Christina roused the sleeping boys and herded them inside. Within moments, Christina was back beside the buckboard, her voice low and strained. "Miranda, you must come. Someone was here while we were gone."

"Hey, Aunt Miranda, where's that shotgun?" Sean was on Christina's heels, looking wide awake now and very belligerent for a twelve-year-old. Rory was right behind him, looking more scared than belligerent.

"I think maybe somebody robbed us. Everything inside is torn apart," Sean said quickly.

Tobias felt himself reaching for a pistol where he no longer wore one. He swore under his breath and spun about for the shotgun. "Give me that," he ordered Miranda. "You and the boys wait here by the buckboard with Christina."

"I will not," Miranda replied indignantly. "This is my home, and my trouble, for that matter. You've no cause to get caught up in it."

Christ, this was no time for them to get into an argument. "I'm not going to ride away and let you go into that house by yourself. What sort of man do you think I am?"

"One who knows more of books than guns and violence, and I'm rare glad of it," she fired back at him.

He should have seen that one coming. "Just hand me that damn shotgun," he said, biting back a string of profanities which would have shocked all present.

"Do you know how to use it?" Sean asked him suspiciously.

"Any fool knows how to use a shotgun," he gritted. "You

just point it in the right direction and let fly with both barrels. Now, Miranda, let me have it so I can check and make sure your place is safe.''

"All right, then''—she handed the gun over to him—''but I'm coming with you. Christina, you and the boys wait here.''

They did as she told them, their eyes wide in their worried faces. He wanted to make Miranda stay behind as well. He'd seen too many bullets cut down women just as easily as they killed men, and the idea of Miranda Kilpatrick hurt or bleeding made a blinding panic rise up inside him. But he was also aware that she would likely come after him at the first sound of trouble, and they would both be much safer if he knew exactly where she was.

"Come along, then, but stay right behind me, and don't say a word,'' he told her curtly.

Face pale, she nodded. She followed right on his heels as he circled the outside of the house once. The back door was wide open. Chances were, whoever had come and robbed the place was long gone, but Tobias wasn't going to take any unnecessary chances. Christina had left the lantern shining in the front hallway. He decided to avoid making easy targets of either himself or Miranda and headed for the back door.

He walked quietly up the back steps. As soon as he entered the dark kitchen, he heard spilled salt or sugar crunching beneath his boots. It took them little time to check every room on the first floor and second. They both tripped over toppled pieces of furniture, and several times Tobias stepped on broken glass or porcelain.

When he was certain the place was empty, he fetched the lantern from the front hall. By its light they both saw the wreck someone had made of the house. Whoever it was had gone through the entire place, spilling out trunks and wardrobes, cutting open sacks of food and tossing furniture about.

Miranda looked about her front parlor, her face white with shock.

"Why would someone do this to us?" she asked in a shaken voice.

Instinctively he understood this was one of the hardest blows for a woman to endure, to have hearth and home invaded and violated in this way. Wordlessly, he took her into his arms and simply held her while shivers racked her body.

In the meantime, he fought down the boiling rage he felt at whoever had made Miranda tremble like this. He forced himself to consider the question she had asked. The more he looked around him, the more he doubted robbers had done this to her place. Someone had been searching through her home for something they wanted, something they wanted badly. But now wasn't the time to tell her that. Miranda would have her hands full during the next few hours simply putting her house together and comforting her family.

At last she drew in a long breath and pushed away from him. "We better go get Christina and the boys. They'll be worried sick wondering what happened to us."

"I'm going to check around outside," he told her. She looked at him sharply, but then she nodded. "Be careful, Tobias," she called after him.

He disappeared into the night, determined to make sure whoever had turned her house upside down was definitely gone from her land. If they had been foolish enough to stay, he was going to make sure they paid for the fear and pain they had just caused Miranda.

He paused behind the barn to wrench off his boots. He was going hunting, and he didn't want the man or men he was after to hear him coming. He hadn't felt this kind of killing rage in years. He was hardly surprised to find he could still feel like this. For all he'd like to think that dark side of him was gone, he knew he'd only managed to bury it deep inside him.

As silent as a stalking mountain lion, he prowled Miranda's land, working out from the cabin in widening circles. He found the place where four riders had left their horses while they searched the house. Their tracks led off to the northwest, away from town. He stared down at the tracks, appalled to discover he was disappointed to find the men gone.

When he returned to the house, he found Miranda, Christina and the boys had all started straightening up. Because the ticks upstairs had been torn apart, there were feathers all over the bedrooms. Miranda was concentrating on making the parlor habitable, for she obviously meant to bed the boys down before the fireplace.

"Four men who rode in from the northwest did this," he told her in an undertone. "I'm guessing they're long gone, but I'd like to go fetch the sheriff and Lucas for you. Will you be all right if I ride into town? I'll only be gone for a half hour or so."

"We'll be fine," Miranda said firmly. "I'd appreciate it if you fetched Lucas. I think we'd all sleep better if he was here."

He handed her the shotgun. "I'll be quick," he promised.

On the way back to town, he gave Romeo his head. When they reached the Shamrock, Tobias tossed the reins over the hitching post and headed straight inside. Ignoring the curious stares he received, he headed for the corner where Ransom stood dealing faro.

"There's been trouble out at Miranda's place," he told the old gambler. "Someone ransacked her house. They left before we got there, but Miranda's some shaken up by it all."

That old man sure could move fast when he'd a mind to. He told Otis the news, and the two of them had that saloon emptied and shut down within five minutes of the time Tobias walked in the door.

"You got any notion who done it?" Lucas's voice was hard and cold as he locked the door to the saloon.

"I expect you'd know more about that than I would," Tobias replied laconically. "I do know this. I've never seen robbers take the time to rip open every flour, bean, and sugar sack in a kitchen before. I figure whoever was out there tonight wanted to find something, and that person knew she'd be gone for a long while in town because of Founder's Day.''

''You sure see and figure a lot for a schoolmaster,'' Lucas said caustically as he strode to a fine sorrel mare tied before the saloon.

Tobias decided he was better off not replying to that comment. ''I'll go roust out the sheriff,'' he suggested, ''while you ride on out to Miranda's. If I'd thought she was in any real danger, I never would have left her, but I think she'd appreciate your coming as soon as possible.''

''All right,'' Lucas replied as he untied the sorrel's reins and swung up into the saddle. ''You can try to fetch Al Carson, but I'll wager you five dollars you won't be able to get his lazy hide out to Miranda's until tomorrow. He's a church-going, teetotaling type, and Miranda don't vote in the sheriff elections.'' With that, the old gambler sent the sorrel galloping down Main Street.

Tobias turned back toward the meadow where well over a hundred people still danced and milled about. It didn't take him long to find Al Carson standing with a group of men tending the bonfire. In a few brief words, he explained what had happened out at Miranda's.

Just as Ransom had predicted, the sheriff didn't seem particularly concerned. ''Reckon it was robbers, right enough. I'll probably hear some other house got robbed while the owners were in town today. Now, what exactly did you say you was doin' out at Miranda Kilpatrick's place?'' The leering curiosity in the sheriff's eyes made Tobias long to put a fist into Carson's face.

''I was escorting her, her housekeeper, and her nephews home from Founder's Day,'' he replied shortly. He considered dragging the lazy son of bitch out to Miranda's place, but he realized there was little to gain. If Carson cared so little about a robbery taking place in his jurisdiction, he sure as hell wasn't going to put any effort into figuring out who did it.

Tobias spun away and headed back to his horse, aware that all the men about the bonfire were watching him.

He was still fuming when he reached Miranda's place. When he knocked on the front door, Lucas opened it, the shotgun slung under one arm.

"Didn't have much luck with Carson, did you?" the old gambler asked with a mirthless smile.

"You were right about him," Tobias replied grimly. "I doubt he lifts a finger to find out who did this."

"I'll look into it. Miranda said you saw tracks."

"I found them beyond that little grove of aspen directly northwest of the barn."

"I'll take a look at them later." The old man made no move to invite him inside. Christina appeared at his elbow. "Miranda is reading a story to the boys now. She asked me to tell you thank you, but she is busy putting Rory and Sean to bed." The accusing look in Christina's eyes made him wonder just how much she'd seen tonight when she brought the boys back to the buckboard.

Tobias stood on the doorstep, suddenly feeling very much like an outsider. The message was clear. Miranda's adopted family would look after her, and she would look after them, and none of them needed Tobias E. Johnston.

*And that's the way you want it. That's the way you've always wanted it.* Wordlessly, he stalked from the porch and mounted Romeo. *Old son, how could you let yourself get so caught up in someone else's problems? As the Good Lord is your witness, you should know better by now.*

Riding back to his own home, he had to face a sobering fact. If he had come face to face with the men who had torn apart Miranda's place tonight, he could have easily killed them, and killing was something he'd sworn he'd never do again. Hell, he'd promised himself he'd never touch a gun again, and he'd just about snatched that shotgun out of Miranda's hands. And the heavy, cold barrel and smooth, carved stock of that old

Parker twelve bore had felt completely right and natural in his hands.

To see the resolutions he'd built the last seven years of his life upon crumble to dust just because he was worried about a woman left a bitter taste in his mouth and a hollow feeling in his stomach. To make matters worse, he was coming to want Miranda so desperately he couldn't think straight around her anymore. He'd always trusted his instincts, and his instincts from the start had warned him that Miranda Kilpatrick was trouble.

Now it was even more clear to him than ever. He was going to have to stay away from her, and whatever mysterious trouble stalked her, or he was going to come face-to-face with the kind of violence he'd turned his back on seven years ago.

# Chapter Eight

Miranda stood up from scrubbing the kitchen floor and rubbed her aching back. So much for Sunday being a day of rest. She would have liked to have spent the day going to mass and playing with the boys, but she and Christina had a whole house to put back together. The boys had manfully done their share all morning, sweeping up feathers and spilled food, and carting away broken glass to the rubbish heap behind the house. Miranda had relented after dinner when she saw the wistful way they kept looking out the window. Because there weren't going to be many more fine days before winter set in, she let Sean and Rory play outside and left the rest for her and Christina to finish.

Right now Lucas was busy out in the barn gluing together two chairs and a small chest the robbers had smashed, and Christina was starting to restuff and resew the ticks upstairs.

Miranda fought back the tears that had threatened to overwhelm her all day. She had probably lost over a hundred dollars in ruined foodstuffs, money she could ill afford to spend. More than the lost food, she ached for the small family treasures that had been destroyed. She'd lost most of her mother's china plates, and a crystal vase her father had given her mother for their twentieth anniversary. The silver mirror she'd inherited from her grandmother had been smashed along with a lovely little porcelain box her da had given her for her twelfth birthday. At least they hadn't found Da's pocket watch. That would have been the worst blow of all if the robbers had taken that. Because she kept it carefully wrapped up inside two old woolen socks, the robbers had missed it.

*People are far more important than possessions,* she told herself firmly, *and you should just thank heaven that everyone in your little family is all right. But will they stay that way?* Shivers went down her back when she considered what could have happened if she and the boys had come home when she had originally planned, before the dancing started. They might have come face-to-face with the men who had brutally wrecked their home. She sat down at the kitchen table and buried her face in her hands.

Lucas came in quietly and poured them both cups of coffee and sat down beside her. "You ready to talk about this now? I figured it was a good time with the boys outside."

Miranda lifted her head from her hands and nodded.

"That schoolmaster of yourn had an interestin' idea last night," Lucas said.

"He's not my schoolmaster," Miranda countered before Lucas could go any farther.

"The man looked mighty upset when he came charging into the saloon last night to tell me what had happened out here. You may not have staked a claim on him, but he's mighty close to staking his claim on you, and you best be thinking how you feel about that. But right now we're supposed to be figuring out who turned this house inside out last night, and your Mr. Johnston had a pretty sharp notion about it."

Miranda sighed and decided there wasn't any point in trying to straighten Lucas out over the topic of Mr. Tobias Johnston right now.

"He thinks whoever did this was looking for something particular," Lucas continued on, "and I'm inclined to agree with him. Robbers are a greedy bunch, but they're also lazy. I ain't never heard of robbers being so damn thorough that they ripped apart every tick and every flour sack in a house."

"But what could they have been looking for?" Miranda shrugged her shoulders helplessly. "I don't own anything of real value. All my savings are tied up in the Shamrock, and you know we put each night's take right into the bank in the morning."

"I don't think someone tore this place apart lookin' for fifty dollars or mebbe even a hundred they'd figure you'd have from the Shamrock. They put this much effort into it, they were after something worth a hell of a lot more."

"I can't imagine what that would be."

"I've been thinking Ben Slaughter had something to do with this." Lucas's blue eyes were worried. "Those tracks led off to the northwest, and he and his men have them a hideout somewheres back in those mountains."

Even as Lucas made the suggestion, Miranda knew he could be right. Her house being ransacked could be connected to the unfinished business Slaughter claimed to have with her uncle.

"The way I see it," Lucas continued on thoughtfully, "they were after something your uncle had, and now they think you have it. We need to figure out what that something is before Slaughter and his men get to be too much for us to handle."

Miranda stared at Lucas in astonishment. "I can't imagine Uncle Shamus owned anything of much value besides the Shamrock. As much as I loved my uncle, I know he was a dreamer. He schemed and hustled most his life, and none of his schemes or plans ever came to anything. All he left me was the Shamrock, this house, and the Kilpatrick family bible."

"Well, it's just an idea." Lucas scratched his chin. "I've been kind of surprised Slaughter hasn't paid us a visit before now. He meant what he said when he swore he'd be back. Maybe next time he'll tell us straight out what he wants."

Miranda rubbed her hands up and down her arms against a sudden chill. "I hate to think he was the one who was here."

"He's a bad man, all right," Lucas said soberly, "and he's not going to forget we forced him to back down at the Shamrock. You keep your eyes peeled for trouble, missy, and don't you go anywhere without your rifle or the shotgun, you hear?"

"Yes, sir," Miranda said meekly.

Lucas went back to his furniture mending out in the barn. By four o'clock, Miranda decided she had done enough cleaning for one day. She and Christina still had another hard day of work ahead of them, but they had managed to restore order to most of the house. She told Christina to relax and take some time for herself.

Intending to do likewise, Miranda headed for the barn and saddled up Lady Luck, the sweet sorrel mare she and Lucas shared. To placate Lucas, she brought along the Spencer rifle she'd inherited from her uncle, a much lighter weapon than Lucas's old Parker shotgun. She had practiced with the Spencer enough to feel comfortable shooting it, and it was much easier for her to handle. Before leaving, she asked Lucas to keep an eye on the boys for her.

As she rode up the ridge behind the cabin, Lucas's words kept replaying themselves in her mind. She supposed he was right, but it still seemed hard to believe Uncle Shamus had possessed anything that Ben Slaughter or anyone else would want. If her uncle had owned something of great value, she couldn't understand why he hadn't mentioned it in his will.

She pulled the mare to a halt when she reached a high point on the ridge with a fine view over the Pine Creek valley. She often came up here when she wanted to be alone. For the first time she had a free moment to think about Tobias and what had happened between them in the shadows beside the buckboard last night.

She touched her own lips softly with her fingertips as she remembered the fiery way he'd claimed her mouth. She'd been kissed by men before. There had been a handsome young man named Jimmy Dugan in Da's troupe she'd fancied until he ran off with a butcher's daughter in Chicago. Jimmy Dugan had kissed her with a finesse that set her heart aflutter, but Jimmy's skillful kisses were nothing like Tobias Johnston's.

When Tobias had taken her in his arms last night, it was as if he wanted to devour her. A strange ache pulsed low in her belly when she thought of how he'd pressed her against the buckboard. She could still feel the way his big hand had cupped her breast so gently. He'd wanted her, and she'd wanted him so badly in return her knees had gone weak with it and her body burned.

If he'd asked her to go lie with him in the dark woods in that moment, she wondered if she would have had the strength to say no to him. For the first time, she began to see why young women risked their reputations and their whole futures for a brief moment of passion with a man they desired.

A cold voice inside her whispered, *And now you can begin to understand what Mary had and what Mary lost when Jake Broden walked out on her.*

Miranda clenched her fists. She had nothing in common with her poor, sweet sister. Mary had been foolish to give her heart to a footloose man who made his living with a gun. She had been reckless to want Jake so badly that he destroyed her when he left. Miranda would never open herself to that kind of hurt. She was too intelligent, and too strong, and too many depended upon her for her to indulge in that sort of stupidity.

Deliberately, Miranda made herself relax. She must try to spend little time alone with Tobias Johnston from now on. For some odd reason, she was far too vulnerable to that big man with his stern face and lonely eyes. Her peace of mind and his reputation were at stake. Both were worth far too much to risk for a quick tumble in the hay. *The next time you see him, Miranda Kilpatrick, you are going to treat him like a polite acquaintance, and that is that.*

Resolutely, she ignored the part of her that wanted to break down and cry. She started the sorrel down the ridge, taking a new trail. She was surprised when that trail led her directly to a small cabin. She thought she had explored all of her uncle's land, but she had never come across this cabin before. She pulled the mare to a halt and dismounted.

When she pulled on the latch string, the door swung open. The cabin was full of mining equipment. As she prowled about looking at picks, shovels, single jacks and rockers, she remembered a conversation she had overheard a long time ago between her parents.

*You Kilpatricks are all the same,* her mother had scolded her father. *Your brother chases his dreams of gold while you chase after dreams of fame and fortune on the stage. The real fortune in life is love, and that you would find in plenty at your own hearth if you only owned one. Shamus would find real gold awaited him in a home with a strong woman and friends to stand by him in good times and bad.*

It was an argument they had had many times over the years until Da had given up his theatrical dreams for the farm his wife wanted, and in the end, that decision had killed them both. Da had died laboring like a slave in the fields, and Ma had died a year later, too worn from hard work to put up much of a fight against the typhus that killed her.

Uncle Shamus had gone west to hunt for gold right after the war. When her parents heard he was keeping a saloon, they had figured he'd given up prospecting. But now, looking at all this equipment and thinking about Ben Slaughter, she wondered if her uncle had kept looking. Could he possibly have found his bonanza at last?

More questions plagued her as she left the cabin and closed the door behind her. If Uncle Shamus had found a rich claim, why hadn't he developed it? Why hadn't he told the rest of his family about it? Always a generous man, her uncle would have shared his good fortune with his brother and his family in an instant.

Still pondering that puzzle, Miranda turned to mount the sorrel. She froze when she heard a twig snap in the spruce grove behind the cabin. She had just pulled the Spencer from its sheath when Tobias Johnston rode out of the trees.

Her heart lifted at the sight of him. In his dark suit and gold spectacles, he looked like a college professor fresh off the streets of Boston, except for the comfortable way he sat his saddle.

"You shouldn't be out here by yourself," he said woodenly.

She studied him, puzzled by how closed and shuttered his face appeared. He had never seemed this distant toward her, not even that first day when they met in the street and he had treated her so politely.

"This is my land, and I refuse to hide in my house like a frightened mouse," she declared. "What are you doing here?"

"Just checking to see if your company from last night decided to pay you another visit today. Did Ransom make certain you know how to use that rifle?"

"He did," she replied, growing more irritated with his blunt tone by the moment. "In fact, I probably know how to use it better than you do."

"Good," he replied tersely. "I hope he also taught you that if you carry a gun, you'd better be prepared to use it."

Unaccountably, the coolness in his voice made a lump rise in the back of her throat. Of course, just moments ago she'd been telling herself the next time she saw him, she would treat him like an acquaintance. The fact he'd done it first made her both hurt and angry. Obviously, he'd come to his senses just as she had. The way they had been heading could have only caused problems for them both.

"I didn't know you were such an expert on guns," she tossed at him.

"I saw more than a few in Kansas in my younger days." His voice was even, but something in his tone reminded her of the way he had spoken of Kansas that first night he came to her house for supper. *Bleeding Kansas was a dangerous place for lots of folks before the war,* he had said. She wondered if he'd lost someone dear to him in Kansas, and if that was why she often saw such bleakness in his eyes. But she had no right to ask him about the wounds in his past when she meant to keep him at arm's length from now on.

"I wanted to thank you for fetching Lucas out to the house for us last night," she said, taking some satisfaction from the fact her voice sounded just as cool and polite as his own.

"I hope he escorts you back and forth to the Shamrock from now on. I don't know what sort of trouble you've gotten yourself into, but you obviously need to be more careful."

"It's kind of you to be concerned, but I believe that's my business. You've no claim on me, and I clearly have no claim on you." Even as she echoed the words Lucas had said to her just an hour ago, she searched Tobias's face for some sign of the man who had taken her into his arms and kissed her as if he couldn't bear to let her go. A cold voice reminded her that it was better this way, better for both of them, but she still felt as if she might burst into tears at any moment.

"Fine," he said with a sudden savagery which had her lifting her hand to her throat. "I'll see you home, and then I won't bother to poke my nose into your business again."

He swung Romeo about and waited with his back to her while she mounted. She was a little surprised when he led off, taking a trail that led directly toward her house. In fact, now that she thought about it, he seemed awfully familiar with her property. She considered asking him why and when he had come to learn his way about her land so well; but she was afraid her voice might not be steady, and she simply didn't have the courage to provoke him with another question. Despite his calm exterior, she was more certain than ever that Mr. Tobias Johnston had a temper to match her own.

It was a quiet, strained ride back to her house. He still hadn't spoken by the time she dismounted in front of her barn. He stared at her, his face as hard as the granite foundations of the mountains surrounding Pine Creek. He started to say something, but then he obviously thought better of it. Instead, he whirled the big bay about and sent it galloping down the lane.

Miranda let go a long breath as she stared after him. Although he'd actually said very little to her, he clearly had been furious. She couldn't help wondering if that anger had been directed at her, or at himself.

Miranda strolled up the boardwalk from Peabody's store admiring the bolt of periwinkle blue winter wool she had just bought for Christina. Like it or not, her housekeeper was going to have a pretty new dress, even if Miranda had to sew every seam and buttonhole of it herself. Now that she knew Rob McGregor was seriously interested in Christina, Miranda was determined to help their romance along.

With all her heart, she wanted someone's romance to progress well. Her brief flirtation or infatuation, or whatever she had been enjoying with the schoolmaster, was clearly over. She hadn't even spoken to Tobias in a week. She often saw him from a distance as they went about their daily business around town, but he never made any effort to talk with her or even look her way. Miranda sighed and told herself once again that it was better for them both this way, but she still couldn't forget how much she had liked dancing with him, talking with him, and trying to make him laugh. And the one kiss they had shared still haunted her dreams at night.

Besides the physical longing he stirred in her, Tobias Johnston had made her consider something she had never thought she had wanted for herself, a life with a husband and children of her own. For a brief, heady, foolish time, she had actually imagined sharing the rest of her days with the schoolmaster, even though she'd seen few marriages end happily for those she loved. Marriage had brought her sister and her parents mostly pain. She had always treasured her independence and her ability to provide for her own too much to marry. It was just as well Tobias Johnston no longer had the time of day for her. Thinking about him had started her dreaming foolish dreams indeed.

She had just stepped off the boardwalk to cross the alley between the livery and the blacksmith shop when Ben Slaughter and Tyrel Reynolds walked straight out in front of her and blocked her path. From the way they stood grinning at her, she knew they meant trouble. With them were the three rough men who had come into the Shamrock with Slaughter three weeks ago.

She thought longingly of the shotgun she had placed beneath the bar at the Shamrock. Lucas was still back at her house. They hadn't anticipated her running into trouble like this on Main Street, in broad daylight. Miranda bit her lip. She was going to have to try to brazen it out. Surely there were limits as to what Ben Slaughter would try in front of a townful of witnesses.

"Red, it's time we had a little talk."

"All right," she said, doing her best to look calm and cool. "What is it you wanted to discuss with me?"

"I'd rather do our talkin' in private." Her heart fell when he grabbed her arm. He proceeded to twist it cruelly behind her back. She tried to dig in her heels, but it hurt her arm too much when he started dragging her down the alleyway.

One thing she knew for certain. She wasn't going anywhere with a man like Ben Slaughter. Miranda opened her mouth and screamed as loudly as she could.

# Chapter Nine

"I don't believe the lady cares to go with you," a deep voice said, stopping Slaughter in his tracks.

Miranda looked over her shoulder. Tobias stood in the middle of the alley looking unflappable and scholarly as ever. Miranda almost groaned aloud. Now she had to worry about getting them both out of this nasty situation in one piece.

"She ain't no lady." Slaughter gave a short bark of laughter. "Can't you see through those spectacles you're wearing?"

"I can see just fine," Tobias replied evenly, "and I see a young lady who has no interest in accompanying you."

"Please, Tobias," Miranda broke in desperately. "I can handle this. Just go back to your schoolhouse. I'll be fine."

Ben Slaughter looked Tobias up and down with his one good eye and snorted. "A schoolmaster, eh? That figures, dressed the way he is. Well, schoolmaster, you best follow the lady's advice, or I'll smear you all over this alley with my fists."

"I don't want to fight anyone, but I'm not leaving until you let her go." Miranda blinked at the steel in Tobias's tone.

"All right, schoolmaster, you were warned. Boys, show this feller what happens to fools who meddle in Ben Slaughter's business."

Suddenly, Slaughter's men surrounded Tobias. "For heaven's sake, man, run and fetch the sheriff," she cried to him, but Tobias didn't look the least bit inclined to run. He didn't look like he was inclined to defend himself, either. He did remove his spectacles and place them carefully in the pocket of his jacket. He raised his arms only when the first tough took a swing at him.

Moving with surprising speed, Tobias blocked the punch and buried his fist in the man's stomach. Pivoting swiftly, he bloodied the nose of his second attacker. He sent the third sprawling with a flying mare.

"Here, you hold her," Slaughter said, handing Miranda over to Reynolds. "I want to take a shot at this feller. It ain't every day you get to slug a schoolmaster who can fight."

When all four men converged on him at once, Tobias started to take a beating. Miranda winced at the dull thud of fists meeting flesh. She got out two loud yells for help before Reynolds clapped his gloved hand over her mouth. Desperate to fetch the sheriff, she tried to kick Reynolds in the shins, but his legs were well protected by the chaps he was wearing. He swore at her for her efforts and twisted her arm viciously.

For a brief time, it looked as though Tobias might be able to hold his own. He landed a punch so hard on one attacker's jaw, the man sat down for several moments looking dazed and sick. Seconds later, Tobias sent Slaughter reeling back from the fray with a split lip, but soon the schoolmaster disappeared beneath a pile of swearing, struggling bodies.

Worried about the punishment Tobias must be taking, Miranda bit Reynolds's hand through his work glove as hard as she could. Reflexively, he caught his hand back, and she managed to get out another good shriek for help.

"You try that again, whore, and I swear to God I'll break

your arm,'' Reynolds hissed in her ear and clapped his hand over her mouth once more.

Slaughter and his men stood up one by one, all breathing hard and looking considerably worse for the wear. Tobias, she saw with dismay, lay completely still, face down in the dirt.

"Say, what's going on here?"

Miranda glanced up to see Al Carson standing at the entrance to the alley, looking more apprehensive than officious. Reynolds let go of her at once. Miranda stumbled over to Tobias, ignoring the burning pain in her arm and shoulder. After she knelt by his side, she was relieved to see he was still breathing.

"Don't worry, Sheriff. We was just leaving," Slaughter told Sheriff Carson.

"And as for you, Red, this ain't over between us, not by a long shot," Slaughter warned her with chilling menace. "Your uncle owed me a share in that mine he found. I figure it's worth at least ten thousand dollars, and by gawd, I intend to collect it." With that, Slaughter turned away and strode toward the horses. His men followed him.

The sheriff simply stood there, looking relieved. Miranda stared at him in disbelief. "You can't just let them ride away," she told him indignantly. "Those men are wanted for robbery and murder, and they just beat the schoolmaster to within an inch of his life."

"And whose fault is that?" Carson's heavy face grew flushed. "It's clear enough what happened. You're the reason he got himself beat up. If he'd minded his own business, none of this would have happened. I ain't riding after Ben Slaughter unless he kills someone in Pine Creek or robs our bank. And then I'll wait until I have a full posse at my back." With that, Carson simply walked away, leaving Miranda alone with Tobias.

"Carson, you're a lily-livered coward and one poor excuse for a lawman," she shouted after the sheriff. Yelling insults at

Carson wasn't going to change anything, but it did let her vent a little of her pent-up fear and anger.

She turned back to Tobias. He was already beginning to stir, which she hoped was a good sign. Gently she rolled him over on his back. Tears rose in her eyes when she saw his swollen eye and the cut on his cheek. The gray suit which he always kept so immaculate was dirty and torn, and his white shirt was stained with blood. Lord only knew how badly he had been hurt, and it was all because of her, just as Sheriff Carson had said.

She reached out and smoothed a lock of his hair away from his forehead. She was just about to check his body for broken bones when Rory and Sean appeared in the alley.

"Say, we just heard the schoolmaster was in a fight," Rory announced, and then his eyes widened when he saw his teacher lying in the dirt.

"Boys, I need you to go fetch Doc Wheeler now," she told them in a shaky voice.

"He doesn't look so good," Sean commented dubiously.

"I'd like to see you look any better if you took on four outlaws to save me," Miranda told Sean with exasperation. "Now go fetch Doc Wheeler." Startled into silence for once, the boys went racing off to do as she asked.

When she turned back to Tobias, his eyes were open, and he was watching her with curious intensity. For the first time, Miranda realized she was seeing him up close without his spectacles on. His eyelashes were long and dark, quite at variance with the severity of the rest of his features. His irises were a gorgeous pewter color, darker at the center and lightening to silver around the edges. Somehow he seemed even more masculine, more intimidating, and just plain heartbreakingly handsome without his spectacles. All at once, she realized this was hardly the time to be admiring him.

"How do you feel?" she asked him as she wiped a streak of blood from his cheek with her handkerchief.

"Like a herd of Rob McGregor's prize Herefords just ran over me," he admitted. "I don't think anything's broken, though."

"We're going to have Doc Wheeler check you over to make certain, and then you're coming out to my place for a good meal. Christina and I can clean up your suit and mend it. It's the least I can do."

Tobias lay back and let her fuss over him. He was surprised by how much he liked it. He felt like hell now, and he knew from past experience that he'd feel even worse tomorrow.

He could be in worse shape, all things considered. Although he might be foolish enough to take on four men at once, he wasn't a complete idiot. In keeping with his schoolmaster image, he'd gone down early and made no particular effort to get up again. There was no reason to prolong his punishment when he'd already accomplished what he'd set out to do when he challenged Slaughter. He wanted to make sure the outlaw didn't continue to bother Miranda, and by allowing those men to beat him, he'd caused enough of a scene that Sheriff Carson had to investigate.

Tobias decided his dignity wouldn't allow him to stay lying down any longer. The groan that escaped his lips as he sat upright was hardly feigned. At first the world threatened to spin away from him, but gradually his dizziness faded. He'd taken a kick and several hard punches to his body which were going to make him sore for a long time to come. The only bright spot was the fact he could look forward to a delicious supper at Miranda's house.

He supposed he shouldn't allow her to take him home with her, but hell, he deserved some special treatment after the beating he'd just taken for her sake. He'd managed to stay away from Miranda for a full week. He'd still be holding fast to his resolutions concerning her, except for the fact he'd seen Slaughter and his men surround her and drag her toward the alley.

He staggered to his feet, ignoring Miranda's orders to stay still. He was trying to slap the dirt from his clothes when Rory and Sean arrived with Doc Wheeler in tow.

"Well, you don't look so bad," Doc Wheeler told him with an ironic smile. "If you can stand, chances are you're going to live."

"Thanks for that expert medical opinion, Doc," Tobias told him.

"You're welcome. Now, take in a deep breath, and tell me if you feel any sharp pain."

Tobias closed his eyes and did as he was told. "Just about everything hurts," he admitted after he opened his eyes again, "but I can't say there's a pain that's particularly sharp."

"I reckon you don't have any broken ribs, then, but you'll have a lollipaloozer of a shiner by tomorrow. Get some rest, and stay away from Slaughter and his men. That will be two bits for your exam and the time I took walking over here."

Tobias reached into his jacket pocket and gave Doc Wheeler his fee. He also pulled out his spectacles and put them on once more. Although he didn't need them to see, he'd worn spectacles for so long now, he almost felt undressed without them.

"Sean, you go fetch the buckboard and bring it behind the livery," Miranda told her nephew as soon as Doc Wheeler left.

"You mean, I get to drive the team by myself?"

"With Rory's help. Just make sure you two don't run anyone over on your way back here."

"Yes, ma'am," Sean said with a huge smile, and then he dashed off with Rory at his heels.

Miranda turned about to face Tobias and flashed him a defiant look. "You're coming home with us, Mr. Johnston, but I see no reason to advertise that fact to the entire town. If we take that lane which runs along the south side of town, fewer folks will see you riding in my buckboard."

"That's fine by me, ma'am," Tobias said meekly. Right now he didn't care who the hell saw them together, as long as he had a chance sometime soon to rinse some of the grit from his mouth. In no time he was settled on the seat next to Miranda, for Sean managed to bring the team around quite competently. They stopped briefly at the schoolhouse to tie Romeo behind the buckboard.

On the way out to the house, Tobias had to listen to Miranda's account of the fight. She described to her curious nephews in detail his efforts to stop Slaughter and his men from carrying her off. Tobias was startled to hear the whole incident had reached rather heroic proportions, in her mind at least. He thought he'd just gone and got the tar beat out of him.

He considered contradicting her a time or two, but when he saw the boys looking at him with new respect in their eyes, he held his tongue. The way Sean had completely dismissed him as a sissy had stuck in his craw, more than he wanted to admit. Now perhaps he could make a little more progress in getting the boy to apply himself to his lessons. Sean was obviously a bright youngster, but since that first day in town when Sean had seen him swallow a series of insults from the two loafers before Peabody's store, the boy had clearly lost all respect for his teacher.

During the last part of the drive, Tobias contemplated the irony of the situation. It had been extremely hard for him to walk away from a fight with those idiots that day in front of the store, and relatively easy to let a gang of owlhoots beat the stuffing out of him. Yet the boys thought he was a hero for getting beaten. None of it seemed to make a great deal of sense. At least he had the satisfaction of knowing Ben Slaughter's face had to hurt as much as his own did right about now.

When they reached Miranda's barn, Lucas came out to greet them. His smile soon changed to a frown when Miranda told him what had happened with Slaughter.

"I'm glad you were there for her," the old man told Tobias shortly. He tended to the team while Miranda led Tobias inside to the boys' room. There she left him while she went to fetch him some clean clothes which had belonged to her uncle. Tobias just managed to squeeze into the plaid shirt and overalls Miranda brought. Shamus Kilpatrick must have been broad through the shoulders and waist, but several inches shorter than himself, Tobias concluded ruefully when he looked down at his legs and realized a fair bit of his shins were showing above his boot tops.

A knock came on the door just as Tobias finished dressing. When the door swung open, he started to make some humorous comment about the clothing to Miranda, but he found Sean, instead, standing in the doorway.

"I came to thank you for helping Aunt Miranda," Sean announced. "Lucas and me, it's our job to look out for her. We should have been there for her today."

As he studied Sean's set expression, Tobias's heart went out to the stubborn boy. He knew saying those words couldn't have been easy for Sean, but his sense of responsibility and honor had demanded it. Tobias had to quell a sudden urge to smile. *With all his prickly pride and stubbornness, Sean reminds you of a certain preacher's boy in Kansas who fought the world to keep folks from thinking he was a "sissy."*

"That's all right," Tobias said, keeping his response light and simple. "I know you two could have handled the situation if you'd been there."

"Well, Lucas could have, anyway," Sean said, flashing him a smile full of surprisingly adult humor. "Does your eye hurt? Lucas says you're going to have a heck of a shiner by tomorrow."

"My face feels like Romeo stepped on it," he admitted candidly.

"When Freddie Atkins gave me a shiner last year, it ached like the dickens. But Aunt Miranda will make it feel better. You'll see." With that, Sean obviously felt honor had been satisfied. He left the room and went pounding down the stairs.

Tobias picked up his suit and shirt and followed him more

slowly. He hoped he could make progress now in forging a better relationship with Sean. He'd liked young Sean Broden from the start, and he wanted to be a friend to the boy if he could.

Miranda's eyes brimmed with mirth, but she wisely made no comment about his appearance when Tobias appeared in the kitchen with his too-short pants. She took his blood-stained shirt and set it to soaking and gave Christina his suit to brush.

"All right then, let's see what we can do for you," Miranda said briskly as she set down a washbasin and clean rags on the kitchen table beside him.

"I'm not sure there's anything you can do that would make much of a difference," Tobias said doubtfully as he eyed the various household ingredients she laid out upon the table next to the rags. Was she planning to treat him or bake him in a cake?

"There's always something one can do to make a body feel better," Miranda contradicted him cheerfully. "That's one thing I've learned looking after the boys' cuts and scrapes this past year."

Tobias sat in the comfortable rocker and let her doctor his hurts with her homemade recipes. The boys hovered close, ghoulishly intrigued with the proceedings until she shooed them away.

"I don't think this cut needs stitches, but a little sticking plaster will help hold the edges together until it heals," Miranda declared after inspecting the cut on his cheek. It stung like hell when she flushed the cut out with vinegar, but mindful of the boys watching from the door, he managed not to swear aloud. He winced again when she applied the cool plaster to his cheek.

"That's the worst of it now," she assured him, and she was right.

He closed his eyes in sheer pleasure when she gently washed his face and sore hands with warm water and baking soda. Occasionally he could catch the scent of her when she drew close. She smelled like roses, soap, and fresh-baked bread. He longed to reach out and pull her to him, so that he could nestle his face against her softness.

This new need he had to touch and be touched by Miranda disturbed him. He was well aware he'd gone half a lifetime without the gentleness of a caring woman's touch. Until he knew for sure he could live a life of peace, he had no business developing a taste for the kind of cherishing only a caring woman could give a man. And so he kept his hands to himself while she fixed cold compresses for him to hold against his eye, cheek, and jaw to keep the swelling down.

After she finished with her doctoring, Tobias was content to remain in his rocker holding compresses to his face while the two women went about fixing supper. His ribs ached from the various punches he'd taken, his face pounded, and yet he felt strangely happy as he watched the comings and goings of the Kilpatrick household, and savored the delectable smell of slumgullion stew cooking on the stove.

Rory and Sean were in and out of the kitchen constantly while doing their afternoon chores. No matter how busy she was with her cooking, Miranda always made time to talk with her nephews when they came bursting into the room to ask her questions or tell her things about their day. At one point, Rory smuggled in a young rabbit and held it out silently for Tobias to admire.

"Rory Broden, I won't have that animal in my kitchen." Miranda shook a wooden spoon at him when she turned about and spotted the rabbit before he could whisk it out of sight under his shirt. "If you don't keep your wild creatures out of my kitchen, they'll end up in my stew pot."

"Aw, Aunt Miranda, you know you couldn't cook Sylvester now. You said so just the other day."

"If we were hungry enough, I'd cook Oliver himself, scales and all, to feed my boys." She said the words lightly, but there was an underlying seriousness to her tone which made Tobias wonder if she had faced starvation in the past.

He watched her with undisguised admiration as she moved about the kitchen and set the table. She looked just as pretty to him now as she had on Founder's Day all done up in her Sunday best. Tonight she wore a simple blue gingham dress, tendrils of her brilliant hair escaping from the bun at the back of her head. Her cheeks were flushed from the heat of the stove, and her eyes were bright with a special light he was fool enough to hope came from the excitement of his presence.

By the time they sat down to eat, Tobias was just about drowning in his own saliva. Supper itself tasted even better than it smelled. Tobias ate three helpings of the stew, two portions of coleslaw, and four slices of the bread Miranda had baked just that morning. He topped off the meal with two pieces of the best peach pie he'd ever tasted. He would have felt self-conscious packing away so much food, but the table was mounded high with it, and Ransom and the boys ate like Sherman's army marching through Georgia. Miranda looked just plain delighted that he liked their cooking so. When he was done, Tobias sat back with a contented sigh.

"That was one fine meal, ladies. I thank you both."

Christina, he saw with some surprise, actually smiled at the compliment. Perhaps she was starting to thaw toward him, now that he'd shed a little blood trying to help Miranda.

"It was the least we could do for you," Miranda declared with a smile. "After we clear the dishes, I want to mend those tears in your suit jacket."

"That's kind of you to offer," he countered, "but I can mend my suit well enough when I get home. I've been doing my own mending for years now. What I was really hoping you might do is sit down at that piano I saw in your front parlor and sing us a song or two."

As soon as the words were out of his mouth, he realized he might be putting her on the spot. Anything to do with the

Shamrock seemed to embarrass Miranda, but for a long time now he'd been wanting to hear her sing. Unfortunately, he knew full well the proper element in town would have frowned on the schoolmaster patronizing a saloon, and so he had stayed away from the Shamrock when he would have greatly enjoyed watching her perform.

She looked at him steadily across the table, the color in her cheeks rising only a little. "I'd be pleased to sing for you, Mr. Johnston. Why don't you menfolk go out on the porch, and I'll call you back inside when we're done cleaning up in here?"

Lucas rose at her suggestion and headed for the porch. Tobias followed him and found the old gambler had taken a seat on the porch steps. Tobias sat down on the wooden porch swing. He thought Lucas might take this opportunity to resume the inquisition he'd begun the first night Tobias ate at this house. He was agreeably surprised when the old man seemed disinclined to talk. Instead he pulled out a pipe and lit it. They sat in companionable silence, watching the twilight sky darken into night.

"That little gal sure can cook," Lucas commented after he took one final puff on his pipe. "Reckon I went sober just for the joy of sitting down at her table on a regular basis." He stood up and knocked his pipe against the last porch step. He lit a lantern and hung it up on a hook so it lit the whole porch. When he finished, he turned about and studied Tobias, his eyes shrewd and cool.

"I still can't read your sign, schoolmaster, but you stuck your neck out for her today, and for that I'm beholden to you. Miranda's taken a real shine to you, and that worries me because I'm damn sure you ain't what you seem. If you hurt her, I'll hunt you down and skin you alive."

Tobias smothered the surge of irritation he felt at the old man's belligerent tone. "For what it's worth, she's the last woman on earth I'd want to hurt in any way."

"I figured you probably felt like that, which means you're

already a goner." Lucas sighed and looked out over the darkening ridges and mountains. "I just don't see how this could turn out right, but no one's going listen to an old codger like me." With that, he turned and wandered off toward the barn.

Tobias was still staring after him when Miranda stepped through the doorway. "Would you like to come back inside now? I've time to sing for you if you still want to hear a short performance," she said with a shy smile. Light from the porch lantern shone off her hair and turned it the color of polished copper. Inside, lamplight shed a welcoming glow over the parlor and front hallway.

Tobias knew he should listen to the old man's warning. A part of him realized he'd be much wiser to take his suit and ride off into the mountain night. But he couldn't face returning to his own lonely cabin just yet, and so he forced his aching body to its feet and smiled at her as best he could with his sore face.

"I've been waiting a long time to hear you sing," he told her truthfully, and followed her inside.

# Chapter Ten

Tobias followed Miranda into the front room which served as a formal parlor and music room. It looked warm and cozy, with a fire burning on the stone hearth and two oil lamps casting their soft yellow glow over the simple old furniture. Christina was already there, he saw with some amusement, doing her knitting in a corner and clearly prepared to act the part of a chaperone. Miranda sat down at the piano bench and gestured that he should take a seat on the settee on the far side of the room.

Instead, he chose to sit in a chair beside the piano so that he could watch both Miranda's face and her hands as she played.

"What would you like to hear?" she asked him after she had settled herself and her skirts with a careful precision which made him smile.

"Whatever you're in a mood to sing," he replied easily.

She made a small moue with her lips in exasperation, and then a gleam came into her eyes. "All right then, here's a fine

one in your honor since you seem so fond of the poet Robbie
Burns.''

As her hands stroked the opening chords to the popular song
"Flow Gently Sweet Afton," he realized at once that she was
a fine player. He loved music, and one of his favorite pastimes
back east had been attending concerts and recitals whenever
he wanted to take a break from his studies. He forgot his
admiration for her skill at the piano, however, the moment she
sang the first line of the song in her sweet, expressive soprano.

He sat there mesmerized as the lovely notes washed over
him. No wonder men rode fifty miles to hear Miranda sing. They
probably came the first time to ogle her while she performed, for
she was a fine figure of a woman in a land where beautiful
women were scarce. They most likely stayed and came again
because for a brief, bittersweet time she gave them back their
homes and loved ones left behind.

He sat completely still as she sang a series of songs that
invoked in him deep, instinctive memories of happier times,
times of innocence, times of joy, times all men longed for but
rarely appreciated properly while they lived them. At last she
drew her little concert to an end and gently shut the piano.
Tobias sat blinking in the lamp-lit room, feeling as if something
precious had just been closed away from him.

"Well, is my audience so silent because he's impressed or
merely tired from what he endured today?" she asked, lifting
one brow.

"I'm impressed." He managed to shake off the strange,
nostalgic mood that had seized him. "I'd heard you were a
good singer, but I had no idea your voice was this fine. You
could sing at the best concert halls in New York if you had a
mind to. Why are you wasting such talent singing in a saloon
in Colorado?''

"That's as nice a response to my singing as a woman could
ask for," she said lightly, her cheeks coloring. "I thank you
for the compliment."

He folded his arms and studied her curiously. "You're welcome, and you didn't answer my question."

She sighed and trailed her fingers lovingly over the piano. "Then, here's your answer, for what it's worth. I know God gave me a lovely voice, but it was never trained properly. One needs training, connections, and backing to become a success in the music world you described, and I lack all three. It's too late for me now, and besides, my dreams have changed."

"You talk as if you were all washed up, at what, the sedate old age of twenty?"

"Twenty-three to be exact, and didn't your mother ever tell you it isn't polite to be asking after a woman's age?" she teased him with a flash of her usual humor, but then her tone sobered again.

"I'll be admitting to you honestly, I don't want that life for myself any longer. There was a time when I longed to set the world afire with my singing. I dreamed of being the toast of America and Europe. Da found me a fine voice teacher in New York who told me I had the talent to sing with the best if I worked long and hard. But Da's theatrical troupe couldn't make it in New York, and he was determined to go on the road. I couldn't bear to be parted from my family, and so I gave up my lessons with Madame Desarte, and all they might have led me to."

"What are your dreams now, Miranda Kilpatrick?" he found himself asking her gently.

"One of them is easy enough to fulfill," she said with a smile with such sweetness and wistfulness in it, he wanted to change the world so that all her dreams came true. "That is, if you don't mind doing a little playacting in a moment. I've always dreamed of entertaining a suitor on my front porch swing like proper girls do in their proper neighborhoods while their proper parents wait just inside. I know well enough you're no suitor for my hand, and my parents are long gone, but for tonight it would be grand if we could just pretend you were."

In reply, he rose to his feet and held his hand out to Miranda. He glanced across the room at Christina. The Swedish girl opened her mouth, obviously to voice a protest. Then she saw the dreamy expression on Miranda's face, and Christina's eyes softened. She looked down at her knitting and didn't say a word.

Miranda took his hand and followed him into the front hallway. He paused when he saw the warm shawl hanging there from a hook. He took the shawl and carefully draped it about her shoulders, his fingertips brushing the soft skin at her nape. And then they both went out onto the porch. Tobias crossed to the lantern Lucas had lit earlier and turned it down low.

Miranda sat down on the swing, and he sat next to her, close enough that their shoulders brushed and her skirts spilled against his thigh. He reached out and took her hand again. It felt warm and remarkably small tucked inside his own. After a time, they began to swing slowly, just as courting couples did.

For a long while they simply sat, drinking in the coolness of the mountain night, and watching the stars shimmer over the dark mountains to the north and east. Although he hated to diminish Miranda's pleasure in this moment, he wasn't sure when he'd have a time like this alone with her again, and he had to find out why Slaughter had been after her today. He knew too much about Ben Slaughter. Tobias was frightened for her if the notorious outlaw was the cause of the problems she'd been having recently.

"We need to talk about what happened today in town," he said at last.

He felt her stiffen beside him.

"And why would that be?" she asked, releasing his hand and turning so that she could look him directly in the eyes.

"I'd like to know what sort of trouble you're in. Someone's been watching your house, and likely it's the same someone who ransacked it the other night. You're in a world of trouble if that person is Ben Slaughter."

"I believe I told you before, you've no reason to get involved in my problems," she told him in a frosty voice.

"Slaughter made it my business when he took a swing at me."

She looked at him for a long moment, and her indignation faded. "You've a point there, I have to grant you. It's sorry I am that you've been touched by my trouble." She drew in a breath and twisted her hands in her lap.

"Ben Slaughter came into the Shamrock three weeks ago and claimed he had some unfinished business with my uncle. When he became offensive, Lucas forced him to leave."

Tobias let go a soft whistle. "That I would have liked to see. That old man sure has sand."

"Aye, that he does. But Lucas isn't as young as he once was, and I'm sore worried he'll get hurt before this trouble with Slaughter is done."

"Ransom is a canny and dangerous old man. The West breeds men who are hard to kill. It might take more than Slaughter and his whole gang to do your Lucas in."

"I know Lucas had a formidable reputation once, but I'm not the least bit interested in discovering whether or not it was well-earned," she said coolly. "I want to figure out why Ben Slaughter seems to think my uncle owned a valuable gold mine and owed him ten thousand dollars, and I want to know what it will take to convince him to leave me alone."

"Short of giving the man what he wants, you aren't going to be able to convince him of anything," Tobias told her shortly.

"For a man of books and learning, you seem to feel you know a great deal about Ben Slaughter and his ilk."

"You forget, I grew up in Kansas, and Slaughter and his gang used to ride in those parts. I understand only too well how his mind works. My guess is your uncle found gold in the general area Slaughter and his gang consider to be their territory. That's enough reason for Slaughter to believe he deserves a share of your uncle's profits."

"But that wouldn't give the man any legal rights to the gold my uncle found."

"Not in any court of law, but we aren't talking about legalities here," he explained grimly. "We are talking about a lawless man who's made up his mind he's owed something by you, which means you've got a problem. Do you have any idea where this gold mine might have been? I'm guessing that information is what Slaughter and his men were looking for the night they ransacked this place."

"That thought occurred to me, too," she admitted, "when we were driving back from town this afternoon. If Uncle Shamus found a valuable mine, he didn't leave any mention of it in his will or in the papers his lawyer turned over to me." Miranda pursed her lips while she considered his question. "There is that old cabin where you saw me on Sunday. It's full of Uncle Shamus's prospecting equipment. I suppose there might be a clue of some sort up there."

"You'd be well-advised to take a look around that cabin the next time you have an hour free. Slaughter isn't going to believe you have no idea where your uncle's mine is located. The fact that that sort of information is public knowledge makes me think your uncle found a valuable claim but never had a chance to record it."

"Thank you for your concern, and for your help today, but that's enough of Ben Slaughter and my problems for now," Miranda said firmly. "I don't think outlaws make a proper topic for front porch swing conversation."

Tobias bit back a caustic retort. He wanted so desperately to make her understand what she was up against. Today had shown her only a glimpse of the kind of vicious violence that Slaughter was capable of. With an inward sigh, he decided he had done all he could for the moment to make her think. Hopefully today's incident would make her take even greater care in the future. It was an awful, helpless sensation to realize that until Slaughter found that mine, Miranda was in danger, and there was pitifully little he could do to shield her from it.

With a conscious effort, Tobias tried to push his worry for her to the back of his mind. It occurred to him he was finally alone with Miranda, a situation he'd been dreaming about since he'd kissed her beside the buckboard. Of course, the rational, controlled side of him had meant to make damn sure he never got close enough to Miranda to be tempted to touch her again.

But now he was more than close enough. Miranda—warm, lovely and vital—sat just inches away, and he knew a lifetime of control and restraint was about to fail him once again.

"What would you like to discuss, Miss Kilpatrick?" he asked as he deliberately put his arm about her shoulders and shifted closer.

"I want to talk more about you," she replied promptly, but her voice had gone tight and breathless.

"That seems like a boring topic to me," he objected. "Schoolmasters tend to lead sedate and uninteresting lives."

"You're different, then, from most the men who come into the Shamrock," Miranda informed him jauntily. "As far as I can see, most men are happiest when they are talking about themselves."

He would have smiled at the truth in her sally, but he was too busy worrying about what she was going to ask him. "What do you want to know?" he asked cautiously.

"Tell me a story about yourself when you were a boy. I've come to think a man's personality is often formed in his youth, and I want to understand you better."

He cast his mind back, trying to find details of the happy time in his life before the violent passions ignited over abolition tore his world apart. He rarely thought about his past, for he was tired of being angry and sad. Sitting on this porch swing brought back memories of the swing they had had at the house in Abbotsville. He smiled when he thought of a story he could tell her.

"I had a sister named Amy. She was five years older than I, and pretty as a picture. When she turned sixteen, she was the belle of Abbot County. The only problem with Amy was that she knew she was pretty, and she spent an awful lot of time thinking about her looks and trying to flirt with boys. There was nothing Amy liked more than getting all gussied up and sitting on our porch swing while poor fellows from all over came and paid court to her. She'd only let the ones she really liked sit next to her.

"Amy and I loved each other, but we had our differences just as brothers and sisters do, and I liked to play tricks on her. One night, when I knew a gent she'd really set her cap for was coming to call, I worked a bunch of porcupine quills into the cushion of that porch swing. She sat down on her side like she always did, but when poor Oscar Felden tried to sit down, he got a bottom full of quills.

"He let go a curse I'd never heard before—and being a preacher's kid I made a point of knowing as many as I could. He jumped up and went running off that porch like a swarm of bees was after him. The other fellows on the porch just about split their shirts from laughing because Oscar had quills a-hanging off his trousers every which way. Of course, Amy was so furious she wouldn't speak to me for a month afterward. Our father made me scrub out the hen house for that one, but it was worth it.

"There's your story," he finished, still smiling over the memory he hadn't thought about for years.

"What happened to Amy?" Miranda asked him, her gaze serious. "That's the first you've ever spoken of anyone in your family except your parents."

"She died before the war," he replied shortly.

"Oh," Miranda said in a small voice.

That was why it was better to keep the doors to the past tightly closed. Tobias felt the all-too-familiar waves of hatred and anger sweep through him, threatening to destroy his equilibrium and his pleasure in Miranda's company and the entire evening. The bitter tide was rising higher and higher inside him when she reached out and put a gentle hand on his sleeve.

"I'm sorry," she said. And with that gesture, and those words spoken with a wealth of sympathy behind them, the floodwaters of his rage eased.

She reached down and took his hand and linked her fingers through his. They swung back and forth until Tobias could trust his voice again.

"Perhaps we could talk about the weather," he suggested, although more talking was the last thing on his mind.

"That topic sounds fine by me," she replied quickly.

"It was quite warm today, for October, wouldn't you agree?" he asked as he reached out and slipped a tendril of her hair behind her ear.

"That it was, indeed," she said, her eyes wide and wondering as he smoothed the line of her cheek with his palm.

"Should be sunny again tomorrow, I should think," he said in a deep, mesmerizing voice.

This time Miranda could only nod in response to his comment. She was still wondering about his sister, and the tragedies in his past which Tobias seemed so determined not to discuss. Yet she was drowning in his closeness. She couldn't help but be aware of the hardness of his leg pressed against her own, and the warmth of his arm against the top of her shoulders. His hand, strong and deliciously heavy against her collarbone, held her and urged her to turn more fully toward him. With one large forefinger, he delicately traced the outline of her lips until she thought she might go mad from longing for a proper kiss.

"Then again, in high country like this, it's always hard to tell what the weather's going to be like from one moment to another. It could turn stormy soon." His gray eyes looked at her with a heated intensity which made her insides go all shivery.

"Lord, man," she groaned, "forget about the weather and get on with kissing me."

"I'm happy to oblige you, ma'am," Tobias said with amusement in his voice, and then his lips covered her own. Within moments she decided being kissed by him was just as heavenly as she remembered. He went about kissing with the same single-minded concentration that marked everything he did, and it left her breathless.

His arms went round her and pulled her closer. She'd never felt so warm and safe. His lips left hers and slanted across her face, kissing her eyelids, her cheeks and her temple. When he kissed the skin beneath her earlobe, shivers of delight went tracing down her back. More joined them when his hand slipped lower and began to massage the side of her rib cage. She had no idea she could feel so sensitive, or that his touch on one part of her body could trigger such strong responses in the rest of her.

Impatiently she placed her hands on his cheeks and guided his mouth back to hers. She hadn't gotten nearly enough of the taste of him. Greatly daring, she kissed him in the bold way he had kissed her on Founder's Day. She didn't know whether she should be shocked or pleased by his immediate response.

He groaned. His hands closed on her shoulders. Abruptly he picked her up and placed her so that she was sitting crossways in his lap. He started kissing her with such passion she thought she might grow faint. His hands ranged across her, caressing, touching, rousing her body to life, creating an unbearable hunger within her to find some way to be closer to him.

Boldly, she slipped her hands beneath his jacket. His body felt warm and firm, his arms corded with muscle. Allowing herself free rein, she let her hands explore upward, running her fingers through the soft, curling hair at his nape. When she kissed the skin at the side of his neck, he drew in a long breath.

He leaned back a little so that he could look at her. She trembled when she saw the blazing hunger in his gray eyes. All at once, she remembered the way he had looked that day before Peabody's store when Red and Randy had been tormenting him. Inexplicably, she trembled again.

"I'd like to touch you in a way few courting couples probably do on a porch swing," he told her hoarsely. "I know you're not a fast or easy woman. I swear I'll stop the moment you ask me to. I'd never hurt you."

She wanted to tell him. *Yes, yes, show me anything and everything right now*. This heady, sensuous world he'd introduced her to was intoxicating. She wanted to experience more of it with a kind of reckless greed completely foreign to her. She knew she might regret her actions tomorrow. A stern, inner voice warned her Tobias could easily hurt her heart in the long run, but she ignored that voice.

For tonight, she wanted him to show her more of the joy lovers could give each other. Deep in her heart, she trusted Tobias. Despite his great strength and size, he never would use that strength to hurt her in a physical sense. Today, instead, he had shown his willingness to protect her at great cost to himself.

She found when she tried to speak, her mouth had gone dry, so instead, she simply nodded.

He swallowed once, the stark planes of his face tight with strain. Slowly, he raised the hem of her dress, his big hand caressing the inside of her calf and knee through her knit stockings. Unable to meet the heat in his eyes any longer, she hid her face in his neck. He smelled of soap, horse, and some spicy male scent all his own. The night was completely quiet except for the occasional whisper of the night breeze in the aspens surrounding the house.

She bit her lips and tightened her grip on his shoulders as his hand ranged higher. There was a strange dampness now between her legs, and a pulsing sort of intense pleasure. Gently he placed his hand over the opening to her drawers and stroked her there.

Startled by the flare of feeling his touch unleashed, she twisted her legs away from him. The sudden movement set the swing to moving so wildly, she let loose a little shriek and clung to his neck.

Tobias withdrew his hand from beneath her skirts and wrapped his arms around her waist to steady her. "Now I see why they put courtin' couples on a swing," he said with such disgust she had to laugh.

Hoping to recapture some of the mood they had just lost, she squirmed on his lap, trying to cuddle closer. Suddenly Tobias went completely still beneath her.

"Don't move," he told her in a choked voice and shifted his legs. Suddenly, she realized what she had been sitting on, and her cheeks began to burn. She remained completely still until he leaned his face against her own.

"Miranda Kilpatrick, I swear there must be a witch back in your family tree somewhere. I've never met a woman who could make me want like this, especially on a damned porch swing."

"And I'm thinking there must be a conjurer in your own. You've made me forget my own sweet nephews are sleeping just upstairs, and I've no business to be spoonin' with any man with them to look out for."

"We've got a problem, and it's time we both faced up to it," he told her soberly. "Each time I see you, it's getting harder and harder for me to keep my hands off you."

"And I'd like to come visit with you at the schoolhouse every day of life, but you've been seen with me too many times already. I'm sure people are starting to talk, especially after what you did for me today. I could never live with myself if your reputation in Pine Creek was damaged because of me."

She touched her palm to his cheek. He closed his eyes and leaned into the caress.

How starved for a woman's touch he must be, to savor such simple gestures the way he did. She was beginning to think there had been little tenderness or caring in his life for a very long time. She leaned forward and brushed a kiss along his hard cheekbone. His arms tightened about her. His eyes opened, and from the look in them, she had an idea they were about to go for another round, despite what they had just said about staying away from each other.

Miranda grinned in anticipation. She was beginning to think she liked spoonin' with Mr. Tobias E. Johnston better than just about anything else she'd ever done.

"Figure Otis could probably use a hand down at the Shamrock sometime tonight," Lucas drawled from the shadows.

Miranda hastily slipped from Tobias's lap, her cheeks heating once again. She could tell from the way his hands lingered at her waist that he was reluctant to let her go.

"You can start harnessing the team," she called out to Lucas. "I'll say goodnight to Mr. Johnston, and I'll be ready in no time."

"I won't hold my breath," she thought she heard the old man mutter as he stamped off toward the barn.

"He's right. Otis does need a hand," she told Tobias apologetically. "I should have been at the Shamrock quite a while ago. Some of my regulars will get angry if I don't perform right on time."

"By all means, don't let me keep you," he said in a perfectly polite tone, but she could tell he was angered by something she'd just said.

"I'll just go inside and fetch your suit and shirt. The shirt ought to be dry by tomorrow. You can send my uncle's clothes home with Rory and Sean."

"Thank you, and please relay my thanks to Christina as well. It would have taken me a long time to make my suit presentable again."

"It was the least we could do." Miranda drew heavily on

her acting experience to keep her tone light and airy. From the moment she'd mentioned the Shamrock, he'd retreated back behind that polite, formal facade he wore. She knew it was foolish to care. She knew it was folly to keep trying to break down the formidable walls he kept erected about himself. Still, it hurt that one moment he could be kissing her as if she were the most desirable woman on earth, and at the mere mention of what she did to make a living, he turned back into a proper, inscrutable schoolmaster once more.

With a lump in her throat, she went inside to find his clothes. When she returned to the front porch, she found him standing at the base of the porch steps, his eyes shadowed by the brim of his hat. Clearly, Mr. Tobias Johnston was impatient to take his leave.

"Here you are, then," she said as she came down the steps. She handed him his suit and then retreated quickly to the porch. She wasn't going to linger near him, for she didn't want him to think she was hoping for a final kiss good night.

"Thank you for the delicious supper, and the singing," he said, a hint of his former warmth in his tone.

"Thank you for stopping Ben Slaughter." She drew in a deep breath and decided to take the risk of telling him what was on her mind. "I know there's a dozen good reasons why you'll never truly come courtin' me. I've a dozen more for why I could never let you. Still, I want you to know it's a great favor you did me today, and Kilpatricks always pay their debts. If you ever need anything, even if it's just wanting your socks mended or a good meal served to you, you're always welcome here."

She thought his harsh expression softened a little, but it was difficult to tell in the uncertain light.

"I will remember that," he told her gravely. "Few folks have ever been kind enough to offer me such a warm invitation." He tugged the brim of his hat to her and went to his horse.

Miranda stared after him, shaking her head. Even though

she should have been getting ready to go to the Shamrock, she remained on the porch for a long time after Tobias left, wondering why one moment he made her so angry she wanted to break a fence post over his head, and the next he made her want to cry for him.

# Chapter Eleven

Tobias gave a sigh of relief as the last of his pupils rushed out the door. It was Monday afternoon, and he'd had one hell of a day. From the moment his students had spied his shiner, they had been a-titter with excitement and speculation. He couldn't blame them for not concentrating on their lessons today. During his own childhood, if his teacher had come to school looking like he'd been beaten by a lumberjack, he'd have been in a tizzy over it, too.

He turned and began to write tomorrow's lessons and exercises for the different classes upon the chalkboards surrounding the room. He dropped the chalk on the floor and winced when he had to lean over to retrieve it. His day had been made immeasurably longer by the fact he was just plain sore all over. *Tobias E. Johnston, you are not getting any younger.* He'd taken more than a few beatings in his day, several of which had been much worse than this one. He couldn't, however, remember any of them making him ache this much.

He'd spent all day Sunday reading and loafing about the

cabin, reluctant to show his face in town. He had a sinking feeling schoolmasters weren't supposed to get into fistfights, particularly ones involving Irish saloon keepers. He guessed Al Carson had probably had a fine time over the past few days telling the story to anyone who would listen about the schoolmaster getting beaten by Ben Slaughter and his gang. Those parents who didn't know the schoolmaster had been in a fight would by the time his pupils sat down to supper tonight. Most likely there were going to be repercussions for what he had done, but if he had to make the same choice again, he knew he would go down that alley in a heartbeat to help Miranda.

The distinctive sound of a female clearing her throat made him pause in his writing. For a brief moment an irrational hope surged in him that it might be her. Of course, he wasn't going to seek Miranda out, but if she stopped by the schoolhouse of her own accord, he could enjoy looking at her.

Saturday night had only served to harden his resolutions concerning Miss Miranda Kilpatrick. Two nights ago she had come far too close to making him lose control of his desire, and control was the one thing he'd come to pride himself on. Self-discipline and restraint had kept him alive when so many men he'd known who had lived by their guns were dead now.

Being with Miranda had also made him come perilously close to losing his temper. He still saw red over the notion of her tarting herself up and sharing that sweet voice of hers with a bunch of slavering cowpokes at her saloon. If she was going to sing for anyone, he wanted her to sing for him. He knew he was hardly being fair, for her voice was a major part of the reason the Shamrock was a success, and the saloon was how Miranda managed to support herself and the boys.

But when he turned away from the chalkboard, he discovered it wasn't Miranda standing in the doorway to the schoolhouse. It was Mrs. Josiah Smith, and she looked like she was loaded for bear. She took in his bruised face with a single, disdainful look.

"So it's true. You did get involved in a brawl over that saloon keeper," she said in a scathing tone as she stalked down the aisle between the desks and halted before him.

"I wasn't about to let an outlaw molest a woman in broad daylight," he said, doing his best to hide his mounting irritation. "If that lazy sheriff this town hired had done his job when all the commotion started, I wouldn't have gotten involved."

"I remember very clearly the discussion we had about that Kilpatrick woman's nephews. At that time I agreed to help make certain those boys were treated decently by our town's citizens, but their aunt is completely beyond the pale. I am one of the founding members of our school board. My visit today is in an unofficial capacity for that group. I have to tell you that concern about you is mounting within our community."

Tobias gripped the rag he had been using to erase the boards and bit back a scathing profanity that probably would have gotten him fired on the spot. He thought of the joy he took in his teaching, even on a day like today when his students had been as unruly as young squirrels. Teaching was at the heart of this new life he was building for himself. If he wasn't a teacher, he didn't know what he was.

"Indeed, what sort of concern?" he managed in a polite voice.

"Concern about your fitness for this job," she replied in a crushing tone. "Until recently, we have been very pleased with your performance. Having a schoolmaster with credentials like yours from such a fine eastern university has been a great honor and a tremendous contribution to our town's standing. But no matter how excellent your credentials, we are not going to tolerate a schoolmaster who displays loose morals and consorts with persons who peddle vice in all its lowest forms."

She paused and tilted her head a little to the side. "Do I make myself perfectly clear?"

Briefly he considered tossing Mrs. Josiah Smith out the door of his schoolhouse. He was certain the thick bustle she wore would pad her landing adequately. But once again, he wanted to keep his job, and so he replied grimly, "You certainly do, Mrs. Smith."

Finally she must have sensed some of the fury he was feeling, for she paled and moved back from him a step. "Very well, then." She looked away and fussed with her reticule. "I'm certain after this we'll have no cause to be concerned about your performance."

Taking savage pleasure from her discomfiture, Tobias didn't say a word. He did let a little more of the contempt he felt for her and her so-called Christian ways show in his eyes. When he stepped forward, she retreated again. "Good day to you, sir," she gasped and withdrew as quickly as her dignity would allow her.

Tobias sighed and ran a hand through his hair after she left. He sat down at his desk, feeling more weary and depressed than ever. His gaze fell on the apple little Suzy Ellers had brought him just that morning. He smiled wistfully when he remembered how proud and excited she'd been to bring a present to school for her teacher. The idea that anyone wanted to give him a present, much less such an innocent six-year-old, still made a sweet sort of amazement unfurl deep inside him.

Tobias got to his feet and began to pace up and down the aisle of the schoolhouse. Just as he had feared, it had come down to a choice between Miranda and his teaching. He wondered if there was a town anywhere in the world where people minded their own business instead of sticking their noses into the affairs of others. Human nature being what it was, he doubted there was such a place.

If he wanted to be a part of civilized society, he had to play the game by its rules, no matter how much he disagreed with them. From now on, he was going to make sure no respectable citizen in Pine Creek saw him come within spitting distance of Miranda Kilpatrick.

He sighed again when he pictured how pretty she'd looked playing the piano for him Saturday night, and how right and welcoming she'd felt in his arms. He'd known it would be just plain loco to start caring about Miranda Kilpatrick, but care for her he did.

He was eaten up with worry about her trouble with Ben Slaughter. Try as he could, he couldn't see any clear way out of the tangle she found herself in. Slaughter wasn't going to give up until he was absolutely convinced she knew nothing about that mine he believed Shamus Kilpatrick had found.

Until that day came, Miranda Kilpatrick was in terrible danger. And if Tobias E. Johnston wanted to keep his job, there was nothing he could do to help her.

As the days passed, Tobias held to the pledge he'd made himself. He never rode out to Miranda's place, and he never spoke to her the times he saw her around town. In turn, Miranda made no effort to approach him, or even to catch his eye when they passed each other on the wooden boardwalk. It was well they both were so careful, for Tobias frequently caught townsfolk watching them both with avid curiosity.

The fear he felt for her, however, deepened until he could hardly sleep at night. He knew only too well the sort of man Ben Slaughter was. If he wanted to take Miranda, and try to force the information he wanted out of her, Lucas Ransom wouldn't be able to stop him.

One night Tobias awoke from a particularly terrifying dream about Miranda and Slaughter. Unable to go back to sleep, he saddled up Romeo and rode into town. He waited in the trees behind the Shamrock for Miranda to close down the saloon. When she and Lucas finally drove home, he followed them. He was careful to stay far enough behind the buckboard he was certain even Lucas had no idea he was tailing them. All the while, he kept his eyes peeled for any sign of Slaughter or his men.

Every night after that Tobias got up at one o'clock in the morning, rode into town, and followed Miranda back to her place. After she reached home safely, he usually circled her land once or twice, making sure no outlaws lurked back in the trees, before he returned to his own cabin to fall into an exhausted slumber.

Although he'd never needed a great deal of sleep, the nights of watching over Miranda began to take their toll. At school he found it was harder for him to be patient with his students. After his pupils had gone home, it became more difficult to concentrate on devising his lessons for the following day.

One night as he sat on Romeo's back watching the Shamrock and cursing the cold, Tobias decided with a grim sort of satisfaction that this situation couldn't go on indefinitely. Slaughter would be making his move soon. He and his gang had held up a bank in Rock Springs last week. Needing money to last them through the winter, Slaughter had probably been busy for the last few weeks planning this heist. Now that he'd been successful, he could turn his mind to other matters, like trying to coerce gold mines out of lovely saloon keepers.

Tobias pulled the collar of his sheepskin jacket up higher against the chill wind. It was early November now, and the nights had grown longer and colder.

*Tobias E. Johnston, what the hell are you doing out here?* he asked himself for the hundredth time. He'd swore he'd never kill again, yet helping Miranda against Slaughter was pulling him relentlessly into a situation where he was going to have to use a gun. He hoped he could give Ransom warning, or find a way to help him in a fight without actually killing a man. *Your only other choice, to ride away and let an old man and a young woman with more spirit than sense face a man like Slaughter on their own, is no choice at all.*

And so Tobias stayed right where he was, wishing like hell

that Miranda and Lucas would finish closing up the saloon soon so that he could go back to his own cabin and get some sleep.

Because he was so tired, Tobias was slow to spot the group of men riding quietly down the road which led into Pine Creek from the north. Romeo pricked his ears and noticed them first. Tobias was off his back in a flash, stroking his nose and whispering to him to keep the gelding from neighing a greeting to the other horses. When the men turned off the road before they reached the main part of town and approached the back of the Shamrock, Tobias knew they meant trouble. The cold night wind brought with it the scent of kerosene.

Silently he eased back into the saddle and sent Romeo trotting as fast as he could through the trees toward the south end of town. As soon as he reached the road, he kicked the bay into a gallop and headed for the front door of the Shamrock.

He reined Romeo to a plunging stop before the saloon. Looking through the front windows, he could see the place was already empty, and Miranda, Lucas and Otis were in the process of closing it down for the night. Tobias leapt from the saddle and reached the door in three strides. When he tried the handle, he discovered the door was already locked. Impatiently he pounded on it, willing Miranda to hurry.

Miranda came to open it, Lucas one step behind her. Her eyes were wide and startled when she recognized Tobias. "What on earth are you—" she started to ask, but he cut her off.

"A group of five men just rode up behind the saloon. I think they mean to fire the place."

Lucas didn't waste time talking. He spun about and ran to the bar. Within moments, he had pulled out a small arsenal of pistols, rifles, and shotguns. Obviously, the old man had been expecting this moment would come.

Tobias looked at the guns spread out upon the bar and swallowed hard. "I'll shoot at Slaughter's men," he told them tersely, "but I'm not killing anyone."

Lucas didn't look up as he grabbed a gun belt and slung it about his hips. "Suit yourself. They ain't goin' to be so particular."

Swearing under his breath, Tobias grabbed a pistol and spun the cylinder quickly. When he was certain the six-shooter was fully loaded, he stuck it in his waistband. He also picked up a Winchester repeating rifle and checked its load. Otis chose the Sharps buffalo gun and a pistol. He likewise checked to see if the weapons were loaded, with a calm efficiency that made Tobias wonder if Miranda's piano player had served in the war.

"You know I can shoot a rifle as well as most men." Miranda reached for the remaining rifle on the bar, looking pale but determined.

"I know you can, missy," Lucas replied as he filled the pockets of his jacket with shotgun shells, "but you'll be a bigger help to us if you run upstairs and grab some blankets, and fill whatever buckets we've got with water. You be ready to help us put the fire out if they get one started, but don't you come outside until we tell you it's safe. Remember, this place is important to you, but it ain't worth dying for."

"The same goes for all of you," she told them fiercely, and then she turned and ran upstairs.

"Speaking of staying alive, I'm not all that keen on charging out the back door of this place with five men waiting for us," Tobias pointed out.

"Who said anything about going out the back door?" Lucas asked even as he hurried to the front door. "Otis, you can fire through the storeroom window off the back. Johnston, you go down the right side. I'll take the left."

Tobias spared a half-moment to wonder why Lucas seemed so certain a schoolmaster could hold his own in a gunfight. Then he stepped out into the cold, dark night, and there was no time left to think. His belly tight with a familiar tension, he ran down the side of the Shamrock, the Winchester cocked and ready to fire. When he reached the corner of the building, he peered around it warily.

Four of the five riders had already dismounted. Two held lit torches, and two more were busy using kerosene to douse the lean-to where Miranda left her team. Slaughter's men had already led the horses out, clearly intending to add horse thieving to their night's activities. It was difficult to tell in the uncertain light, but Tobias was fairly sure Slaughter himself wasn't present. Tobias ran forward two steps and ducked behind a rain barrel which would give him good cover and a better field of fire.

One of the men holding the kerosene had just started toward the back of the Shamrock when Ransom's big Parker shotgun boomed. All of the outlaws started swearing and grabbing for their guns. Buckshot must have caught two of their horses, for they started rearing and plunging madly. Otis's buffalo gun thundered from the back of the saloon, and one of the men holding a torch cried out and fell to the ground.

To keep the pressure on Slaughter's men, Tobias opened fire from his position behind the barrel. He was careful to aim over their heads, but he was sure enough of his marksmanship from this distance to make the outlaws feel the wind from his bullets.

Tobias swore aloud when he heard the crack of the rifle from the second floor of the Shamrock. Damn Miranda. Of course that woman wouldn't have the sense to stay out of it. He levered the Winchester swiftly, firing shots as fast as he could, determined to drive Slaughter's men off before they aimed a hail of lead at Miranda's window.

Getting raked by fire from four positions broke their nerve. The outlaws started scrambling for their horses. The second man with a torch pitched it onto the roof of the lean-to as he raced for his mount. The outlaw who had remained mounted throughout leaned over to catch up the halter ropes for Miranda's team. Coolly, Tobias shot him in the arm. Clutching his sleeve, the outlaw spun his horse about and went pounding off into the dark.

Tobias leaned the Winchester against the side of the saloon and went running toward the lean-to, which was fast going up in flames.

"Miranda," he hollered up at her window, "get those blankets down here, and then go get some people for a bucket brigade."

The lean-to was close enough to the saloon, sparks from it could easily set the rough-hewn boards of the Shamrock afire. He ran and caught the halter ropes of the restive team, then led the frightened horses away from the burning lean-to and tied them to the corral behind the nearby livery.

When Tobias ran back to the Shamrock, Otis and Lucas were pulling the buckboard away from the blazing lean-to. Miranda appeared within a minute, blankets under one arm, a bucket in the other.

"Is everyone all right?" she asked them breathlessly.

"We're fine," Tobias replied as he helped the other men with the buckboard. "We're going to do what we can to keep this fire under control, but we're going to need help. Folk should start coming soon to see what's happening back here. You tell them that with this wind, the whole town could go up if the Shamrock catches fire."

Miranda wasted no time on words. Instead, she simply nodded and disappeared back inside the Shamrock. Embers from the burning building were landing everywhere now.

Tobias had just caught up a blanket to slap some of those embers out when Lucas suddenly shouted, "Watch out, behind you!"

Tobias reached for the pistol at his belt even as he spun about and dropped to one knee. One of the raiders stood weaving on his feet, his pistol drawn, his side a bloody mess from the bullet he'd taken from the buffalo gun. In the light cast by the leaping flames, Tobias saw the man's wild eyes focus on him.

From a lifetime ago, he read the moment when the outlaw made the conscious decision to fire.

At this distance, Tobias knew he had to shoot for the heart. Wounding him wasn't an option if he wanted to survive. Cursing fate and his own weakness which had brought him to this moment, he reached up to fan the hammer of his pistol. Just as he touched the hammer, Ransom's shotgun boomed a final time, and the wounded man fell backward like a toppled tree and lay still.

Tobias staggered to his feet, the acrid smell of gunpowder strong in his nostrils. A wave of nausea rose in him. He doubled over and retched, and retched again, wishing he could purge his heart and soul of bloodshed and violent death even as his stomach seemed bent on purging his body. After Tobias had finished, Lucas laid a hand on his shoulder.

"He's dead," the old gambler said briefly. "I'm sorry. I should have checked him more carefully."

"It doesn't matter." Tobias forced the words through his throat, his heart as bitter as the taste in his mouth. He'd been a second away from killing a man, an act he'd sworn he'd never commit again. He caught up a blanket and went after an ember he saw glowing on the back steps of the Shamrock. Within minutes, people started appearing, drawn by the sound of gunfire and the smell of smoke.

They hastily formed a bucket brigade. He knew few of them cared about Miranda's lean-to or her saloon; but they didn't want their own businesses and homes to catch fire from windborn embers, and so they pitched in with a will. Two men even joined Otis up on the roof of the Shamrock to make sure no embers lit there. Within a half hour, the lean-to was a smoldering, steaming mass of burnt timber.

When he was certain the danger to the Shamrock was past, Tobias slipped away from the crowd of folk who had gathered behind the saloon. Plenty of people had seen him fighting the fire, but there would be time enough later to answer their questions about why their schoolmaster had been in town at two o'clock in the morning when he should have been sound asleep in his cabin a mile away.

For the moment he had his own demons to wrestle with. He pointed Romeo toward the cabin. Tired though he was, those demons were likely to keep him up the rest of the night. If Lucas hadn't fired his shotgun when he did, Tobias knew he would have killed that man. Any court of law would have justified the shooting as self-defense, but there was no way he could justify his actions and his choices to himself.

*You were given a heaven-sent chance to try again, you fool, yet within months of coming back to the West, you're neck deep in the kind of trouble that leads to shooting and killing.* Not for the first time he had to face the bitter possibility that violence and killing might be a fundamental part of his nature. *Maybe trying to change is a misguided, idiotic waste of your time.*

He clenched his fists as he rode down the darkened road. He'd tried so hard, studied so long to become a man of letters and a man of peace. He wasn't going to give up on his new life yet, just because he'd been tempted to kill tonight.

But one gut-wrenching fact remained. He cared about Miranda Kilpatrick, and she was up against trouble too big and dangerous for her and Lucas to handle on their own. Tonight was proof of that fact. If he hadn't given them warning, the Shamrock and Miranda's whole livelihood would have gone up in flames.

Yet a painful truth stared him in the face. He was going to have to stop looking out for sweet Miranda. Helping her was destroying him.

# Chapter Twelve

A delegation from the school board came to see Tobias after school the next afternoon. He was hardly surprised to see them. Mrs. Josiah Smith was there, along with Cyrus Reed and Thomas Goodwin. All three looked at him with concern and disapproval evident in their glances.

Tobias wasn't the least bit surprised when Mrs. Josiah Smith led the charge. ''We've come to ask what you were doing in town last night at two o'clock in the morning. In light of the recent conversation you and I had concerning that Kilpatrick woman, we believe we have a right to know if you were seeing her last night.''

''I was waiting behind the Shamrock at two o'clock in the morning to make certain Miss Kilpatrick arrived home safely.'' He knew they would put the most salacious interpretation possible on his actions, but he was damned if he was going to lie or make excuses to save his job.

They looked stunned that he would admit to his wrongdoing so openly.

"I've reason to believe Miss Kilpatrick is being persecuted by Ben Slaughter. Since the lawman you folks elected doesn't seem inclined to help or protect her, I've been lending a hand where I see fit. If I hadn't been in town last night, Slaughter's men probably would have succeeded in setting fire to the Shamrock, and several of your homes and businesses easily could have gone up in flames with it."

There, at least he'd gotten a word in for himself, not that it would do him a damn bit of good. He knew a hanging jury when he saw one.

"We didn't hire you to offer your protection, if that's what you want to call it, to a saloon keeper," Mrs. Smith said with biting sarcasm. "You were hired to teach our children and, by your own example, promote the highest standard of moral, ethical behavior in our town. We now have good reason to wonder if you can possibly fulfill the second half of that job description for the young of Pine Creek."

"What we mean is," Thomas Goodwin broke in anxiously, "if you have something goin' with that Kilpatrick woman, it's got to stop. The town won't stand for it."

"If it becomes obvious the two of you are keepin' company," Cyrus Reed added, "we're going to have to fire you. Myself, I think that'd be a shame. My boy likes you, and for the first time since we opened this school four years ago, I think he's actually learning something."

Tobias was too infuriated by their sanctimonious meddling to appreciate Cyrus Reed's compliment. "Very well, I will take your warning under advisement. Good day to you all."

With that he swung away and busied himself with putting the next day's lessons up on the board. After a long, awkward minute, they accepted their dismissal and left the building. At that moment, Tobias was very glad he didn't have a shotgun at hand. He might have been tempted to send three of Pine Creek's finest, most upstanding citizens home with buckshot in their drawers and britches.

His second visitor that afternoon was a surprise. When he went out to saddle Romeo, he found Lucas Ransom waiting for him by the corral.

"Wanted to thank you for your help last night," the old man began in his straightforward way. "They would have caught us with our pants down, and most likely burned the place if it weren't for you."

"I'm glad for Miranda's sake that we managed to stop them," Tobias said shortly. He opened the gate to the corral and stepped inside. When Romeo came over to nuzzle him, Tobias fed his horse a bit of carrot and set about saddling and bridling him.

"Been thinkin' ever since I saw the way you handled that pistol last night," Lucas said in a conversational tone and hung his elbows over the top rail of the corral. Tobias shot him a quick look. The old man clearly had more on his mind than saying thank you.

"I heard about a gunfighter once," Lucas said thoughtfully, "a man named Jonah. Men who'd seen him in action swore he was fast as lightnin' and cool as ice during a fight. He was a big man, from Kansas most believe, and supposedly he had a real fondness for books.

"After fighting in cattle wars and working as a marshal in some pretty rough towns, this Jonah up and disappeared. Lot of folk figure some kid hunting a reputation probably got him, or a renegade injun. All I know is that Jonah dropped off the edge of the earth about seven years ago. I figure that's just about the time you headed east and got yourself all educated. Course, that timing could just be a coincidence."

"You're probably right about him. Jonah's most likely dead and buried in some town's Boot Hill. Most his kind come to a bad end," Tobias said stonily.

"That would be a good thing, I reckon." Lucas scratched his sideburn. "You see, I'm not sure she realizes it yet, but Miranda's just about head over heels for you. She's got no use for gunfighters, though, because of what that worthless Broden did to her sister. If Miranda ever found out you had made a living as a hired gun, it would break her heart.

"Don't get me wrong, son," the old man's cool blue eyes softened for a moment. "I don't hold anything against you. This ain't personal. In fact, I appreciate what you done to help Miranda, and I admire what you done tried to do with your life. I just ain't sure you're gonna be successful. A man can't change his nature, and that's a fact."

"And you think because I carried a gun once, I'm a killer through and through?"

Lucas sighed and looked toward the snow-capped peaks. After a long moment he answered in a surprisingly gentle tone, "That ain't a question for me to answer, son. That's the question you've got to answer for yourself."

That night at the Shamrock was one of the busiest Miranda had ever experienced. Almost being burned down by outlaws seemed to add to the Shamrock's standing amongst the saloon-goers in town. As Miranda dashed back and forth behind the bar serving up drinks, she decided wryly that she might have tried torching the place herself if she'd realized it would be this good for business.

The room was buzzing with talk about the men who had come and tried to burn down the saloon. Miranda soon grew weary of fielding her patrons' curious questions about the incident. For the most part she tried to close her ears and concentrate on her work and ignore the gossip about her and the speculative glances men were giving her.

She was just coming back from the storage room at the rear of the saloon when she overheard Red Dooley and Randy Murchinson talking in the hallway about the schoolmaster's role in last night's events. For Tobias's sake she stopped in the doorway of the storeroom and listened quietly to their conversation.

"He was in town last night, all right," Red was saying. "Peabody swears he was just about the first one there, and the schoolmaster was helping Otis and Ransom put out the fire."

"So Johnston was here with her in the wee hours of the morning. Then all that talk about them must be right on the money." Randy paused to take a long drink from his glass. "Whoooeee. Who'd have thought that prissy, citified schoolmaster would manage to get into her drawers right away when the rest of us have been trying for a half a year now?"

"It's probably because he has such fancy manners and such," Red said wisely. "Women set store by such things. But underneath, that schoolmaster must be just as randy as the rest of us gents."

Growing angrier by the moment, Miranda was about to give them both scathing setdowns when Randy's next words stopped her cold.

"Well, he got his comeuppance. I heard tell a delegation from the school board went and told him this afternoon that if he doesn't stop sniffing around her, they're gonna fire him for sure."

Miranda's stomach twisted. So it had come to that. It was bad enough that people were gossiping about them both, but it was far worse to know his job was actually in danger. And it was all her fault.

She cleared her throat loudly and launched herself down the hallway. When they spun about in surprise, she sent both Red and Randy killing glances. "I'll just be taking your drinks, *gentlemen*," she said with particular irony. "I'd appreciate it if you left the Shamrock immediately. I might consider serving you again another night. For the moment, I want both you 'randy gents' out of my sight."

"Aw, come on, Miranda." Red actually had the grace to look

embarrassed. "We was just talking. We didn't mean nothing by it."

"You leave now, or I'll ask Lucas to help you leave."

"All right, we're going," Randy said sullenly. "There's no need to sic that mean old man on us."

She stared after them, her stomach still tied in knots. Sweet St. Agnes, the last thing she'd ever wanted was to have any of the scandal attached to her name rub off on Tobias. From the way his face softened when he spoke about his teaching and his students, she knew his job meant the world to him. And now, that job was in jeopardy because he had helped her.

Miranda wandered back to the storeroom and sat down on a keg of beer. She started to wish he hadn't come to warn her about Slaughter's men; but then the Shamrock would probably be a smoldering pile of burnt timbers right now, and her ability to provide for her family would have gone up in flames with it, so she couldn't wish that, exactly. She could wish that Tobias had had the sense to leave before the rest of the townsfolk arrived and started wondering just what their proper schoolmaster was doing in town at that improper time of night. But, of course, he had wanted to stay until he was certain the fire was under control, and now he was going to pay for that kindness and concern.

*What was Tobias doing in town at that hour?* For the first time during the craziness of the last twenty-four hours it occurred to her to wonder about that question. Had he been watching out for her, or had he been in town on some mysterious business of his own? How and when had a schoolmaster become so comfortable around guns? Most frontier men knew how to hunt with rifles, but the competent way Tobias had picked up that pistol and spun the cylinder to check its load spoke of plenty of experience with that kind of weapon.

There was something disturbing, too, about the way he had looked from the moment he strode through the door of the Shamrock to warn them about Slaughter's men. He hadn't seemed the least bit flustered or excited. Instead, he had looked grim and icy cool, and he had remained that way throughout the gunfight and the chaotic time afterward when they had struggled to keep the saloon from burning. Perhaps he was simply the sort of man who stayed calm during a crisis.

But that didn't explain the strange eagerness in his eyes, as if a part of him welcomed the chance to strike at the men threatening her and her business. *Miranda Kilpatrick, you're imagining things*, she told herself sternly. *But what about that day before the dry good? Did you imagine the wild, fierce look in his eyes then*? And she shivered.

Tobias Johnston was coming to mean far too much to her. She thought about him all the time. She found herself longing to see him again, even if it was just to catch a glimpse of his gold-brown hair or his broad shoulders as he passed by on the opposite side of the street. She remembered every moment of the times they had talked and the way his beautiful gray eyes warmed the rare times he smiled. At night when sleep too often eluded her, she lay in her lonely bed remembering the times he had set her nerves afire with his touch and kissed her in that all-consuming way he had.

*Miranda Kilpatrick, you are perilously close to losing your heart to this man.* 'Twas stupid and foolish, for she had known all along nothing could come of a relationship between an Irish saloon keeper and a schoolmaster. It didn't surprise her, this agony she felt in her heart at the prospect of loving him. *You've known all along love can lead to pain.* But now, after last night, she realized a particular danger in caring for the schoolmaster she hadn't considered before. She was beginning to wonder if she knew the man at all.

She was still sitting on the keg in the storeroom when Lucas came hurrying in the door to find her.

"There you are," he said with considerable relief. "The boys are asking when you're going to sing again, and Otis can't keep up with the drink orders."

He looked at her more closely and frowned. "Are you all right?"

"I'm fine," she lied brightly. "I'm just a little tired after last night. I was stealing a moment to rest my feet. I'll be along in a moment."

"Maybe we should close down early tonight. I'm betting we've already taken in three nights' worth of revenue, and last night was plenty hard on you."

"All the more reason to stay open until two," she replied and rose to her feet. "We'll make four night's money in one, and we'll be that much closer to buying that new faro table you've been wanting."

Lucas reached out and touched her shoulder. "When are you going to stop pushing yourself so hard? I've never seen a gal work the way you do."

"When I know I never need worry again about being able to feed my boys," she said tersely. Determined to change the subject, she asked, "Do you have any idea why Tobias Johnston was in town last night?"

Lucas sighed and rubbed his chin. "I think mebbe he was looking out for you. I've seen tracks from that big bay of his all around your place. I'm guessin' he follows us home from the Shamrock most nights."

She stared at him in astonishment. "How long has this been going on?"

"I'm not rightly sure. I first noticed the tracks a week or so after he had that go around with Slaughter and his boys in town."

"Why didn't you tell me?"

"I figured you'd be all bothered and worried by it, and to tell the truth, I didn't mind the notion of having a little more help looking out for you. That schoolmaster is a man to be reckoned with, and I'm not sure I can handle Slaughter and his gang all by myself."

"I see," Miranda said slowly, and she was afraid she did

see. Tobias Johnston had been giving up his nights to protect her. He was the kind of man who possessed a deep sense of responsibility. He could be looking out for her simply because he knew she was in trouble. He also could be doing it because he was falling in love with her. That possibility made her heart twist and tears burn in her eyes.

She never, ever wanted to hurt him. It was as clear as the nose on her face, he had been hurt in the past. But she never intended to marry, and the schoolmaster was obviously the marrying sort. She could just imagine him teaching in Pine Creek for the next twenty years, and she could picture him settling down with a prim, proper woman and living in one of the prim, proper houses on the edges of Pine Creek. That whole vision made her so depressed two tears slipped down her cheeks. Resolutely, she wiped those tears away with her hands and brought her mind back to focus on the current problem facing her.

He certainly had to stop following her home from the Shamrock at night. Especially since he'd received that warning from the school board. Taking a deep breath, she decided she'd go see him at his cabin after school let out tomorrow. She needed to talk with him one last time, and make certain that from now on the townsfolk of Pine Creek had absolutely no reason to fire their schoolmaster.

With a sigh, Miranda left the storeroom and closed the door carefully behind her.


When Miranda set out for Tobias's cabin the next afternoon, the sky was gray, and the air raw with the damp chill that heralded snow. By her feet on the floor of the buckboard was a basket containing a warm dinner for him, since he seemed to take such pleasure in the meals she and Christina made. She also had the Spencer loaded and kept it right beside her on the seat where she could reach it in a hurry. Before Lucas rode into town this afternoon, she hadn't mentioned to him that she meant to make the trip to Tobias's cabin. Lucas would probably be furious with her when he found out that she'd gone out on her own without him, but she wanted to talk with Tobias in private.

The drive took less than an hour, for her house and his cabin were both on the south of Pine Creek. It seemed like a lifetime, though, as she rehearsed again and again what she wanted to say to Tobias.

When she finally pulled the team to a halt before his cabin, she heard the sound of someone hammering out back. The hammering abruptly ended when her team whinnied to Romeo, and Romeo neighed back lustily. Tobias appeared around the side of the cabin moments later, still carrying a hammer. He was clad in jeans and a red plaid shirt open at the neck. He must have been working hard, for he wore no jacket. He'd rolled up his sleeves, baring his strong, muscular forearms.

Miranda did her best not to stare at the dark shadow of hair curling at the vee in his shirt. She was struck by how different he looked in work clothes. His shoulders seemed even broader, his hips leaner, his legs longer. His gold-brown hair had grown longer since he first arrived in town. Now it curled over the collar of his shirt.

He looked rough, rugged, and confident—much more like a western frontiersman than the eastern scholar she met that first day at Peabody's store. It wasn't fair that Tobias Johnston in either his schoolmaster or western garb made her heart leap.

He frowned as he strode toward her buckboard. "Why isn't Lucas with you?" he asked abruptly. "He should know better than to let you go haring off on your own."

"Good afternoon to you, too, Tobias." Miranda forced herself to smile brightly at him. They weren't exactly getting off to a good start. "For your information, Lucas had some business of his own he had to take care of in town today."

"What are you doing here?"

Resolutely, Miranda kept smiling, even though she was afraid deep down inside that her visit was quite unnecessary. She was beginning to think Tobias had taken the school board's warning to heart, and he had already decided they mustn't see each other again.

"I have a few things I want to discuss with you," she matched his cool tone.

"All right. Say what you have to say, and then I'll saddle up Romeo and make sure you get back home safely."

That did it. She wasn't going to tolerate such rude behavior from anyone. "Tobias E. Johnston, you are one of the most ill-mannered louts I've ever had the misfortune to encounter. I've just driven an hour through the freezing cold to come call on you, and the least you could do is invite me inside so that I can warm up a little before I drive home again."

His lips twitched at this burst of temper. "Fine. You can come in for a few minutes, thaw yourself out, and then I'll see you home." He reached out to help her down from the buckboard; but she was very aware of the fact his hands didn't linger on hers, and he didn't offer her his arm to escort her into his cabin.

Miserably she picked up her basket and wished she had never come. Obviously, Tobias didn't need a lecture on staying away from her. The school board's visit had already killed his interest in her once and for all. She still wanted to thank him for everything he'd done to help her, though, and she needed to apologize for jeopardizing his job and tarnishing his reputation. Her pride demanded it. Then she'd be on her way, and that was the last time she'd ever lay any claim on Tobias Johnston's precious time.

He opened the door to the cabin and let her pass before him. The starkness of it made her draw in a breath. The cabin was so painfully neat and clean. Only the books in the rough bookshelf in the corner gave any sign that Tobias had occupied the dwelling for two months now. Her gaze skittered past the iron bedstead covered with a lovely old double wedding ring quilt and came to rest on a large rocking chair. That and a fat, sawed-off log seemed to be the only chairs in the place.

He drew the rocker closer to the stove. "You can sit here while I put more wood in the stove. I don't have anything to eat but some old biscuits. You can have coffee, but I warn you that it's strong enough to float a horse's shoe."

"Your gracious hospitality overwhelms me," she said nastily. Despite her resolution just an hour ago to save him from hurt, now she was wishing heartily that there was some way to make him feel at least a portion of the embarrassment and mortification scorching through her at this moment.

"I don't believe I remember inviting you here," he commented in a cold voice as he walked to the stove and shoved several logs inside it. He swung the stove door shut with a clang.

"And I surely won't ever be trespassing on your precious privacy again." Her blood was up now. She was going to state her piece to this great boor of a man and be on her way.

"I wanted to say I was sorry about the warning you received from the school board. I'm also sorry that because of me you've become a source of gossip in Pine Creek. I know you wanted to help me, and having your good name and reputation tarnished seems like a poor reward for your charitable actions. I'll always be grateful for what you've done, and I understand that under the circumstances there's no way you'll be helping me further, or socializing with me in the future. Good day to you, sir."

With that, she spun about and headed for the door. She was just opening it when he reached past her and slammed it shut. She stared at the back of his hand splayed across the door. She swallowed hard when she realized he was standing right behind her.

"You're right," he said harshly. "Having my good name tarnished is a poor reward. But I can think of a better one you could offer me."

And then his arms went around her waist, and he pulled her back against the hard length of him. She tried to pry his arms loose, but it was like trying to loosen bands of iron. Furious with him now, she tried to stomp on his boot. He simply lifted her off her feet and tightened his grip about her waist. She shivered when she felt his warm breath on her neck, and then he began to trail kisses along her hairline, her ear, and her temple.

Somehow all that anger she had felt toward him moments ago suddenly transformed itself into a fierce hunger. She wanted him to touch her. She wanted him to make her feel need and desire the way he had before. She stopped trying to fight him. Instead, she reached up behind her and ran her hands through his hair.

He nipped at her neck in appreciation. She was appalled to hear herself moan aloud. He loosened his grip around her waist and let her slide slowly down him, their bodies rubbing against each other with tantalizing friction until her feet were touching the ground. She shuddered when one of his hands slipped to her hip and pulled her more snugly against him. Even through her petticoats she could feel how much he already wanted her.

His other hand moved upward slowly, teasing her, making her breasts harden before he ever cupped her gently. This time he took greater liberties, fondling and caressing her through the fabric of her dress until that treacherous pulse of pleasure started up once more deep in her belly. Suddenly he stepped back, leaving her bereft and cold.

She made an inchoate sound of protest until she realized he was undoing the back of her dress, his big hands surprisingly clever with her hooks. Outside the light was starting to fade.

The cabin was completely silent, except for the sound of their quick breaths and the occasional pop and hiss from the fire in the stove. She felt the coolness of the cabin air on her skin as her dress slipped forward. Tobias's warm lips kissed her neck, sending lovely shivers down her spine. He moved lower, kissing her back through her chemise. Now she was sinfully glad she hadn't worn a corset. She waited, anticipation making her heart slam in quick strokes, and wondered where he would touch her next.

When he had finished with her fastenings, her dress front fell forward about her waist. She tipped her head back when his arms went round her, and he stepped close once more.

His palms spread wide, he grazed the very tips of her breasts through her chemise, the fine lawn tantalizing her skin in an exquisitely pleasurable way.

Just when her legs were about to buckle, he reached lower and touched her gently between her legs, pressing her petticoats against that place which was growing almost painfully sensitive. He massaged her until she grew damp and her legs did start to give. She had never experienced such intense pleasure. She had no idea her body could feel like this.

Tobias's strong arms wrapped around her waist once more, steadying her and pulling her back until she could feel his jutting arousal pushing against her. He kissed the side of her neck and thrust against her in a slow, sensuous rhythm.

When she could stand the delicious torment no longer, she twisted about in his embrace. She reached her arms up and wrapped them around his neck. He pressed a quick, hard kiss on her lips, and then he pushed her dress down about her hips and made quick work of the ties to her petticoats. As her undergarments collapsed about her feet, he slipped his arms beneath her knees and picked her up. After three quick strides, he lowered her gently onto his bed. He came to lie beside her, the hunger in his gray eyes at odds with his forbidding expression.

"God help me, Miranda, you never should have come here," he said, raising himself up on one elbow to look down at her. "I know I have no right to you, but I don't have the strength to let you go." His voice was rough, his tone violent, but his touch was tender when he reached out and smoothed a tendril of hair which had fallen forward across her cheek.

Miranda gazed up at the strong lines and planes of his craggy face. She was honest enough to admit to herself this was what she had wanted from Tobias all along. At least she knew now that despite the school board, despite Pine Creek's rumormongers, he still wanted her with a desperation that made her giddy.

She reached up and pulled his head down to hers. And then he was kissing and touching her everywhere, his skillful hands stroking and caressing her until she was breathless. He shifted one leg until it lay warm and heavy across her thighs. Impatiently she undid the buttons of his shirt, smoothing her hands over his chest and savoring the contrasting textures of smooth skin, soft springy hair, and hard muscle she discovered there.

Impatiently he tugged his shirt completely off and tossed it over the side of the bed. She drew in a breath as she watched the play of muscles in his arms and chest. He was so beautiful in a lean, hard kind of way. When he turned back to her, he took the hem of her chemise and pulled it up over her head, baring her to his view, and then he stilled to look at her.

Miranda felt her cheeks warm. It took all her self-control not to cover herself with her hands. Sweet St. Agnes, she hoped her body pleased him even as his pleased her.

"Miranda, you're even more lovely than I dreamed you'd be," he told her in a thick voice. And then he bent his head and kissed her mouth reverently. She parted her lips in an invitation he accepted with alacrity. After a long, luscious kiss, he moved lower and kissed her breasts as well.

Miranda closed her eyes, swept away on a whole new wave

of sensation. She loved the feel of his lips on her. She relished the softness of his hair brushing against her skin. Her hands ranged over his shoulders, marveling at the glorious male strength of him. And then her fingers found the scars, and her eyes flew open. Tenderly she traced two rough, round spots on his back.

Because they were too rough to be birthmarks, she guessed they might be from bullet wounds. Tobias had mentioned fighting in the war, the first night he had come to her house. But he had never mentioned being wounded. She closed her eyes against the pain it gave her to think how much he must have suffered, and how little she truly knew about his past.

Her thoughts returned to the present with a rush when she realized she could feel his warm breath on her belly now. He lowered his head and kissed the skin above the line of her drawers at the same time his hands began to dance tantalizing patterns along the insides of her thighs.

She drew in a breath when his hands moved higher and touched her in that intimate place where he had touched her before. She moaned and clutched the quilt as a wondrous wave of pleasure shot through her. He stroked her again, and the pleasure intensified. As he continued to work his sensual magic, she felt a rush of warmth between her legs.

Just when she thought the intensity might overwhelm her, he shifted upward and settled himself between her thighs. He bent his head and began kissing her fiercely. His weight felt just right, although her body still ached for closer contact still. Tobias rocked against her, his breath coming in gasps. Instinctively, she arched her hips up against his, writhing and twisting, trying to ease the growing tension inside her.

Suddenly, he caught her head between his hands and lowered his forehead to hers. "Miranda," he said hoarsely, his breath warm on her face, "if we go any farther, I'm not going to be able to stop. I have to ask you now, are you sure this is what you want?"

She fought back the desire clouding her mind. A part of her was amazed at his self-control. She could only guess at what it had cost him to stop and ask her that question. A less honorable man would have taken what she was offering without a second thought. As she stared up at his familiar face gone taut with strain, she forced herself to consider what he had asked.

Was this truly what she wanted for herself? Her body longed to join with his, but her mind wasn't sure. In that cold moment while she hesitated, rational thought came flooding back to her, and with it all the reasons why she shouldn't make love with him. They had no future. As much as they cared for each other, they didn't truly love each other—and that would make the conjugal act between them the worst of sins. And finally, she couldn't face the risk of bringing a child into the world when she already had her hands full providing for Rory and Sean.

"I'm sorry," she said, her voice less than steady. "I had better go."

For a moment she thought he might try to dissuade her. All he would have had to do was touch her with his clever hands, or make her forget her conscience with one of his soul-drugging kisses. Instead, he closed his eyes, drew in a deep, shuddering breath and rolled away from her. Without his large body close to shelter and warm her, she became aware of how cold the cabin had grown.

Shivering and suddenly feeling terribly embarrassed, she reached for her chemise. She pulled it over her head and quickly retied her drawers. Without a word he brought her petticoats and dress. Greedily she gazed at him, storing up memories for the desolate time ahead without any hope of seeing him. He'd shrugged his shirt on, but he had yet to button it. Through the gap in the fabric she caught an enticing glimpse of a muscular chest and a pelt of brown hair which made her long to reach out and touch him once again.

When she realized she was staring, she ducked her head, and her hands grew clumsy with the ties to her petticoats.

"Let me," he said, and the gentleness in his voice almost proved to be her undoing. She stared down at her feet, hoping the tears in her eyes wouldn't spill over while he did up the ties and helped her with her dress hooks as well. When he had finished with her fastenings, he draped her jacket carefully about her shoulders.

It took him just a few moments to finish dressing himself. In the meanwhile, Miranda kept her back to him and made a show of warming her hands before the stove. Before they went out the door, he picked up the basket she had brought.

"No." She stopped him. "That's supper for you. It was meant to be a part of the apology I came to give you, although an apology seems so useless. I am terribly, terribly sorry to have jeopardized your teaching position."

"I made my own choices, sweet Miranda." He reached out and smoothed her cheek. For a moment, his gray eyes softened. "Thank you for the supper, and thank you for caring. It's been a long time since anyone has worried about me."

She wanted to ask him why that was. She wanted to ask him about the awful scars on his back from injuries that must have come far too close to killing him. But whatever she had with Tobias was ending, and it was for another woman to learn about the wounds in his soul and heal them if she could.

They didn't speak during the entire drive back to her house. Dusk was deepening into night, and the wind was rising by the time they reached her barnyard. She looked at Tobias and tried to form some jaunty phrase of thanks and farewell, but instead her treacherous eyes filled with tears once again. He must have seen the wetness in her eyes, despite the fading light, for he looked away from her and cleared his throat.

"I'm sorry," he said harshly. "I'm sorry about the whole bloody mess. You deserve better than me, Miranda Kilpatrick, and don't let the rest of them convince you otherwise."

"And you deserve to be happy," she told him in return. "I

know some day you will find the right woman who will give
you a world of love.''

She could tell from the bleakness in his eyes that he didn't
believe her.

He turned and rode off into the dark November night, leaving
her more alone than she had ever been before.

# Chapter Thirteen

It was the first Saturday in December. The peaks to the west wore a dazzling cape of white, and the brilliant sun shone off the packed snow on the road. Tobias sent Romeo along at a fast walk toward the Ladder M. Rob McGregor had invited him out for supper that night. He had begun spending more time at Rob's ranch since he had stopped seeing Miranda. For a man who used to be content wandering months at a time by himself, he was developing an odd need to be with people.

He'd spent a quiet Thanksgiving with Rob, his son Robby, his Mexican housekeeper and his ranch hands. Tobias had enjoyed himself thoroughly, much to his surprise. That Graciella sure could cook, but he didn't think her meals could touch Miranda's.

A few minutes later, he came to the turn off to Miranda's place. He found himself pulling Romeo to a halt. He had stopped following her home at night, and only once during the past three weeks had he given in to the temptation to ride out to her place and make sure she was safe and well. He had made certain no one saw him, and he hadn't stayed long. *This afternoon,* he promised himself, *you'll do the exact same thing again. You'll catch one glimpse to make sure she's fine, and then you'll be on your way.*

He missed Miranda. He missed her smile. He missed her lilting voice and the way she laughed. And he worried about her and the boys every day. He told himself that he had made the right choice, that he had to put himself and his new life ahead of her. Caring for Miranda had put him on a collision course with the kind of trouble he'd never wanted to face again. To help her, he was afraid he might end up becoming his old self again, a man who could take a life without flinching. But still he wondered how he could possibly live with himself if Slaughter hurt her and he hadn't done all he could to stop the man.

Tobias grimaced at the blue sky overhead. He'd managed to get his quiet, peaceful, lonely life back, all right. If he continued to mind his own business, he knew the school board would have no reason to fire him. *But the fact remains, old son, that you've been miserable as a lovesick skunk since that day Miranda came to see you, and so far you aren't getting any better.*

When he drew close to her place, he turned off the lane and took a game trail which led up to the top of the ridge above her home. He'd found a little glade up there where he could watch her house and barnyard and be certain no one below could see him.

He reined Romeo to a stop and dismounted. Smoke was coming out of the chimney of the house, and the barnyard was as neat as ever. There was no sign of the boys outside. He was just about to turn Romeo about when he saw Miranda step out the back door. He smiled wistfully. There was no mistaking the gleam of her red hair, even from this distance. She made her way straight to the barn, walking in a purposeful manner. The lady was obviously on her way someplace.

Sure enough, she emerged several minutes later leading the sorrel mare. She mounted the mare and rode toward the trail that led up to the old cabin full of mine equipment. Perhaps she was following his advice and trying to find some clue that might help her figure out if her uncle's mine existed, and where it might be located. After Miranda's mare disappeared into the trees five hundred feet below him, Tobias pushed his hat back on his head and tried to make up his mind.

It would be easier, and wiser, if they didn't speak to each other again, particularly in such a private place. *You probably couldn't keep your hands off her for more than a minute without ornery old Lucas around to play chaperone.* At the same time, he wanted to make certain she reached the cabin all right. Making up his mind, he remounted Romeo. He'd stay back in the trees and watch for her to reach the cabin. Then he'd head out for the Ladder M.

He guided Romeo down the ridge and found a thick stand of spruce not far from the old cabin. He left Romeo tied there and moved to a large deadfall on the south side of the cabin. He hunkered down behind that deadfall and watched Miranda ride up.

A wave of longing so intense that it was painful swept through him at the sight of her familiar features. She'd caught her hair back in a long, fat braid which hung down over her right shoulder. Her braid made her look young and innocent and very pretty. Another pang went through him when he realized she appeared thinner than the last time he had seen her. As she tied the sorrel's reins to a small pine, her expression was sad and pensive. He wondered if she'd had more problems with Slaughter at the saloon. She went straight inside the cabin and left the door open behind her.

*Go on and leave her be, you damn fool,* he told himself. *You'll have to light a shuck as it is to reach McGregor's place by dark.* But he stayed right where he was, crouching in the snow while his toes started to turn to ice. Enduring the cold was worth it, just to catch one more good look at her. He waited ten minutes for Miranda to come out again, but she must have been searching the cabin thoroughly.

He was just about to stand up again and slip away when two riders appeared out of the trees, coming up the trail Miranda had just taken. His heart missed a beat. He recognized Slaughter's battered black hat and the big buckskin he always rode. The other rider was probably that young kid Tyrel Reynolds, the one who fancied himself a gunhand. Tobias could see the gleam of ivory from the handles on his tied-down six-shooters.

He swore under his breath. The cabin didn't have a back door. There was no way he could reach Miranda and warn her in time without the two men seeing him.

As he studied Slaughter's harsh features, he found himself almost regretting the pledge he had made never to carry a gun again. Somehow he had to find a way to stop two armed men, and he had to find it fast. If the outlaw wanted information that could lead him to gold, he wouldn't hesitate to hurt Miranda. Remembering the light in Slaughter's eye when he had looked at Miranda that day in the alley, Tobias knew the outlaw would rape her first and ask his questions after.

Tobias clenched his fists, feeling a familiar rage rise inside him, along with a desperate fear that he wouldn't be able to save her. He looked around him, searching for something he could use as a weapon. Leaning up against the side of the cabin was an old ax handle. It wasn't much, but it was better than going after the two men empty-handed.

Both men dismounted. Slaughter gestured for Reynolds to stay outside.

At least that evened the odds a little. He had a ghost of a chance if he could take them on one at a time. Tobias eased back into the trees. When the cabin was between him and Reynolds, he dashed out of the aspens and grabbed the ax handle. Moving as soundlessly as he could, he ran back into the trees and worked his way around to the front of the cabin.

He heard a muffled shriek and a crash as something fell inside. He redoubled his pace, leaping over fallen logs and dodging through the aspens, trying to avoid stepping on dry branches which would crack and give away his presence. It was hard not to imagine what was happening to Miranda. It took all his self-control not to rush straight to the door of the cabin and tear Slaughter apart for laying a hand on her. First he had to deal with Reynolds.

Right now the young gunfighter was staring at the door of the cabin, obviously trying to see what was going on inside. The first thing a gunfighter learned, Tobias thought with grim satisfaction as he slipped out of the trees, was to always watch one's back. Reynolds was still new enough to his chosen occupation that he hadn't learned that lesson yet.

At the last moment, Reynolds must have heard or sensed something behind him. He twisted about, clawing for the guns at his hips, but it was too late. Tobias sent the ax handle swinging through the air. It connected with the side of Reynolds's head with a sickening thud. The young gunfighter dropped like a stone. Tobias glanced down at him, mildly relieved to see he was still breathing.

He stared at Reynolds's pistols. It was tempting to lean over and pick one up. But if he had the gun in his hand, he knew with a sick feeling in his belly that he'd use it, and everything he had tried to become in the last seven years would vanish the moment he put a bullet into Slaughter. Not that the man didn't deserve killing. He just didn't want to be the one who did it.

Tobias picked up both of Reynolds's pistols and hid them out of sight behind a spruce. He was almost sure there was another way he could still take Slaughter. For Miranda's sake, as well as his own, he hoped the gamble he was about to make was going to pay off.

"Slaughter," he bellowed, "come on out here. You and me have some unfinished business to settle."

"What the hell—who's out there?" Slaughter appeared in the doorway a moment later, hauling a struggling Miranda along with him. He held a pistol in his hand, and he pointed it straight at Tobias. "You're that damn fool schoolmaster we whupped in town," he snarled, recognition dawning in his one good eye. "You must really be carrying a torch for Red here. Where's Reynolds?"

"He's taking a little siesta. This is between the two of us." Tobias fought the burst of fury he felt when he saw the red mark on Miranda's face where Slaughter had obviously struck her. The neck of her dress was torn, and her hair was falling down about her shoulders. She had stopped struggling, and her blue eyes were wide with shock. He had to drink in deep breaths to keep from launching himself right at Slaughter. If he got himself killed, he wouldn't be of any use to Miranda.

"Hell, I don't know if I should shoot you or him for being just plain stupid," Slaughter said, staring down at Reynolds with disgust.

"I'm unarmed." Tobias held his arms out slowly. "Where's the sport in shooting an unarmed man when you could whip me first? It took you and three of your men to lick me last time. I don't think you can take me by yourself."

"Is that so? It might be sportin' at that." Slaughter squinted at him while he considered the idea. "I always hated schoolmasters. I done fixed the one where I grew up. I beat him to a pulp with his own paddle and shot him in the gut afterward. I'll do the same for you," he finished with a mirthless smile. "And while you're dying, you can think about the fine time I'm having riding your pretty little whore."

"You can always try to beat me, but I don't believe you're man enough to do it on your own."

Slaughter let loose with a particularly vicious obscenity. "You just wait while I take care of Red here. She might try to put a bullet into my back while I'm tearing down your meathouse."

Slaughter disappeared inside the cabin, dragging Miranda with him. He reappeared moments later, a length of old rope in his hands. Tobias bit his lip when Slaughter roughly tied Miranda's wrists together. He dragged her over to a big pine and forced her to stand against it, then used a final loop of the rope to tie her to the tree. He squeezed her breast roughly and pressed a hard kiss on her lips.

"Don't you worry none, Red. This won't take me long, and then we can get back to having a good time just the two of us."

Once again Tobias had to still the urge to run straight at Slaughter. The outlaw had holstered his pistol, but he was too quick with a gun to risk rushing him. Before today was over, the man was going to pay. Tobias quickly removed his jacket, vest, and glasses. He studied Slaughter, hoping to find some weakness he could exploit. The outlaw was a big bear of a man, going to fat at his belly, but still immensely strong. Unlike many who lived by the gun, Slaughter had a reputation for liking to fight with his fists. Rumor had it he'd killed three men in bare-knuckle brawls. Tobias was about to do his damndest to make sure he wasn't the fourth.

"You know, schoolmaster, you remind me of someone. I just can't quite recollect who," Slaughter said as he undid his gun belt and hooked it over his saddle.

"I'm sure we've never met," Tobias said shortly. Slaughter's stomach definitely looked soft. He'd try to concentrate his punches there. Although he probably was in better shape than the outlaw, he had his work cut out for him. And he couldn't take his time about it, for he wasn't sure when Reynolds might start to stir.

Tobias looked over to make certain the young gunfighter still lay where he left him. He glanced up from Reynolds just in time to see Slaughter running toward him, holding the butt of his Winchester high like a club.

"I never said nothing about fightin' fair," Slaughter announced with a grin.

Tobias thought longingly of the ax handle, now lying beyond his reach by the cabin, and then Slaughter was on him. He ducked under the first sweep Slaughter made with the rifle and buried his fist in the outlaw's gut. The big man just grunted, spun about, and drove the rifle butt into Tobias's kidney. Tobias stumbled to his knees as the red-hot pain burned through him.

Slaughter would be coming again. He twisted about and managed to raise his forearm just in time to deflect some of the power behind the next blow. His forearm went numb, but the rifle butt still connected with the side of his skull with enough force to make him see stars. The ground came rushing up, and a black wave threatened to engulf him. Tobias stubbornly clung to consciousness and rolled away from Slaughter.

When Tobias fetched up on his back, he opened his eyes to see the outlaw smirking down at him.

"Shit, can't you do any better than this, schoolmaster? Guess I'm just going to have to shoot you and put you out of your misery." Slaughter started to raise the rifle to his shoulder. Tobias threw himself against the outlaw's legs. The rifle went off. Tobias felt the wind from the bullet as it whipped past his ear, and the report almost deafened him. He knocked Slaughter off his feet and kicked the rifle out of his reach.

They rolled across the ground, hitting, gouging and kicking each other. Tobias had fear and anger on his side, but he was hampered by the fact he didn't want to kill Slaughter unless he absolutely had to. The outlaw, however, wasn't restrained by any such considerations.

At one point they broke apart and lurched to their feet. They stood there slugging it out, pounding each other mercilessly. Slaughter split Tobias's lip. Tobias managed to land a blow that broke Slaughter's nose. They had just stumbled back from each other to catch their breath in the thin mountain air when Slaughter's one good eye widened.

"Christ, I do know you. You're Jonah. Son of a bitch. You were too damn clean for me to recognize you before. They said some punk had killed you up Montana way. Son of a bitch."

Tobias took advantage of Slaughter's shock to wind up with a punch with all his weight behind it. He landed a right uppercut on Slaughter's jaw with such force the outlaw's eye rolled up in his head and he pitched backward onto the ground. Tobias fell on the stunned man and hit him again and again, making him pay for daring to hurt Miranda, and trying to obliterate the name Slaughter had called him. Through the red haze clouding his senses, he gradually became aware that Miranda was crying and calling out his name.

"No, Tobias, no. For the love of God, you're going to kill him."

He drew in a shuddering breath and pushed himself away from Slaughter's still form. He rose to his feet and stood there swaying and gasping for air. Some deep-seated instinct made him think to check Reynolds, who was still out cold. He stumbled to the tree where Miranda was tied.

His eyes fastened on her pale face. Her cheeks were still wet with her tears. He wanted to tell her how sorry he was. He knew the violent fight she had just seen must have been terrible to witness. But his mouth was too dry and his tongue too thick. He reached out to stroke her face. His heart lurched when she flinched away from his hand. He lowered his arm and turned away to hide his own hurt and went to find a knife to cut her loose. His hands were so stiff from the fight, he knew he wouldn't be able to undo the knots Slaughter had tied.

He took a swallow of water from Slaughter's canteen and found a knife in his saddlebags. When he returned to the pine, Miranda was watching him warily.

"Tobias, who is Jonah?" she asked in a low voice.

"Jonah is a man who died seven years ago," he said so roughly she shrank back against the tree. When he finished cutting Miranda loose, she sank down on her knees and covered her face with her hands. He wanted to take her into his arms to comfort her, but he was afraid she'd turn away from him again. Walking like a stiff old man, he took the rope over to Reynolds and began to truss up the young gunfighter as best he could. He had just started on Slaughter when a familiar voice rang out across the little clearing.

"Sweet Jesus." Lucas sat on his horse, surveying the scene with some amazement. "I heard the rifle shot and decided I'd best get the hell up here. Son, it looks like you tangled with a grizzly and came out on the losing end."

"Believe it or not, he looks worse," Tobias said with some satisfaction as he gestured to Slaughter. He finished with the last of the knots and stood up wearily.

"I'm going to haul these two off to the jail in town," he told Lucas. "They're wanted in this state and Wyoming and Lord knows where else."

"You mean they're both still alive? I thought you must have killed one for sure." Lucas dismounted and came over to peer at the two outlaws.

"Hell, no, I didn't kill them. I wouldn't look like this if I'd taken the easy way and just shot them," Tobias said irritably.

"Well, I'll be goddamned."

Tobias ignored the old man and glanced over at Miranda worriedly. She still hadn't moved. "Will you look after her? Slaughter was alone with her inside that cabin for a good five minutes. He hit her and handled her pretty rough, and she's still shook up."

Lucas looked from him to Miranda and back again, his gaze troubled. "Of course I will. You sure you can make the ride into town?"

"I'm sure," Tobias replied. With Lucas's help, he soon had both unconscious outlaws tied to the backs of their horses. By the time Tobias swung into his own saddle, Lucas was kneeling beside Miranda, and she had yet to raise her face from her hands.

Tobias swallowed hard and kicked Romeo into a jog. Even though he managed to keep from killing Slaughter today, the violence inside him had just destroyed whatever regard Miranda might have had for him. It didn't really matter that she knew the truth about his nature now. When Miranda found out who Jonah had been, she would never want to see him again. His heart heavy as a boulder, Tobias rode from the clearing and didn't look back.

Miranda lay in bed and picked at her supper tray. Bed was where Lucas and Christina had insisted she go immediately after she returned home. She had wanted to stay in the kitchen and help Christina make supper. She would have preferred to remain busy, rather than have time in her room to think about this afternoon. Her little family seemed more upset than she was, though, about what had happened, and so she put on her nightgown and let them fuss over her.

They all had been wonderful. Christina had insisted on fixing chicken and dumplings, one of her favorite meals. Sean and Rory had been quiet as church mice all afternoon, an amazing feat for either boy. Sean had read a whole chapter in *Lorna Doone* to her, and Rory had brought in his collection of pressed flowers and plants for her to look at. This evidence of how much her rough-and-tumble boys cared warmed Miranda's heart.

Her family was downstairs now, eating supper. She tried to make inroads on her own meal; but the food tasted like sawdust in her mouth, and her stomach roiled with every swallow. She sighed and pushed her supper tray away. She knew she should feel grateful to Tobias. Without his timely aid, Slaughter would have raped her. He probably would have killed her as well when he found out she knew nothing about the gold mine he seemed convinced Uncle Shamus had found.

But instead of feeling grateful, she was furious. The certainty was growing in her that Tobias Johnston wasn't the man she thought she knew at all. The notion he might have been lying to her all along made her stomach clench even tighter.

Lucas knocked quietly on the door. He stepped inside when she called to him.

"I've come to fetch your supper tray." He frowned when he saw how little she had actually managed to eat.

"Lucas, who is Jonah?"

Lucas swore aloud, something he rarely did in her presence. "Where did you hear that name?" he asked, obviously stalling for time.

"Before they started fighting, Slaughter said something about Tobias looking familiar to him," she replied, watching Lucas carefully all the while. "Then, right in the midst of it, Slaughter got this stunned look on his face and called Tobias Jonah. Then Tobias hit him so hard he knocked Slaughter off his feet. When I asked him about Jonah, Tobias would only say that Jonah was a man who died seven years ago."

Lucas sighed and rubbed his chin. "I don't suppose you're going to let this go, so I'm going to tell you what I know, and then you best talk about the rest with Johnston yourself." Lucas wandered over to her window. He looked out into the dark winter night, his face expressionless as he spoke.

"Jonah was a gunfighter. He was one of the fastest gun hands folks had ever seen, and he was hell on wheels during a fight. He tamed a couple of real tough mining towns and fought for a few big cattle outfits. If he'd kept on the way he was going, he would have become as famous as Clay Allison or Wyatt Earp. But Jonah just dropped out of sight seven or eight years ago, and no one knew what had become of him." Lucas swung away from the window and stuck his hands in his back pockets.

"You aren't telling me everything you know about Jonah," Miranda accused him, for Lucas still wasn't meeting her eyes.

"All right, then," he said grimly, "here's all of it. Supposedly Jonah was a big man, and he hailed from Kansas. He was also partial to reading. I knew a man once that rode for the same brand Jonah did, and he swore Jonah always kept a book or two in his saddlebags."

"Do you think Tobias is Jonah?"

"I think it's possible, 'specially if Slaughter recognized him. Slaughter and several of his boys are from Kansas, too, and it stands to reason Jonah and Slaughter crossed paths there years ago. From the start, somethin' about your schoolmaster just didn't add up. There's a kind of wariness in men who've lived that sort of life, and Johnston has it in spades. Then there's the way he handled himself that night Slaughter's boys tried to burn down the Shamrock. Lots of men get flustered when the lead starts flying, but he didn't turn a hair.

"I got to say this for him," Lucas said firmly. "I respect Johnston, or Jonah, or whatever his real name is. It would have been a hell of a lot easier for him to shoot both them owlhoots today once he got a pistol away from Reynolds. Instead, he took a big risk with his own life and took Slaughter alive."

"You respect him when he's lied to all of us?" She couldn't keep the bitterness out of her voice.

"It takes guts for a man to change himself. If Johnston really is Jonah, he's done a remarkable thing, gettin' an education and trying to start a new life for himself. I don't know if he's got a snowball's chance in hell of succeeding, but I admire him for trying. You might think on that before you chew his ear off the next time you see him."

With that, Lucas slipped out the door and left Miranda alone with the bitter confusion of her thoughts.

# Chapter Fourteen

Miranda heard the loud clatter of boots on the stairs and looked up from the clean sheets she was putting on Rory's bed. No matter how often she asked the boys not to run inside the house, they still charged up and down the steps like a herd of wild buffalo. Moments later, Sean appeared in the doorway, breathing hard from racing to find her.

"Aunt Miranda, Mr. Johnston just rode up. He's out in the barnyard right now talking with Lucas."

The excitement in his eyes made Miranda grit her teeth. She was afraid that Sean's case of hero worship had grown worse than Rory's. If Tobias Johnston did prove to be the notorious gunfighter Jonah, he was the last man in the world she wanted her nephews to idolize.

"Thank you, Sean. I'd like you two boys to stay in this room with the door shut while I talk with him. Please fetch Rory and bring him back up here."

Sean must have sensed some of the distress she was feeling, for the protest he was about to make died on his lips. He turned about and went clattering back down the stairs. "Come on, Rory," she heard him corralling his reluctant brother.

When both boys were settled in their room, she closed their door firmly behind her. She went downstairs and stood before the front window, trying to compose herself. Somehow she had known he would come to see her today.

She watched Tobias's familiar, long-legged stride as he walked up to her front door. His walk might be familiar, but she was afraid the man himself was a complete stranger to her now. She'd never thought she'd known him well, but she had believed along with everyone else in Pine Creek that he was an erudite and peaceful man, dedicated to his teaching. She knew from firsthand experience that he was a man capable of great kindness and caring. Now she had to wonder if he was a man capable of great violence as well.

She told herself it didn't really matter who or what Tobias Johnston was, since he never could be a part of her life. And yet when she walked to the front door to answer his knock, her stomach was churning and her mouth was dry.

When she opened the door, he had already taken his hat off. She bit back a gasp when she saw his mouth. His lip was split and puffed out to almost twice its normal size. The right side of his face was bruised as well. He should have looked grotesque, but somehow he just looked rough and dangerous.

Dangerous. Now there was a word she had never associated with Tobias Johnston until yesterday, she thought painfully. He'd taken some care with his appearance. His beautiful hair was clean and neatly combed, his schoolmaster suit carefully brushed, his white shirt as immaculate as ever. But he didn't look like a schoolmaster to her anymore, and that fact made her heart ache.

She was so busy studying him that she was slow to realize he was staring at her cheek. He reached up to touch the swollen place where Slaughter had hit her; but then he seemed to remember himself, and he dropped his hand to his side.

"I'm sorry I couldn't stop him before he hurt you," he said quietly.

"You kept him from doing a great deal worse, and I'm grateful," she said. "Would you like to come in?"

"I wanted to say a few things to you, and then I'll be on my way."

"All right." She led him inside. She sat down on the settee in the parlor, but he remained standing, his hat clenched in his hands.

"You asked me yesterday who Jonah was, and last night I decided I owed you the truth," he began with no preamble.

She closed her eyes. After a sleepless night of railing at him in her mind for hiding the truth from her, now she suddenly didn't want to hear it.

"Slaughter had good reason to think he recognized me," Tobias said, his face set in somber lines. "I once was the gunfighter people called Jonah."

Miranda felt bile rise in her throat. So it was true. This gentle, scholarly man wasn't gentle or scholarly at all. He was a killer, a footloose gunslinger just like Jake Broden, who had broken Mary's heart. Miserably Miranda wished the earth would open up and swallow her. Of all the sins he might have been able to forgive, his was the one she couldn't face. She could not, she would not, let a gunfighter break her own heart.

Drearily, she realized he deserved for her to hear him out, after all he'd done for her. Making a supreme effort, she tried to concentrate on his words.

"I told you that my father was a preacher in Kansas," he was saying, "and a fervent abolitionist. That was all true. My mother also believed in the cause. They traveled throughout Kansas holding revival meetings and speaking out against slavery. They became quite well known, which cost them in the end."

He paused for a moment, and when he spoke again his voice was as harsh as she had ever heard it.

"One night pro-slavery guerrillas raided our farm. They cursed my father and called him a slave lover. While my mother, my sister and I watched, they hanged him from a rafter in our barn. They shot me in the head when I fought to keep them from raping my mother and my sister. When I came to in our barnyard hours later, everyone was dead. Our house had been burned to the ground."

Miranda stilled an urge to reach out and touch him. From his remote, forbidding expression, somehow she sensed he didn't want her comfort right now. Yet the fury and the bitterness in his quiet words made shivers trace down her spine.

"I decided then that God must have let me live for a purpose. The raiders had been careless. They let us see their faces, for they hadn't meant to let any of us survive that night. I knew what they looked like, and for the next ten years, before the war and during it, I hunted each of them down and killed them all."

He looked past her then, as if he were staring at the life he had once led. "By the time I was done, I had earned myself quite a reputation with a gun. I was twenty-five, and all I knew how to do was shoot and fight. I drifted west and found work as a sheriff in a couple of rough mining towns and fought in some range wars for various cattle outfits. To honor my father's memory, I always tried to fight for men with law on their side, but as the years went on, the lines between good and bad seemed to blur. As my reputation grew, there was always another young punk eager to challenge me to a gunfight.

"One day in Abilene I was forced to kill a boy who couldn't have been more than seventeen. I'll never forget the stunned look in his eyes when he lay dying in the dirt where my bullet had put him. I still see his face in my dreams. He had freckles, for God's sake."

Tobias paused for a moment and closed his eyes. "He was so young he couldn't even grow a proper mustache. He died crying for his mother."

He opened his eyes again and seemed to collect himself. "After that, I tried to change my name and bury myself in small settlements on the far edges of the frontier, but my reputation always seemed to catch up with me.

"Seven years ago, a young punk named Arizona Jack found me in Montana. I wouldn't face him in a gunfight, so he waited in ambush and shot me twice in the back. I played possum and killed the boy when he came to gloat over me. I rode out into the sagebrush, figuring the two bullets he'd put into my chest would certainly kill me. While I was lying on the ground waiting to die, I told myself if I had a second chance, I'd surely make different choices with my life."

Tobias paused, shifted his weight, and looked at Miranda once more, his gray eyes begging for her understanding. "As fate would have it, those bullets didn't kill me. An old Mexican sheepherder found me, and he nursed me back to health.

"Jose Ramirez was a remarkable man. He was seventy years old, and he had survived the Mexican war, countless Indian attacks, and outlived three wives and several of his children. None of the hardship or tragedies in his life could diminish the joy he took in living every day.

"At first I was bitter and angry that he hadn't let me die. What was the point of living when some young punk might come along any day and plug me again when I wasn't looking?

"Jose helped me see I could live any sort of life I chose. I decided the only way to escape my reputation as Jonah was to go east and start over. I'd always loved books, and I decided to attend university.

"Eventually the big cities and the press of all those people wore on me. I'd always loved the wildness of the West, and a part of me felt dead the whole time I lived away from it. Once I finished with my studies, I decided to come back out here. I had hoped in seven years people might have forgotten about Jonah. I had hoped in seven years I had changed. To make certain no one I knew from the old days recognized me, I started wearing these glasses and had my hair cropped short. And then I took the teaching job here in Pine Creek, as small and quiet a town as I could find, and you know the rest.''

When he fell silent, he bowed his head as if waiting for her to deliver judgment. Her mind whirling from his account, Miranda could only think of one question to ask him. ''Is Tobias Johnston your real name?''

He looked at her again and his lips curled in a smile with little humor in it. ''Tobias Elijah Johnston is my legal name. Men started calling me Jonah after I went on a particularly ill-fated cattle drive. After we lost half the herd to rustlers and half the trail crew to Indian attacks, the remaining hands decided I must be the source of all their bad luck, and they first gave me the name. It seemed to fit me better than the name my parents had used to christen me, and so I kept it.''

He lay his hat on the oval table beside the settee and began to pace back and forth.

''Last night I did some hard thinking. I couldn't figure out why I kept coming back to you, even though I knew it would be better for both of us if I stayed away. I knew I'd have the school board down on me and I'd have to tangle with Slaughter sooner or later if I became involved in your life. But I went right ahead and barged in anyway. In the middle of the night I realized why my heart made me do the exact opposite of what my head was telling me. Somehow you had come to mean more to me than my teaching and the new life I was trying to build for myself. Somehow I had come to love you, when I thought I was incapable of loving anyone again.''

He halted his pacing to look at her, and the stark longing in his eyes made her throat go tight. ''Miranda Kilpatrick, you're everything I've ever wanted in a woman. You're loving and sweet and giving, and you're brave as any person I've ever known. I'd say to hell with them all, and come courtin' you proper, if you thought you might be able to care for me some day. I know a gunfighter walked out on your sister, and you blame him for her death. I know what I told you about myself today most likely will kill any chance we might have had, but I have to hear it straight from you.

"Could you . . . ?" He paused for a moment while he straightened his shoulders and watched her face searchingly. "Do you think you could ever love a man like me?"

Miranda looked away from him and stared down at her lap, humbled and panicked by the risk he had taken. Instinctively she understood that it was the hardest thing this guarded man could do—sharing his past and his feelings with her. As much as she felt for him, she knew what her answer had to be.

"No," she said gently and met his gaze again. "I'm quite sure I could never learn to love you. I'll always be grateful for what you did for me. I'll always be grateful for the kindness you showed me from the first day we met in town. But I never planned to marry at all. My parents' marriage was full of frustration and disappointment. My sister's marriage cost both her happiness and her life. It's my duty to provide a good, safe home for Rory and Sean. I have too many people depending on me to take the risk of loving the wrong person. I'm sorry."

"I figured that's what you'd say, and I can't blame you." He turned about and picked up his hat. He stared at it for a moment as if he couldn't remember what to do with it.

"I can let myself out," he declared gruffly and strode from the room.

Miranda stood up and hurried after him. She watched with growing consternation as he walked right out the front door. She couldn't let him leave like this.

"Tobias," she said suddenly. He looked back at her over his shoulder, that expressionless mask she hated firmly back in place. Now, at least, she knew how and why he had learned to wear that mask.

She wanted to tell him to take care of himself. She wanted to say she admired him for trying to become something better. She wanted to tell him someday a wonderful woman would fall in love with him and give him all the joy and tenderness he deserved. But her throat grew too thick for her to speak, so instead she darted forward, raised herself up on her tiptoes, and kissed him on the cheek.

He raised his fingers and touched the place she had kissed. "Sweet Miranda," he said with a crooked smile. Her eyes flooded with tears. He leaned over and pressed a gentle kiss on her lips with the battered mouth he'd earned protecting her, and then he turned and walked down the porch steps. As he mounted Romeo and rode away, he never once looked back at her.

As she listened to the sound of his horse's hoofbeats fading into the distance, Miranda had to face the bitter truth. She had just lied to Tobias. He had been courageous enough to bare his soul to her, and she had taken the coward's path and used her skill as an actress to disguise her true feelings. She already did care for Tobias, so much she felt as if her heart was shattering into a hundred pieces. But she was too frightened of love to take the risk of telling him how she felt.

Now she was left to wonder if she would ever know peace or happiness again.

Monday morning, Tobias's students were more quiet than usual. It wasn't every day they learned that their teacher had apprehended a notorious outlaw. The children watched him out of big, wondering eyes as he taught them their lessons for the day, and some of the littlest girls would hardly speak to him at all.

Rory and Sean were quiet along with the rest, but during the noonday break, Sean marched up to Tobias with Rory in tow. "We just wanted to thank you for saving Aunt Miranda," Sean declared. "That's three times now you've helped her." The older boy drew in a deep breath and squared his shoulders.

"I thought you were a coward," he forged stubbornly on,

"and a sissy ever since that day you wouldn't fight Red and Randy to get your hat back. I guess I was wrong about you. I'm sorry for all the times I was so rude, and I promise I'm going to work ten times harder in school from now on."

"That's all right, Sean." Tobias managed to keep from smiling. "And I'm very glad to hear you are going to study harder. You've got a good mind. You could be anything you want when you grow up."

"I already know what I want to be. I'm going to be a sheriff. Then I could keep good people like Aunt Miranda safe."

Tobias looked into Sean's earnest brown eyes and felt his heart twist. "That's a worthwhile goal, son, but to be a lawman in these parts, you have to be handy with a gun. You might even have to kill someone someday, and that's a hard thing for any man to have on his conscience." He could tell Sean wanted to argue with him, but Rory broke in before Sean could say another word.

"Is it really true you caught Slaughter and Reynolds without using a gun?" Rory's freckled face was ablaze with curiosity.

Tobias sighed. "It's really true I got danged lucky on Saturday. I could have gotten myself shot full of holes, and then your aunt would have really been in a fix. Now, you boys go eat, and I'll see you in an hour."

Tobias half expected a visit from the school board that afternoon, but no one came to give him a lecture on his latest escapade. He wasn't sure what Mrs. Josiah Smith and the rest would say about his actions on Saturday, and he didn't really care. He rode home after school and put in another hour of work on the shed for Romeo. He was just sitting down to supper at his own table when a knock came at his door.

He opened it to find Rob McGregor standing on his doorstep. Surprised but pleased, Tobias invited him in for a cup of coffee.

After he went over to the stove to pour the rancher a cup, he looked up and caught McGregor watching him. "What are you looking at?" he asked him irritably.

Rob grinned. "I'm looking at the man who brought in Ben Slaughter and Tyrel Reynolds all on his lonesome. Rumor has it that you tamed them both with your bare hands."

"Rumors have a funny way of being wrong most the time."

"I'm almost inclined to believe this one. You sure have a way of staying in the limelight for such a quiet gent," Rob McGregor said quizzically.

"Is there any particular point to this visit, or are you just enjoying flapping your jaw on general principles?" Tobias asked as he sat down at the table opposite Rob.

"Besides enjoying twisting your tail a bit, I do have a real serious reason for coming by." Rob's smile faded. "I thought you'd better know the news right away. Slaughter broke himself out of jail this afternoon."

Tobias shot to his feet, anger and fear for Miranda rushing through his veins. "How the hell did Carson let that happen?"

"He was fool enough to let Slaughter get ahold of his pistol when they went out to the privy. He shot up Carson pretty bad, and then he and Reynolds stole two horses and lit a shuck. The town's in an uproar over it. Mayor Wright has already wired Denver asking for a U. S. marshal to chase down Slaughter."

"It's about time someone got serious about taking him in."

"The question is, will he have time to settle up some scores before they chase him out of Pine County?" Rob's brown eyes were worried. Tobias sat down at the table again. He was still furious, but a part of him was also startled and warmed by the rancher's obvious concern. It had been a long time since he'd had a friend who cared about what happened to him.

"There's one more thing you should know," Rob said slowly. "Did you stop by the jail today?"

"Couldn't see much point in it. There's nothing I wanted to say to Slaughter."

"Well, talk has it he had plenty to say about you before he escaped."

Tobias closed his eyes. He had been afraid of this, but short of killing Slaughter, he didn't know how to stop it.

"That owlhoot's been telling anyone who'd listen," Rob continued on evenly, "that the schoolmaster who brought him in isn't a schoolmaster at all. He claims you're actually that gunslinger Jonah who made such a name for himself a few years back. Now, I think it riled Slaughter plenty gettin' caught after dodging the law for so long, and it sticks in his craw that a schoolmaster was the one to fetch him. That's why he made up such a whopper about you being Jonah. That's the story I've been telling folks, but I'm not sure many are listening. Some fools rather fancy the notion they have a famous gun-fighter living in their town."

Tobias rubbed his face with his hands. "I doubt many parents would want that man teaching their children."

"I guess it depends on how good a teacher he was," Rob countered. "So far as I can tell, you're the best damn schoolmaster we've ever had."

"I doubt our school board is going to see it the same way."

"They may be fine, upstanding citizens, but I'm not sure they know a good teacher from a hole in a wall," Rob admitted. "Well, I best be getting on home." He stood up and drained his cup. "You know, you'd be welcome to come stay at the ranch for a few days, just until we know Slaughter's caught or on his way to Mexico. My cowboys are a pretty salty bunch when it comes to a fight."

Tobias stood up and forced a smile. "That's a mighty kind offer, especially considering what a good cook Graciella is, but I think I'll stay put." The last thing he wanted to do was bring shooting trouble down on Rob and his son.

"Somehow I thought that's what you'd say." Rob shook his head. "I stopped by Miss Kilpatrick's place before I came here and gave her the same news and the same invite. You might be interested to know she turned me down, too."

"That woman is too stubborn and independent for her own damn good," Tobias growled.

"The way I see it, you two stubborn fools were made for each other," Rob said with a hint of a smile, and with that he headed out the door. Tobias followed him and watched Rob mount up. Before he rode off, the rancher said simply, "You watch yourself. If you need help, you know where you can find me."

Sobered by the news Rob had brought, Tobias went inside. He finished eating and cleaned up his supper quickly. When he was done, he gathered his bedding and headed out to the shed he'd built for Romeo. Until Slaughter was caught and accounted for, he wasn't going to take any chances. The first place Slaughter would come looking with his boys would be the cabin. Out here, Romeo would give plenty of warning if he smelled horses coming.

Cursing the cold, Tobias built a bed for himself in the hay. He planned to get a few hours sleep and then ride into town and make sure Miranda made it home from the Shamrock safely. Rob was right to think Slaughter might want to settle some scores, and in his twisted mind, the outlaw probably blamed Miranda for the fact he'd been beaten within an inch of his life and hauled off to jail to boot. And there was still this blasted business of the mine he thought he had a claim to.

Tobias stared at the stars through the open door of the shed and tried not to think about Miranda, but it was no use. Quiet times like these she haunted his thoughts.

He still felt hurt and angry that she'd rejected his suit so quickly. The least the woman could have done was take some time to think about it. But he knew he was being petty. If he was a woman with two boys to raise and support, he supposed he wouldn't have anything to do with an ex-gunfighter either.

How he wished, though, that she could have given him a different answer. His mind was filled with her these days. A loving woman with hair the color of cedar and a smile full of joy had stolen her way inside his heart. He never had felt this way about anyone, and he wasn't sure how he was supposed to make himself stop.

He was still wide awake pondering that question when it came time for him to ride into town and see Miranda home.

Tuesday morning, Miranda frowned at the ledger in her hand as she checked inventory in the saloon storeroom. The Shamrock was closed, and she was trying to decide if she needed to send to Denver soon for more whiskey. Business had been booming ever since she'd started having problems with Slaughter. Last night the Shamrock had been packed once again. Men from miles around Pine Creek had come into town to talk about Slaughter and Reynold's escape from jail.

Wearily, Miranda put down her ledger on a whisky barrel and rubbed her forehead. It was hard to concentrate when she was constantly listening for footsteps or the sound of someone breaking down a door. Lucas was by the bar, keeping a sharp eye out for trouble. He was always with her now, the shotgun never far from his grasp.

Although he didn't say so, she knew Lucas was worried. Tobias must be worried, too. Last night after she and Lucas had finished closing up the Shamrock, Tobias had appeared out of the shadows. He hardly said a word; but she knew he had come to make certain she made it home safely, and she was glad for his presence. Nothing untoward had happened during the ride home, but the wary way the men had kept watching the trees on either side of the road had made the hair on the back of her neck prickle.

Slaughter had always frightened her, but after the beating Tobias had given him, she guessed he would be particularly vengeful now. And she still hadn't been able to find any information on her uncle's mine to placate him. The search Slaughter had interrupted inside her uncle's old cabin had been frustratingly unsuccessful.

Maybe she should pack up her entire household and go to Denver for a week or two. It irked her to run away from trouble like a scared rabbit. More seriously, it would hurt her finances to shut down the Shamrock for any length of time. *But what if Lucas or Tobias is hurt because of you? You won't be able to live with yourself if harm comes to either of them. Tobias came far too close to getting killed on Saturday saving you from Ben Slaughter.*

She decided to give more thought to leaving Pine Creek until Slaughter was apprehended and brought to justice. She could always go in person to place her liquor order with her suppliers in Denver, and take the boys, Lucas, and Christina with her.

Wondering if Otis could possibly run the saloon while she was gone, she went back to working on her inventory. Five minutes later Sean appeared in the doorway to the storeroom. His cheeks were flushed, and he was struggling to catch his breath.

"You and Lucas gotta come quick," he managed to say between pants. "That fellow Reynolds is back in town. He came to the schoolhouse, and he's trying to challenge Mr. Johnston to a gunfight."

# Chapter Fifteen

Miranda picked up her skirts and ran for the front door, Sean and Rory one step behind her. She stopped just long enough to catch up her jacket before she darted outside. As quickly as she moved, Lucas was ahead of her. When she reached the boardwalk in front of the Shamrock, she could see Lucas running up the street, his shotgun slung under his arm.

She fought down a sob of panic. Surely Tyrel Reynolds wouldn't shoot down an unarmed man. He'd be wanted for murder then.

She tried not to think of the story Tobias had told her, of the young punk who had shot him in the back just to gain the fame of being the man who killed Jonah. And what if Reynolds gave Tobias a gun? Or what if Tobias had started to carry one because he knew this moment would come? Slipping and sliding on the snowy boardwalk, Miranda followed Lucas as fast as she could, and prayed Tobias would be all right.

Word of violent trouble had obviously spread in the mysterious way such news always traveled like wildfire through a small town. Those few folk who had ventured outside stood by the corners of buildings where they could duck out of the line of fire when the shooting started. Pale faces appeared in the windows of businesses. Everyone peered up the street toward the school, where two still figures stood facing each other in the center of the snowy street.

When she reached Peabody's store, Miranda whirled about to face her nephews. "Sean, you and Rory go inside and wait until this is over."

"But we want to see—" Rory started to protest, and Miranda cut him off.

"If they start shooting, one of their stray bullets could hit you. I couldn't bear it if one of you was hurt." The boys must have read the fear and desperation in her expression, for without another word of protest they both slipped inside the store.

Ignoring her own warning, Miranda ran on up the street. Reynolds was shouting at Tobias now, but she couldn't make out his words yet.

Tobias must have hurried out of the schoolhouse, for he wore no hat or jacket. She knew his first concern would have been for his students when Reynolds came looking for him. He had walked a good hundred feet away from the school building. Not a child lingered in the school yard. He must have managed to send them all away.

Light snowflakes swirled down out of the gray sky. It would have been a peaceful scene except for the two tense men standing before the school, completely focused on each other. Miranda halted, out of breath and trembling when she reached Lucas's side.

He had stopped in front of the tailor shop, which was the closest building to the school. Tobias and Reynolds stood directly across the street from him, less than twenty feet apart from each other.

"Now look here, missy," Lucas told her in a quiet voice, his eyes never leaving the two men. "I'll do what I can to keep this fair, but in the end a fight like this is between the two of them. If I do have to shoot, Reynolds may snap off a shot or two my way, and you've got the boys to think of. Get back by the corner of the shop, and don't you move until this is over.''

Afraid she might distract Lucas, or Tobias for that matter, Miranda bit back a protest and retreated behind the shelter of the shop. She still could see both men, and she could hear Reynolds quite clearly now.

''You are one sorry excuse for a man,'' Reynolds raged. ''Pick up that pistol, or I'm going to shoot you down where you stand.''

For the first time, Miranda noticed the gleam of a pistol in the packed snow at Tobias's feet. He didn't even look at the weapon. He simply stood there wearing that grim expression she knew too well, his hands hanging empty by his sides.

''People always told me Jonah was the fastest. Jonah was the best. Well, Jonah looks like he's a lily-livered coward from where I'm standing. Damn it, pick up that pistol,'' Reynolds shouted, his pale eyes glittering with frustrated fury. Deliberately, he raised his pistol and pulled back the hammer.

Miranda clapped her hands over her mouth to stifle a cry when the shot rang out. Tobias didn't even flinch as a small plume of snow spurted up by his right foot. Reynolds pulled back the hammer on his pistol, and shot again. This time a spurt of snow kicked up by Tobias's left foot.

''This is your last chance, you yellow son of a bitch.'' Reynolds pulled the trigger again. When the third shot blasted the quiet, Tobias staggered back, clutching his left shoulder. Miranda heard Lucas swear under his breath. The old gambler raised the shotgun to his shoulder and waited. Tobias regained his balance and stood motionless once again, still refusing to reach for the pistol by his feet.

''Hell, Slaughter must have been wrong about you. You can't be Jonah. I ought to kill you for wasting my time.'' Reynolds raised the pistol again, and from the rabid look in his eyes, Miranda feared he was furious enough to do exactly that.

"That's enough, boy. It's over," Lucas spoke up. "You put another bullet into an unarmed man, and you're going to get your neck stretched when the law catches up with you."

Reynolds spun about. Miranda knew she'd never forget the expression of rage twisting his young face.

"I ought to shoot you for interferin', old man," the young gunfighter threatened and shifted his six-shooter to cover Lucas.

"Use your head, boy. I've got a shotgun pointed at you, and you have a pistol pointed at me. You might take me, but I'm sure as hell going to take you. Besides, I don't figure killing an old has-been like me would do all that much for your reputation anyways."

Reynolds stared at Lucas for a long moment. Then he let loose a string of profanities and stalked away. Lucas kept his shotgun trained on Reynolds until the young gunfighter mounted his horse and galloped off. By the time Reynolds left, Miranda was already on her way to Tobias.

He started a little when she laid a hand on his arm, but his gaze fastened hungrily on her face. "Sweet Miranda, you are a sight for sore eyes." And the smile he gave her went straight to her heart.

"You've been crying," he said wonderingly. "I'm not worth a single one of your tears."

Miranda raised a hand to her cheek. She was surprised to find it was wet. "I'll cry over you if I've a mind to. How bad are you hurt? Can you tell?" she asked. Dimly she was aware that Lucas had come to stand beside her.

"He just grazed the top of my shoulder. It hurts like hell, though." Tobias's eyes looked dark and almost dreamy. "When I caught two slugs in the back seven years ago, they hardly hurt at all. Isn't that the damndest thing?"

"It certainly is," she agreed with him gently. "Why don't

you come along with us now to Doc Wheeler's and get that shoulder looked at?''

"All right," he agreed. He started to let her lead him away; but then he noticed Lucas and he stopped dead in his tracks.

"Thanks," he said to Lucas, "I owe you one. He was going to drill me for sure."

"Hell, it was my pleasure. I should've killed him. He's going to cause a world of grief before he gets his."

"But you didn't. Maybe you're getting tired of killing, too."

"Maybe I am at that." Lucas looked down at the shotgun in his hands, a strange expression on his face.

Frightened by the scarlet she saw seeping through Tobias's fingers, Miranda urged him toward the doctor's office once again.

"I'll go fetch his coat from the schoolhouse, and then I'll catch up with you," Lucas called after them.

Doc Wheeler met them at the door. "Someone came by and told me I might be having a patient to tend to shortly. For a schoolmaster, you sure manage to give me a lot of business," the old doctor told Tobias wryly. "First it was you, and then it was Slaughter, and now it's you again. Come on into my surgery, and let's take a look." The doctor ushered Tobias into the surgery and closed the door. Miranda had no choice but to sit down on an old wooden bench in Doc's small office and wait.

Lucas arrived moments later with Tobias's jacket. "What did the doc say?"

"Doc Wheeler didn't say much of anything yet. He's looking at him now."

"Well, I reckon it wasn't too serious. It looked like Reynolds just winged him," Lucas said comfortingly and settled himself beside her on the bench.

"Lucas, is he going to be all right? He seemed so strange just now."

"I seen men acting like that a time or two. I reckon he

figured he was going to die, and now he's mighty surprised to find out he's still alive. He'll be more himself in a little while, you'll see." He patted her arm reassuringly.

"How could he have done it?" she asked him wonderingly. "How could he possibly stand there and let that vicious young man shoot him?"

Lucas scratched his sideburn. "He's got sand, all right. I think he needed to prove to you and himself that come hell or high water, he's giving up the gunfighting. It's a damn shame, though. When word gets round that Jonah is still alive, there will be more like Reynolds coming after him."

"Why can't they just leave him alone?" she cried, appalled at the idea Tobias might never be left to live his life in peace.

"I told you before. The papers out here and those penny dreadful magazines back east are to blame. They make gunfightin' sound real exciting, and they make the men who do the most killing into heroes. Young punks come west and figure the fastest way to get famous is to kill someone famous. The papers don't talk about what it's really like afterward. At the end of a gunfight, someone's lying on the ground gasping out his last breath and wishing like hell he'd never touched a six-shooter." Lucas's face was bleak.

She was silent for a time, digesting his words. "He's such a good man. It just doesn't seem fair," she said in a small voice.

"It's not fair, but it's best now you realize how it is for him. As much as I like him, I don't give a plugged nickel for his chances, 'specially when he seems so dead set on not shooting back."

Miranda rubbed her arms and thanked every saint she could think of that Tobias hadn't ended up lying in the street today. During that horrible race up the boardwalk when she had waited and wondered if Tobias was going to die, she had realized the truth. For all she had wanted to protect herself from hurt, it was too late. She loved Tobias, and a part of her would have died today if he had been killed.

*You've gone and done a foolish, foolish thing, Miranda Kilpatrick. If Lucas is right, you've no more hope of a future with Tobias than you ever had.*

But for now he was alive, and she decided to cling to the joy and relief that fact gave her, rather than dwell on the gray and distant future. After a little while, Lucas went and fetched the boys.

"Is he gonna be all right, Aunt Miranda?" Sean asked in a subdued voice the moment the boys entered the office. They made a beeline for her—a measure of how shaken they both were by the shooting. She made space for them beside her on the bench. She held Rory's hand while she smiled as brightly as she could at Sean.

"He said the bullet just grazed him. He's a big, strong man. I'm sure Mr. Johnston will be fine," she said with more confidence than she actually felt.

"I don't understand why he didn't pick up that pistol and shoot Tyrel Reynolds," Sean shook his head, his eyes puzzled. "Jimmy Smith told me Jonah used to be one of the fastest gunfighters in the whole West. He should have just killed that skunk."

"Mr. Johnston doesn't want to kill anyone, and he risked his life today to prove that to all of us. Please don't say the name Jonah in front of me again," Miranda said tightly.

"Yes, ma'am," Sean replied, obviously startled by her anger.

"Mr. Johnston doesn't want to be a gunfighter anymore," she told him in a softer voice. "Killing Reynolds wouldn't have solved anything."

"Yes, ma'am," Sean said after a long moment, but she could tell he wasn't convinced.

They all sat quietly in the small room after that, waiting for the doctor to finish. Miranda wondered a little at the way none of them questioned being there. They all cared for Tobias in their various ways, and perhaps they were the closest thing he had to family in Pine Creek.

A half hour later, Tobias emerged from the surgery, looking pale and tired, his left arm in a sling.

"I'd wish you'd think about boarding with Mrs. Fisher for a week or two," Doc Wheeler told him, obviously continuing a discussion they had been having inside the surgery. "You're going to find it awkward looking after yourself."

"I'll be fine, but thanks, Doc," Tobias said shortly.

At just that moment, a sharp knock came on the front door to the office. When Doc Wheeler opened it, they all saw Mrs. Josiah Smith, Mr. Cyrus Reed, and Mr. Thomas Goodwin standing on the threshold. "We've come to see Mr. Johnston," Mrs. Smith announced. "Is he still here?"

"He's here all right." Doc Wheeler opened the door wider and let the three march inside. Suddenly, the small office seemed very full. Miranda looked at their set faces and felt her stomach sink.

"Mr. Johnston, we regret to inform you that because of this morning's gunfight, you are fired," Mr. Reed declared.

Doc Wheeler looked at the man in disbelief. "Hell, Cyrus, he wasn't in a gunfight. Johnston didn't do any shooting. He's the one who got shot."

"Nevertheless, we cannot tolerate this sort of spectacle in Pine Creek," Mrs. Smith broke in. "One of his pupils easily could have been hurt. The events of this past week have demonstrated that Mr. Johnston is simply not the sort of man we wish to have teaching our children."

"Well, that's just fine by me," Tobias declared in a cold, hard voice. "I like the children of this town fine, but their parents and their school board are getting to be a real pain in the ass. Good day to you all." With that, he stalked past them all and slammed out the door of the doctor's office.

Miranda was the first to react. She hurried past the stunned school board members and slipped out the door. For the second time that day, she found herself rushing along the slippery boardwalk. Tobias was walking toward the schoolhouse so swiftly on his long legs, she couldn't catch up to him. At last she had to call out, "Please, Tobias, wait. Wait just a moment."

Reluctantly, he stopped and turned about to face her.

"Are you sure you wanted to do that?" she asked him anxiously when she fetched up beside him. "Surely you could try talking with them. What happened today wasn't your fault."

His expression was set. "There was no use arguing with them. Their minds were made up. Besides, they were right. I did endanger their children, and I definitely am not the right sort of man to be teaching their young."

As she stared up into his bitter gray eyes, Miranda damned each and every one of those sanctimonious school board members for doing this to him.

"I think both you and they are very wrong," she told him softly. She stepped forward and slipped her arms about his waist. His body stiffened for a moment, and then his good arm went around her and pulled her close. She felt him lower his head until his cheek rested on the top of her head.

"Sweet, sweet Miranda," he said with a sigh, and they stood there while the snow drifted down about them. She savored the feeling of being in his arms once more. She didn't care in the least who saw them. For the moment all that mattered was Tobias was alive, and he needed what comfort she could offer him. At last, she grew worried that he might be getting chilled standing out here in the cold. Reluctantly, she let go and stepped back from him.

"Well, since you are no longer employed by the school board of Pine Creek," she said briskly, "I see no reason why you can't come home with us. Christina and I can look after you far better than Mrs. Fisher could. And don't you even dream of going back to that Spartan place you call a home."

He stared down at her, and then his lips twitched. "I don't believe I ever did call it a home," he said mildly.

"And well you shouldn't." She linked her arm through his elbow and walked him back toward the doctor's office where her family waited.

Once Miranda got Tobias settled in her bedroom, he fell fast asleep. The smell of cooking must have roused him around supper time. Using the little bell she left by his bedside table, he rang for her and admitted he was both hungry and thirsty. She brought him a tray of food and a pitcher of water, then sat down in the rocker in the corner while he started on his supper.

It was hard for her not to stare at Tobias in her uncle's nightshirt. The simple white garment clung to his broad chest and wide shoulders. Because of the blood he'd lost today, his strong cheekbones and jaw appeared more blunt and rugged than ever. The shadow on his cheeks from a day's growth of beard made him look more like a desperado than a schoolteacher. He made quite a contrast to her feminine room with the lace doilies covering her nightstand and dresser, and the little glass and porcelain knickknacks she had scattered about.

Watching him lying in her bed, propped up against her pillows and covered by her own sheets and blankets, gave her a queer, restless feeling. She hoped she hadn't made a terrible mistake, offering to care for Tobias while he recovered from his injury.

After a few unsuccessful attempts to engage him in conversation, she left him alone. When she went in to remove his tray, he was sleeping again. She checked on him a few hours later, and he was awake once more, staring moodily at the far wall. Some books Lucas had fetched for him from his cabin lay unopened on the nightstand.

"I know you aren't in much of a mood to talk, but would you like some company anyway?" she asked him tentatively.

"I could read in here for a little while before I go to sleep."
Tonight she would be using the trundle bed they kept in Christina's room.

"I'd like that just fine," he replied with a ghost of his former smile.

She sat down in her old rocker and opened *The Three Musketeers*. She was reading the book to the boys right now, and she had gotten so involved in the story, she meant to cheat and read ahead of her nephews a chapter or two. She also had a sneaking suspicion that if Tobias had any interest in being read to, he might enjoy Alexander Dumas.

"Aren't you going to the Shamrock tonight?" he asked her suddenly.

"I decided to take the night off."

"Good," he said gruffly. "You're safer here."

When he said nothing more, she bent her head and began to read.

He shifted restlessly under the bedclothes. "Aren't you afraid your regulars are going to miss you?"

Her head went up at that, and her eyes narrowed. She couldn't mistake the veiled challenge in his tone.

"I know they may miss me, but they will just have to survive without me for a night," she replied evenly.

"Aren't you going to miss them? I've heard most performers live for their audiences."

She shut her book with a snap. Obviously, he was looking for a fight. Perhaps she ought to give him one.

"That statement is true for some actors and actresses, but it's not true for me," she managed politely enough.

"Indeed," he said, his disbelief obvious.

He might be tired. He might be hurt and angry about losing his teaching position today. But she wasn't going to let him take his anger out on her. She rose to her feet and placed her hands on her hips.

"For your information, Mr. Tobias E. Johnston, I don't

exactly enjoy prancing about on a tiny stage in a smoky saloon, showing off my ankles and the rest of me to a bunch of salivating men.''

"Why do you do it, then?" he countered swiftly. "Surely you make enough at the Shamrock to get by without your singing. I'd wager you make enough profits off that place you don't need to go into the saloon at all. You could probably hire someone to run it for you.''

"Why do I run the saloon myself? Why do I sing myself hoarse performing bawdy songs night after night? Why do I smile and flirt with my patrons and dodge their groping hands? Because it costs money to hire people to do my work, and the nights I perform we double our revenues. You can ask Lucas if you don't believe me. And I'm dead set on making that extra money because I'm putting every red cent I can into the bank.''

He started to say something, but she cut him off. Her temper was up now, and he could damn well hear her out. "I'm going to make every penny I can, and I'm going to save every penny I can, because I'm never, ever going to let my boys go hungry again. Back in Nebraska we almost starved on that benighted farm when a drought shriveled our crops in the field. Our neighbors couldn't help us because they were starving, too. I watched Rory and Sean grow so thin I could count their ribs. One afternoon, Rory fainted out in the field because he was dizzy from hunger, and Sean insisted on giving him his pitiful share of corn pone that night and going hungry himself.

"That's when I went to Johnny Nolan, the proprietor of the only saloon in town. If I hadn't been able to convince him I could earn more for him singing, I would have sold my body in one of his rooms upstairs to earn a loaf of bread I could take home to my nephews. I almost became a harlot that night, and I never want to be that desperate again.

"I don't mind prostituting my voice, because it's a hell of a lot better than prostituting the rest of me. I'm going to use the Shamrock and the men of Pine County to make so much money I'll always be able to provide for Sean and Rory. I'd even like to be able to send them off to a school like the one you attended if I'm able—not that any of this is your business in the first place.'' With that crushing line, she stormed from the room.

The problem with being a nurse, she realized with some chagrin down in the kitchen a few minutes later, was that she had to go back to her patient when he called no matter how angry she was with him. She thought about asking Christina to take over for her, but Christina had already gone to bed, and besides, that solution seemed cowardly. When Miranda heard his bell ring five minutes later, she drew in a deep breath, squared her shoulders, and marched upstairs again.

''I was out of line, and I'm sorry,'' he said the moment she entered the room, stealing most of the wind from her sails. ''The fact is,'' he said, his gaze falling to the bedclothes before him, ''I think I'm jealous of those gents who come from all over to see you sing.''

That confession melted her hurt and resentment in a second.

She walked to his bedside and knelt beside him. He reached out and took her hand.

''You've no reason to be jealous of any of them. They mean nothing to me.'' Diplomatically she refrained from pointing out he had no right to be jealous.

He looked down at their joined hands, and his mouth twisted. ''You know, I've always admired your pluck, from the first time I learned why you ran the Shamrock. I'm sorry you had such a rough go of it in Nebraska. Dryland farming's a mighty tough way to make a living. Those nephews of yours are lucky to have an aunt who cares so much about them. Tonight I'm just a sore old bear, and I apologize for hitting out at you.''

''Well, you sore old bear, your apology is accepted. Now, before I go downstairs for the night, is there anything I can do to make you more comfortable?'' The moment the question was out, she wished she could catch it back and rephrase it.

He looked at her with such a gleam in his eyes, her cheeks began to burn.

Suddenly, she became very aware of the fact he was lying in her bed, in the privacy of her room, and the rest of her household was already sound asleep. The fact he was clad in a nightshirt only added to the intimacy of the situation. She stood up abruptly and pulled her hand out of his grasp.

"You could give me a kiss good night. I'm sure it would help me cope with the pain better. I'm probably in for a rough night of it," he suggested plaintively. She could tell he was trying to look as woebegone as possible.

"That isn't the reason I invited you to my home while you heal up, Mr. Johnston," she informed him primly.

"You can't blame a man for trying," he said, abruptly abandoning his sorrowful expression. "Lying in your bed can give a fellow ideas."

"I think I'd rather not know what sorts of ideas you might be referring to," she countered, her cheeks warming again. "If you are set for the evening, I really should go downstairs now."

"It would help if you could just leave that pitcher of water where I can reach it with my right hand."

Relieved he had stopped teasing her, she moved around the bed to do as he asked. As she looked down at his strong brow and the stark planes and angles of his familiar face, she remembered what he had risked today to prove a point to himself, and possibly to her as well. Once she had moved the pitcher for him, she leaned over and pressed a kiss on his forehead.

"You were remarkable today, Mr. Tobias E. Johnston. It took a rare sort of courage to face Reynolds the way you did."

He tilted his head and looked at her, longing so evident in his beautiful gray eyes that her throat went tight.

"Miranda Kilpatrick"—his deep voice was rough with real emotion now—"I wish I had met you a lifetime ago."

She wished the same as well, but it was wiser to leave those words unsaid. Using every iota of self-control she possessed, she refrained from leaning over, framing his face with her hands, and kissing his lips with all the longing pent up inside her own lonely heart. When she left the room, she glanced back over her shoulder. Pain lanced through her when she realized her patient was back to staring broodingly at the wall.

Ben Slaughter shifted closer to the fire in the smoky old stove and cursed Tyrel Reynolds under his breath. After the kid tried to brace Jonah on his own, a posse from Pine Creek had followed Reynolds's tracks straight back to the gang's hideout. Because that damn fool sheriff had up and died, the posse had been after blood.

He always kept a man on lookout, and Smitty had given them enough warning to saddle up and ride out. Slaughter had no taste for a pitched gunfight against twenty law-abiding citizens set on evening a score. One of the idiots might have gotten lucky and hit someone. The frustrated posse had fired the ranch, though, and now Slaughter didn't have a decent place to winter. The abandoned ranch house was no mansion, but it had been warmer than this pitiful old mine shack they had retreated to farther up the mountain.

Slaughter swore again, but he was careful not to let his anger show when he looked toward Reynolds. He needed the kid for the moment. Tyrel was amazingly fast with a pistol, and the men feared him. Down the road, Slaughter was going to make the boy pay for defying his orders. When the time was right. That was how Ben Slaughter had survived this long. He was damn smart about choosing the right time for things.

And Reynolds wasn't the only one who was going to pay. Jonah and his red-haired whore were going to be damn sorry they ever crossed him. It was Jonah's fault he'd ended up in jail. It was Jonah's fault he'd had to shoot that sorry excuse for a lawman. It was Jonah's fault he couldn't blow his own goddamned nose without flinching. It was Jonah's fault that whore hadn't told him where the mine was, a mine so rich he and the boys could stop robbing banks and live like nabobs for the rest of their days.

Jonah would pay when the time was right. And that time was coming soon.

# Chapter Sixteen

Despite the burning pain in his shoulder and his disappointment over losing his teaching position, Tobias almost enjoyed himself the next day. Life was never dull in Miranda Kilpatrick's home. To begin with, he relished the pleasure of having Miranda at his beck and call. Whenever he wanted to see her, he simply thought up some reason for ringing the bell, and she promptly came and shared her cheerful presence with him.

The boys were constantly in and out of his room, too. Having summarily dismissed their schoolmaster, the school board had to close the Pine Creek school while they scrambled to find a replacement for Mr. Johnston midterm. The boys didn't trouble themselves over the reason for their freedom. They were just thrilled to find themselves with an unexpected holiday, and they made the most of this time to talk with Tobias.

Sean was the first to appear in the doorway, soon after Miranda disappeared with Tobias's breakfast tray.

"How's your shoulder feel?"

"It hurts like the dickens," Tobias admitted honestly. "Getting shot is a mighty uncomfortable business. You might think on that fact if you're still so set on being a sheriff."

Sean wandered into the room and stood at the foot of the bed, his hands thrust in the pockets of his overalls.

"How come you didn't shoot Reynolds?" Sean asked suddenly. "Were you too scared to reach for the holster and gun he left by your feet?"

Tobias thought hard, searching for an honest answer which a twelve-year-old boy could understand. "You bet I was scared," he admitted after a long moment. "I was darn scared that if I buckled on that gun belt and drew on that punk, he might kill me, and I wasn't ready to die. Then again, I might have killed him. Then I would have had his blood on my hands. It's a terrible thing to take a man's life. With one bullet, I could have stolen away his future, including his chance to have a wife or children or to leave any sort of mark on the world."

He could tell from the stubborn look on Sean's face that he wasn't really reaching the boy, and so he decided to take another tack.

"Do you ever have nightmares?"

Sean looked puzzled by the question. "Once in a while, I suppose."

"Well, I have nightmares plenty often, and in those nightmares I see the faces of the men I killed. I didn't need another face to haunt my sleep at night. I reckon your dreams are pretty peaceful right now, and I hope they stay that way for a long time to come.

"The other reason I didn't reach for that gun is simple. If I had killed Reynolds, I'd be Jonah once more, and I'd never know a moment of peace again."

Tobias lay back against the pillows and stared out the window, thinking of the desolate years he'd lived as Jonah. "Once you get a reputation for being quick with a gun, you always have to be on your guard. There's always going to be someone out there who thinks he's faster and tougher. And sooner or later there will be someone who is faster, tougher, or luckier, and then you're dead. Before you decide to be a lawman, you best think about whether or not you want to live like that.''

"But wasn't any of it fun?" Sean asked, his eyes full of disbelief and disappointment. "Didn't you like having people everywhere you went know your name?"

Tobias closed his eyes wearily. "That's one thing I can tell you for sure. Not a moment of it was fun. Not a single moment.''

He'd forgotten what fun was, until Miranda Kilpatrick had burst into his life. He'd forgotten what joy was until a spirited young woman with a loving heart had taught him how to experience that emotion once again. But now word would be getting out that Jonah was alive, and soon he would have to move on, unless he wanted to face another Reynolds. Suddenly too tired and too disheartened to talk with Sean anymore, he kept his eyes closed, and moments later the boy slipped away.

Tobias dozed for an hour, and when he woke up he found Rory sitting in the chair by his bedside, watching him eagerly. Tobias couldn't help smiling. Rory reminded him of a gangly young puppy he'd had as a boy. Always cheerful and happy, Horatio had been perpetually eager to play.

"Would you like to see my collection of pressed plants and bugs?" Rory asked so hopefully, Tobias didn't have the heart to say no to him. To his surprise, he enjoyed the next hour greatly as the two of them tried to identify the various plants and insects Rory had collected. Toward the end of the hour, Sean returned to the room and joined their discussion.

Tobias was disappointed when Miranda discovered the boys and chased them out of the sickroom. Their company had lightened his mood and kept his mind off the pain in his shoulder. Throughout the rest of the day, the boys returned frequently when their aunt wasn't watching. The fact he was no longer their teacher seemed to lift much of the restraint the two had formerly shown in his presence. Sean in particular was remarkably talkative, smuggling in animals from his menagerie and bombarding him with questions about hunting and horses.

"You don't need to chase them away. I enjoy their company," he told Miranda when she came up the stairs to shoo them away from his room for the fourth time.

"I don't know what's gotten into them," she said with exasperation. "Usually they mind me better than this."

"I expect a guest is a fairly major event in their lives," he suggested diplomatically. A part of him wondered if the boys' fascination with him might be due to the fact they were at an age where they needed more contact with men who could talk with them at length about manly topics. Tobias didn't know how to point that out without hurting Miranda's feelings, and so he kept quiet on the subject for now.

Rob McGregor stopped by midday.

"I hear you let Tyrel Reynolds use you for target practice," he said as he entered the room. "And here everyone in town thought you were such a bright sort of a fellow."

"You can go to hell," Tobias told him cordially.

"Yep, looks to me like you'll live," Rob told him with a grin and settled himself in the rocker. "I hope you don't get well too soon, though. You're being here gives me a heaven-sent opportunity. I plan to be a mighty good friend and stop by most every day to see how you're doin'."

"That way you can see a certain young Swedish lady every day, too," Tobias guessed shrewdly.

"You bet. If you could just manage to spin this convalescing business out for a week or so, I should have made real headway by then, me being such a charming, sweet-talking gent and all."

"I'm glad to be able to help you out. In fact, now that I think of it, I'm sorry I didn't let Reynolds fill me full of holes. Then you could have come visiting here for a month of Sundays."

"Well, I expect there are probably some limits as to what one friend should do to help another's romancing,'' Rob allowed judiciously. He settled back in the rocker and entertained Tobias with his company. After a half hour Tobias gave a big yawn on purpose. Rob was on his feet in a moment, obviously eager to try his luck at charming Christina.

After a delicious midday meal brought up the stairs by Miranda, Tobias fell sound asleep until Doc Wheeler came to change his dressing. When that ordeal was finished, he slept again.

He awoke just before supper and realized he felt a great deal better. His shoulder still hurt every time he moved it too suddenly, but he didn't feel so weak. He ate every bit of the beef stew and biscuits Miranda brought him and asked for seconds. After supper he wanted to get dressed and come downstairs, but Miranda wouldn't hear of it.

"Dammit, I'm not used to being cooped up like this all day in a small room," he growled at her. "Reynolds just winged me, for God's sake. It's not like I've been at death's door."

"The man must be feeling better if he's swearing at me," Miranda said philosophically to the room at large.

In the end, they both compromised. Miranda allowed Tobias to come downstairs for a few hours, dressed in the nightshirt and her uncle's old dressing gown. He asked her to play and sing for him, and she seemed happy to oblige.

While the boys were still up, Tobias was amused to see they sang along enthusiastically with Miranda, arguing cheerfully with each other over which songs they wanted her to play. Even Lucas and Christina participated, requesting songs they particularly liked and joining in on the choruses. When the steeple clock on the mantel chimed eight, Miranda finished the impromptu concert and declared it was time for the boys to go to bed.

Tobias remained in the front room while Miranda went upstairs with the boys. Christina retreated to her own room, and Lucas went off to the barn where he had living quarters of his own. Although he pretended to read, Tobias was actually enjoying the novel sensation of being in a house full of people he cared for. He'd lived in boardinghouses before, but sharing space with polite acquaintances and spending time in Miranda's warm, happy home were two completely different experiences.

He grinned as he found himself listening to Miranda's spirited reading of D'Artagnan's latest adventure. She must have been a fine actress. He could see her throwing her heart and soul into her roles. She would be a fine mother, too.

Tobias stopped smiling abruptly. Although he sincerely hoped she would have a chance to raise children of her own, the idea of another man fathering those children and raising them with her made him see red. *Tobias E. Johnston, you have absolutely no right to feel this way, but you'd probably go loco if you saw another man touch her.*

When Miranda returned, she sat down on the piano bench facing him. "There's a question I've been meaning to ask you for a long time now," she said in a tentative voice very different from the direct way she usually addressed him. That tone had him shutting his book at once and looking at her with some concern.

"What is it?"

"I've noticed you never sing. Are you tone deaf, or do you just not much care for singing in general?"

Tobias stared back at her, completely nonplussed. Of all the things he thought she might be worried about, his talent or lack of it for singing hardly topped the list. She was watching him so earnestly, he decided she deserved an honest answer.

"I used to be able to carry a tune," he admitted. "I always sang in my father's choir when I was a boy. But since then, I guess I just haven't had much occasion to sing." He refrained from pointing out he hadn't felt much like singing ever since his family had been killed. He figured whatever singing voice he possessed had probably atrophied from disuse.

"In every day of life, there's occasion to sing," she contradicted him softly. "Will you do something for me?"

He looked at her, a dark suspicion growing in the back of his mind. He might be willing to lay down his life for her, but singing for Miranda was a whole different matter.

"Tell me a song you like, and come sit beside me on the piano bench while I play it."

That request seemed safe enough. Besides, he could hardly turn down an opportunity to sit closer to her. Miranda was looking exceedingly pretty tonight. He'd been admiring her all evening long with bittersweet pleasure. She wore that dark blue dress again with a fine lace collar which just matched the lovely color of her skin. She'd dressed her hair differently, pinning it in coils at her neck, which made her look even more feminine than usual.

She settled herself on the piano bench and patted the space beside her. He rose and sat down next to her gingerly, wondering if the piano bench could hold them both. He'd had more than a few chairs collapse beneath his weight. But the piano bench held, and so he looked over at Miranda and found she was watching him expectantly. Hell, she was still waiting for him to name one of his favorite songs.

It was on the tip of his tongue to tell her that he didn't have any. But he didn't want to hurt her feelings. And then he realized he did have a song he liked. His mother had had a favorite song she'd often sang to his father, a sweet, old-fashioned ballad about a young man in love and the girl he had to leave behind.

"I don't suppose you know 'Annie Laurie'?"

"Indeed I do. That's a lovely old tune." She gave him a wide smile, and Tobias's gaze went to her lips. Sweet heavens, she had a beautiful mouth. Tobias shifted a little on the bench as his loins tightened. As always, staying this close to Miranda was starting to wreak havoc with his senses. He was keenly aware of the place her skirts spilled over on his thigh. He could smell roses and a wonderful scent that must be the essence of Miranda herself.

As she reached out and played the opening chords to the song, his physical awareness of her receded a little, to be replaced by a wave of nostalgia so intense it almost hurt. In that moment, he could see his parents smiling at each other while his mother played this song on the pump organ in the parlor. His mother had been a petite woman with gold hair, smiling brown eyes, and endless energy. His father had been a big man with a remarkable gift for eloquence, put to good use for the causes they had both believed in so passionately. Tobias had forgotten until now just how much they must have loved each other.

"You can sing the chorus with me," Miranda urged him. Tobias came back to the present with a start.

He opened his mouth to protest. As he stared into her eager eyes, damned if he didn't find himself actually singing the refrain. He had to pause once to clear his throat, but to his own critical ear, his voice didn't sound too bad.

She sang the next verse alone, and on the chorus they sang together, his baritone mixing remarkably well with her soprano. Miranda brought the ballad to a close with a flourish of chords.

"There," she said triumphantly, "I knew you could sing. I knew it from the first time you spoke to me. That wonderful voice of yours was just meant for singing."

"Thanks for the compliment, but I'm not joining your saloon act," he said dryly, "just because I'm currently unemployed."

"Now there's an idea with real promise. A singing ex-gunfighter might really fill the house," she countered, her eyes alight with devilment.

Even though he knew she meant to make him smile, it still hurt to hear her name what he had been. He looked down at the piano keys.

"Why don't you sing one more song," he suggested gruffly. "One of your own favorites this time."

He could feel her gaze on him. The teasing note was gone from her voice when she said, "Very well," after a few moments. She sat still and thought, and then she smiled.

"Here's one I've always liked. The one we just sang reminded me of it." She played "Drink To Me Only With Thine Eyes," another sweet old love song which suited her voice perfectly.

Tobias turned a little on the bench and watched her profile as she sang. The yearning her music roused in him soon turned into a different kind of yearning. His awareness of her as a woman, a woman he had wanted for months now, returned in a rush. He toyed with the notion of leaning over and kissing her nape where small tendrils of her hair drifted downward. It would be so easy to steal a quick taste of her ivory skin. But she had invited him to stay under her roof out of friendship and gratitude. He had no right to begin something that could be disastrous for them both to finish.

More than ever he was aware of how little he had to offer her. His run-in with Reynolds had convinced him he would have to move on soon. Once word got out Jonah was still alive, more young fools like Tyrel Reynolds would come, and he would be forced to kill again or be killed. Miranda was the kind of woman who would take loving seriously. It was obvious that she already cared for him more than she should, and he'd be selfish to make their parting any harder on her.

Instead of leaning over and kissing Miranda as she sang, he sat and imagined the various ways he would like to touch and be touched by her. His mouth went dry at the thought of her long, white fingers, so clever and skillful on the piano keys, stroking him. The lamplight brought out the rich shades in her hair, from dark cedar to the pale copper color of a new penny.

He could just picture pulling the pins out of the demure coils she had fashioned and letting that wild, wanton hair of hers loose so that he could bury his hands and face in it. He'd lay her back on that braided rug before the fire and kiss her lovely lips and the rest of her until she was breathless and twisting beneath him.

"Tobias, are you all right?"

He looked up from the piano keys, startled to realize she'd finished playing. She had turned sideways toward him on the piano bench. Concern for him darkened those gorgeous indigo eyes of hers.

"I knew coming downstairs was too much for you."

It was too much, but not in the sense she meant. He used every bit of self-control he possessed to keep from taking her in his arms and fulfilling some of those lascivious fantasies he'd just been having. Afraid he still might give in to temptation and worried that she might read the hunger in his eyes, he rose to his feet abruptly and turned away from her and the piano bench.

"I guess you're right. I'm more tired than I realized." From someplace he managed to dredge up the wits to add, "Thank you for the concert."

"It was my pleasure," she told him warmly and stood up as well. "Do you need any help getting ready for bed?"

"No," he replied harshly. Out of the corner of his eye he saw her step back and pale a little. If she came upstairs with him now, there was a damn good chance they would end up in her bed together.

"I know your shoulder's probably hurting you, but that's no reason for you to snap at me," she pointed out with great dignity.

His shoulder wasn't exactly the part of him that was hurting at this moment. "I'm sorry," he said. He walked stiffly to the base of the stairs.

"Before you go up, I just wanted to know if you had any particular meals you liked. Christina and I were going to plan what to cook for you over the next few days."

"There's no need for you to bother," he said without turning around. "I'll be going back to my place first thing in the morning."

"But why on earth—" Before she could work up steam, he cut her off.

"If I stay here another night, I won't be able to keep my hands off you." He turned around slowly to face her.

She stood in the middle of the parlor, her blue eyes stricken, color seeping into her cheeks. "I see," she said in a low voice and crossed her arms tightly across her chest.

"I want you to know I'm going to be leaving Pine Creek soon," he added. "I promise I'll stick around long enough to make sure that marshal does his job and that Slaughter's no longer a threat to you. Then I have to be on my way. Too many people heard Slaughter and Reynolds call me Jonah."

She took a deep breath and let her arms fall to her sides. Her chin lifted. "I understand," she said in a cool voice. "I think that would probably be best, for everyone."

Since there really wasn't anything else to say, he turned around and climbed up the steps. As he shut the door to Miranda's bedroom behind him, he wondered why doing the best thing for everyone felt so hellish.

Miranda remained in the parlor for a long time after Tobias walked upstairs, her body aching and her mind awhirl. From the moment he had come downstairs tonight, she had been aware of Tobias in that wonderful, peculiar way she never had been aware of anyone else. It had been a delicious sort of torture to sit next to him on the piano bench, so close she could smell the scent of his shaving soap and feel the warmth of his shoulder almost brushing hers. When she had cajoled him into singing, goose bumps rose all over her at the sound of his deep voice. She had sung that last song for him, expressing through her music the love that was too dangerous to say to him directly.

She had been so caught up in her own desire for him, and

her need to hide it, she had been unaware that he had been feeling much the same way.

She picked up an oil lamp and walked to the front hall. She stared at her reflection in the hall tree mirror. Although she had faced hardship and tragedy in her life, in many ways she had been fortunate. She had been raised by two parents who loved her. She had traveled extensively with her father's theatrical troupe and known a kind of freedom few young women her age ever had a chance to enjoy. Currently she was blessed by the love of two young boys who meant the world to her.

But as she looked at her face in the mirror, she realized she was twenty-three years old, and she hadn't shared her body with a man she loved. There was a good chance she never would. The sort of decent man she might love would be repelled by her occupation. The kind of man who was attracted to her at the saloon repelled her.

She never meant to marry, but did that mean she never would know the act of love? Tobias was leaving. She closed her eyes against the pain that thought gave her. Instead, she concentrated on the present. *You have so little time left with him. Da always said, "Seize the day."*

Her courses were due in a few days. The chances of her having a child were slim, and the notion of bearing Tobias's baby gave her a secret kind of joy. *Miranda Kilpatrick, if you don't go to him tonight, you'll always wonder what it might have been like, and you'll regret that choice for the rest of your life.* That thought, in the end, was what decided her.

As if in a dream, she turned the lamp down low and slipped into Christina's room. Quietly she changed out of her dress and underclothes and into her nightgown. Slowly, her body thrumming with both nervousness and anticipation, she unpinned her hair and brushed it out. Rather than braid it, she decided to leave her hair loose. Tobias had always seemed fascinated by it. She had a feeling it might not be easy to break down that careful control of his, and she needed every feminine weapon at her command to breach his defenses.

She wasn't exactly sure how to go about seducing a wounded ex-gunfighter, but tonight she was going to give it her very best shot. Her heart in her throat, she closed Christina's door behind her quietly and headed for the stairs.

# Chapter Seventeen

Her pulse was racing by the time Miranda reached the top of the stairs. Panic assailed her as she stared at Tobias's door. What if he laughed at her? What if he didn't really want her? But then she remembered the burning look in his gray eyes and the strain in his voice when he'd told her he was leaving in the morning.

Tobias Johnston wanted her, all right, but whether or not she could overcome his gentlemanly instincts was another matter. She drew in a deep breath, squared her shoulders, and stepped inside.

"If I had a gun, I might have shot a hole in you by now," he told her in a conversational voice. "Lurking by people's doors in the middle of the night is never a wise idea."

Miranda looked across the room. He was leaning back against the pillows wearing only her uncle's nightshirt. As he took in her appearance, his eyes narrowed and his brows came together in a scowl.

"You're not asleep yet." She couldn't keep the relief from

her tone. She hadn't fancied waking him from a sound slumber to try seducing him.

"No," he replied shortly. "What the hell are you doing in here?"

She closed the door quietly behind her and set the lamp down on the nearby dresser. Marshaling all the courage she possessed, she turned to face him. "I want you to make love to me tonight."

He left the bed with alarming swiftness. In three strides he crossed the room and grabbed her shoulder with his one good hand.

"Don't you have the sense God gave a turnip?" he demanded.

"I'd appreciate it if you didn't speak to me if as if I were an idiot."

"Then don't act like one. This isn't what you really want." His eyes had turned as cold and hard as flint.

"Don't you dare tell me what I want."

"Well, someone has to think clearly for you since you obviously aren't." He let go of her shoulder and swung away from her.

"I'm thinking perfectly clearly, thank you very much. I know exactly what I'm asking. I don't want to turn into a wizened old maid without knowing what every matron in this town knows. I want to know what it's like to be loved by a man I care for."

"Miranda, trust me on this. You are not going to turn into an old maid. Some good, upstanding fellow is going to come along and sweep you off your feet."

"That sort of man is truly going to court a saloon keeper?"

She had him there, and they both knew it; but he hardly hesitated with his rejoinder. "I know some day a good, decent man is going to realize what a prize you are. He's going to fall head over heels for you, and spend the rest of his life trying to make you happy."

"I think I'm looking at that man now," she said softly.

He gave a harsh laugh. "I'm neither good nor decent, and I'm the last man in the world who would have a chance of making a woman happy. Women as a rule don't enjoy being widows, and there's a mighty fine chance any woman fool enough to tie the knot with me would end up wearing black."

"You could make me happy. I'm not asking for a lifetime. I'm just asking for one night."

"Lord, Miranda, I don't want to hurt you. What if we made a child together?"

"We won't," she said firmly, her cheeks warming. "It's the wrong time for that."

He ran a hand through his hair, but she was encouraged by the fact he couldn't seem to stop looking at her.

"I'm afraid if we do this, it will make it that much harder for you when I leave."

"And what about you?" she asked in a low voice. "Will it be harder for you to leave me?"

That question seemed to take the wind out of his sails. "I don't think anything could make it any harder than it seems now," he admitted. He glanced away from her, but not before she saw the vulnerable look in his eyes.

Some womanly instinct told her this was her final chance. She crossed the room and slipped her arms about his waist. She was heartened when he didn't push her away. She laid her cheek on his chest and listened to the quick thud of his heart. After he gave a long sigh, his arm went round her, and he pulled her closer. She smiled to herself when she felt him toying with her hair.

She tilted her head back to look at him. "Show me how it can be between a man and a woman. Love me tonight."

He smoothed her hair back from her face. In his eyes she read his worry for her warring with his desire. "I wish I was strong enough, but I can't tell you no another time. A man's only got so much willpower, and I've just reached the end of mine. You're offering what I've been wanting from you for months now.''

''And I've been wanting just the same from you,'' she said teasingly, trying to lighten his somber mood. ''I had designs on you from that first day I saw you on Main Street. When I saw those broad shoulders of yours and heard your voice, I knew I was in trouble.''

He didn't even seem to hear her. Instead, he was studying her. ''This is your first time, isn't it?''

Her cheeks warmed again. She hid her face in his chest and nodded once.

''Christ.''

The dismay she heard in his voice made her heart sink. ''I-I thought men liked making love to a virgin,'' she faltered.

''They do—I mean I do. Not that I ever have. Christ,'' he swore again. ''What I'm trying to say is that I'm honored. I just want to do this right. I want to make it good for you, but it can hurt the first time.''

''Tobias, I've trusted you with my life. I certainly trust you with my body.'' She had to swallow a laugh. She had never seen this poised, strong man so rattled. Obviously it was up to her to get the ball rolling. She reached up and wrapped her arms around his neck. Careful of his wounded shoulder, she pulled his head down to hers. Whatever protest he was about to make next died on his lips.

And then he was kissing her in that all-consuming way he had, and she knew it would be all right. The tension that had smoldered between them all night flared to life. His hands caressed her, teasing, smoothing, kindling the longing deep inside her into flame, and all the while his demanding mouth drove her wild and left her breathless. Encouraged by his boldness, she let her own hands have free rein, relishing the rough stubble on his cheeks, the silkiness of the hair at his nape, the solid strength of his arms holding her tightly against him.

She was so caught up in this burning onslaught on her senses, she was startled when she felt her mattress pressing against the back of her leg. Somehow they had moved from the window to her bed, and she hadn't even noticed. He had ahold of her hips now, for he had wedged his hard leg between hers and pulled her forward until she was straddling him. If it weren't for his hand on her shoulder, she would fall. She didn't really mind the precariousness of her position, for it brought their lower bodies into deliciously wicked proximity.

At last she had to pull her mouth away from his just long enough to gasp, "Tobias, please, I can't breathe. I can't get my balance."

"Good. You've kept me off balance since the first day I met you." Humor glinted in his gray eyes along with that familiar hunger which made her head swim. He bent to kiss her once more, and he sent them both toppling back onto the bed. He landed beside her, their legs entwined. She felt that familiar pulse low in her belly when he twisted about and threw his leg across her hips. She was quite aware of the fact that all he had on was a nightshirt, and her nightgown was now rucked quite immodestly up about her thighs.

She had to still the urge to tug her gown lower and cover her legs. *Miranda Kilpatrick, you're being plumb foolish. Before this night is over, you're going to see a great deal more of him, and he's going to see a great deal more of you.* Nevertheless, now that she was lying on her back with a very large, male Tobias right beside her, some of the nervousness she had been feeling earlier returned with a rush.

She looked up to see Tobias had propped his head on his hand, and he was watching her intently.

"I reckon you're probably having some second thoughts right about now."

"No," she said as firmly as she could. "I-I'm just trying to get used to the notion that you're lying in my bed."

"I've been lying in your bed for nearly two days now," he pointed out reasonably, but she could tell he was teasing her.

"All right, I'm trying to get used to the fact we're both lying in my bed," she said with some exasperation.

"How about we just take this one step at a time? I do anything you don't like or you aren't comfortable with, you let me know."

"All right. Can we go back to kissing first?" she asked hopefully. "I like kissing you."

"And I damn well like kissing you," he growled. "In fact, I'm planning on kissing just about every inch of you before we're through tonight."

"Oh, my," Miranda said, a wave of warmth washing through her at the thought.

"Woman, I love your fair skin. Now I know when you blush, you do really blush all over," he said as he surveyed her with a wicked gleam in his eyes.

"When are you going to stop talking and get on with that kissing you promised me?" she asked plaintively.

"Now that I'm sure you're feeling less skittish, I'd be happy to oblige, ma'am."

She closed her eyes, expecting him to kiss her lips again. Instead, he began kissing the side of her neck, sending shivers up and down her. While his lips teased and caressed her, he made quick work of the top buttons on her nightdress. He moved on to the hollow at the base of her throat, causing more shivers, for now she could feel the softness of his hair against her chin.

With exquisite gentleness, he moved the edges of her night-gown apart. His breath was warm above her breastbone, the air of the bedroom so cool on the rest of her that she puckered and hardened. When he bent and kissed the tip of her breast, her toes curled against the old quilt which covered her bed. Lord, his mouth felt so good on her. With the sober concentration that seemed to mark everything he did, he tugged gently with his teeth and laved her with his tongue. The torment began all over when he lavished the same care on her other breast.

She was panting by the time he had finished. Although she loved the tumultuous sensations he had aroused in her, she wanted to make him gasp and pant as well. He stilled when she reached up and began working at the buttons to his nightshirt. Then he took her hands, kissed them, and sat up.

"Let me," he said and started to pull the nightshirt over his head. When he had problems managing it with his one good arm, she reached over and helped him.

"Oh, my," Miranda found herself saying again as she watched the play of muscles across his rib cage and shoulders. The white of the bandage wrapped around his left shoulder made a contrast to the darker color of his skin. She couldn't bring herself to look any lower just yet, but the view up top was plenty impressive for the moment. He was wide and lean and beautiful in a purely male way. His chest was covered with fine, curling brown hair which tapered in a vee down to his belly. A sort of possessive joy went through her to realize his wonderful male body was hers to learn and explore this night. The only barrier now between their bodies was her nightdress.

That was hardly any barrier at all, she realized moments later when he came back to lie beside her. She felt the heat of his body through the thin cotton fabric, and the muscular strength of his legs against her own. Greatly daring, she reached across and traced the line of his collarbone with her fingertips. He closed his eyes in pleasure and rolled on to his back. Encouraged, she leaned over and followed that line with her lips. At the same time, she let her hand wander across his chest, running her fingers through his springy hair and exploring the supple hardness of the skin beneath it.

When she gently kissed one of his nipples, he drew in a breath. She raised her head and looked at him.

"Did I do something wrong?"

"If you do this any more right, I'll probably die on the spot. But at least I'll die a happy man."

Reassured by his words, she went back to her exploring.

About the time she had reached his belly and was summoning the courage to adventure lower, he groaned aloud and gently pushed her questing hands away.

"As much as I love your touch, sweet Miranda," he said in a strained voice, "I made a pledge to you to go slow, and I'm not going to be able to hold to that promise much longer."

A part of her was greedy to know and feel everything as soon as possible. Another part of her, the part that was still worried about the physical reality of sharing her body with him and the possibility of experiencing pain, was reassured by his determination to abide by his promise.

"It's my turn now," he announced and reached for the hem of her nightdress. "Let's get this damn thing off you," and he urged her gently into a sitting position.

In one fluid motion, he skimmed the nightdress up and over her head. His gaze darkened as he looked at her.

"Sweet heaven, Miranda Kilpatrick, you're even prettier than I remembered."

The heat in his eyes made an answering heat warm her loins. He reached out and caressed her gently. They sank back into the pillows together, kissing as though they couldn't get enough of each other, their bodies twisting together, striving for the ultimate intimacy.

He stroked her gently until he caused a rush of warmth between her legs. As she clung to his shoulders, a coiled tension began to build inside her. Restlessly she shifted beneath his touch, wanting something, needing something more.

"Easy now, sweet Miranda," he whispered in her ear. Despite the dizzying waves of pleasure overwhelming her mind and her senses, she was aware of how much it was costing him to keep hold of his control. He rolled her beneath him and nudged her legs wide with his own. She felt him probing at her entrance, and suddenly her nervousness returned. She waited for the pain she knew most virgins had to endure, but the pain didn't come.

Instead, he entered her until he encountered the barrier of her maidenhead. Then he withdrew, and thrust shallowly again, and again. Miranda swallowed as her fear receded and the tension began to build in her once more. He rolled his hips and stroked her with his hand. The combined sensations were so pleasurable, she was almost surprised when he said suddenly, "This is where I have to hurt you, just a little, my sweet Miranda."

She nodded to show she was ready. Slowly, relentlessly, he pushed all the way into her and nipped her lip at the same time. It did hurt, a burning, stretching flash of pain; but then the burning subsided, and she was left with the overwhelming sensation of his filling her completely. He stayed still while her body grew accustomed to his. He leaned down and kissed her forehead.

She tensed when he moved, thinking surely it would hurt again, but it didn't—at least not much. With his second slow thrust, she realized she didn't hurt at all. And by the third, that wonderful tension had returned, and she longed to have him deeper inside her. He gripped her hips and showed her how to meet him.

"Miranda, I'm sorry, but I can't take this slow any longer," he ground out, and he began to drive into her with a wildness she welcomed. Soon she was raising her hips of her own accord, the tightness inside her making her wild as well. There was a place she needed to reach, a place where the sweet burning tension inside her would ease. She held on to Tobias for dear life, somehow knowing he would take her there.

She was almost past coherent thought when he reached down to stroke her a final time. She looked up at his harsh, rugged face. Their gazes met, and in that moment, she saw the fierce warrior within Tobias. His grim intensity almost frightened her. Then he smiled, his heart in his eyes, and she knew she never need fear him. Her body burst into flame beneath his touch. He thrust into her a final time, shoving her back against the pillows. He bent his head and kissed her, muffling both their cries as his big body convulsed, and he joined her in a joyous firestorm of sensation.

Tobias lay awake for a long time after Miranda's even breathing told him she was asleep. He considered blowing the lamp out, but he decided to keep it burning so that he could watch her lying beside him. She lay with her head on his shoulder, her hair spread in riotous abandon across the pillow. Her full lips were still swollen from his kisses. Toward the end, he'd gotten rougher than he meant, but she didn't seem to mind.

It didn't surprise him that Miranda had participated in the act of making love with her usual enthusiasm and generosity of spirit. Despite her lack of experience, she'd been remarkably adventurous—and determined to give back to him the pleasure he gave her. He was awed and frightened by how different it was to make love to a woman he cared for, rather than the faceless girls down on the row he'd gone to in the past when he needed release.

He knew making love to Miranda was a mistake. He knew from the moment she walked in his door that he should have forced her to walk right back out again. Now he had to add another wrong to the long list of wrongs he'd committed in his life. He had absolutely no right to take Miranda's innocence this night. It was no consolation knowing she had wanted him as badly as he had wanted her. Despite her occupation, Miranda was a decent woman, and she deserved to go to her husband on her wedding night a virgin. Knowing her honesty, she'd most likely tell a serious suitor she'd had a lover, and that would scare off more than a few of the God-fearing, proper kind of men she probably wanted to marry. She hadn't been thinking about that aspect of her future tonight, and selfishly he hadn't pointed it out to her.

He sighed and picked up a lock of her hair and rubbed it

between his fingers. He'd marry her in a moment because of what he'd taken from her tonight and because he was damn certain being with Miranda was the only way he'd ever be happy. In her company, he knew a kind of contentment he had never experienced before. But she had made it clear she had no interest in a gunfighter, retired or otherwise, courting her, and he had to respect her resolve.

Besides, he meant what he'd said earlier. He didn't give a wooden nickel for his chances of surviving more than a few years once word got out he was Jonah. He'd lost the edge one needed to be a good gun hand. He cared too much now about living, and he didn't want to kill anyone anymore. He wasn't willing to retreat back to the East. There were too many people, too many towns and cities for him. He belonged in a less settled place surrounded by plenty of wild country.

He let go of Miranda's hair and lay back on her pillows. She rolled over and cuddled up to him. His body stirred, aroused by her nearness, but he refrained from waking her. Along with doing her regular household chores, she'd waited on him all day, and she had to be worn out. Besides, he took remarkable pleasure from simply being with her like this. He never realized how wonderful it could be to lie with someone you loved. He'd spent a whole night with a whore once when he was too drunk to leave her bed, and the hollowness of the experience had haunted him afterward.

He dozed only a little, for he was determined to make the most of the only night he'd ever have with Miranda. Occasionally he looked at her father's pocket watch which she had placed on the bedside table for him. An hour before dawn he woke Miranda by kissing her softly beneath her ear. He was already hard, for he'd been thinking of every way and every place he wanted to touch her. That kind of thinking had made his body ache and pound with desire. Even though he wanted Miranda so much he felt ready to explode, he was determined to go slowly this time. Last night when they had come together, he had indulged his own reckless need. Now, this morning, he wanted to show her all the tenderness he could.

He kissed the line of her collarbone, relishing the smoothness of her skin and the womanly scent of her. When her eyes fluttered open, he gave her a long, lingering kiss on her lips. He pulled back to study her, hoping she wasn't regretting the choice she made last night.

"I believe that's the nicest way anyone's ever woken me up." She dispelled his fears with a warm smile.

"It's five o'clock. I figured you might want to leave before the boys were up and about."

"They won't be up for another hour or two."

"I figured that, too, just in case you were interested in a second helping of what we had last night."

"When the cook is as good as you, I'm always interested in another helping," she replied in a husky voice and reached her arms out to him.

But he was the one who feasted. He turned her gently on her stomach and sampled her just as he had promised himself, exploring every sweet, feminine inch of her. He kissed her back, the sides of her rib cage, the backs of her knees. He trailed his fingers across her and smoothed her with his palms, relishing her satiny skin. She soon became pliant beneath his touch. Her quick breaths and stifled moans told him how much she, too, enjoyed this sensual banquet.

At his urging, she lay once more upon her back, and he lavished the same care upon the front of her until she was gasping and twisting beneath his hands. No longer willing to remain passive, she reached up and touched him in the shy, passionate way that made his blood boil in his veins. When her hands ranged lower and closed around him, it took every ounce of his self-control not to take her right then. He'd promised himself he'd give Miranda tenderness, and for her sake he was damn well going to fulfill that promise.

But Miranda wouldn't allow him to go slowly any longer. She stroked him, kissing his chest and the base of his neck, and rubbed her legs against his own until he thought he would go wild. When he couldn't stand the delicious torment a moment longer, he gripped her hips and rolled her beneath him. Spreading her legs wide, he entered her with a single, swift plunge.

She welcomed him with a smile and a sigh even as her body welcomed him inside her. They stayed completely still for a long moment, gazing into each other's eyes and savoring the sensation of being completely joined.

"Dammit, Miranda, I'm not a gentle man, but I was trying to be gentle for you."

"When I want you to be gentle, I'll be letting you know," she countered, her Irish accent much stronger in her passion. She raised her hips, inviting him to move, and he obliged her. Within moments they were racing toward the top once more, Miranda urging him onward with her clever lips and hands and wild, wanton movements beneath him. He drove deep and fast, forgetting the past, forgetting the future, caring only about this woman and the incredible peace and pleasure she gave him.

She climaxed first, her body tightening around him. Her hands clutched at his shoulders, hurting his wound, but he hardly noticed. With his lips he muffled the cry she made, and then her shudders sent him over the edge. Miranda gave him ecstasy which spiraled on and on, taking him over the edge into dark, sensual oblivion.

They lay limp and panting while she stroked his cheek and kissed him gently, her glorious hair spread across his chest like a silken curtain. He gathered her closer with his good arm and relished the feel of her cuddled against him.

In that too-brief moment, he felt as if he had come home at last.

\* \* \*

The sky was just beginning to lighten in the east when Tobias strode into the barn to saddle Romeo. It was so cold, his breath made wreaths of mist about him as he walked.

He froze in his tracks when he heard the distinctive click of a shotgun being cocked. He turned about slowly to see Lucas peering at him from a shadowy corner of the barn. The old gambler wore only his union suit.

"What the hell are you doing out here?" Lucas asked as he lowered the shotgun. "The only company I'm expecting this time of day is Slaughter and his boys."

"I'm getting my horse and I'm heading back to my place," Tobias replied as he carefully hung the lantern he'd been carrying on a nearby hook. For once he took no pleasure from the familiar scents of hay and horse.

"Is that so?" The old man stood looking at him, his eyes narrowed. "Jesus, Mary and Joseph, it's cold as a witch's tit in this barn." He disappeared through a doorway. He returned a minute later, though, wearing woolen socks and a sheepskin jacket over his union suit.

"Did you and Miranda have a row?"

"Not exactly." Tobias slipped a saddle blanket onto Romeo's back.

"You mind me asking why you're so set on lighting a shuck out of here? Last I knew, you looked mighty happy up in her room letting her fuss over you and such."

"I expect I do mind," Tobias replied shortly as he walked from the stall to fetch his saddle.

"Hell, you bedded her," the old man said after a long moment and sat down on a hay bale.

"I didn't exactly force myself on her." Tobias felt compelled to defend himself. He winced at the burning pain in his shoulder as he picked up his saddle.

Lucas gave a dismissive wave of his hand. "I ain't blaming you. I ain't blaming her neither. The way the two of you look at each other, I'm surprised you waited this long. What I don't understand is why you've taken it into your head to leave her now."

"No good can come of it. No good can come of any of this." Ignoring the pain from his wound, he walked into the stall and hefted the saddle up onto Romeo's back.

"Ain't that a bit like closing the barn door after the stock's run off?"

"That isn't the only reason I'm leaving here. Until that marshal gets here on Tuesday, I figure it's my blood Slaughter's after. She'll be safer if I stay well away from her."

"I don't reckon he feels too kindly toward either of you. Well, I can tell when a feller's mind's made up, so I ain't going to waste my time trying to change it."

"Glad to hear it," Tobias said dryly as he tightened his cinch.

"She's going to be madder than a hornet when she finds you're gone."

Tobias took down Romeo's bridle and warmed the bit in his hands. "I know, and I'm sorry. But I'd rather have her mad at me than hurt her." He bridled the gelding and led him from the stall. Lucas was silent for a change while he watched him mount.

"You run into trouble, you know where to find me," the old man said suddenly.

"Likewise. I'm staying around until that marshal catches Slaughter or runs him off. Then I'll be moving on."

Lucas said nothing more, but Tobias thought his lined face looked old and weary in the lantern light. Feeling old and weary himself, he urged Romeo into a jog and headed off into the frozen winter morning.

# Chapter Eighteen

Somehow Miranda managed to get through the next few days. The first morning when she awoke in her own bed and realized Tobias was gone, she had indulged herself in a good, long cry. Then she had dried her eyes and decided to be furious at him instead. She wouldn't forgive him for making love with her and then riding away without even saying goodbye.

*But you were the one who asked him to make love to you,* she reminded herself as she scrubbed Rory's soiled overalls up and down a washboard. *He was only human to take what you offered.* Her cheeks burned when she remembered how bold she had been. Tobias had done his best to dissuade her, but she had gone ahead and thrown herself at him.

After the first day, she decided she was glad she had been so brazen. What they had shared was too remarkable, too magnificent, to regret. To think she might have gone a lifetime without sharing her body with Tobias and learning the joy that could be between a man and a woman—that would have been a real cause for sorrow.

When she started to think more clearly, she could see Tobias hadn't meant to reject her. He probably thought that by leaving, he could protect her heart. Lucas had told her he hoped to protect her from Slaughter as well.

Well, Tobias needn't have worried, she told herself staunchly. She cared for him. She probably even loved him, but the man wasn't going to break her heart. She wasn't going to let any man do that. She would carry on with her life and take what joy she could from the boys. Christmas was fast approaching, and she meant to give her nephews a wonderful holiday time. Already she was starting to make their presents and work on decorations and holiday baking when she had a free hour here and there.

But she was going to miss Tobias sorely. And after that night in her room, she now knew the beautiful intimacy a man and woman could create between them, and that made losing him even harder.

"If love could but erase both time and place." The line from Shakespeare had never seemed more apt to her. In another lifetime, they could have had such a good, happy life together. She knew she would never meet another man who could be the companion of her soul and make her body sing the way he had.

A wave of grief seized Miranda. She bowed her head, letting the tears fall into the washtub before her. She started when Christina appeared in the doorway directly across from her. Miranda had no time to hide the fact she'd been crying.

"I should go out and shoot that man myself," Christina announced, an unusually vindictive look in her sky blue eyes.

"You might be a bit outnumbered." Miranda wiped her eyes hastily on the back of her sleeve. "When that marshal gets here, he'll chase Slaughter all the way to Mexico."

"It's not that awful Slaughter who makes you cry," Christina said shrewdly.

Miranda decided there was no point in trying to dissemble

with her young friend. "Tobias never meant to hurt me. This is all my fault."

"It is always the man's fault," Christina replied, her face stony. "They only treat women well until they get what they want from them."

"Not all men are like that. Your father wasn't. You've told me how much he loved your mother. And I know for a fact Rob McGregor isn't. I've asked a dozen men who know him well, and they all say he treated his wife like gold until she died."

Christina snorted in disbelief. "Of course that is what other men would say. They all stand up for one another."

"Well, I'd ask the women in town about him, too, if I could, but none of them happen to be on speaking terms with me right now," Miranda countered ironically.

"You would be wasting your time. I will never let a man mean anything to me again. I do not know how we ended up talking about that foolish Rob McGregor." Christina shook her head. "I thought we were talking about you. You have been so good to me. I would do anything to keep you from being sad like this."

"Well, it makes me sad to see you turn your back on Rob." Miranda was determined to make the most of this opportunity. She could rarely get her young housekeeper to talk about such private matters. "You have a chance to build a fine life with a good man who loves you. I've seen the way he looks at you."

"*Ja*, he sees a pretty Swedish girl who would be good for a quick roll in the hay," Christina said bitterly.

"You wrong him when you say that," Miranda contradicted her levelly, "and I think you know it. I believe Rob McGregor is head over heels in love with you. Lord knows why, for as far as I can tell, you've never said more than two words to the poor man."

Christina clenched her hands, "I do not think you are a good person to talk to me about love. The only man you've looked at in a year will never make you happy.'' With that, she turned about and stormed from the kitchen.

Miranda stared after her young friend, afraid her words were only too true.

That night at the Shamrock all Miranda's patrons could talk about was the United States marshal who had just arrived in Pine Creek. As Miranda poured drinks, she learned the latest news. Marshal Nathaniel Holloway was heading out tomorrow with a posse of six experienced lawmen. Ben Slaughter, it seemed, had crossed the line by killing a local sheriff, and the governor of Colorado was determined that this elusive desperado and his gang would be brought to justice at last.

Miranda did her best to smile as her patrons congratulated her. Surely her troubles with the outlaw were over at last, they told her.

''Slaughter's going to be so busy running for Mexico, he ain't going to have time to take in the scenery,'' one cowpuncher from the Rafter Eight told another.

''Hell, Slaughter should go pick out a tombstone. Nathaniel Holloway always gets his man, and he ain't too particular about whether he brings them back dead or alive,'' his friend agreed.

And so the comments went. Try as she might, Miranda could only summon a dull sort of relief to know she didn't need to worry about Ben Slaughter any longer. With the threat from Slaughter gone, Tobias would go, too. She wondered painfully if he would stop by to say goodbye, or if he would just slip away.

Just before she started to perform her first set of the evening, the famous marshal walked into the Shamrock and ordered a whisky. A big man with shoulder-length black hair and cool blue eyes, Holloway looked more like a desperado to Miranda than a lawman.

''This is on the house,'' she told him when he tried to pay

for his drink. "It's going to be a real relief to have Ben Slaughter back behind bars."

"Thank you, ma'am," he responded politely enough, but the remote look in his eyes reminded her painfully of Tobias. She slipped away from him as soon as she could and went backstage to change. The marshal stayed throughout her first set, but left soon after.

When she stepped out from behind the velvet curtains to perform her second set of songs for the night, she was stunned to see Tobias sitting at a table right before the stage. Instead of his somber gray schoolmaster suit, he wore a plaid shirt, jeans, a leather vest, and a worn black cowboy hat. That hat was so worn, in fact, she wondered with a little shiver if Jonah had worn that hat seven years ago.

She was startled to see he wasn't wearing his spectacles. It was the first time she'd seen him in a public place without them. Without his suit and spectacles, he no longer looked like an eastern scholar. In fact, he appeared to be a thoroughly western man—larger and more intimidating than most. While the men about him laughed and talked, Tobias sat by himself, his face still and set. His gaze widened when he took in her stage costume, and his expression hardened.

Her chin went up. It was hardly any of his business what she wore when she performed. She sent her brightest smile to the room in general and gave Otis a nod to show she was ready.

She launched into the first verse of "Ta-ra-ra Boom-de-ay," and did the flouncy dance steps which she always performed with this song. About the time she picked up her skirts to show off her ankles, Tobias looked absolutely furious. Just to irritate him, she lifted her skirts an inch higher the next time she twirled around.

Her mind raced ahead. "Drink To Me Only With Thine Eyes" was the fourth song in this set. Now she wished she had never incorporated the song into her act. But if she went to the edge of the stage to tell Otis not to play it, she was afraid

Tobias would guess she had made a change in her song selection because of him. She certainly didn't want him to think his being here tonight had any effect on her at all.

She did her best to ignore his glowering presence and put her heart and soul into the set. When Otis played the opening notes to "Drink To Me Only With Thine Eyes," her heart tightened, and she faltered a little on the first verse. She didn't look at Tobias—she daren't look at him. The song instantly took her back to that night when they had sat together on her piano bench, longing and desire setting their hearts and senses afire. Somehow she made it through the piece, making her voice an outlet for the sadness and regret welling up inside her. After she finished, the saloon was completely hushed. She chanced one quick peek at Tobias. He was staring down at the table top before him.

She quickly nodded to Otis, and he launched into the spirited opening to another bawdy bar song. She finished the show with the popular and humorous song, "Cindy," which she performed with lots of pantomime to make it more amusing. Her audience roared with laughter as they always did, even men who had seen her perform the song fifty times.

When she gave her final curtsey, every man in the saloon leapt to his feet and gave her a standing ovation, every man except Tobias, that was. She watched him drain his whisky and slam the glass on the table. Without a look in her direction, he stalked out of the saloon. Miranda hid the fact her heart felt as if it were splintering into jagged shards. With a laugh and a smile, she went on to perform two more encores.


Rob McGregor stopped by Miranda's place the next after-noon.

"Hello, Mr. McGregor," Miranda greeted him with a warm smile. "It's always nice to see you, but if you've come to visit with Mr. Johnston, I'm afraid you've come to the wrong place. He isn't staying with us any longer.''

''Actually, I just saw him over at his cabin,'' Rob McGregor said, ''and I figured you might want to know he's got it all packed up. Not that he had all that much to pack in the first place, mind you, but he told me he was planning to leave town first thing tomorrow.''

Even though she had been expecting this news, she still felt as if she'd been punched in the stomach. ''I see,'' she managed to say. ''Thank you for coming by to tell me. Do you, would you like to speak with Miss Erickson? She's in the kitchen right now.''

*Tobias is going away. Tobias is going away. And you know he's never coming back.* The litany replayed itself in Miranda's mind, making it almost impossible for her to think, much less have a coherent conversation with Rob McGregor.

''Why, thank you, ma'am, I believe I would,'' he said, his brown eyes warm with unspoken sympathy. He stepped inside and made a beeline for the kitchen. Miranda remained in the front parlor, staring out the window and trying to come to terms with the news the rancher had brought her.

Rob McGregor walked quietly through the house. He found Christina in the kitchen kneading bread. He smiled to himself. Her hands and forearms were covered with flour, and she even had a streak of it across her nose. She hummed under her breath as she worked the dough vigorously on the kitchen table. He leaned against the doorway, content to simply watch her. He had too few chances to see her like this, relaxed and happy.

The moment she sensed his presence, she whirled about to face him. He thought for one brief, unguarded moment she actually looked pleased, but then her expression grew wary. He could almost see the walls spring up around her. He sighed to himself. Why was he so attracted to this prickly young woman? It was more than Christina's pretty face that made him stop by Miranda Kilpatrick's place whenever he could.

Beneath the sullenness she showed him and the rest of the world, he sensed Christina was a warmhearted girl. He had seen the loving care and affection she lavished on Sean and Rory. He knew she had a sense of humor. Despite her efforts not to smile, he could tell she had been amused by the tall tales he spun for her.

He thought she'd even been touched the times he had told her about himself. Over the past few weeks he'd spent hours talking to her, hoping that if he shared his hopes and dreams, she would come to know and trust him. He'd told himself it didn't matter that she said very little in return. It took time to gentle a wild mare, or a mare who had been abused and used cruelly.

"Well, you surely are a fetching sight today, Miss Erickson," he declared.

She grimaced in disbelief at his comment and went back to her kneading. Rob sauntered into the kitchen. He didn't miss the way her shoulders tightened when he drew closer. He stopped abruptly, shoved his hands in his pockets, and swore to himself. Maybe he'd been fooling himself. Maybe he never would be able to get her to trust him.

He moved back to give her more space and leaned against the dry sink.

"Did I ever tell you the story of the time my grandma made biscuits so hard they broke my grandpa's teeth?"

"No," she said shortly, "you did not." She took a deep breath and met his eyes directly. "I do not wish to hear this story. I do not wish to hear any more of your stories. I have made up my mind. Tell Miranda goodbye, and come around to the barn in a half hour. I will meet you in the hayloft. There I will give you what you want, and then maybe you will leave me in peace."

Burning anger flashed through him. It must have shown in

his expression, for although he made no movement toward her, she stepped back a pace. He waited until he could trust his voice.

"I told you before I wanted more than that from you. I'm sorry you won't believe me. I'm sorry that Nolan fellow served you such a bad turn. But someday if you want any sort of life, you're going to have to start trusting folks again. I had hoped you might be able to bring yourself to trust me, but I guess I was fooling myself."

She stared back at him, her blue eyes filling with tears. Even now, when he was so furious with her, he ached to reach out and offer her comfort. Calling himself ten thousand times a fool, he kept his hands to himself. "I'll go say goodbye to Miss Kilpatrick, and I'll leave you in peace just like you want."

With that, he turned on his heel and stalked toward the door.

Miranda was still standing in the parlor when Rob McGregor came striding past. Despite her own turmoil over the news that Tobias was leaving, she was still surprised and disappointed for Christina's sake to see Rob departing so soon. Usually his visits with Christina lasted a good hour or more.

"Mr. McGregor, are you sure you can't stay any longer? I know Miss Erickson doesn't give you much encouragement, but I think she enjoys your visits."

Rob McGregor paused, his hand on the handle of the front door. "With all due respect, Miss Kilpatrick, you are dead wrong about that," he said, his brown eyes bleak. "She made it pretty clear today that I've been wasting my time and hers. I'm sure sorry about that, because she's the first gal to make me feel alive since my sweet Sue died. But I reckon even a stubborn gent like me gets the message eventually. I won't be troubling her anymore." With that, he yanked the door open, clapped his hat on his head, and headed down the porch steps.

When Miranda closed the door behind him and turned about,

she saw Christina standing in the hallway, a stricken look in her blue eyes.

"I guess we've both lost whatever chance we had to be happy," Miranda told her quietly, and climbed up the stairs.

*Tobias is going away. Tobias is going away.* She paced back and forth across her bedroom, unable to escape the despair those words caused her. Damn that man for making her feel this way. She couldn't live with this sort of pain. Yet she had known this moment would come, ever since she had found out he was Jonah. She knew from the start she could never have him. So why was it so hard to accept it?

*Because you didn't even have a chance to say goodbye to him.* Miranda stopped dead in her tracks as she considered a possible solution. If she went to say goodbye to him, surely this pain would lessen. She would exorcise his ghost before it ever began to haunt her.

Before she could change her mind, she put on a warm sweater. She hurried downstairs to find Christina. The girl's eyes were suspiciously bright when Miranda found her in the kitchen making supper for the boys. Miranda promised herself she would talk with Christina later about Rob McGregor's announcement. She asked her to keep on eye on Rory and Sean until she returned.

"Where are you headed in a such a hurry, missy?" Lucas asked her when he emerged from his room in the barn and found Miranda saddling up Lady Luck.

"I'm riding over to Tobias's place to say goodbye. He's leaving town in the morning."

"I see," the old man said thoughtfully and brought her Lady's bridle.

"I reckon you don't much want my company," he said after a few moments, "but I ain't sure it's safe for you to go anywhere's alone until that Holloway feller brings Slaughter in."

"Surely Slaughter is miles away from here by now. He'd

have to be crazy to stay near Pine Creek with that marshal and his men after him.''

''Somehow I got a feelin' in my bones that our dealings with that murderin' snake ain't over yet.''

''I'll take my Spencer, then, and I promise I'll keep a sharp eye out for trouble. But I need to see Tobias on my own.'' Her voice almost broke. Tobias was going away, and she had to see him alone one last time.

Lucas searched her face. What he saw in her eyes must have convinced him. ''All right,'' he said gruffly and looked away. ''But make sure you're back by dark, or I'm goin' to come looking for you.''

Once again as she made the trip to Tobias's cabin, Miranda found herself rehearsing what she wanted to say to him. She wasn't going to apologize for her stage costume last night, the songs she sang, or the way she performed them. She had already told him why she sang at her saloon. He must have guessed what her performance would be like if he'd ever taken in a saloon act before. If seeing her sing and dance before a crowd of rowdy men was going to bother him so, he never should have come.

She did want to tell him to be careful, that he mattered, that someday he could make a happy, contented life for himself. She wanted to tell him that she cared, and that she would miss him sorely. Somehow when she came face-to-face with him, she would find some way to put these sentiments into words.

Tobias opened the door to the cabin and stepped outside just after she rode up. Her treacherous heart leapt at the sight of his handsome face and his golden brown hair shining in the afternoon sun. He stood by Lady's head and held her reins as Miranda dismounted. She stood staring blankly at her saddle, wondering why all the carefully prepared speeches she had made up on the way over here had suddenly fled her mind. When she finally summoned the courage to turn and meet his gaze, his expression was unreadable.

"I'm glad you came," he said simply.

"You are?"

"I was going to ride by your place in the morning to say goodbye, and to ask you for a favor."

So he wasn't going to ride away and leave her without saying goodbye. That softened the hard shell of hurt around her heart a little. "What can we do for you?" she asked, wondering what he could possibly want. He had never asked her for anything before.

"I was hoping you might look after my books. I thought I'd officially put them into Sean's keeping. I don't expect to have any place for them for some time, and this way he can keep up with his reading. If and when I do get settled, I'll send for them."

"We'd love to look after your books," she said, fiercely glad to have even the illusion that she might hear from him again. "Sean will be so pleased and honored that you would trust him with them."

Only slowly did a more sobering interpretation of his request dawn on her. Perhaps he wanted Sean to have his books because he didn't think he'd live long enough to need them again. That notion made her stomach twist in fear for him.

"Do you want to come inside? You took me to task for my poor hospitality at the start of your last visit, and I'd hate to fall short in your eyes a second time."

Miranda blushed when she remembered the angry way she had sniped at him, and what had happened between them after. She took refuge in making conversation while he opened the door and let her precede him inside.

"I'm surprised you're not still angry with me. You looked furious when you left the Shamrock last night."

"I know," he said with a grim smile. "I wanted to punch every slavering fool in that place just for looking at you. By this morning, though, I'd cooled off some, and I realized I don't have the right to be angry about what you wear or how you act on that stage." He pulled the rocker closer to the stove and gestured for her to have a seat.

Miranda stared at him after she sat down. The man never ceased to surprise her.

"I am sorry that you have to do it night after night to provide for your family," he said as he poured them two cups of coffee from the pot on the stove. "It looked like damn hard work to me, and the fellow next to me said you perform like that two or three times a night. Running that whole business is a mighty big job."

"It is," she admitted and took the cup he handed to her. "I'd be lost without Lucas and Otis."

"I'm sure they help, but I know you'd find a way to get by without them. I've said it before, but I mean it even more after seeing you work last evening. You are a remarkable woman, Miranda Kilpatrick."

"Thank you, Tobias Johnston," she told him quietly. She wanted to tell him once again how remarkable she thought he was for trying to change his life, but she was afraid she would just embarrass him. Instead, she sipped the coffee and then set it down on the table. "How is your shoulder?"

"Doc Wheeler says it's healing up just fine."

"I'm glad to hear that. Will you try to find another teaching position after you leave Pine Creek?" She was proud of how steady her voice sounded.

"I'm not sure. I'm afraid my reputation as Jonah will follow me wherever I go. I'd hate to get settled in a new town, start getting to know a new set of students, and then have to leave." He ran his fingers around the edge of his coffee cup. "I didn't realize how much I was going to miss my Pine Creek pupils. Between Reynolds and the fine citizens on the school board, I never even had a chance to say goodbye to my students here."

She reached out and laid her hand over his. "I'm so sorry. You mustn't give up on your teaching. You're the first one who made Sean really care about school. You've a gift for teaching young ones, and it would be such a shame if you wasted it.''

Tobias stared at her hand lying atop his own. Miranda started to pull her hand back, but he covered it with his left hand and gripped it hard.

"Why did you come here today?" he asked, his head still bowed.

Her cheeks warmed. "Rob McGregor rode by to tell me you were leaving. I-I couldn't take the chance you wouldn't say goodbye to me before you left.''

"All I've thought about for the last three days is what it felt like to have you in my arms. All I've dreamed about is what happened between us three nights ago." He lifted his head slowly. A shudder ran through her when she saw a familiar light blazing in his gray eyes.

"I thought I could keep from touching you if I asked you in," he admitted harshly, "but I was lying to myself. I won't lie to you. If you want to leave, leave now. Otherwise, we're both going to end up in my bed, and I'm going to touch a whole lot more than just this pretty hand of yours.''

The indignant protest she was about to make died on her lips. All at once, she realized why she had ridden over to see him. It would be easier to face a whole lifetime without Tobias if they could make love together just one more time. With her hands, her lips and her body she could tell him farewell in a way she could never put into words.

There was no point in being coy. They had only four hours before dark, and they had already wasted ten precious minutes. Her answer in her eyes, she leaned over and kissed him full on the lips. She felt a quiver go through him, and then his hands closed on her shoulders and he drew her gently to her feet.

"Sweet Miranda," he sighed against her lips, and he kissed her with a gentleness he'd never shown her before. He smoothed his hands down her arms and up her back, as if he savored every moment of touching her, making her feel precious and fragile. Her arms went around him, and once again that comforting sense of coming home overwhelmed her. Tobias was meant to be her rock, her foundation, her center. And yet he was leaving in the morning.

She blinked when he pulled her more tightly against him. Despite the chasteness of his kiss, it was clear he was more than ready to make love to her, and another little tremor shot through her. Would any man ever want her, would any man ever need her, the way Tobias did?

Boldly, she deepened the kiss, nipping at his lower lip, encouraging him to taste her more fully. With a groan, he obliged her, plundering her mouth with his own and molding her closer to him. She ran her fingers through his hair and pressed herself shamelessly against him, the hunger inside her building so quickly she was breathless with it.

Impatiently she tugged at the buttons to his shirt, wanting to shed the unwelcome barriers between them. He helped her, undoing the last buttons and pushing the sleeves down his arms. At last she could touch and taste him to her heart's content. He still wore a white bandage on his left shoulder. He stood completely still as she trailed her fingers beneath the lower edge of the bandage and across his rib cage, fascinated by the strong male lines of him. She leaned forward and feathered kisses across his chest. His body was warm, his skin supple, the hair she encountered surprisingly soft. He smelled like wood smoke and horse and the freshness of outdoors. The rapid rise and fall of his chest was the only sign of how much her touch affected him.

Because she wanted to please him, and because she knew this would be their last time together, she found the courage to let her hand drift lower.

He closed his eyes, and his hands clenched into fists when she slipped her fingers underneath the band of his jeans and stroked him gently. He was such a fascinating combination of soft and hard.

"Woman, are you trying to drive me mad?"

"Could I?" she asked, intrigued by the idea of driving the controlled Tobias Johnston to the brink.

"There are days I think you already have." He opened his eyes and looked down at her, his expression somber. But then he added in a lighter tone, "What's good for the gander is good for the goose."

She started to tell him that he had the phrase backward, but he was kissing her so fiercely, she couldn't draw breath to say anything. He made quick work of the buttons on her dress and skimmed it off her. She was still clad in her petticoats, drawers and chemise when he lifted her up on the side of the bed and pulled her knees wide. He knelt between them and shoved her petticoats up about her waist.

"Tobias," she said uncertainly, for there was a look in his eyes she didn't quite trust.

"Sh, now, I've dreamed of doing this for months now. If you don't like it, you can tell me to stop."

There was that promise again. So far, he hadn't done a thing to her she hadn't liked. She started to relax when all he did at first was kiss her lips and rub his hands gently along her legs. Her eyes focused on the square of light where the afternoon sun flooded through the only window. The little cabin was completely silent except for the sound of logs settling in the stove. He kissed the base of her neck and the sensitive skin beneath her ear, causing her to squirm away from him.

"That tickles," she explained breathlessly.

"Hmm. Let's see if this tickles as well."

She was startled when he bent his head and kissed the skin of her inner thigh through the slit in her drawers. When he moved to taste and lave the very center of her, she had to grab on to his shoulders, for the sensations mounting inside her were overwhelming. Although she had overheard the prostitutes at

Johnny Nolan's place talking about such acts, she never dreamed they could feel so wonderful. She never dreamed she would know a man willing to give her such pleasure. She closed her eyes and surrendered to his touch.

"Tobias," she said urgently sometime later, for she was nearing the edge, and the intensity of the feelings he aroused in her were almost frightening now.

"Sh, now, sweetheart, just relax and let it happen."

And it did happen, that amazing, exquisite burst of sensation that seemed to go on and on, and it was delicious and sinful and sensuous all at once. While she collapsed back on the bed, panting and amazed, Tobias stripped off his jeans and socks. When he came to kneel beside her on the bed, she took one look at his set face and the intent expression in his eyes, and the coil of tension began to build inside her all over again.

She wondered if he wanted her to take off the rest of her clothes, but then it became obvious he wasn't in a mood to wait. None too gently, he shifted her legs until she was lying lengthways upon the bed, and then he knelt between them.

He held her hips and entered her with a single, strong thrust. She gasped, and her body closed welcomingly around him. He stayed absolutely still for a long moment. He leaned down and pressed a searing kiss on her lips. Then he began to plunge into her again and again. Her boneless body came to life, catching his rhythm and matching it. She was astonished to feel the need flooding back, more intense than before. She writhed beneath him, pushing her hips up to meet him, locking her legs around his back so that he could enter her more fully.

Soon the sweet tension inside her coiled so tight, she thought she might die of it. He must have sensed she was close, for he looked down at her and said hoarsely, "Come with me."

He lifted her hips and drove into her a final time, and she shattered into a thousand brilliant pieces. Dimly she was aware that he called out her name as he shuddered and filled her with himself. And then he collapsed on top of her, still careful to keep a part of his weight on his elbows.

They lay with their bodies joined while their breathing steadied and their hearts stopped racing in their chests.

"I must be crushing you," he said after a long time and started to shift away from her.

"Oh, no, this feels just right." She stopped him by wrapping her arms around his body, and then he relaxed against her. She sighed contentedly. It was odd how the weight of a man could feel so good and natural. By all rights, Tobias probably should be crushing her, but having him surround her like this was wonderful. The Good Lord must have known what he was about when he fashioned men and women. Miranda blushed. 'Twas a shocking business, to be thinking of her maker at such a time.

After a few moments' reflection, she decided it wasn't surprising her thoughts turned to the divine after such an experience. Tobias had shown her a sort of ecstasy she never dreamed existed. He had given her a piece of heaven, and even though she might never see him again, she was grateful that he had taught her what joy two lovers could share with each other.

"A penny for your thoughts. They must be interesting since you just blushed head to toe again." His chuckle sounded like thunder in his chest.

"It's not fair that I'm so fair skinned. I can never tell when you're embarrassed."

"Perhaps I'm never embarrassed," he suggested with a raised brow.

She snorted at that. "Then you, Mr. Tobias Johnston, aren't human."

"I'm human, all right. Human enough that I need you and want you far more than I should." He held her shoulders and rolled her on top of him. After the first startled moment, she decided she rather liked her new perspective. She rarely had a chance to look down at him.

From just about any viewpoint, she had to conclude Tobias Johnston was a fine-looking man. She loved the strong planes of his face, and the stubborn set to his jaw. Right now, when he was relaxed and content, his eyes were soft silver gray, the color of pussy willows in the spring. She smiled to herself. That was one comparison she was definitely going to have to keep to herself. His hair had grown longer since he first arrived in town, and now it fell down over his forehead, softening his features and making him look younger.

She was so busy admiring him, she was slow to realize his clever fingers were busy undoing the ties to her petticoats. She took notice about the time he tugged them off her.

"It occurs to me that one of us is overdressed for this social occasion," he offered by way of explanation.

"And whose fault is that?" she asked him indignantly.

"It's all yours. If you weren't such a tempting witch, I might have been polite enough to undress you first."

"I'm glad you didn't take the time to be polite," she declared. It was true. There was something deeply stirring about the fact that he had wanted her with such urgency.

"Miranda Kilpatrick, you are a woman in a million," he said with one of his slow smiles.

"Because I let you make love to me while I still had my petticoats on?" she asked him quizzically.

"Because you are direct, and honest, and sincere, and a hundred other wonderful things I had forgotten women could be."

"For a quiet man, you surely have a gift for blarney, Mr. Johnston."

"Not to mention persistence and endurance," he said with a smug look and tugged her chemise up around her shoulders.

Miranda laughed aloud, delighted at this light, teasing side to him she had so rarely had a chance to see. He pushed her gently upright, and then he skimmed the chemise up and over her head. She stopped laughing when she saw his smoldering look return.

His big hands moved up her rib cage, just grazing the sides of her breasts, and down her back, raising little shivers wherever he touched. He teased the tips of her breasts, touching them with his fingertips until they puckered and a fresh rush of pleasure shot all the way through her.

He raised himself up on his elbows and kissed her, pulling her nipples between his lips, razing her gently between his teeth until she moaned aloud. He cupped her buttocks, lifting her and then helping her slip the drawers down her legs, and finally she was as gloriously naked as he.

She was surprised when he urged her back to the position where she had been sitting, straddling his thighs. She was delighted that he clearly meant to make love to her again, but she rather thought she was supposed to be on her back for that to happen.

"You can stay right where you are if you want," he said when she shifted uncertainly.

"I can?" she asked, curiosity and shock warring with one another. How naive she must seem to him, especially for a woman who ran a saloon.

His lips curled in a wide smile. "Miranda Kilpatrick, I don't believe I could ever grow tired of seeing you blush."

*But he isn't going to have a chance to grow tired of you blushing, or you for that matter. Neither of us is going to have a chance to learn if we would ever become bored with each other. Tobias is leaving in the morning.*

Miranda stilled the treacherous thought. This moment was too important, this time together too precious, to let anything, including her fear of the pain to come, spoil it. Instead, she decided to concentrate on the fascinating suggestion he had just made.

"Is it possible—I mean, is it just as pleasurable for you this way?" Sweet St. Agnes, she could feel another wave of warmth tingling her skin. If only she could talk about these matters with a little more composure. She was grateful when he didn't laugh at her.

Instead, he merely smiled and said, "I figure a strong-willed woman like yourself might well fancy this way. It's like taking the reins and setting whatever pace you want."

She had to admit that notion sounded mighty appealing, especially when he shifted and she felt him warm and hard between her legs, and his magical hands began to caress her once more.

Tobias was absolutely right. She discovered that she did like taking the reins and setting the pace. In this position, he filled and stretched her deliciously. At first she felt a little clumsy; but he showed her how to move, and her own body sensed the rest. Soon they were moving together in wanton harmony, driving and pushing each other onward.

Miranda had never felt more free and pagan than when her body suddenly convulsed about him, sending wave after exultant wave through her. She collapsed panting on his chest moments later, dazed and pleased that once again he had given her such an amazing experience. Tenderly he stroked her hair and kissed her cheek. Only slowly did she sense the tension in him.

She lifted her head from his chest and searched his face. "I was right. That wasn't as pleasant for you as it was for me," she said sadly.

"It was plenty pleasant," he got out in a strained voice, "believe me. I liked watching you. I just haven't gone where you went yet."

"What do I need to do?" she asked him shyly.

"Have you got your breath back now?"

She nodded. "Well then, just keep moving the way you were earlier." He gripped her hips and showed her. She raised up and lowered herself slowly. He closed his eyes and said in a tight voice, "This won't take long."

But she made it take a long time, for she discovered the pleasure of watching her lover nearing the edge. Again and again she rocked against him, driving him almost to the peak and then stopping. At last Tobias could take no more. Holding tight to her hips, he bucked beneath her, his big body shuddering as he cried out her name and climaxed. Miranda smiled as she gazed at him, fiercely glad that she could give back a little of what he had given her so generously.

Afterward they rested, but neither wanted to lose precious time sleeping. Instead they talked and touched and kissed in the quiet little cabin and wished the minutes would slip by more slowly.

"Where did you get this quilt?" she asked him, fingering the lovely fabric and admiring the fine needlework in it.

"My mother made it and gave it to one of our neighbors back in Kansas. After my mother died, the woman thought I should have it, so she gave it to me."

"And you've managed to keep it with you all these years." Miranda smiled at the notion of the notorious Jonah packing a wedding ring quilt in his bedroll. "Tobias Johnston, I think you are sentimental deep down inside."

"This quilt's as warm as most blankets and a damn sight lighter."

"I'm glad you still have it. You'll always have a little piece of your mother."

"I still have my father's Bible and his prayer book, too. They were at his church the night our house burned."

His gaze darkened the way it always did when he spoke of his past. Miranda asked him quickly, "Is he the one who taught you to love books?"

She was relieved when she saw his expression lighten. If only Tobias could learn to remember the best parts of his parents rather than dwelling on the cruel way they died.

"He used to read to us by the hour," Tobias said with a faraway look in his eyes, "and not just from the Bible. He read

Shakespeare and Tennyson and Sir Walter Scott. I can still hear his voice. He could make Deuteronomy or Kings sound like the most dramatic tale in the world.''

Miranda propped her head up on her hand and looked down at him while she traced patterns on his chest idly with her fingertips. ''That's what my da could do, too. Whenever he opened a book for us, it was as if we all were starting off on a great adventure together.''

''Tell me about your mother. You don't speak of her as often as you do your father.''

Miranda sighed and moved away to lie on her back. ''She was a kind, motherly soul. She wasn't as talkative or charming as my da, but she was three times as strong inside. I don't speak of her as often, for a part of me still blames her for their early deaths. It's not fair of me, I know, for she had a right to follow her dream. It was bad luck, mostly, that they started farming just before a long drought hit that part of Nebraska. I'm just sorry that she and my father could never be happy together because their dreams were so different.

''She wasn't a brilliant sort of a woman, but she was a loving one. She was always going out of the way to help those less fortunate than us.''

''I see where you got your loving heart.'' Tobias caressed her cheek tenderly. ''I'm sorry I never had a chance to meet your parents. I think they would be proud of the way you've been caring for their grandchildren.''

''I'm not so sure of that,'' she voiced a fear that she had never shared with anyone. It had haunted her since she first took over the Shamrock. Although her parents had been more open-minded than many folk, she had often wondered and worried what they would have thought of her selling spirits and running a saloon.

''I'm sure. Sean and Rory are turning out to be fine boys, and that's because you've provided them with love and discipline. You should always take pride in the way you've raised them, no matter how the citizens of Pine Creek treat you." He leaned over and kissed the place on her cheekbone where he had just touched her with his hand. She turned toward him, offering her lips instead.

*How can I live without him, when he knows exactly the words I need to hear, when he understands me in a way no one else does?*

This time they came together slowly, the first rush of urgency past. Heat still built quickly between them, but they both kept it banked while they took the time to explore and cherish, learning each other's bodies and storing up memories which would have to last them a lifetime. Toward the end, when the blazing heat consumed them both, he slung her heels over his shoulders. He pounded so hard into the center of her, she thought she was branded with the fire of him forever. When it was over, they both were quiet for a long time, holding each other close.

"I may regret most of all not having a chance to see you perform again," he surprised her by saying suddenly.

"You looked so angry, I didn't think you liked any of my act last night."

"Oh, I liked it all right. There was one part of me that liked it too much. That's a good part of the reason why I stormed out of there. I figured if I was getting all steamed up watching you, the rest of the gents in the room must be getting randy, too, and that notion made me just about loco."

"Well, you were the only one in that room who can make me feel randy," she told him saucily, but he just looked at her, the bleakness in his gaze betraying the fact he was thinking of tomorrow once again.

To chase away the shadows in his eyes, she decided it was time to do something outrageous. She slipped from the bed and retrieved her chemise from the pile of her undergarments beside the bed. Wearing only that, she proceeded to give him a spirited rendition of "Ta-ra-ra Boom-de-ay," complete with dance steps, until he laughed aloud. He scooped her up and tossed her back on the bed. After he pulled the covers back over them both, she quickly twined her legs with his.

"Woman, your feet are frozen," he said with a wince. "Don't you know better than to dance half-naked and barefoot in a drafty cabin?"

"True actors never turn down a chance to perform before an appreciative audience," she informed him loftily. "Besides, I'm counting on you to warm me up again."

"I would be happy to be of service." And for a final time, warm her through and through he did.

The sun was nearing the horizon when Miranda stirred in his arms. She reached out and traced her fingers across his cheek. It was rough with stubble. "I have to go," she said, regret making her voice go tight. "Lucas is going to come looking for me if I'm not back by dark."

He closed his eyes. When he opened them again, she saw resignation along with a grief that made her breath catch in her throat. "All right," he said quietly. He kissed her on the forehead and then slipped from the bed and began putting on his clothes. All too soon they both were dressed.

"I'll ride back with you," he said in such an uncompromising tone, she knew there would be no use in arguing with him. Deep in her heart, she was glad to be able to put off their final parting for another hour.

On the way back to her house they talked of small things, neither one wanting to speak of the separation to come. Miranda knew she would never forget that ride through the clear winter dusk, the setting sun turning the snow-covered ranges in the distance brilliant orange and then fiery pink. The cold burned her cheeks and chilled her toes while she listened to Tobias's rich voice and treasured the last moments she would have in his company.

She glanced over at him from time to time, trying to impress his features upon her memory so that she would never forget what he looked like. She loved his thick brown eyebrows, his clear gray eyes, his rugged cheekbones and strong, uncompromising jaw. Her gaze lingered on his well-formed mouth. There, and in his eyes, she saw the sensitivity and the kindness that he had learned to hide from the world.

A little tremor went through her as she remembered the way he had worshipped her with his lips less than an hour ago. No man's face would ever stir her; no one's soul could ever be so dear. Tobias, her friend and her lover, was leaving in the morning, and from somewhere she would find the strength to go on.

When they rode into her barnyard, she stiffened her back. She was a Kilpatrick, she had her pride, and she would not embarrass them both with tears. She was so busy trying to control the grief threatening to tear her apart, she was a second slow in realizing that her house looked too dark, the barnyard too still.

Just as she was about to tell Tobias something must be wrong, the barn door slid open. Ben Slaughter stood in the opening grinning at them both, a rifle aimed at Tobias's heart.

# Chapter Nineteen

Miranda's throat went dry. The cruel, gloating look in Slaughter's one good eye made her heart pound in her chest. Briefly she considered reaching for the rifle in the sheath slung beside her saddle. But she was no gunfighter. Slaughter could shoot her and Tobias before she could get a shot off. The outlaw wouldn't hesitate to kill them both. He had a score to settle. The fact he had taken the risk of staying in Pine Creek when a U.S. marshal was after him showed just how much Slaughter wanted to even that score.

She glanced over at Tobias. His face was cold and remote. He didn't look afraid. He looked like a man who was thinking hard. Miranda tried to draw some comfort from that fact. In her heart she feared Tobias wouldn't be able to save her this final time. Their luck had run out. Now he was going to pay with his life for trying to help her.

Tobias glanced over at her. "I'm sorry," he whispered to her, a world of regret in his eyes.

"I'm the one who's sorry," she said fiercely. "I never should have let you get involved in any of this."

"Surprised to see me, ain't ya, Jonah?" They both turned to look at the outlaw. "Well, old Ben Slaughter is crazy like a fox." He leaned over and spat into the packed snow of the barnyard. "Hell, the best place to hide is always in plain sight. Folks were so sure that Pine Creek is the last place I'd be, I figured I could stick around and take care of a little unfinished business.

"Come on out and join the party, boys," he raised his voice. Moments later, Tyrel Reynolds rode out of the barn leading a horse with Christina bound and gagged on its back. Her blue eyes were wide with fear, her face paper white.

Miranda bit back a cry. Five more of Slaughter's men appeared from their hiding places about the barnyard, their guns all drawn and pointed at Tobias. One of them rode close enough to pull the Spencer from its sheath on her saddle. The wariness on their faces, despite the fact they were facing an unarmed man, made her realize with new clarity the formidable reputation Tobias must have had back in the days he was Jonah.

"Where are my nephews? Where's Lucas?" Miranda couldn't keep her voice from trembling. She was too frightened for them all.

"That old fool decided to put up a fight," Slaughter said, "so we had to kill him. You don't need to worry about those boys, though. I've always had a soft spot for a tough boy, and that Sean of yours is a real hellion. We just trussed them up like turkeys and left 'em inside the house."

Slaughter's tone had softened slightly when he spoke of the boys, but the cruelty returned when he walked over to Christina and stroked her thigh. "We ain't had this pretty little house-keeper of yours yet neither. We was all just about to have some real fun with her when you two rode up. Now we'll just have our fun with both of you gals later back at our hideout."

"Take me instead of the women," Tobias spoke up for the first time, "and I'll go without a fight."

Slaughter burst into a loud guffaw. "You hear that, boys? The great Jonah says he'll go peaceably. Well, from where I'm standing, you don't look so great, and you sure as hell don't have a damn thing to bargain with, you stupid son of a bitch. You are plumb out of aces."

Suddenly Tobias sent Romeo leaping forward, running straight at Ben Slaughter.

The big outlaw paled, but he kept his head long enough to fire. Tobias jerked in his saddle. He kept his seat and charged right at his enemy. Slaughter started to run toward the barn, but other guns exploded from all around the barnyard. Tobias toppled from the saddle and fell heavily. He lay still, face first on the ground.

Romeo reared and danced away; but one of the outlaws caught his bridle, and the big bay gelding settled. Swearing viciously, Slaughter walked over and gave Tobias several brutal kicks. Through a haze of tears, Miranda watched and prayed for some sign of movement, but Tobias lay still. When Tyrel Reynolds came to stand beside him, pistol drawn, Slaughter reached down and roughly turned Tobias over onto his back.

Miranda gasped. The side of his head was covered with blood, and scarlet seeped through his shirt from two different wounds. Two other outlaws stepped forward to stare at the famous gunfighter.

"I think he's still breathing, Ben," one of the men who was peering down at Tobias's body pointed out doubtfully.

"That's all right by me. I want him to wake up and feel them holes we blew in him. Ain't no way he's gonna survive being gutshot. That's just about the most painful way a man can die. Jonah's gonna find out what hell's like, and I'm glad we sent him there."

Slaughter looked around. "I reckon it's time to vamoose. Someone might have heard those shots."

Fighting down the panic that threatened to overwhelm her, Miranda forced herself to think. Should she try to make a run for it? She could try to fetch Doc Wheeler for Tobias and help to get Christina back. But as she eyed the hard-faced men all about her with their drawn guns, she decided her chances of success were too poor. Most likely they would shoot her, and she was determined to live through this, for her own sake and for the boys'.

She sent a quick prayer of thanks to the saints who had chosen to look out for her nephews. But to lose Lucas—Miranda closed her eyes against the pain which seared her heart. The wonderful old man had been her best friend, her protector, and her confidante for years now. And he had died trying to protect her family.

Miranda swallowed a sob and opened her eyes. She couldn't allow herself to give in to her grief and guilt now. She had to keep her head clear.

That resolve almost crumbled when she looked down at Tobias. How long could he possibly survive out here in the cold, bleeding so heavily? Slaughter rode up and snatched her mare's reins. The lecherous gleam in his one good eye as he stared at her made her shudder.

Numb with fear and shock, she was still looking at Tobias over her shoulder when Slaughter led her mare from the barnyard into the winter night.

As Tobias swam up through the darkness in his mind toward consciousness, he was aware of red pain ripping through him. Staying in the darkness almost seemed preferable, for the more awake he became, the worse the pain grew. But there were two voices, young voices which called to him repeatedly, and someone kept shaking his shoulder. Deep inside his own mind he knew he was needed. He couldn't rest and surrender to the peaceful comfort of the dark just yet.

"Mr. Johnston, you gotta wake up. Come on, Aunt Miranda needs you."

Tobias responded to the fear and urgency in that voice. When his eyes fluttered open, he saw Sean and Rory peering down at him.

"See, I told you he was too tough for Slaughter to kill," Rory told Sean with great satisfaction. In that moment, Tobias's memories of what had happened in the barnyard came flooding back. He wished he could be as confident as Rory was about his chances of survival. Right now, he was afraid Slaughter's men had shot enough holes in him to make him quite dead shortly. The only way to be certain was to sit up and inspect the damage himself.

He pushed himself upright, and a most unheroic moan was torn from his lips. His belly felt like it was on fire, and he had a pounding headache. The room started to tilt away from him, and he almost fell over. Sean reached out to help steady him. Tobias glanced about and discovered he had been lying on the floor in Miranda's parlor. Even though the old gambler was dead, he saw Lucas ranked the settee.

"He was lighter than you," Sean said, obviously reading his thoughts.

The boy had a point there. Tobias reached up and touched his head gingerly. He was surprised to find a rough bandage had been tied around it.

"Did you two do this?"

"Well, you were bleeding like a stuck pig from that gash in your head," Sean replied, "and I figured you wouldn't be able to go after Aunt Miranda if you lost too much blood. I've watched Aunt Miranda patch us both up a bunch of times, and it didn't look so hard. We did the best job we could strapping up the hole low on the right side of your belly, but that one is still leaking a bit. You caught another bullet on the edge of your belt buckle. I think that one maybe came from the side.

It tore your shirt and made you bleed some, but the buckle kept the bullet from hurtin' you any worse.''

Tobias tried to think past his blinding headache. ''You boys did fine. Now, get me some water, and fetch whatever guns and ammunition you can find lying about this place.''

Sean nodded to Rory, who got up and hurried off. ''I was thinking now we got you both patched up as best we can, maybe Rory should ride into town and fetch Doc Wheeler for Lucas, and I could ride out to Mr. McGregor's ranch to fetch help. I know if you weren't all shot up and all, you could handle Slaughter by yourself, but maybe you could use some help. And Mr. McGregor's got those great huntin' hounds of his. He probably has a good horse for you, too. Slaughter's men took Romeo with them.''

If Tobias hadn't hurt so badly, he would have laughed over Sean's apologetic manner. Obviously, he was afraid of offending a famous gunfighter's pride. But even back in his prime, Jonah would have thought twice about tackling a tough outfit like Slaughter's on his own.

''Sean, that's a damn good idea. With those hounds, we can set out tonight. You go saddle up and ride like hell for Rob McGregor's ranch. Make sure he knows they took Christina as well as your aunt.''

''The horses are all saddled,'' Sean admitted. ''I was about to go get help when Rory told me he thought you were about to come round. I wanted to make sure you thought I was doing the right thing.''

''You've done everything just right, Sean,'' Tobias said, proud and amazed at the boy's quick thinking in a crisis.

Something Sean had said nagged at Tobias. He looked over at Lucas. ''Is Ransom still alive?''

''Yes, sir.'' Sean's expression sobered when he looked over at the old gambler. ''Slaughter pistol-whipped him pretty bad, and then Tyrel Reynolds forced him into a real, stand-up gun-fight, and he beat Lucas to the draw. He took two bullets in his chest. I don't know if he's going to make it. We strapped him up just like you, but his color ain't so good.''

"How'd you boys get loose, anyway? Slaughter said he left you tied up.''

Sean flashed him a grin. "I used a penknife Aunt Miranda gave me for my birthday to cut us both loose.''

"Well, I'll be damned,'' Tobias swore softly. "You best get going, now. Every minute counts." Every minute did count. The longer they took to catch up to Slaughter, the more danger the women faced. He doubted those animals would kill them outright, but his stomach clenched at the notion of what those men would do to the women when they got back to their hideout.

Sean nodded and left. A few minutes later Rory appeared bearing Lucas's shotgun, an old muzzle loader, and a canteen full of water.

"I'm sorry we don't have any pistols for you,'' Rory said apologetically.

"That's all right. Mr. McGregor and his hands are probably going to bring along an arsenal of guns and ammunition unless I miss my guess. Now you best head for town and fetch Doc Wheeler. Are you going to be all right riding that road in the dark?''

Rory squared his shoulders, and Tobias felt another pang of pride. "You bet. I've ridden old Jimbo lots of times, and I know that road as good as anyone.''

"Make sure you take the time to bundle up, and ride slow enough you don't fall off. A man could freeze to death out there in that cold.''

"Yes, sir.''

Rory looked scared, pleased, and determined all at once.

Tobias stared wearily at the doorway long after Rory had left the parlor. Christ, kids had to grow up young out west. A few minutes later, Tobias heard Rory go pounding out of the barnyard. He prayed and hoped the younger boy made it into town in one piece. Miranda was going to have his hide if anything happened to her nephews tonight. That was, if she survived this sorry business, and he and McGregor found some way to get her out of the clutches of seven armed men. Tobias took a long draught from the canteen and then pulled himself along the floor until he was leaning his back against the settee where Lucas lay.

Rory was right. The old gambler didn't look good. His face was pale, his breathing labored. Anger flared deep inside Tobias. He didn't want Lucas Ransom to die. He was surprised to realize just how fond he had become of this blunt old man. How could Miranda possibly run the Shamrock without him—assuming Miranda lived through the night?

If only he'd killed Slaughter when he had the chance. As he sat there on Miranda's floor, urging two young boys with all his heart to ride as fast as they could, Tobias wondered if he had been wrong to swear off violence. Perhaps there were men who deserved killing. Perhaps it was right for a man to kill in defense of his loved ones. If he hadn't been so stubborn about holding to his new principles, Slaughter would be dead now, and Miranda and Lucas would be safe.

Tobias held his aching head in his hands and decided he hurt too much to make sense of it all. Right now he knew only one truth. If Ben Slaughter had harmed Miranda, if he had raped Miranda by the time Tobias caught up with them, Slaughter was dead. It was as elemental as that.

He had drained the canteen and was considering going in search of more water for himself when suddenly the old gambler beside him stirred and coughed.

"Goddamn, I hate getting shot," Lucas said in a surprisingly strong voice.

Tobias found himself grinning. It sounded like there was some life left in the old man after all. Moving slowly and carefully, he turned about so that he was kneeling next to the settee. Lucas's eyes were open, and he appeared to be studying the ceiling.

"I was just going to get some water for me," Tobias told him. "You want some?"

"Hell, yes. And a shot of whisky. I been dry for nigh on to three years now, but tonight I deserve a drink. Miranda keeps some whisky in the cupboard above the dry sink."

Tobias lurched to his feet. It was nip and tuck there for a moment whether he was going to fall flat on his face. The room started to tilt away from him, and the pounding in his skull intensified until he thought he might be sick.

"You don't look so good," Lucas said dryly.

"At least I'm standing."

By sheer force of will, he managed to stagger into the kitchen and find the water bucket beside the stove. After refilling the canteen Rory had brought him, he found the whisky and poured two stiff drinks.

"I take it Slaughter and his boys surprised you," Lucas said when Tobias returned and handed him the whisky. Tobias had to help him sit up. Lucas knocked back the drink in two swallows. A look of sheer bliss crossed the old man's features. "Lord Almighty that tastes good." He sighed and motioned for Tobias to let him back down on the settee.

"How come you ain't dead?" Lucas asked him between rasping breaths.

"I could ask you the same question. Slaughter told us you were a goner."

"The man's so full of himself, he thinks anyone shot by one of his men should cock up his toes and die." The old man flushed with indignation, and then began to cough. After Tobias held the canteen up to his lips, Lucas took a few swallows and his coughing eased.

"He should know better," Tobias said. "The world is full of men who have caught some lead and lived. He must have thought I was hit worse than I was."

"Did he take Miranda?"

Tobias nodded grimly. "And Christina. The boys have gone to fetch Doc Wheeler and Rob McGregor, his men, and his hunting hounds. I'll head out with them as soon as they get here."

"You plannin' to pack a gun this time?" the old man asked.

"I'll pack a gun, and I'll use it if I have to," Tobias replied.

"You watch Reynolds. That kid is poison fast, and he doesn't have the sense to be scared in the midst of a fight."

Tobias tensed when he heard horses approaching the house. He rose to his feet and walked to the closest window. Rob McGregor was there, and it looked like he'd brought five of his cowhands. He wasn't surprised that the rancher had come a-runnin'. It was clear from the times he had talked with Rob about Christina that his feelings for the Swedish girl ran deep and strong.

Tobias went to the kitchen and brought back the water bucket and the bottle of whisky for Lucas. He also added all the wood he could to the stove. As he shrugged into his sheepskin jacket which the boys had left lying on a chair, he asked Lucas, "Anything else you need?"

"Just for you to git out of here and fetch those little gals back as soon as you can."

"All right." He pulled on his gloves and eased his hat on over the bandage the boys had fashioned for him. "You hang on until the doc gets here. Miranda would be mighty angry if you up and died before she got back."

The old man smiled one of his tight-lipped smiles. "I'll do my best."

Tobias nodded to Lucas and stepped out the front door. It was a clear night out and bone-chillingly cold. Rob McGregor was just coming up the porch steps. The rest of his men remained mounted in the barnyard.

"You got a strong horse for me?" Tobias asked him. "That son of a bitch stole my bay."

"I brought a big mustang cross that should be able to carry you. There's a loaded Winchester on the saddle, and a gun belt and pistol, too, if you want it."

"I do," Tobias said briefly. He followed Rob to the mustang and for the first time in seven years buckled a gunbelt about his waist. "Will those hounds of yours track horses?"

"They'll track just about anything I ask them to. Are you sure you can ride?" Rob asked, eyeing his bloody jacket skeptically.

"I can ride," Tobias replied, and swung up into the saddle. He had to clutch the saddle horn for a moment as a wave of dizziness struck him. But the dizziness eased after a few moments. Ignoring the pounding in his head, he straightened his shoulders and nodded to McGregor.

"Let's go, then," Rob said to his men.

Casting about in circles, the hounds soon struck the scent and led them back down the road toward town. After a half mile, Slaughter's gang had left the road and headed northwest, following a game trail.

The rescue party had one piece of luck. A full moon rose shortly after they left Miranda's place. Its light reflected off the snow-covered ground and turned the mountain valley almost as bright as day. Once the moon rose, they could easily follow the hoofprints of Slaughter's mounts through the snow which had lingered since the last fall. McGregor and his men pushed the horses as fast as they dared along the trail.

The ride was a nightmare for Tobias. His head hurt and his belly burned. Every time he drew in a breath too deeply, a red-hot pain stabbed through his rib cage. He'd wager he had a broken rib on his right side someplace. He could feel wetness trickling down from the wound in his side. But it didn't matter. None of it mattered as long as they reached Miranda in time.

McGregor asked him once if he wanted to stop to rest. He shook his head in answer. He wanted them to ride faster. It drove him mad, imagining what might happen when Slaughter reached his hideout. It made him frantic, picturing what Miranda might have to endure before they could reach her.

*Please,* he sent a prayer to a God he had lost faith in long ago. *Please, let her be safe.*

Miranda sat quietly next to Christina in a corner of the drafty cabin, watching Slaughter and his men wolf the dinner she had just cooked for them. She had been terribly afraid the outlaws might rape them at once, but after a long, cold ride, they were much more interested in sitting by a warm fire and being fed. She had volunteered to cook, to keep from being tied up, and to buy more time. She had cooked their supper as slowly as she dared, despite the fact the men grew surly and impatient.

A part of her knew it was futile to hope that anyone would come to their rescue. Lucas was dead; Tobias, too horribly hurt to be able to help. She refused to believe that Tobias was dead, too, although it was difficult not to fear the worst. No matter how hard she tried, she couldn't stop seeing the image of him sprawled on the snow, blood seeping from his wounds.

She prayed the boys would find a way to free themselves before the house grew too cold and they froze. If and when the boys did get loose, they would ride for help. It might be hours and hours from now before those men arrived, if anyone came at all. Still, she had to cling to that hope. The alternative was too awful to contemplate. And so she did her best to keep her head, watch the outlaws, and look for some chance to escape.

As they finished their food, one man fetched a bottle of whisky, and they all drew long draughts from it. The outlaws began to stare at their captives, and the look in their eyes made Miranda's skin crawl. Time was fast running out.

"Hey, Red, that supper wasn't too bad." Slaughter belched and pushed his plate away from him. "We may have to keep you two on for the winter."

Miranda shuddered at the notion, and beside her Christina paled. Still, the men weren't threatening to kill them out of hand.

"Come on over here, Red. I want to find out if you're as good on your back as you are at slinging hash. Boys, the rest of you can have the blonde, but Red's all mine."

Slowly, Miranda rose to her feet, her heart pounding in her chest, knowing the moment she had been dreading was finally here. Surely there was some way she could delay them a little longer. And then she remembered the one other skill she possessed besides cooking.

"Before we go on with that fun you mentioned earlier, how would you boys like a little show?" Her voice sounded weak and shaky to her own ears. That would never do. Drawing on all her skill as an actress, Miranda placed her hands on her hips and gave a coquettish toss to her head. "You came and left the Shamrock so fast the last time, you never had a chance to take in my act."

"Say, how about that, Ben?" one of the older men, who had been watching Miranda all night, asked eagerly. "Remember that fellow over in Grand Junction told us her show is supposed to be really somethin'."

The rest asked Ben to let her perform, all except for Tyrel Reynolds, who sat staring moodily into space. Miranda wondered if he was sulking because he hadn't had a chance to kill the legendary Jonah on his own.

Slaughter took another slug from the whisky bottle and wiped his mouth on his sleeve. "All right, boys. I guess there's no big hurry. We got all night to enjoy these little ladies. Red, first you come on over here and give me a kiss, and then you can do your show."

Miranda swallowed hard. Trying to look nonchalant, she walked over to Slaughter. He stood up and pulled her hard against him. He mashed his mouth against hers, his breath hot and sour against her cheek. He reeked of stale sweat, and he tasted like whisky and chewing tobacco. While he pinched and fondled her breast roughly, he ground himself against her. When he finally let her go, Miranda staggered back from him, her hand to her mouth, gagging with revulsion. It took all her self-control not to reach out and slap that grin off Slaughter's face. The men seemed to think her reaction was hilariously funny.

She almost gave it up then, but the desperate look in Christina's eyes hardened her resolve. Holding her chin high, she walked before the stone hearth and turned to face the outlaws. *Just pretend it's a rowdy night at the Shamrock,* she told herself. But this cabin wasn't her saloon, and dear Lucas wasn't here to protect her. Sweet Lucas would never protect her again. She caught back a sob of pain and concentrated on the present.

"Pull that table back, boys. I'm going to need a little more room for this," she managed in a stronger voice. And she even sent them a smile.

She took a deep breath and launched into "Little Brown Jug." By the end of the first chorus she had everyone except Christina and Tyrel Reynolds tapping their feet and smiling. By the end of the song, she had them laughing and clapping.

She sang song after song, putting as much energy as she possibly could into her performance. When she thought they were starting to lose interest, she threw in "Ta-ra-ra Boom-de-ay," a rowdier number with wilder dance steps. The danger in this game was, of course, that a lewder song might inflame them. She reminded herself grimly that unless help came soon, she and Christina were going to be violated by these animals anyway. To put off that moment, anything was worth trying.

Just as she feared, the men grew more bold throughout the song. They grabbed at her skirts and yelled profane comments. Miranda's heart lurched when she saw a gaunt man with a long scar on his cheek grab Christina and force her to sit on his lap. To make matters worse, the room was growing so smoky she could hardly sing.

She finished the song a verse early and played her last card. She launched into "I'll Take You Home Again, Kathleen," one of the saddest and most sentimental songs she knew. Despite the smoky air burning her lungs, she sang the song with all her heart. The men quieted. Even they had mothers and sweethearts they remembered from their youth, and the song reached out and touched whatever humanity they still possessed inside their hardened hearts.

"Hell, that was one piss-poor song," Slaughter growled when she finished. The furious look in his one good eye told her he knew exactly what she was trying to do. "Your performance is over, Red," he said menacingly, and rose to his feet.

Miranda closed her eyes. Time was up.


Tobias stalked across the snow, easing closer to an old cabin in the abandoned mine camp. They had tracked Slaughter to his lair. During the last part of the ride he had ridden along in a semiconscious daze, but the news they had found the outlaws' hideout sent a jolt of anger, fear and relief sizzling through him. In its aftermath he felt clear-headed once again.

He circled the cabin soundlessly, trying to find a way to see into the interior. The windows were no use, for they were made of stretched rawhide and their shutters were closed tightly. The chinking on the cabin was poor, though, and at last he found a wide enough gap in the logs he could see through. He heard Miranda's voice a moment before he spotted her before the hearth. He blinked when he realized what she was doing. The woman was actually giving the outlaws a spirited rendition of her saloon act. *Sweet Miranda, that's the way to use your head. Stall them until help comes.*

A wave of pride washed over him. There she was, surrounded by a gang of slavering cutthroats, and she was singing as if she didn't have a care in the world. Now he just had to figure a way to get her out of there alive. He studied the layout of the cabin more carefully. He spotted Christina, sitting on a man's lap in the corner, her face white and strained. If he and Rob burst through the door, guns blasting, there was far too good a chance she or Miranda would get hurt.

He moved back from the cabin and studied the stovepipe. It was an old trick, pulling off the stovepipe to smoke up a room and force men out of a building like this. The noise they would make pulling the stovepipe would alert Slaughter that he had enemies outside, and the outlaws would come out shooting. Once again, that would put Miranda's life in too much danger. Perhaps there was a more subtle way to block that pipe. He made his way back to where Rob and his men were hiding beside a small stand of spruce.

"You're never going to believe this," he told them quietly. "Miranda's in there dancing and singing up a storm. My guess is, she's trying to buy time."

"Is Christina all right?" Rob asked anxiously.

"She looks scared, but neither of them look like they've been hurt. Now we just have to get them out of there in one piece. You think that roof is sturdy enough to hold a man's weight?"

Rob studied the old cabin in the moonlight. "I reckon it might hold someone light. You'd go through it in a heartbeat. If you want to pull that stovepipe off, we could just lasso it from the ground."

"Yeah, and Slaughter would hear it and know he had company, and the lead would start flying. If we block up that pipe gradually, they might not get wise to the fact it's being done on purpose."

"That just might do the trick. And I'm the one to make this play." Rob was among the lightest men present, and Tobias guessed he didn't want to ask any of his hands to take on the risk. If Slaughter and his men heard something on the roof, they would start shooting through the rafters first and ask what sort of critter was crawling around up there later. After searching through their saddlebags, Rob's men found an old slicker to plug the stovepipe. Leaving his rifle behind, the rancher approached the cabin quietly.

Tobias kept his rifle pointed toward the door of the cabin and blew on his right hand while he waited with Rob's cowboys. A loyal group, their faces were tense as they watched their boss climb carefully up the corner of the old cabin, using a rain barrel to get started. Once Rob reached the roof, he continued to move slowly, obviously feeling his way and trying to make as little sound as possible. Tobias breathed a little easier when Rob finally reached the stovepipe and began to plug it with the old slicker.

The minutes seemed to crawl by like hours as Rob gradually pushed more and more of the slicker into the pipe. Tobias shifted restlessly. Miranda was so close. A part of him longed to go charging through the door of the cabin, guns blazing, and trust to his own skill and the element of surprise to see him through. The rational, thinking part of his mind knew his plan was smarter and more likely to get her out of that cabin alive. But he hated the plan he had devised, for the wait and the worry were going to finish him off before Slaughter's gang ever had a chance to.

Slaughter started to reach for Miranda, and then he doubled over coughing. "Goddamn that stovepipe. Buck, I thought you said you fixed it."

"I did," the outlaw with the scarred cheek replied sullenly. "I pulled a whole bird's nest out of it two days ago."

"Someone open the door."

"Hell, I gotta get out of here."

Coughing from the increasingly heavy smoke, four of the men headed toward the door. Miranda watched Slaughter carefully, wondering if she and Christina might find some way to escape during the confusion. Slaughter must have read her mind, for he clamped his hand tightly about her wrist.

"You ain't going nowheres, Red."

Tyrel Reynolds and Buck, the man who held Christina on his lap, likewise showed no inclination to leave. Miranda clenched her fists when she realized Buck was fondling Christina's breasts, and she was struggling with him.

"You leave her alone," Miranda shouted at the outlaw, her eyes streaming from wood smoke and tears of frustration.

From outside came a hoarse, wordless cry of surprise, and then several guns boomed at once. Slaughter cursed and grabbed for the rifle by his chair. The moment the shooting started, Tyrel Reynolds came alive. He snatched one of his pistols from its holster and knelt beside the door. Buck shoved Christina from his lap, blew out the kerosene lamp, and caught up a rifle.

Miranda was tempted to dive for the doorway; but Slaughter still held her arm tightly, and she didn't want to leave Christina behind.

The guns fell silent, and the only sound from outside came from an outlaw who lay moaning in the snow, clutching his belly.

"They didn't nail all four, did they?" Slaughter asked, trying to peer out the door without exposing himself to fire.

"Yep, they dropped every one. Smitty is the only one who's moving at all, and he looks done for." Tyrel could have been talking about the weather for all the emotion she heard in his voice. A shiver went down Miranda's back. How could he be so dispassionate about the deaths of four men he had ridden with? The air in the cabin was growing more smoky by the moment, but she found if she crouched near the floor, the air there was almost breathable.

"I knew we shouldn't have stuck around Pine Creek," Tyrel said bitterly.

"Shut your mouth, Tyrel, or I'll shoot you myself."

"Nobody speaks to Tyrel Reynolds that way," the young

gunfighter said hotly, and he spun about to face Slaughter. The one-eyed outlaw let go of Miranda's wrist and raised his rifle to cover Reynolds. Miranda eased away from Slaughter and began crawling toward Christina across the dirt floor.

"You don't want to draw on me right now, you damn fool," Slaughter told Reynolds angrily. "Three of us stand a hell of a lot better chance shootin' our way out of here than two do."

"You figure it's that marshal out there?" Buck broke in on their arguing.

At just that moment, Miranda touched something smooth and cool lying on the floor. It was a gun belt. Feverishly she searched the length of it until she found a cold, hard pistol still strapped in the holster. She drew the pistol out and hid it in her skirts. Quietly she made her way over to the corner where Christina sat. The girl was shaking with terror.

Miranda put an arm around her. "That shooting means help has come. We're going to be all right," she whispered in her ear with more confidence than she actually felt.

"There's one way to find out who's out there, I reckon." Slaughter paused for a moment, and then shouted out the cabin door, "Who the hell just shot up my boys?"

"Jonah, and some friends of mine," a familiar, deep voice shouted back. "You put down your guns and come on out of there before we burn that place down about your ears."

Miranda closed her eyes as a deep wave of relief flooded her heart. Tobias was alive. He was alive, and he'd come for her.

"I don't think we'll be doing that," Slaughter yelled back. "You see, the way I figure it, we put some lead into you, and a man don't go riding about all shot up unless there's somethin' he wants mighty bad. Now, it could be you want my hide, but I'm bettin' you're fool enough to want this red-haired whore of yourn back."

"You send her and the Swedish girl out, and we might let you live."

"You want her, Jonah," Slaughter countered, "you come and get her. The score between us ain't nowhares settled now that you killed four of my outfit. If you don't walk through this door in five minutes, I swear I'll shoot her deader than a doornail."

Miranda tightened her hold on the pistol. Surely Tobias would say no. He'd be cut to pieces by these three men and their guns. There was a short silence.

"All right. I'll come get her. If any of you harm those women, you'll be sorry you were ever born."

*No,* she wanted to scream at him. *No, don't do this.* Within a heartbeat she realized why he'd said yes to such an impossible challenge. He didn't think he was going to live much longer anyway now that people knew Jonah was still alive. He was willing to give his life to make certain she survived.

Miranda swallowed a sob and gripped the pistol tighter. He was going to live. She was going to find some way to make certain they both lived through this grim night. And in that desperate moment she had to face a final truth. She had known for sometime that she loved Tobias, but she had told herself that it was a limited, safe sort of love. Now she had to face the fact she couldn't imagine going on without him. This quiet, strong man had come to mean everything to her. She didn't care anymore who or what he had been. He was simply Tobias, and her world would come to an end if Slaughter and his men killed him.

"You're really planning to walk through that door?" Rob asked while he watched Tobias check the loads on his pistol.

"Any of you boys have another six-shooter I can borrow?" Tobias asked the rest of the men. Wordlessly Pete Samson, Rob's foreman, handed over a big Army Colt which Tobias stuck in the extra holster on his cartridge belt.

"I'm not exactly looking forward to it, but I don't seem to

have a lot of choice right now,'' Tobias replied. ''Slaughter wants me. With any luck I can take him and Reynolds. That third man in there should throw in the towel right quick with those other two out of it.''

''I've got a better idea. I spotted a place on that roof that is mighty thin,'' Rob spoke quickly. ''I think I could break right through it in a single jump. That might take their minds off you for a moment or two.''

''You're more apt to break your leg and get yourself shot to doll rags.''

''Well, you walking in there and getting yourself gunned down isn't going to help the women any. That cabin is a stacked deck, even for the likes of Jonah.''

''You've got a point there,'' Tobias had to admit.

''You give a loud knock on that door, and that's when I'll jump.'' With that Rob slipped back into the trees to circle behind the cabin.

Tobias stared after him, stifling the urge to call him back. It was a damn fool plan, and it was apt to get them both killed; but for the life of him, he couldn't think of a better one.

''What's taking you so long?'' Slaughter bellowed.

''You shot the hell out of my hip. I can't walk fast,'' he lied on the spot.

Taking a deep breath, Tobias started across the snowy clearing. His feet had grown so numb during the long wait, he hardly had to feign a limp. The outlaw who had been moaning earlier was quiet now. He and three others lay sprawled in motionless heaps near the cabin. All four men were dead or dying now in the snow, but he could not let their deaths touch him. Jonah would not have cared. And for the fight to come, he had to be Jonah once more. He had to be Jonah if Miranda was to survive.

He let the men inside see he was on his way, and then he veered away from their line of fire. There was no point in letting them cut him down before he ever reached the door. Now that the wait was over, the old icy stillness he'd always felt before a fight stole over him. As he approached the cabin, he considered his options and adversaries a final time. Reynolds would be the fastest, but Slaughter was more dangerous. He was a big, strong man, and he was angry, and he would just keep coming unless he took a bullet in his heart.

What if Miranda got caught in the cross fire? Ruthlessly he suppressed the fear spurting through him at that thought. *She's dead anyway unless you get her out of there. Slaughter has never given a damn about anyone's life but his own.*

He walked more slowly the closer he drew to the cabin, careful to make no sound. He wanted the men inside to sweat and worry, and he didn't want them to know exactly where he was. He also wanted to give Rob plenty of time to scale the corner of the cabin again.

"I give you one more minute, Jonah, and then I'm going to put some lead into your purty little whore," Slaughter called out.

This time Tobias didn't answer. When he reached the side of the cabin, he drew the Army Colt from its holster and took a deep breath. He crossed the remaining distance to the doorway soundlessly. He rapped on the half-open door with the barrel of the six-shooter.

Seconds later, a loud, splintering crash came from the back of the cabin, and Tobias lunged inside. Reynolds and Slaughter were standing in the middle of the room. Both were looking toward the back, where Rob McGregor lay sprawled on the floor in a tangle of broken boards, but Slaughter was the first to react to Tobias's presence. Tobias shot him in the chest just as the outlaw swung his six-shooter back toward the door. Tobias snapped his second shot at Reynolds, and then he concentrated his fire on Slaughter.

He put two more bullets into Slaughter's chest. But the big man just kept coming. His teeth bared in a fearful grimace, the outlaw raised his left hand to fan the hammer on his pistol, and Tobias shot him again in the shoulder. That bullet staggered the outlaw and turned him away from the door.

In the back of his mind, Tobias knew there was one other outlaw he needed to account for, but for the moment, he had to stop Slaughter. He posed the greatest threat to Miranda. A part of his mind registered the crack of Rob's pistol, and then a third gun he couldn't identify. Reynolds spun about and fell flat on his face. Out of the corner of his eye, Tobias saw the last outlaw stagger to his feet. The third gun boomed again, and the outlaw fell heavily to the floor.

Slaughter turned about to face Tobias. He reached down to his belly and brought his hand back up, scarlet with his own blood. He seemed fascinated by it. "Damn, Jonah, you fetched me. Guess I'm glad it was you if it had to be anyone. Ain't many of our kind left."

With that, Slaughter's one good eye rolled up in his head, and he fell back on the dirt floor of the cabin like a toppled tree.

Tobias stared stupidly at the three men lying on the floor of the dark cabin, amazed to find he was still on his feet. Miranda came out of the shadows in a rush, holding a big Remington revolver in her hands. So she'd been the one firing the third gun. By taking out that last outlaw, she likely saved both Rob's and his own life. He almost smiled when he saw Christina fly across the room to fuss over the rancher. Perhaps after tonight she would finally give Rob a chance.

He had the presence of mind to gently remove the gun from Miranda's hand, and then she wrapped her arms around him. It hurt like hell when she squeezed his wounded midsection, but it didn't matter. It didn't matter that he had truly become Jonah once more since he had killed, and he had sworn to himself he would never take a life again. The only thing that mattered in this moment was that Miranda was in his arms again, and she was safe.

# Chapter Twenty

Miranda paused in the doorway to her bedroom and studied her patient worriedly. After the shoot-out at Slaughter's cabin, she had insisted that Tobias stay at her place while he recuperated. Right now he was dozing, the stack of books she had left by his bedside untouched. He claimed his head ached whenever he tried to read, and he politely declined her offers to read to him as well.

Doc Wheeler came out to check his wounds every day. The old physician had been relieved when none of Tobias's injuries had become septic. Tobias was healing, thanks to the splendid strength of his body. But there was something terribly wrong inside him. He was brooding and unhappy, and she couldn't get him to talk about what was bothering him. There was a distance in Tobias since that grim night he had been forced to kill Slaughter, and she couldn't seem to reach past it no matter how hard she tried.

She wished she had more time to spend with Tobias, but she was always on the run these days, tending to two recovering invalids, keeping the household going, minding the boys, working at the Shamrock at night, and preparing for Christmas, which was less than a week away now. Despite the recent turmoil, Miranda was determined to give the boys a wonderful holiday. After what they all had been through, every member of her household deserved a festive time. Whenever she could steal a moment away from her chores, she worked on making presents for everyone and her holiday baking.

A bell tinkled from the front parlor. Miranda sighed. That meant Lucas wanted her to fetch him something. She hurried down the stairs to the parlor where she had set up a temporary bedroom for him.

"I want a glass of water, and this damned bed has lumps in it. I'd probably be better off if I just bedded down in the barnyard."

"The bed feels that way because you've been lying in it for a week now." Miranda smiled at him as she plumped up his pillows and poured him a fresh glass of water. "I'd be happy to move you out to the barnyard. Of course, it might get a little chilly tonight. I think it's going to snow again."

"Hell, I'll stay in here," Lucas said gloomily.

"Do you want me to bring you your whittling? Christmas is only six days away now. That doesn't leave you a lot of time to finish your presents for the boys." Before he'd been shot, Lucas had been working on a carved figure of a horse for Sean, and a bird whistle for Rory. When Lucas brightened at her suggestion, she went to fetch his whittling tools.

Lucas was proving to be an irascible patient. One moment he was apologizing for making more work for her; the next he was complaining about his every discomfort. She didn't mind his crankiness, for she had come far too close to losing him.

When he had first treated the old gambler, Doc Wheeler had been pessimistic about his chances. He had lost too much blood, the doctor had told Miranda gently, and he was too old to survive two such terrible bullet wounds. But contrary to the doctor's prognosis, every day Lucas grew a little stronger. Just yesterday Doc Wheeler declared cheerfully that if the old cuss had managed to live this long, chances were he was going to keep on breathing. Lucas Ransom was just too ornery to die.

She wished Tobias would be cranky or demanding. Instead, he was merely quiet. It was as if his heart and soul had already left her, before his physical body could heal enough for the rest of him to move on as well.

Miranda had just given Lucas his whittling pieces and his knife, and spread a rag across his bedding to catch the shavings, when Christina called from the kitchen, "Miranda, I'm ready to leave now."

Miranda hurried to the kitchen to see Christina off. "Stay at the ranch all afternoon if you wish. I can handle things here," Miranda assured her.

Rob McGregor had broken his ankle when he crashed through the roof of the old cabin. So far, the break seemed to be healing well, but Rob couldn't get around much on his crutches. Christina had been using that fact as an excuse to go see him every day, and Miranda was happy to have her visiting Rob regularly, even if it left her a little shorthanded.

"I do not know if Rob wants me to stay that long," Christina said, color rising in her cheeks. "I'll just go and tidy up his room and help Graciella a little."

"I think Rob would be delighted to have you stay all afternoon. In fact, I'm willing to bet he wants you to stay at the Ladder M permanently. I have a feeling I'm going to have to find myself a new housekeeper before long," Miranda said with a mock sigh of resignation.

"After all you have done for me, I would never leave you," Christina pledged earnestly.

"The very best way you could pay me back is to accept that brave, wonderful man in a heartbeat when he proposes, and go on and raise a brood of children out on the Ladder M."

Christina blushed again and looked at her feet. "Do you

think he could possibly want a woman like me to be his wife? After all I have been and done?'' she asked in a low voice.

''Rob McGregor sees you as a lovely, decent young woman. Why else would he have risked his life to save you? I think he cares very much about you, and very little about the foolish mistake you made when you were fifteen. If he doesn't care what you were, why should you?''

''Oh, Miranda, every day I thank God you knocked on my door and gave me a way to leave Nolan.'' Christina stepped forward and gave her a quick hug. ''I will think about what you have said.'' With that, she hurried out the door to the barn.

Miranda gazed after her, warmed by such a display of affection from her usually reserved young friend. Christina deserved her chance at happiness. She sighed and went to the kitchen to prepare Tobias's supper tray. *Miranda Kilpatrick, your own chance is fast slipping away from you. Just what are you going to do about it?*

Since that awful moment when she had seen Tobias fall from his horse to lie bleeding in the snow, she'd had to face the fact she loved him with all her heart. She was prepared to gamble her own future happiness and marry him. She was even ready to wager the boys' futures as well. The more time he spent with Sean and Rory, the more she realized what a fine role model Tobias was for them. He was intelligent and kind, and endlessly patient with her nephews and their countless questions.

She no longer thought of Tobias as a gunfighter. He had so little in common with a man like Jake Broden. That day on the street when he had refused to draw a gun against Reynolds had proven to her that Tobias was no longer a killer. True, he had killed Slaughter, but he had shot the outlaw only to save her. She had even been forced to kill that awful night. Miranda shuddered at the memory of the cold pistol kicking in her hand and the stunned look in Buck's eyes as he sank to the ground with her bullet in his chest.

As much as that memory haunted her, she wasn't sorry she had shot that man. *Surely it's right to take a life to protect one's own, or the life of someone you love.*

*There must be some place, some way you and Tobias can be together.* But it would take both of them working together to plan a future that could make them happy, and right now Tobias would hardly even speak to her. Taking a deep breath, Miranda picked up the finished tray and decided today she was going to find some way to make him start talking.

"Here's your dinner," she told him with deliberate cheerfulness as she stepped through the doorway and laid the bed tray across his lap. With a white bandage wrapped about his head, he looked like a rather somber and heartbreakingly handsome pirate. She ached to reach out and smooth away the frown lines between his brows with her fingertips, but she was afraid that in his current mood he would reject her touch.

"Thank you," he said in that polite, distant tone she hated.

"You could thank me by showing a little more enthusiasm for the meals we've been working so hard to make for you. You hardly touched your breakfast."

"I'm sorry. I'll try to do better by this one."

She could tell by his set expression that nagging wasn't getting her anywhere, and so she decided to try a different approach. "Christina rode over to Rob's yesterday, and she's going again today. She won't talk about it much, but I think a real romance is brewing between those two at last."

"I'm glad," he said simply. "I'm glad for both of them." Before he looked down at his tray, she caught a glimpse of the turmoil in his gray eyes.

"What's wrong?" She crossed swiftly to his bedside and laid her hand over his. "Can't you be telling me?"

"There's nothing wrong. My head just hurts a little more than usual."

She snatched her hand away and strode across the room.

"Tobias E. Johnston, you are one of the biggest liars on God's green earth."

The frustration and pain in her voice must have reached him. He looked across the room at her, his gray eyes full of concern for her. "Sh, now, I'm not worth a moment of your worrying. I'll be fine."

"You make me so furious when you talk like that. You are worth plenty of worrying. Besides, if I don't worry about you, who will?"

"I got along well enough for a number of years without anyone worrying about me. And you have plenty of other folks to worry about."

"Well, I'm going to keep worrying about you until you leave, and then I'll probably be fool enough to keep worrying about you for a good time after."

"Then you would be a damn fool. There's only one end for a gunfighter like me, and you would be better off if you accepted that fact now."

He spoke with such bitterness, Miranda drew in a breath in surprise. She stared at him, her mind whirling. Could this be the source of his trouble? Could it be he saw himself as a gunfighter once again just because he had been forced to kill Slaughter to save her life?

"The gunfighter Jonah is dead," she told him firmly. "I have it on very good authority that he died seven years ago."

Tobias stared at his hands, and his mouth twisted. "Is he? The one thing I swore to myself when I headed east and started to build a new life for myself was that I would never, ever kill again. Yet I killed Ben Slaughter just the same, and at the time, I was damn glad about every bullet I put into him."

"He was an evil man," she countered, "and he was going to kill you and me and Christina."

"I know Slaughter was one poor excuse for a human being, and he would have killed us all without a single iota of remorse.

But the fact remains, I killed him, and someday when pressed I could kill again.''

He was silent for a long moment, and when he finally spoke, his voice was rough. ''I've thought a lot about what Slaughter said right before he died, and he was right. He said there weren't many of our kind left, which is a hell of a good thing. There's been too much killing here in the West, and I'm sorry I was ever a part of it.''

Miranda looked at him in horror and disbelief. ''You are not his kind. Just the fact you are sorry shows how different you are from him. You have a conscience. You made a conscious decision to change yourself, and you succeeded.''

''Sweet Miranda, you shouldn't waste your breath talking about this. A leopard can't change his spots, and I was a fool to try. You told me once you could never trust your heart to a gunfighter, and you were wise.''

She drew in a trembling breath. It was time to share the truth with him.

''You asked me once if I could ever love a man like you. That day you looked as if my answer meant the world to you. And the answer I gave to you was false. I told you I could never come to care for you, yet I knew I was already falling in love with you, and that fact frightened me to death. Love only brought misery to my parents and my sister. I couldn't afford to take the risk of loving the wrong man when Rory and Sean need me so badly.

''When I thought Slaughter had killed you, I realized none of those fears mattered. Slaughter made me face the truth at last. I love you with all my heart. I do trust you, and I know you would be kind and caring toward my boys. I refuse to give up the wonderful life we could share. Surely there is some way we can be together.''

Tobias stared at her, the naked pain in his eyes making her throat go tight. She crossed to the bed and reached both of her

hands out to him. He took them and drew her down to sit beside
him.

"Miranda Kilpatrick," he said, his voice thick with emotion.
"You turn me inside out." He stared down at their joined
hands. "Of all the gifts you could have given me," he said
slowly, "this is the most humbling. I wanted your love more
than anything else I've ever dreamed of, and now I can't accept
it."

Gently he released her hands. She felt tears burn in her eyes.
Fiercely she blinked them back. She didn't want to ask the
question, but a part of her had to know the worst. "Does this
mean you no longer want to marry me?"

"What kind of a life could I offer you and the boys?" She
almost started back from the suppressed violence in his voice.
"We'd be on the move constantly. And you'd always have to
worry that someday some young punk would recognize me and
put a bullet in my back. What if you or Sean or Rory got caught
in the cross fire? That possibility haunts me the most."

Her heart sank at his answer, but she refused to give up just
yet. "So you do still love me?" she prodded him brazenly.

He looked up at her again, his gray eyes despairing. "I love
you as much as a man like me can love anyone," he admitted,
"and because I love you, I know the best thing I can do once
I'm healed up is ride on out of here and never come back."

Miranda swallowed her rising frustration and fear that she
wouldn't be able to reach him before he left. There had to be
some way to make him see reason. "I'm sorry you feel that
way," she said quietly and walked to the door.

With her hand on the door handle, she met his gaze once
more. "It's just plain foolishness to think killing Ben Slaughter
turned you back into Jonah. Any man has the right to protect
his own life and those he cares for, and Slaughter meant to kill
us all. I'll leave you to eat your meal in peace." *And chew on
what I just said to you, you stubborn man,* she thought to herself

as she hurried down the stairs, the tears she had refused to shed in his presence streaming down her cheeks.

Over the next few days, Miranda came to the discouraging conclusion that her words had made absolutely no impact on Tobias. He continued to be remote and uncommunicative the times she had to enter his room. He never once spoke of the declaration she had made to him, and she had too much pride to face another rejection. He did start to eat a little better, which would have lifted her spirits except for her nagging fear that he was only consuming his food so that he could heal faster and leave her all the sooner.

The only time he seemed to smile was when the boys slipped into his room to talk with him. He must have realized how excited they were about Christmas coming, for one day he asked her to fetch a couple of his books from the barn. She'd hired a man to bring over all of Tobias's books from the cabin, hoping that reading might help divert and entertain Tobias while he was laid up. After asking her opinion on what she thought the boys would like, he wrote inscriptions in *Treasure Island* for Sean and *Tom Sawyer* for Rory, and then she wrapped both books for him and hid them under the bed.

That day was the first time she'd seen a ghost of the old Tobias who used to laugh with her. For the most part he remained cool and withdrawn. She was surprised, therefore, one afternoon when she arrived with his tray and he declared, "I want to talk to you about something."

Miranda nodded cautiously, wondering what could possibly be on his mind. Sitting upright against his pillows, he appeared more alert and focused than he'd seemed in days.

"Lying around like this, I've had lots of time to think about that mine Slaughter was convinced your uncle found."

Happy that he was finally willing to talk to her, Miranda

settled herself in the rocker. "And have you come to any conclusions?"

"From what you've told me about your uncle, he seemed to be a man who prized his family greatly. He certainly went to some trouble to make certain you would inherit the Shamrock and this house if anything happened to him."

"That's true," Miranda said slowly. "We didn't see much of Uncle Shamus after he moved to Colorado, but he wrote to us often, and he always sent Mary and me boxes full of wonderful presents at Christmas time. He also sent my mother what money he could after Da died."

"Now, if a man like that found a valuable mine, don't you think he'd go to some trouble to make certain his family would benefit from it, just as they would from the sale of his saloon?"

"I've wondered about that ever since Slaughter first mentioned the mine," Miranda admitted. "Perhaps Uncle Shamus meant to leave his mine to us, but he died before he could change his will. Perhaps there is no mine at all. Perhaps Slaughter took some of my uncle's blarney and bluster more seriously than he should, for Uncle Shamus always liked to spin tales."

"That's always a possibility, a possibility which means you won't inherit a rich gold mine. But what if your uncle did discover a promising claim? What if he was afraid Slaughter would jump his claim if he ever knew the exact location of the mine? In that case, your Uncle Shamus would have been very careful about leaving you information concerning its location. He feared Slaughter would try to take it from you as well. Remember that night your house was torn apart? I think Slaughter and his men were looking for a map or a letter or some sort of document your uncle had left you describing where his claim was."

"What's the use of going on with this? It's all a pipe dream." Miranda laid her head back against the rocker, the long day of waiting on two invalids, preparing for Christmas, and minding her household suddenly catching up with her. "I searched Uncle

Shamus's old cabin from top to bottom, and I didn't find a single hint of where that mine might be located. If he left any clues as to its whereabouts, I simply don't have time to look for them."

"I have plenty of time on my hands right now," Tobias said firmly. "If there was such a mine, and Slaughter doesn't strike me as the type to go chasing after rainbows, the proceeds from its sale could be considerable. You wouldn't have to work at the Shamrock anymore. You wouldn't have to stay in Pine Creek where most of the folk treat you like dirt. You mentioned the fact you wanted to send Sean and Rory to college some day if they wanted to go. This mine could make all those things possible for you."

"Don't you think I've already thought of all this?" she asked him tiredly. "I've lived with two generations of Kilpatrick men who chased rainbows most of their lives for all the good it did them. My first responsibility is to keep a roof over Sean and Rory's heads, provide them with food and clothes, and love them as much as I can."

"I understand why you feel that way," he said, a resolute look in his eyes, "but I'm going to keep after this just the same."

*And I'm going to keep after you,* she told herself firmly, but deep inside her heart, she was afraid she'd already lost him.

Christmas Eve day dawned clear and cold. Rob McGregor and his son were coming to spend the afternoon and evening with the Kilpatrick household, and they were bringing a Christmas tree the Ladder M ranch hands had cut down. Despite the cold and a foot of new snow on the ground, Rory and Sean spent the later part of the morning by the road waiting and watching for the McGregors to arrive. Miranda was happy to have the boys out from underfoot. She had plenty of last-minute holiday preparations which were much easier to complete when Rory and Sean weren't watching her every move.

As she and Christina bustled about, placing evergreen branches on the mantel and setting the table for a grand dinner, Miranda decided her young friend looked radiantly happy. She was wearing the dress Miranda had insisted she make from the bolt of bright blue winter wool, and Christina looked very pretty indeed in it.

There was nothing like being in love to make a woman look her best. Miranda refused to be envious, but today she was having a hard time feeling happy herself. She always threw herself wholeheartedly into celebrating holidays, and Christmas was by far her favorite day of the year. But this morning she found it difficult to get into the Christmas spirit.

Before breakfast she had found Tobias out in the barn, checking his saddlebags and travel gear beside Romeo's stall. At first, when she had spotted him dressed in his jeans and sheepskin jacket, she had thought for one heart-stopping moment that he meant to leave this very day. He must have noticed her stricken expression, for his mouth had twisted.

"Don't look like that," he had told her gruffly. "I'm not leaving now. I couldn't leave you or the boys on Christmas. I know how much this holiday means to all of you."

*But you will leave us after the holidays. You will leave me.* As she stood in the cold, dim barn, a part of her had wanted to plead with him to stay, but she had too much pride. Instead, she had commented in the most offhand tone she could manage, "The boys have been taking good care of Romeo for you."

"I can see that."

Miranda had taken a deep breath and lifted her chin. "Whenever you are ready to leave, let Christina and me know, and we'll fill up those saddlebags for you with some good trail food."

"Thank you," he had said in his deliberate way. "I'd appreciate that. I appreciate everything you've done for me."

"When will you go?"

"The day after Christmas," he had said, his gray eyes as barren and empty as the high peaks in winter.

She had longed to cross the distance separating them and throw herself into his arms. But she knew his iron will was set on leaving, and she had been afraid he might reject her outright, or worse, offer her pity. Instead, she had left him there and returned to the house to take what joy she could from the only Christmas she would ever spend with Tobias.

Miranda roused herself from her musings when she heard the boys' cheering outside. The McGregors were here. She crossed to a window and watched as Rob and his son drove a sleigh into the barnyard with a lovely large spruce tied on the back of it. With stars in her eyes, Christina flew out the door to greet them, forgetting to put on a coat or scarf despite the chill outside.

During the bustling, busy hours of Christmas tree raising and trimming which followed, Miranda could never quite forget that moment in the barn this morning. Drawing on all her skills as an actress, she smiled and laughed and pretended for the boys' sake that she was having a wonderful time. And all the while she was thinking of poor Mary, who had given up on life when the man she adored left her. *Tobias is leaving in two days.*

She knew she was stronger than Mary. She could never give up completely when Sean and Rory needed her so, but how was she ever going to learn to live with this tearing, burning pain? *Tobias is leaving me.*

Throughout the afternoon, she stole looks at him, trying to memorize his face once again. Now she wished with all her heart that she had insisted he have his portrait made at the photography studio in town. Yet a part of her knew she would never forget what Tobias looked like. His silver-gray eyes, hard face, and gentle mouth would haunt her forever.

When they finished trimming the tree, most everyone stepped

back to admire their handiwork. Tobias, though, watched Rory and Sean. The boys were awestruck by their very first Christmas tree. A lump rose in Miranda's throat when she realized Tobias was clearly enjoying the boys' reaction just as much as she was.

Rather than burst into tears, Miranda launched into, "Oh, Christmas Tree," and soon everyone joined her in a caroling session about the piano. When she paused between carols, Miranda was surprised to find Tobias staring at the large, old leather-bound Bible sitting atop the piano.

"Miranda, didn't you tell me once all you inherited from your uncle was the house, the saloon, and the Kilpatrick family Bible?" he asked her, an oddly intent expression on his face.

"I did indeed," she answered in a gay tone. "Six generations of Kilpatrick births, weddings and deaths are recorded within its pages. Would you like to look at it?"

"Yes," he replied instantly and took the heavy book from the top of the piano.

"Some men will use any excuse to get out of singing." Miranda rolled her eyes at the rest. "We expect you to rejoin our chorale shortly."

"I will," he said absently. He wandered over into the corner, sat down, and began leafing through the pages of the old Bible.

Shaking her head mentally over Tobias's addiction to books, Miranda led her chorus in a spirited rendition of "Joy to the World."

"Miranda, would you mind if I pried up the lining in this?" Tobias asked the moment they had finished the carol. "I think there may be something hidden under here."

Miranda was about to say she very much minded him tampering with a family heirloom, but Lucas said sharply, "What do you think you've found there?"

Tobias met Lucas's gaze across the parlor. "I don't want to get anyone's hopes up, but it occurred to me that Shamus

Kilpatrick might have thought the family Bible was a good place to hide something important.''

"Like a map or a letter about that mine Slaughter was so sure Kilpatrick had found.'' Lucas let go a crow of laughter. "It'd serve that murderin' skunk right if he turned this whole house upside down, and what he was looking for was right there under his nose in this parlor all the time. Slaughter would never look twice at a Bible, and Shamus Kilpatrick knew it.''

Miranda crossed the room to Tobias's side, her legs suddenly weak. Rory and Sean were already beside him, their eyes wide and excited. "Do you really think you've found it?'' she asked him.

"I can't be sure what it is, but there's definitely something under this liner. Look for yourself. There's a raised area here, and the binding in the back's been tampered with since this book was originally bound.''

"We'll only know for sure if we take a look,'' Sean said eagerly. "Come on, Aunt Miranda. Please let him do it.''

Miranda took a deep breath and looked at everyone watching her expectantly. "All right, then,'' she made up her mind suddenly. "Let's see what's under that lining.''

# Chapter Twenty-one

While they all looked on, and Lucas strained to see from where he lay on the settee, Tobias took a penknife from his pocket. Gently he pried up the edges of the old parchment lining. Beneath it lay a folded letter. Wordlessly Tobias handed the letter to Miranda.

Her mouth dry, Miranda opened the letter and stared down at her uncle's familiar handwriting.

*September 21, 1885*

*My Dearest Niece,*

*I'm praying to all the saints above that you find this letter and not that blackguard Ben Slaughter. I've finally found the bonanza of my dreams; but my health is failing me now, and I won't have the chance to develop the Sweet Kathleen the way I wished. After I took ore from the mine to be assayed in Grand Junction, the clerk from*

*the assay office told one of Slaughter's men what a rich
claim I'd found. I've not known a moment of peace since
that day.*

*Slaughter's men have been watching my every move,
and Slaughter himself has threatened to tear my heart
out if I don't tell him where my mine is. I'm going to
thwart him in the end, for he doesn't realize how weak
my lungs are now. I hope that with my death, Slaughter
will forget about the mine and move on. Then you can
claim it properly and sell it. I've sketched out a map and
the legal description for the mine on the back of this
letter.*

*May God keep you and my dear grand nephews Sean
and Rory. Know that you are in my thoughts constantly
as I prepare to meet my Maker and see my darling Kathleen once again.*

> *Your Loving Uncle,*
> *Shamus Kilpatrick*

With shaking hands, Miranda turned the letter over. On the
back was a remarkably clear map, and the legal description of
the claim, just as her uncle had promised.

In all the hubbub which followed Tobias's discovery, Rob
McGregor noticed Christina quietly slip away to the kitchen.
He heaved himself to his feet and hobbled after her using his
crutches, hoping he finally might have a few precious moments
alone with her. He was startled to find her leaning against the
kitchen table, tears cascading down her cheeks. The moment
she saw him, she turned away and covered her face with her
hands.

"Christina, honey, what's wrong?" In his concern for her,
he let the endearment slip. He'd been calling her that in his
mind for a long time now, but he'd never said it aloud. He'd

been a mighty happy man, broken ankle and all, since the night he'd helped to rescue the women from Ben Slaughter and his gang. A busted ankle was a small price to pay to have Christina talking with him at last. He was well pleased with the progress of his courtship these days.

"There is nothing wrong. I am just so happy for Miranda. You do not know how much she hates it here. The women in this town are horrible to her. Finally, she will have a chance to move away someplace where she and the boys can be accepted."

"Is that the only reason why you're crying?" he asked, his heart lurching at the news Miranda would probably move her household away from Pine Creek. Just when he was starting to make real headway with his little gal, Christina just couldn't up and leave him.

Christina slowly lowered her hands. The misery he saw in her eyes made his heart slam in hopeful strokes. "No," she said softly, "there is another reason I am crying. When I first came here, I didn't care at all where I lived. I didn't care about anything. But now, I-I do not want to leave Pine Creek."

Rob crossed to her side as quickly as he could on his crutches. He reached out and took her hand between his own. His mouth felt dry as a desert. Hell, he hadn't felt this scared when he climbed up on that flimsy roof above Slaughter and his gang of cutthroats. But this was as good a chance as he'd have as any to make his play.

"There's a question I want to ask you. You may not be ready to give me the answer I want yet, but I have to ask it just the same. I don't want you to leave Pine Creek. I want you to stay on the Ladder M with me. I talked it over with Robby, and he's all in favor of it. What I'm trying to ask is, Christina Erickson, will you do me the honor of becoming my wife?"

Christina sobbed aloud and flung her arms around him. Rob grabbed his crutches and manfully managed to keep his balance.

She burrowed into his shoulder, crying so hard her whole body shook.

Rob let go one crutch to gather her closer. He loved the feel of her soft hair against his cheek and the wonderful, sweet female scent of her.

"Christina, honey, it's heaven to have you in my arms," he said patiently after a long moment, "but you mustn't cry like this. You'll make yourself sick. Besides, you should have pity on a poor fellow. Are you meaning to tell me yes or no?"

She pulled back from him, her lovely blue eyes awash with tears. "Of course I mean yes, you foolish man. I cry now because I am so happy. I did not think I could ever feel clean or decent again. But loving you has made me feel like a new person."

"I'm so glad, honey. You make me whole and happy in a way I never thought I could feel since Sue died." He took full advantage of the fact her face was tilted up toward him and pressed a long kiss on her lips. Christina wrapped her arms about his neck and kissed him back wholeheartedly. When he started to lose his balance, she steadied him.

All in all, it was a long time before they returned to the parlor and shared their good news with the rest.

Miranda sat by the stove in her kitchen, relishing a last bit of peace and quiet before going to sleep on the trundle bed in Christina's room. Sean and Rory were sound asleep upstairs, worn out from the day's festivities. She smiled to herself. She had wanted to give them a wonderful Christmas, and they had had a fine time today. They had loved the Christmas tree, and the presents they received. Rory had particularly liked the bird whistle Lucas had carved, and both boys had been thrilled by the books Tobias had given them.

As the McGregors were leaving, young Robby McGregor had shyly told her it was the best Christmas Eve he'd had in a long time. She guessed he meant it was the best Christmas Eve he'd had since his mother died. It felt good knowing she had helped give another family joy besides her own.

Miranda shook her head over the two greatest surprises of the day. She was thrilled for Rob and Christina, and she was certain they would be happy together. She was a little less sure how she felt about Tobias's discovery. She still couldn't believe it. She'd worked herself to the edge of exhaustion and beyond these past two years to provide for herself and the boys. Now it was possible she was a rich woman, so rich she might never have to work again. The idea was so foreign she couldn't quite grasp it.

She started when Tobias opened the back door and stepped inside. She had thought he was sound asleep upstairs. He was bundled up in his jacket and hat. He also was wearing the scarf she had given him as a Christmas present. She eyed the scarf critically as he stamped snow from his boots. Knitting wasn't her best skill, but the scarf was a nice rich brown color, and it had turned out surprisingly well. She liked the idea that during his travels this winter Tobias might wear something she'd made for him.

"The stars are beautiful tonight," he said, looking at her across the kitchen. "Will you come look at them with me?"

She rose to her feet in answer and went to fetch her own coat and scarf.

It was piercingly cold outside, but she didn't mind the cold with Tobias standing right beside her. They walked together out to the middle of her garden where they could see the full sweep of the black heavens above. The stars were lovely, just as Tobias had said. But Miranda couldn't focus on the stars when the man she ached to touch stood so close.

"I think I missed these stars the most during those years I spent back east," he admitted. "Somehow the night skies there were never this clear or the stars this bright."

*Will you miss me during all the endless years which lay*

*ahead of us?* she longed to ask him, but instead she merely said, "They are glorious. Da used to show us pictures in the stars and make up the most lovely tales about them."

"Tell me one, please."

Miranda thought for a moment as she scanned the heavens. "Do you see that perfect little circle of stars right above us? Da used to say that was a crown of a princess who lived in the sky. She was good and kind and did her best to make all her subjects happy. One day she found a wounded soldier beside a well. She nursed him back to health, and they fell in love with each other. Her father would not let them marry and cast the soldier and his daughter into his darkest dungeon. Several of the poor folk she had aided over the years helped both the princess and her lover escape. The princess left her crown of stars on her father's throne and ran off with her soldier. He was tired of fighting, of course, and so they took up farming and lived happily ever after."

Miranda was silent for a moment while she considered the story she hadn't thought about for years. "I think my father added that last bit about farming to please my mother," she added wryly.

"I see where you inherited your optimistic outlook on life," was all Tobias said.

At last her body couldn't ignore the deep cold of the mountain night any longer, and she began shivering. Tobias noticed at once. She longed for him to reach out and put an arm around her. Instead of touching her, he declared, "You're going to freeze out here. We should go back inside before you catch your death."

"I suppose," she said, trying to hide her disappointment and reluctant to let this time with him end.

When they stepped inside, the kitchen was warm and quiet. She'd already pulled the door shut to the parlor earlier to give Lucas some privacy. After they took off their coats, Tobias pulled two chairs up beside the stove. Miranda turned up the lamp on the table and accepted his unspoken invitation. Inside the little halo of light, they sat side by side warming themselves.

"You've had some day." Tobias slanted a glance at her. "Your housekeeper got engaged and you inherited a gold mine."

"I'm so happy for Rob and Christina," Miranda said and stretched her cold fingers out toward the stove.

"I'm happy for them, but I'm more happy for you. Have you thought about what you'll do with the proceeds from selling the mine?"

"I haven't really," she admitted. "I haven't had a free moment until now to think about it. I suppose I'll stay put here in Pine Creek until I've sold the mine. If we get enough for it, I'd love to move away and start someplace fresh, where no one will know I ran a saloon, and all the singing I'll be doing will be at mass on Sundays."

"I think that's a fine plan for both you and the boys," he said in a hearty tone which belied the wistful look in his eyes.

"I haven't told you thank you yet for finding my uncle's letter. I gave up on finding that mine, and you didn't. Because of that, you've my changed life." *In so many ways.*

"I'm glad," he replied.

They both were silent for a long time, enjoying the quiet of the warm, dark kitchen and wishing time would move more slowly.

Finally Miranda sat more upright in her chair. "I have one more present for you. I wanted to wait until the rest were asleep before I gave it to you."

Today, before the others, he had presented her with a beautiful edition of Shakespeare's plays and sonnets, finished in gold leaf with an embossed leather cover. It was a handsome present, and one she would treasure always. His generous gift had confirmed her own desire to give him something that was important to her.

"You shouldn't give me anything else. That scarf you made me is a mighty fine present," he said in protest.

"Nevertheless, there is something I want very much for you to have."

She rose to fetch his present from her bedroom. When she returned to the kitchen, she handed him a small cardboard box wrapped in brightly colored fabric and then sat down in a chair close to him at the end of the kitchen table.

She hid a smile as she watched Tobias. He studied the present carefully as he turned it over in his hands. Despite his protest, she could tell he was pleased. Today he had made quite a production out of opening his other gifts, looking each one over and drawing out the process of unwrapping them all. She would have teased him about it, except that she guessed part of his pleasure in his gifts stemmed from the fact it had been years since anyone had given him a Christmas present.

At last he undid the fabric wrapping and opened the box. He sat looking at her gift for so long she became worried.

"Don't you like it?" she asked him falteringly.

"Miranda, this is your father's watch. I can't take this," he said, a queer, strained note in his voice.

"Why not?"

"I can't take this," he repeated. He glanced up at her then, and his gray eyes looked dark and haunted. "Your father was a good man, and I know he meant the world to you. I don't deserve this."

He thrust the box into her hands and stood up. "You've given me so much, and I don't deserve any of it."

"That's it, isn't it?" She looked up at him wonderingly. "That's why you're leaving me. That's why you're leaving all of us. You think you don't deserve a happy life with decent folk. You don't think you deserve to be loved."

"I've tried to make you understand," he countered roughly, "but you just won't listen. You don't understand what I am. I'm not fit to stay one more night under your roof. I was a damn fool to think it could be any different. There's blood on my hands no amount of right living will ever wash away."

She looked him straight in the eye and prayed to all the saints to give her the eloquence to convince him how wrong he was. "Tobias, I know you've killed. I know you've done things you regret with all your heart. But you can change. All people can change. The Good Lord gave us free will so that we could make choices, for good or ill. You are not the same man who rode east seven years ago. You made yourself into a better person, a man who could give a great deal to any community.

"You had to kill Slaughter. That was not an evil act. That was a necessary act to protect your own life and mine. Slaughter was the cold-blooded killer. It haunts me to think he's a part of the reason why you feel you have to leave. If you walk out of my life, he will have succeeded in hurting me far more than any physical harm he could have done."

Tobias stared back her, his face as bleak and harsh as she'd ever seen it, and she knew then that she had failed.

"My staying on is just making it harder for both of us," he said. "I'll go fetch my things." He walked quietly out of the kitchen and went upstairs.

Miranda stared at the table top and drew in deep breaths. Stubbornly, she blinked back the first wave of tears. She had her pride, and she was determined she wouldn't cry until Tobias walked out the door.

She almost broke that promise to herself when he came back down the stairs carrying the nature book of pressed plants and leaves the boys had made him for Christmas.

"Tell the boys and Lucas goodbye for me," he said as he put on his coat.

"All right. You take care of yourself." She knew her voice would break if she tried to say anything more.

"You do the same," he said and wrapped the scarf she had knit for him about his neck. "I hope you sell that mine for so

much money that you never have to work another day in your
life." He opened the door and started to step through it. Then
he paused and looked back over his shoulder. Light from the
lamp on the table lit the planes of his rugged profile and shone
off his gold-brown hair. One last time she tried to memorize
his features so that she could summon his face to mind during
the barren, lonely future that lay ahead of them both.

"I'm sorry, Miranda."

"I'm sorry, too," she said, regret rather than anger in her
tone. She understood now that he was right to leave. Until he
could forgive himself for what he had been and done, he would
never be content.

They both knew there was nothing else to say. Tobias stepped
out into the cold winter night and shut the door behind him.

Miranda buried her face in her arms and let the tears come.


The bitter cold clawed at Tobias the moment he rode away
from the shelter of the barn. He didn't mind. The freezing night
suited his mood. Right now he felt cold to the marrow of his
soul. He would probably feel that way for the rest of his life—
even though that life was apt to be a short one once word got
out Jonah was still alive.

The moon, a broken silver disc in the dark sky, had just risen
over the peaks to the east. It provided plenty of light to travel
by. He pointed Romeo down the snow-covered road away from
Pine Creek. He decided to head for Hendersonville, some eight
miles to the south. There he'd put up for the rest of the night.
He didn't mind freezing, but he did feel some remorse for
hauling Romeo out into such glacial cold. It was a damn fool
time of night to start traveling, but he couldn't bear to stay
with Miranda any longer. Prolonging his inevitable departure
was hurting them both too much.

Anger flared to life inside him as he thought over what
Miranda had told him in the kitchen. Why couldn't she see

what he was? Why couldn't she just accept the truth? He had done his level best to change, and within a few months of returning to the West he had killed a man. Killing was simply a part of his nature, and violence would follow him wherever he went. *You're doing that woman a favor by riding out of her life.*

But no matter how he tried, he couldn't forget the way she had looked just before he walked out the door. Miranda had always been so joyous and full of life. But tonight, for the very first time she'd looked defeated and weary, and her eyes had been full of sorrow. *You know you're the son of a bitch who's responsible for that change in her.*

If he could undo the damage of the last three months, he would. If only he hadn't gone looking for her that very first day at Peabody's store. If only he hadn't asked himself to supper at her place, and danced with her at Founder's Day. But a part of him didn't want to erase a moment of the past three months. Every instant he had with Miranda was too precious to discard or wish away.

He'd rather undo his whole sorry life. Well, not every bit of it. His parents had given him a fine start. He'd only headed down the wrong path after Hawkins's raid. Tobias grimaced when he thought of the man who had so brutally destroyed a family—dozens of families in fact—all over Kansas in the angry, lawless days before the War Between the States. Jeb Hawkins and Ben Slaughter were cut from the same cruel, violent cloth, using the thin disguise of the slavery issue as an excuse to rape and steal.

Jeb Hawkins was the very first man Tobias had ever killed. Try as he might, Tobias couldn't regret that act. With a shiver which had little to do with the wintry cold, he thought back to that desperate night. Armed with only an old Dragoon Colt he'd bought at a trading post, he'd tracked Hawkins down to his hideout. He walked in while Hawkins and his men were in the midst of a drunken orgy. The bastard had been about to rape a young Negro girl who couldn't have been more than thirteen years old. Tobias had started shooting, and when he finished, Hawkins and three of his men lay dying. Two others slipped away, and three more weren't at the hideout that night.

Something Miranda had said to him tugged at his memory. *The Good Lord gave us free will so that we could make choices, for good or ill.* He'd surely made more than his share of ill choices. He remembered a sermon his father had given on that very topic. It was more clear in his mind than most, for his father had given it the Sunday before he was killed.

*The very worst of sinners shall be forgiven by the love of God if the sinner truly regrets and repents the wrong choices he has made in life.* Tobias stared down at his gloved hands and thought back on the men he had killed. Slaughter, like Hawkins, had deserved killing. Miranda was right about that. Slaughter would only have gone on murdering and hurting others until someone stretched his neck or put a bullet into him. Young Arizona Jack had proved he, too, was a cold-blooded murderer when he ambushed Jonah and shot him twice in the back.

But the rest of the men he had killed weighed heavily on Tobias's conscience. After he shot Hawkins, he had spent the next ten years of his life hunting down the remainder of his gang one by one. Now he sorely regretted the loss of those years and taking those lives. The rest of Hawkins's men were probably killers as well, but he was sorry he was the one who pulled the trigger. With every man he shot, he became a little more used to killing, and his reputation as Jonah had grown.

After he killed the last member of Hawkins's gang, there had been two men he'd shot in towns he'd "tamed" and two other hired guns he killed in range wars riding for the brand. They were rough men all, men who knew the price they could pay for living by the gun, but still he felt sharp remorse for having ended their lives.

Killing Johnny Tucker, the youth with the freckles in Abilene, was the death that haunted him most of all. That boy wasn't a killer. He was just foolish and too full of bravado the way young men were. Tobias reined Romeo to a halt and looked up at the pitiless stars in the sky. That one act shamed and pained him more than all the rest combined. That boy hadn't understood the price he might have to pay when he belted on a six-shooter and went hunting a reputation. That boy hadn't deserved to have his life and dreams stolen away from him.

Tobias suddenly felt a strange moisture on his cheeks. He raised his gloved hand to his face. When it came away wet, he realized that he was crying. He hadn't cried in all the years since his mother, father, and sister died. But tonight, he felt crushed by the full weight of the harm he had caused. For the first time the true cost of his crimes was clear to him—forfeiting all chance of happiness with sweet Miranda. He bowed his head and gave in to a deep, wrenching sorrow too much for even cold, callous Jonah to bear.

At last, Romeo grew restless. He tossed his head and pawed at the snow. Tobias let him have his head, and the bay started walking down the road toward Hendersonville. Every step the horse took sharpened Tobias's grief, for each step took him farther away from Miranda.

Through the dark waves of despair washing over him, something prompted Tobias to look upward once more. This time when he looked up at the black heavens, he spotted the lovely little circle of stars Miranda had pointed out to him. Just thinking of her and the sweet story she had told him made him want to smile in the midst of his torment. If only the princess could heal the wounds of the soldier's soul as well as the wounds of his body.

In that single, crystalline moment, Tobias realized the truth. Miranda had already healed him. He wouldn't kill carelessly or callously ever again. He valued life too much now, for Miranda had taught him how precious it could be. She had given him back his memories of his youth and childhood, a time when he had known how to live right and peacefully. His parents had taught him well, even if he had forgotten their lessons about life and love in his pain over their cruel deaths.

If an evil, brutal man like Ben Slaughter forced him to it, he would kill to protect Miranda's life, or the lives of other innocents threatened by such savagery. But he prayed he never again would have to face the difficult choice of taking a man's life, and he would do his damndest to live a quiet, peaceful existence where violent trouble would never find him again.

He wasn't a good man, but he wasn't a bad man, either. And he would surely do his best from now on to live as well as he could. Perhaps he could find atonement by loving Miranda and her nephews, and devoting the rest of his life to protecting and caring for them.

Tobias drew in a deep breath. He reined Romeo about and sent him back down the snowy road at a quick trot. He would go back to her. He would go back and see if Miranda still wanted him. If she was willing to throw in her lot with a book-loving ex-gunfighter, they would try to figure out some way and some place they might be able to spend the rest of their lives together.

# Chapter Twenty-two

It was still dark when Tobias rode into Miranda's barnyard, and no lights shone in the house. Tobias guessed it was five or so, still too early for Miranda or the boys to be stirring. After he finished unsaddling Romeo in the barn, he turned about and found Lucas standing in the doorway. Tobias swore under his breath when he realized the old gambler looked hopping mad. He also had the barrel of his big shotgun trained on Tobias's belly.

"You mind tellin' me why you're pointing that thing my way?" Tobias asked him.

"I'm givin' some serious thought to filling your worthless hide full of buckshot. Miranda is sound asleep in the kitchen, and it's damn clear she fell asleep crying because of you. I heard you ride out of here in the middle of the night. Have you made up your mind about whether you're a-comin' or a-goin'?"

A shaft of pain went through Tobias to hear Miranda had cried herself to sleep over him. To hide his own dismay, he countered sharply, "Miranda's going to have your hide if she finds out you've gotten out of bed."

"I reckon it's my hide to lose. You should be more worried about your own right about now." The old man lifted the shotgun a little higher and pulled back both hammers. "You'd be well advised to answer my question."

"I'm planning to stay with her," Tobias admitted quickly, "if she'll still have me."

"Hell, she'll have you." Lucas spat into the straw. "Miranda's the biggest damn fool for forgivin' folks I ever seen. If you walk in her door, this time you're staying with her for keeps. We're gonna get you hitched to that gal proper-like as soon as I can round up a sky pilot."

"That's what I had in mind. You can put that thing away now. Miranda's not going to be too keen on the notion of having a shotgun wedding."

"I reckon you're right about that." Lucas eased the hammers back on the shotgun, lowered it, and sent Tobias a wolfish grin. "But I did kind of like having the drop on Jonah."

"That's a name that neither of us is going to say again," Tobias told him seriously. "Jonah is dead and buried, and he'd better stay that way if Miranda and I have any chance of building a life together."

"I been thinkin' about that. The sooner you leave these parts, the better. I spent some time in Minnesota and Wisconsin when I was a boy. That's mighty pretty country up that way. I hear tell there's plenty of wild land there still, and nobody gives a tinker's damn about gunfightin' and such. I can make sure Miranda's mine gets sold for a fair price next spring and send the money along to you."

"I'll give that notion some thought," Tobias said as he turned Lucas's suggestion over in his mind. He'd heard there was nice country up north. It was also probably too damn cold up there for people to care about gunfighters.

"When you see Miranda, you might think to wish her a

Merry Christmas. Womenfolk set store by that kind of thing.''
With that, Lucas scratched himself and headed back toward
the house.

Tobias had to grin as he watched the wiry old man hurry
across the barnyard. Lucas Ransom was surely one of a kind.
Tobias appreciated the warning about the holiday. He had forgotten this was Christmas morning.

An idea suddenly occurred to him. He rummaged through
his saddlebags until he found a present he wanted to give
Miranda. Holding the large bundle under his arm, he marched
towards the back door. He hesitated on the doorstep for a long
moment, surprised to discover his heart was pounding. Deep
down inside, he knew this was his last chance to escape his
desolate existence as Jonah. Sweet Miranda was everything he
needed and wanted to be happy. Hopefully, if he worked hard
at it, he could make her happy, too.

Quietly, he opened the door and stepped inside. He saw
Miranda at once. She slept at the kitchen table, her head pil-
lowed on her arms. The lamp still burned beside her. He eased
the door shut and took off his coat. He walked over and placed
her present on the table. He cursed to himself when he saw the
handkerchief still clutched in one of her hands. Lucas had been
right about her crying.

Although the room felt considerably warmer than the winter
cold outside, the kitchen had grown chilly during his absence.
He took several logs from the wood box and stoked the stove
as silently as he could. Despite the pains he took, he wasn't
quiet enough. Miranda stirred and then lifted her head. He was
still kneeling by the stove when she spotted him and their gazes
met.

Her eyes widened. "You came back," she said softly.

He waited for what seemed like a lifetime to see what her
reaction would be. And then she smiled, a glorious, wide, joyful
Miranda smile, and he knew he was saved.

"Merry Christmas," he told her, his heart so full he couldn't trust his voice just yet to say any more.

"Oh, Tobias." Moments later, she stood and launched herself into his arms. He caught her and held her close. And then she raised her face to his, and they shared a long, sweet kiss. Full of promise and joy, that kiss helped to banish much of the despair they both had endured during the long night.

At last he broke off their embrace, for he wanted to make certain everything was clear between them. He wanted so much from her, and he had only his heart and his name to offer her in return. "Miranda Kilpatrick, will you do me the honor of becoming my wife?"

"There's a question I have to be asking you first." She met his gaze levelly. "Are you absolutely sure you want to take on the responsibility of raising Sean and Rory with me? The man who marries me has to care for my nephews as well. They can be a little wild, and they can try the patience of a saint, but they are good boys."

"I've come to care a great deal about both Sean and Rory, and I swear I'll do my best to help you raise them," he pledged solemnly. "I've known all along that the three of you came as a package."

"Here's my answer for you, then. I will honor you, only if you will honor me by becoming my husband."

"Then, we'll honor each other and get hitched as fast as Lucas can round us up a sky pilot, because I'm damn sure I can't live without you," he growled into her neck. He swung her up into his arms and went back to kissing her.

Sometime later they ended up in the rocker beside the stove, Miranda tucked snugly in his lap. "Whatever changed your mind?" she asked him. "You looked so set on leaving, I was sure we'd never see you again."

"I was halfway to Hendersonville when I got to thinking about that story your father told you about the crown of stars in the sky. I think that princess didn't just heal the soldier's wounds. She healed his soul as well, and all at once I realized you'd performed the same miracle for me. I've done plenty of things I regret, but I hope you'll help me learn how to be a better man in the future.''

Miranda framed his face gently with her hands. ''You already are a good man. You're as fine a man as I've ever known. I'll be happy to spend the rest of my life helping you realize that.''

She dropped her hands from his face. That dark, brooding look was back in his eyes, and she wanted him to feel as gloriously happy as she did. Tobias had come back to her and he wanted to stay. 'Twas the most wonderful and miraculous Christmas present she could possibly imagine. But now she needed to find a way to cheer him, for a man should feel only joy the morning he proposed to a woman who loved him with all her heart.

She sent him a teasing glance and added in a lighter tone, ''I'm fair glad you liked my story, but you don't really want to take up farming, do you?''

''I'm not cut out to be a farmer. Lord knows why, but I'd rather try to convince a room full of wild young heathens that book learning is worth their while. School teaching suits me just fine,'' he reassured her, a smile back in his eyes.

''Lucas had an interesting idea,'' he said in a more serious tone. ''How would you feel about moving to Wisconsin or Minnesota? There aren't too many cities up that way and plenty of wild country still. Few folk will have heard of Jonah much less care about whether he's alive or dead.''

''We traveled through that region with Da's troupe several times. I always thought it was pretty. It gets plenty cold come winter, though.''

''You just need someone to keep your bed warm during those long northern nights.''

''Are you volunteering for the job?''

"I've never been a husband before, but that's one part of the job I think I'll take to just fine," he said with such a smug, self-satisfied look she burst out laughing.

When she finished, he smoothed a lock of her hair back from her cheek, and that serious look was back in his eyes. "If Wisconsin doesn't suit you, I'm willing to go just about anywhere gunfighters aren't. We could even try New York City and see if you could pick up your singing career again."

She stared at him, humbled by what he was offering. She knew how much he hated cities. She shook her head and said firmly, "I told you before, that dream's not for me anymore. All I want now is to live in a nice town and have a few good friends who accept me for what I am. I will miss this house," she added.

She looked around at the dear little home which had become such a refuge and a haven for her during the past year, and a lump rose in the back of her throat. Hopefully the next owners would love and cherish Uncle Shamus's home even as she had.

"I expect there are plenty of good houses, though," she continued on with hardly a catch in her voice, "and nice towns and good people up in Wisconsin. Some of those towns are going to need a mighty fine schoolteacher come fall. If we don't find a place which suits us right away, we'll just ramble about until we find one which does. The boys are old enough now, a little more travel won't hurt them."

"Sweet Miranda." He shook his head. He looked at her with such tenderness in his gray eyes that she melted inside. "I'm glad I'll have a lifetime to get used to your cheerful way of looking at things. I've come to realize you remind me very much of my mother. She had the same remarkable gift you do—the ability to find joy in every day of life. I had forgotten how wonderful it is to be close to someone like that. And speaking of my mother, I've one more present for you. You can consider it a betrothal gift if you want. It's over there on the table.''

As much as she loved opening presents, Miranda had a hard time making herself leave her cozy seat on his lap. She went over to the table and poked at the mysterious bundle wrapped in a slicker.

"I like the wrapping," she laughed. "It's always a good idea to protect a present from sudden downpours inside a house." Her laughter died when she unrolled the slicker and saw the double wedding ring quilt inside it. Tears rose in her eyes as she reverently touched the lovely old quilt.

"I can only accept your mother's quilt if you agree to accept my father's watch," she told him, her voice not quite steady.

"I'd be proud to carry your father's watch. God willing, we might even have a boy someday to carry it in his turn."

"Now there's a thought." She smiled at him through her tears. "I can just see us raising a brood of singing Shakespearean scholars."

"That's one project, Miss Kilpatrick, that I wouldn't mind getting started on as soon as possible."

He stood up from the rocking chair, a hungry look in his eyes, and took her into his arms once more. They were just getting into the spirit of another long, luscious kiss when some small sound alerted them that they were no longer alone. The boys stood in the doorway in their nightshirts, their hair still tousled from sleep. Rory's eyes were wide with surprise, and Sean was frowning.

"Mr. Johnston," Sean declared abruptly, "if you want to keep kissing Aunt Miranda like that, I think you better marry her."

Miranda hid her face in Tobias's shirt, her shoulders heaving with silent laughter.

"If you boys don't object to the notion, that's exactly what I had in mind," he managed to reply gravely.

Rory and Sean exchanged excited glances, and then Rory

let loose an Indian war whoop. Both boys began a wild dance about the table, accompanied by more whoops and yells.

"I gather they're pleased." Tobias eyed the two boys quizzically.

"Oh, yes," Miranda said with a serene smile. "They only do their Cheyenne war dance when they're quite happy about something."

Christina emerged from her room. She looked at them still standing with their arms about each other and gave them a hopeful smile. "Do you have good news for us?"

"You and Rob aren't the only ones about to tie the knot," Miranda informed her gaily.

"This makes me very happy. Congratulations to you both." Christina crossed the room and gave Miranda a warm hug.

"I gather from all this racket goin' on in here, you're done with your proposin'." Lucas stuck his head in the door from the parlor. "Sure took you two long enough. It's about time someone thought about rustlin' up some breakfast. A sick old gent like me could starve to death before a soul noticed."

"A sick old gent like you should be in bed," Miranda tried to keep her voice stern and failed miserably. Shaking her head at her recalcitrant patient, she went to fetch her apron. Lucas blithely ignored her scolding and sat down at the table across from the boys. The three of them promptly began a spirited debate over whether they wanted flapjacks or biscuits for breakfast.

Miranda had just finished tying the strings to her apron when Tobias stepped up behind her and slipped his arms about her waist.

"Thank you," he said simply and kissed the side of her neck.

She turned about in his arms to face him. "That's a fine way to thank me, but just what is it that you are thanking me for, Mr. Johnston?" she asked him with a curious smile.

"For all this, Miss Kilpatrick." He gestured to her warm

kitchen full of people he cared for. "And for you. You most
of all. I can't imagine a happier place this side of heaven."

"I can't either, now that you're about to officially be a
part of our family," Miranda admitted with a contented sigh.
"Merry Christmas, Tobias. Merry Christmas to us all."

# Put a Little Romance in Your Life With
# Fern Michaels

__Dear Emily  0-8217-5676-1  $6.99US/$8.50CAN

__Sara's Song  0-8217-5856-X  $6.99US/$8.50CAN

__Wish List  0-8217-5228-6  $6.99US/$7.99CAN

__Vegas Rich  0-8217-5594-3  $6.99US/$8.50CAN

__Vegas Heat  0-8217-5758-X  $6.99US/$8.50CAN

__Vegas Sunrise 1-55817-5983-3  $6.99US/$8.50CAN

__Whitefire  0-8217-5638-9  $6.99US/$8.50CAN

---

Call toll free **1-888-345-BOOK** to order by phone or use this coupon to order by mail.

Name_____

Address_____

City _____ State _____Zip_____

Please send me the books I have checked above.

I am enclosing         $_____

Plus postage and handling*    $_____

Sales tax (in New York and Tennessee) $_____

Total amount enclosed     $_____

*Add $2.50 for the first book and $.50 for each additional book.

Send check or money order (no cash or CODs) to:

**Kensington Publishing Corp., 850 Third Avenue, New York, NY 10022**

Prices and Numbers subject to change without notice.

All orders subject to availability.

Check out our website at **www.kensingtonbooks.com**